The Forget-Me-Not Bakery

CAROLINE FLYNN

ONE PLACE. MANY STORIES

HQ
An imprint of HarperCollins*Publishers* Ltd
1 London Bridge Street
London SE1 9GF

This edition published in Great Britain by
HQ, an imprint of HarperCollins*Publishers* Ltd 2020

Copyright © Caroline Flynn 2020

Caroline Flynn asserts the moral right to be
identified as the author of this work.
A catalogue record for this book is
available from the British Library.

ISBN: 9780008409029

MIX
Paper from
responsible sources
FSC
www.fsc.org   FSC™ C007454

This book is produced from independently certified FSC™ paper
to ensure responsible forest management.

For more information visit: www.harpercollins.co.uk/green

Printed and bound in Great Britain by
CPI Group (UK) Ltd, Melksham, SN12 6TR

For the real Caroline ...
I miss you every day, Grandma.

Prologue

Cohen

Eight Years Ago ...

There are days that change everything. Change our lives. Change us.

Cohen Beckett didn't understand the razor-sharp truth of that statement. Until now. Now that he stood at the edge of the room, surrounded by all the people he knew and just as many that he didn't, aching with the painful loneliness of a man stranded on foreign ground without a soul in sight. Now that he was left behind, to carry on living a life he didn't know how to live alone. Now that his family of three, content and constant and perfect, was only a family of two.

Cohen didn't remember who he was before Stacey. Try as he might, he couldn't summon up recollections of his time before he'd met her by chance at university, all wide-eyed and beautiful and ready to take on the world. It seemed like a lifetime ago, yet those days, in the beginning, as he careened over the edge and fell madly in love with her, were etched in his brain with a sharp vividness that made them seem like only yesterday. He prayed that haunting vividness would never dull.

Before that, though? Nothing. The realization left him cold, and scared of what it truly meant. The thought niggled at him that he hadn't yet begun to live, to do and be anything worth remembering, until he'd met the woman he would call his wife. And if that was the case, he wasn't just scared. He was petrified. Because he would never be that man again, the one he saw reflecting back at him in Stacey's pretty emerald eyes.

Stomach in knots, shoulders tight with the facade of strength he fought to wear nobly, Cohen ached for another glimpse of his beloved wife's stare in his direction. The smile on her face that forced her long-lashed eyelids to squint with the sheer authenticity of it in the gold-rimmed picture frame beside her matching casket, the smile that seemed to follow him from across the room no matter where he stood, was a poor substitute for the beauty now housed in that closed box. No picture could do Stacey Beckett's smile justice. No memory, regardless of its clarity, would ever do *her* justice.

He'd found his one. The one who was his best friend and his lover and his rock. It pained him to think about whether he'd managed to be those things for her, adequately and fully. His chest constricted as he hoped with every fiber of his being that he had been. It hurt even more to realize that his love for her hadn't been enough to save her, hadn't been enough to protect her in the first place. The rational part of Cohen's brain understood that he could never have prevented the fluke accident that stole Stacey from him and their young son, but there were moments during the darkness of the seven nights that had followed her death when his rational mind didn't stand a chance against the grieving, guilt-stricken part that took over and threatened to drown him in his own numb disbelief.

'Dr Cohen?'

In the distance, as though through a thick veil of cotton but more accurately of dazed distraction, a voice filtered through to him. Cohen turned, and Sonya Ritter stood near him, her back turned to protect him from any oncoming folks intent on bestowing their condolences. Judging by the added lines that marred her forehead and the slight narrowed angle of her eyelids, she had said his name a few times without gleaning a response. Sonya knew nothing of impatience with him, though. As Port Landon's designated mother hen and knower of all that went on within the town's limits, the short elderly woman had taken her role more seriously when the tragedy of Stacey's passing befell their little town and rocked their community to the core. The woman was a fixture in their tiny town, and a friend to all despite her overzealous nature and overbearing personality. But she'd been a godsend to Cohen in the past week. He didn't know how he would have gotten through any of this without her. Didn't know how Bryce would have gotten through it.

Bryce. His son. The last remaining thread to Stacey that he could touch and hold. Only two years old and left without the beautiful mother he adored. Cohen didn't know how to quantify the torturous pain he was battling, but he was sure it was multiplied a thousand times over with the added weight of the grief he harbored on his young son's behalf.

'Sorry, Sonya. What were you saying?' He shook his head, desperate to hold himself together. Not for Sonya; she could handle whatever emotional turmoil Cohen – or anyone else, for that matter – tossed at her. The woman was strong and sturdy as an oak tree despite her age. It wasn't her he worried about.

The toddler in her arms was another story. The little boy he now lived solely for. Not because anything or anyone had ever come before him in his father's eyes, but because he was all he had left.

Sonya looked uncertain of Cohen's current emotional stability. She wasn't the only one. But she thankfully kept her sentiments to herself. Cohen didn't know if he could stand to hear *Are you okay?* or *How are you holding up?* one more time. People meant well, but it didn't make having to form an answer any easier.

'The director says he's about ready to start the service,' she informed him. 'I figured you would want Bryce with you?'

Bless the woman's heart. She was giving him an out, phrasing it as a question and allowing him the chance to admit he couldn't handle sitting in the front row of his wife's funeral, with his son in his arms asking why Mommy's picture was on display but she was nowhere to be found. It was going to be hard. Damn hard. There would be tears eventually, though the icy numbness that spread through him like a biting frost hadn't allowed those tears to fall yet, and there would be moments when Cohen wouldn't know how he was going to get through them.

Today was one of those days. One of those moments. That changed everything. Changed him.

But he couldn't allow this to swallow him up. He couldn't let it, as easy as it would be. Bryce needed him now. More than ever. And Cohen needed Bryce just as urgently. He held his hands out, his fingers twitching with the instinctive urgency to feel the solid form of his son against him.

'I wouldn't want him anywhere else.' He hugged the boy tight to his chest as Sonya gave Cohen's jacket lapel a gentle pull to straighten it, then she pressed her lips together and headed back toward the rows of chairs, leaving him with only his thoughts and his son to keep him steady. He had more faith in his two-year-old than his own frazzled mind to level him out.

'You all right, buddy?' Cohen pressed his thumb into Bryce's palm, squeezing his fingers gently. The boy's eyelashes fluttered before his eyes fixed firmly on his father.

Stacey's eyes.

'I want Mommy.' Bryce played with the edge of Cohen's pocket, flipping the fabric up and down, his gaze flitting from it to Cohen's face then back again. Waiting for an answer. Waiting for his daddy to fix this.

Cohen felt desolate, helpless. But, despite his throat constricting, thick with all the things he couldn't find the strength to say and all the things he couldn't change, Cohen leaned forward and kissed Bryce's forehead, his soft skin warm against his lips.

'I know, my boy. Me too.' He shifted his son in his arms, needing him to focus his waning attention on him, needing him to understand the sincerity of the words he fought to say out loud. 'But we're going to be okay, me and you.' He pressed his forehead to his son's, swallowing hard past the lump in his throat, desperate for his son to believe him more than he believed himself. 'We'll get through this,' he choked out. 'Together.'

Cohen just wished he knew how.

Chapter 1

Paige

Present Day …

Paige Henley had heard a lot of things about Port Landon. Mostly from her cousin, Allison, a long-time resident, and mostly that the tiny town was largely made up of people with big hearts and even bigger mouths. It ran on gossip and small-town gumption, and not always necessarily in that order. Of course, that was just gossip, too, when she really thought about it.

But she knew one thing for sure. When the folks of Port Landon talked about The Cakery's grand opening later on that evening, huddled back into their cozy homes with their own personal choice of sugar fix, their recollection of just how well the new bakery's grand opening had gone would be anything but exaggerated hearsay. It would be the truth.

'I can't believe this is really happening,' Paige exclaimed, bending down to pull two chocolate cupcakes with mint frosting from the glass display case. Rising to her full height, she closed the takeout box and met Allison's gaze. "I guess what I really mean is I still can't believe you talked me into this."

Allison expertly rang the sale through the cash register and bid the customer – Mrs O'Connor from Huntington Street was how she'd introduced her to Paige – a good day before turning to her cousin, eyes gleaming so bright they sparkled. 'Oh, please. You can pretend you're still unsure about this whole venture, but you're not fooling me. Either you've laced the baked goods with some damn good stuff that's making people *think* it tastes good, or maybe, just maybe, the people of Port Landon have spoken, Paige ... and The Cakery is officially a hit!'

Paige couldn't hide her smile. Leave it to Allison to decide that the only two plausible options were either real, honest-to-goodness success or the clandestine addition of hallucinogenic drugs.

She might not have had a clue what she was doing as a first-time business owner, but, by God, she was learning on the fly. And she was doing something right. It felt like the entire population of Port Landon had left their homes and jobs on this cheery sunny day to get a chance at the free coffee and sweet treats being handed out in celebration of Paige's first official day up and running on the bustling downtown street.

Or, if Paige was honest, to catch a glimpse of the newest addition to the small portside town they all called home – *her*. Most customers weren't even trying to hide that they were just as interested in the New Yorker who had snatched up old Wilhelmina Morrison's bakery within days of it hitting the real estate market as they were the baked goods that were strategically displayed about the room. It was like they'd never seen a girl from New York before. Like she was something akin to a Yeti from the Himalayan Mountains, something they'd heard of but never truly witnessed.

Well, they were witnessing her now, a real live city-girl-turned-small-town-entrepreneur, living in what she hoped would remain her natural habitat, her very own dream come true.

And that's what this grand opening day was turning out to be – a dream come true. With Allison graciously allowing her own business, the coffeehouse too-conveniently located beside the bakery, to be solely run by her two employees so she could volunteer to help Paige 'control the impending chaos' – Allison's words, not hers – the doors had been unlocked for the very first time at nine o'clock sharp. The coffee Allison had donated for the event had been brewed and piping hot, ready to be sipped by the patrons who attended. Paige had expected there to be a handful of people who would come out, mostly for the free food that had been mentioned in the *Port Landon Ledger* advertisements, but she never would have expected the line-up of people that waited patiently outside for the heavy glass door to be unlocked, or the way the cupcakes, mini cheesecakes, and scones that had been on display had sold out in a matter of hours, leaving Paige with no choice but to begin cutting the large cakes into individual pieces and sell them by the slice so that everyone would have a chance to try the different frostings and cake flavors she'd boasted about in the ads.

If this day was any indication, The Cakery was going to need to be better stocked on a daily basis than she ever dreamed. The thought had Paige bursting with pride. Every sliver of fear she'd had about leaving her marketing career back in New York, every not-so-subtle hint from Allison that she should take a chance and follow her dreams of owning her own bakery, every doubt she'd harbored since giving her notice and selling her closet-sized condo in the heart of the city …

It was worth it. Crazy and reckless, but absolutely worth it. And it made Paige feel more alive than she had in years. Maybe ever. Even if she had to spend her evenings whipping up buttercream frosting just to keep up, she would do it, because this was her dream, and it was coming to fruition in front of her sapphire eyes.

Yeah, it was definitely worth it.

'Paige, this is Sonya.' Allison's voice cut through Paige's thoughts. She turned to see a slender woman with short, gray hair cut smartly into a bob hairstyle. She wore a black T-shirt identical to Allison's, with the round Portside Coffeehouse logo on the front. The woman looked to be at least sixty-five, which Paige hadn't expected by the way Allison talked about her.

'Oh, Allison's told me so much about you,' Paige gushed, dusting her hands on her block-patterned apron. 'You help her to run the coffeehouse, right?'

'I do what I can,' Sonya replied, nodding as she shook her hand with a surprisingly firm grasp. She leaned forward, a faint grin on her lips as she added in a whisper, 'Which is pretty much everything.'

'Easy, now. I can hear you plotting your stealthy takeover from here.' A wider grin crossed Allison's face as she placed her hands on her hips. This was obviously a running joke between the two of them. 'Taking a break, are you?'

Sonya pointed toward the brick wall to the right that divided the bakery from the coffeehouse. 'I've got Adrian running the place for ten minutes while I grab myself a treat. Got anything with peanut butter in it?'

Paige jumped into action immediately, gesturing toward the other side of the room where a long table with trays of colorful cupcakes and squares were on display. They'd been picked over a bit, but a good selection still remained. 'I put chocolate fudge cupcakes with peanut butter icing on the treat trays this morning! Help yourself to those. They're free for the taking.'

Sonya glanced back at the setup, but she quickly turned back to the front counter where Allison and Paige stood, pulling a crumpled ten-dollar bill from her pocket. 'Anything with peanut butter in it that I can *buy*?' She waved the bill in her hand.

Paige tilted her head, curious. 'Of course, but you don't have to—'

'Look, sweetheart …' The older woman leaned in as though about to reveal a deep, dark secret. 'Around here, we shop local. We help each other out as best we can. It's what we do, in case Allison, here, hasn't told you. So …' She slid the bill across the counter, her deep brown eyes never wavering. 'Sell me ten dollars' worth of sugary goodness, and let me be on my way, will you?'

Paige's cheeks burned hotly at having been put in her place by the older woman, but at the same time, her heart swelled with adoration and respect for Sonya … and for the town. 'A handful of peanut buttery decadence coming up,' she announced, pulling a takeout box from the shelf behind her and beginning to place an array of sweet treats into it. She was just about to disappear into the back of the shop where the kitchen was hidden by a wall when another voice broke into the conversation.

'Sonya, are you giving this poor lady a hard time?'

The voice brought Paige back around to see who it was. It was unfamiliar and deep, the voice of a man.

Sonya had turned around at the front counter, and judging by both her and Allison's easy smiles, they recognized the owner of that voice.

He was tall, standing over by the table of treat trays, pouring himself a cup of coffee from the large coffeepot Allison had brought over from her shop that morning. The steam billowed up from the paper cup in his hands, and his hazel eyes shone with amusement.

'You got one thing right, Dr Cohen. The lady's definitely going to be poor if she doesn't start letting us folks pay for the stuff in her shop.' Anyone else might have sounded crass, but Sonya's tone was anything but. She was blunt and to the point, but there was heart behind her words, not malice. 'Speaking of that, you'd

10

better come up here and see what you can find to buy that sweet boy of yours, yeah?'

'Don't you worry, I've been given my orders,' he assured her, placing a plastic top on the cup before making his way to the front counter. 'I don't believe we've met, yet. I'm Cohen.'

A glass display case stood between them and he jutted his hand out over it. His smile was the first thing Paige noticed about him, genuine. His eyes gleamed with just as much sincerity, and a gentle kindness seemed to emanate off him in waves. He wore dark stonewash jeans and comfortable looking loafers, but the ensemble was paired with a solid green scrub top that made the flecks of gold in his eyes shine all the more brightly.

'Hi,' Paige greeted him, shifting the box into one hand to shake his with the other. 'I'm Paige.' She could hear a sudden shyness tainting her own voice. 'Paige Henley.' She couldn't bring herself to tear her eyes away.

Cohen gave her hand a gentle squeeze, his gaze meeting hers and holding it for what could have been a minute but was probably only seconds. 'This town's been talking nonstop about you and your bakery, Paige. It's good to finally put a face and a name to all the chatter.'

'The novelty will wear off, I'm sure.' She had been living in Port Landon for the past three months, but for the first time, Paige idly wondered just what exactly the gossip was that Cohen had heard.

'As quickly as the sugar fix?' Cohen arched an eyebrow, a crooked grin dancing on his face.

'Well, hopefully not quite that fast.' She laughed.

The sound of a throat being cleared made both Paige and Cohen turn at the same time. Allison and Sonya stood there, their lips pursed, unable to hide their mischievous intrigue. It was too alight in their eyes to go unnoticed.

'Find something you like?' Allison asked, crossing her arms.

Paige didn't know if she was addressing Cohen or herself, but she quickly realized it didn't matter. What did matter was that she and Cohen were still standing there, her small hand enveloped in his.

She pulled her hand from his as easily as she could. 'Right.' She glanced down as she smoothed her apron out, giving herself a moment to compose herself and stamp down her embarrassment. 'Anything I can get you, Cohen?'

'That's *Dr* Cohen,' Sonya interjected, still rooted in place, watching their exchange with distinct interest.

Paige shot her a pleading glance, silently begging the woman to stop making this worse, but quickly tried to cover it up. 'Sorry, Dr Co—'

Cohen chuckled, shaking his head. 'No, just Cohen is fine,' he insisted. He glanced over at Sonya. 'I see what you're doing Sonya, and you can put the brakes on anytime.'

'I could.' She shrugged, waving a dismissive hand. 'But you know I won't, sweetheart.'

Paige wasn't sure whose expression was more amused, the older woman's or Cohen's, but whatever passed between them was a silent, mutual understanding. They had history, those two. Cohen turned back to Paige, unfazed. 'As I was saying,' he began again. 'I got a specific request from my son this morning for something that's double fudge, and I promised I would come and see if I could make good on that request before he got home from school. Unfortunately, I got behind in my appointments and it took longer to get here than planned. Am I too late?'

'I've got just the thing, *Just* Cohen.' She flashed him an excited smile, relieved that she did, in fact, have something that would fit the bill. She ducked down, intent on seeking out the cake she had in mind. Paige didn't even realize she was still holding the box – Sonya's box – in her hand until she was about to set it down and retrieve another one for Cohen.

Immediately, Paige stood up, her eyes wide as she came face

12

to face with the older woman. 'I'm sorry, Sonya. I didn't finish getting everything for you! I'll be right back.' She whirled around, sending an apologetic glance at Cohen for making him wait as well, then scurried into the kitchen to add a slice of the chocolate peanut butter pie she'd made to have as her own dessert tonight, mortified at forgetting what she'd been doing the moment Cohen had entered the shop.

What in the world had come over her?

She knew all too well that Allison wasn't going to let her live that one down. And if her first impression of Sonya was anything to go by, she wouldn't, either.

Paige put on a brave face after slipping the piece of pie into the box and made her way back out to the counter. 'An assortment of cupcakes and a slice of gourmet chocolate peanut butter pie,' she announced, sliding the box across to Sonya. 'You'll have to let me know what you think.'

Sonya didn't bother to open the box and inspect the choices Paige had chosen. Pushing the ten-dollar bill closer to her, Sonya tucked the box under her arm. 'Trust me, Paige, I always let people know what I think.' She cast a fleeting glance from Cohen to Paige and back again, then winked. 'It was good to meet you, sweetheart.' She turned to leave, but not before adding, 'Have a good day, Dr Cohen,' as she closed the door behind her.

The void of Sonya's absence was felt the moment she left, but her words hung in the air like a thick veil. Allison had advised Paige on more than one occasion that the woman was a force to be reckoned with, but her spitfire personality was even more fiery than she'd expected.

'Now, about that order for double fudge anything ...' Paige turned back to Cohen, unable to look Allison in the eye just yet, and went about cutting an enormous slice of chocolate Oreo cake with chocolate fudge icing and double chocolate fudge drizzle on top, carefully boxing it up. She added in a pair of mocha chocolate cupcakes for good measure. 'If that doesn't fit the bill for your son, I don't know what will.'

'It looks like he's going to be swinging from the rafters till midnight once the sugar in that hits his bloodstream.'

He was smiling, but Paige immediately wondered if he thought it was too much. 'I guess the doctor in you would be worried about the effects of all the refined sugar.'

'Nah, it's the dad in me that's worried about that,' he chuckled. 'Besides, I'm not that kind of doctor. I'm a veterinarian. Believe me, I understand the need for a good sugar fix every now and then. What do I owe you, Paige?'

Allison stepped back, gesturing for her to take her place at the cash register. Paige punched a few buttons, ignoring the smug grin on her cousin's face. When the amount came up on the screen, Cohen arched a brow. 'That can't be enough.'

'It's just for the cake,' she advised happily. 'The cupcakes are on the house.'

He pulled his wallet out and held out a twenty-dollar bill. 'Thanks, Paige. Looks like I owe you one.'

Paige counted out his change and handed it to him. 'You owe me nothing. I'm just glad I could fulfill the request of a boy with dreams of chocolate fudge.'

'One forkful of that chocolatey masterpiece and I'll bet you'll be seeing my son and me in here a lot more.'

'I'm looking forward to it, Cohen.'

He shoved his wallet back into his jeans pocket, his eyes gleaming when they met hers once more. 'Me too,' he assured her. 'But I'd better get back to Jazz. She's probably scaling the walls looking for me. It was nice to meet you, Paige. Have a good day, you two.' He offered a slight nod toward Allison, and then they both watched as he made his way out of the shop, the bell above the door tolling lightly to announce his exit.

With the shop empty for the first time since the doors opened that morning, Paige turned to her cousin, who was still grinning.

'What?' Paige asked, rolling her eyes. She knew exactly what her cousin was thinking. They had been best friends too long not to know. 'You're looking at me like something big just happened.'

'Something big did just happen,' Allison exclaimed. 'You, Paige Henley, just met Port Landon's most eligible bachelor.'

Chapter 2

Cohen

'You're right. They almost do look too good to eat.' Cohen carefully closed the box of cakes and placed it on the table in the lunchroom. 'You'd better head over there now if you want half a chance at anything being left. She's going to sell out by the end of the day, I'm sure of it.'

'Really?' Rhonda, the technician at his veterinary clinic, pointed toward the waiting room. 'But what about the next appointment?'

'Don't you worry about Mr Rutherford and Max,' he insisted. 'It's a quick appointment for vaccines and itchy ears. I can handle it. You go on and check out the bakery, or else you'll be stealing Bryce's chocolate fudge cake before he gets here, getting us both in trouble.'

'I'm not sure either of us could handle that kind of wrath.' Rhonda plucked her leather purse from the lunchroom table and headed for the front door of the clinic.

Cohen chuckled to himself. There wasn't a person in Port Landon brave enough to come between a strong-willed boy like Bryce and his love of chocolate fudge. He was only ten, but there

16

were times when Cohen forgot he was still so young. He acted older, and he was terribly smart. Cohen often wondered if it was his genetics that made him so mature for his age, or the enormity of what he'd been through in his short life thus far.

He shook his head, brushed some dog hair from the hem of his scrub top – left there by Coby, the Andersons' always-shedding Labrador retriever, during an earlier appointment – and met his next patient in the waiting room. 'Mr Rutherford, hello. How about we bring Max into the exam room and see what's going on with those ears, shall we?'

Max was a five-year-old cocker spaniel with a robust love of life. He also had a love of water, getting into any puddle, stream, or lake he could find. Mr Rutherford's neighbor, who owned the biggest inground pool in Port Landon, didn't much appreciate Max's love of water, or the fact that Mr Rutherford let Max run loose in the yard every now and then. Or in *his* yard, based on the gossip that permeated the clinic walls daily. The dog had been caught paddling around in the pool more than a few times.

However, Max's love of water was hard on his ears and he'd developed a couple of infections over the years because of it.

One look and Cohen knew he'd better send the dog home with a course of antibiotics and a follow-up appointment in ten days. Max squirmed the entire time, but Cohen managed to get his ears cleaned as best he could, then he applied a few drops of a topical antibiotic into each ear, much to the dog's dismay. Max shook his head, letting his floppy ears flap dramatically, but his tail still wagged wildly. The dog had been there many times before; he knew the drill. And sure enough, after directions to apply the drops twice a day and try to keep the ears as clean and dry as possible, Cohen reached into the glass treat jar on the edge of the countertop and offered Max the beef liver treat he'd been waiting for since the moment he arrived.

'I'll see you in ten days,' Cohen advised Mr Rutherford with a smile. He crouched down and patted the dog on the head affectionately. 'And I'll see you, too, Max. Heal those ears up and be good, for heaven's sake.'

He made sure Alice, the receptionist, was helping the elderly man to settle his bill at the front desk, then made his way back toward the pharmacy room, intent on typing his shorthand notes into the computer system. But as Cohen rounded the corner, he barely registered hearing the back door of the clinic swing open before he was hit by a sprinting Bryce.

'Oomph!' Bryce made an incomprehensible sound before reeling back to stare up at his father with wide, excited eyes. 'Dad! Did you make it to the bakery yet? Josh says his mom went to get him some apple pie, but they were sold out!'

'It's good to see you, too, Bryce.' Cohen chuckled. 'Glad you're so happy to see me.' He held the boy out at arm's length, checking him over, as he did almost every day. A familiar sensation washed over him daily around this time, just as Bryce made his way home from the public school, located two streets over. It was relief. Relief that his son was home, safe and sound. Relief that he could see him again, like laying eyes on him equated to knowing everything was okay.

'I *am* happy to see you,' his son replied, beaming. 'I'm just happy to see chocolate cake more!' Bryce cast a glance through the doorway into the lunchroom, eyed the takeout box, and dove for it.

Cohen leaped forward in a half-hearted attempt to stop him from reaching the box. He managed to get a hold of Bryce's T-shirt near his shoulder and pull him back against him just inside the lunchroom doorway, holding the boy against his chest with one hand and picking up the box of cakes with the other. He held it away from him, causing laughter and cries of feigned desperation to erupt from his mouth.

'Dad, that's mine! You bought it for me, remember?'

'One more false move and Jazz gets it!'

As if on cue, Jazz wandered in, her docked tail wagging excitedly at the sight of Bryce, her eyes squinted from the big smile on her face.

'You wouldn't give the cake to Jazz,' Bryce hollered, arms outstretched and flailing wildly in hopes of snatching the box from his hand. 'You can't give chocolate to dogs. What kind of veterinarian *are you*?' The boy laughed as Cohen expertly placed a foot behind his own, purposely causing him to trip backwards as his father lowered him to the floor.

Jazz was on him in seconds, attempting to lick his face and communicate her happiness at seeing him despite Bryce's attempts to crawl away from her.

'See, even Jazz thinks you don't need cake,' Cohen laughed, his heart swelling at the sight.

'Well, Jazz would be wrong, Dad!'

Hearing her name from Bryce's lips again only heightened the brindle boxer's excitement, and she bounced happily on her front paws as though playing some sort of game. One that only she knew the rules of, and if there were rules, they were likely: Rule #1 – Jazz wins. And what was the name of the game? Jazz Wins.

And Jazz was definitely winning.

'Okay, okay, I give up!' Bryce cried out, laughing so hard tears glistened at the corners of his eyes. 'Get the attack dog off me, Dad!'

'All right, Jazz,' Cohen chuckled. 'Come on back, girl. Let him at least stand and fight for the cake he loves.'

Jazz had traipsed into the lives of those who worked at Beckett Veterinary Hospital last year. Surrendered by her elderly owner due to unforeseen health reasons, the plan had been to place her into a rescue group for foster placement until a new forever home could be found.

A year later, Jazz still called the clinic her home, and she owned the clinic employees and anyone else who scuttled through the door. Someday, someone special would come along and fall for

Jazz the way everyone who worked there had, Cohen and Bryce included. It was inevitable when she was such a companionable, loving animal without an angry bone in her body. She rarely barked, was trained to ring one of the bells hanging from each door of the clinic when she wanted to go outside, and she adored absolutely everyone she met. But, so far, no one had come forward.

No one but Cohen, Bryce, and the team who worked there, as a collective whole. Jazz was just as much a part of the Beckett Veterinary Hospital family as the employees. No one was rushing out to try to find her another place to live.

Most veterinary clinics had a clinic cat, because cats were more independent and simplistic to own. In theory, anyway. But they had a clinic dog, and she fit in perfectly.

Bryce stumbled to his feet once Jazz relented, and he immediately jutted his hands out. 'Dad, please! Let me see the cake. Please!'

Cohen held it further away. 'You can't have it until after supper, though. You know the drill.'

'I didn't say I was going to eat it, I said I was going to look at it!'

'Why put yourself through the misery?' Cohen pursed his lips, thoroughly enjoying himself.

'Because I need to make an educated opinion about the new bakery, and that opinion starts with the presentation of the cake!' Bryce wiggled his fingers for the cake to be passed to him.

Inwardly, Cohen groaned. When did his sandy-haired, green-eyed, ten-year-old son grow up so much that he needed to form 'educated opinions' about the artistic presentation of cake? It was just one more moment in a long list of them when he realized that his boy wasn't a baby anymore.

Mostly because he was anticipating seeing Bryce's face when he caught his first glimpse of the cake Paige had boxed up for him, Cohen gave up, passing the box to his son. 'It was all I could do not to try a bite,' he admitted. 'Rhonda's over there now. Once she saw your cake and cupcakes, she couldn't help herself.'

'Whoa ...' The animated look on Bryce's face as he opened the box and revealed the fudge-drizzled cake slice was worth ten times the price Cohen had paid for it. His eyes grew so round, his mouth dropped open – his father's chest tightened a little.

There he was – his little boy, with wide eyes full of wonder. His baby was still in there somewhere.

'Dad, it looks like it's out of a magazine!' With his gaze fixed on the box of treats, Bryce reached a finger out, intent on scooping a bit of frosting off the top of one of the cakes.

'Hey!' Cohen chuckled. 'What did I say about supper first?'

'Just one taste!' his son pleaded. 'Just one, Dad! Please?'

The desperation in Bryce's eyes was enough to break down Cohen's resolve. Sometimes, battles had to be picked. It was just cake icing, after all. 'Try the frosting on one of the cupcakes. But leave the other one untouched – that one's for me.'

Bryce didn't hesitate, scooping the end of his index finger into the mocha frosting. The boy's eyes crossed and he moaned dramatically. 'Oh, wow, Dad! That's seriously some of the best frosting I've ever had. You've got to try it.' He held out the box to Cohen, but Cohen held up both hands.

'I've still got one more appointment, then I can sit down and have dinner with you. There's lasagna in the crockpot. After that, we dine on chocolate fudge cake and mocha frosting. Deal?'

'Best deal ever,' Bryce said with a grin.

'Good,' Cohen replied. 'Because you've got homework first while you wait for me.'

'But, Dad, I wanted to walk down to the bakery and look inside.'

Cohen halted his footsteps. 'Not today. I've got one more appointment scheduled, and you need to get your homework done.'

'I will, but the bakery's only open for another half an hour and—'

'I can't take you today, Bryce. I'm still working, I'm sorry.'

Cohen felt a familiar ache, painfully aware of how often his son heard those words – 'I have to work' – come from his mouth. It pained him every time he had to deny his son any activity or outing he wanted to attend because of it.

It might have been eight years since Stacey passed away, but it felt like only yesterday in many ways to Cohen. He knew Bryce didn't really remember his mother, having been only two years old at the time. That didn't mean the boy didn't acknowledge the void of a mother figure's presence, though.

'I could go alone, Dad,' Bryce insisted. 'It's only up the street.'

He couldn't fault his son for his logic. The veterinary clinic was on the corner of Clinton Street and Main Street. There was a vacant lot beside it where the first in the row of downtown shops had once begun, but the first shop had burned down two decades ago and was never rebuilt. In its place, a park had been built across both lots, with picnic tables and a variety of different children's playground structures. Beside that was the Portside Coffeehouse, owned by Allison Kent. And besides that, Paige Henley's new bakery.

Any other day, Cohen probably would have caved in and let Bryce meander over to the bakery on his own. But he prevented himself from giving in to his son once again during this conversation, and not just because he didn't want to seem like a pushover.

He selfishly also wanted an excuse to go back again. To see Paige again.

She seemed friendly enough, and kind-hearted. Such a drastic contrast from the slew of rumors that whirled around town for the months preceding her bakery's grand opening. No one had really seen her or been formally introduced until today, but that hadn't been enough to stop the public opinion from forming that the bakery's new owner was an uppity city slicker who undoubtedly believed she was better than the residents of little ole' Port Landon.

But, boy, had she proved the gossipmongers wrong today. Paige was anything but arrogant, and her gentle demeanor emanated from her like a warm embrace.

Her pretty blue eyes didn't go unnoticed, either.

He knew exactly what Sonya Ritter had been hinting at earlier. The old woman was notorious for trying to set him up with every single woman that crossed the Port Landon town limits. She had been hell-bent on playing matchmaker since the year after Stacey's passing. Very unsuccessfully, to Sonya's dismay. Cohen, however, hadn't cared one way or the other, and that told him everything he needed to know. Either the woman Sonya was trying to pair him up with wasn't the right one, or Cohen just wasn't ready. He put his bets on the latter.

He hadn't put much effort into looking for love, anyway. Okay, more accurately, he hadn't put forth any effort. His main priority was Bryce, and Bryce alone. While he knew his son needed a mother figure, he had been content to raise him on his own without a second thought, for no other reason than the fear of losing someone else and his son getting hurt in the process. He couldn't take that chance. Losing Stacey had almost wrecked him. He couldn't let his son witness that kind of pain again.

Despite everything, Bryce had grown up well-rounded, he thought. He was a smart kid, did well in school – save for history and English, but those had once been the bane of Cohen's existence, too – and he was polite and well-liked in the community. He helped their neighbors rake their leaves in the autumn and knew enough to hold the door open for other people and use his manners. Cohen thought he'd done pretty well, all things considered, and there were no words to describe how proud he was of Bryce and the boy he'd become. They were content just as they were; Cohen, Bryce, Norman the black cat – who despised Jazz – and Jazz, the brindle boxer, who loved everyone, Norman included.

Sonya Ritter was another story. She couldn't and wouldn't

believe Cohen was truly content until there was a woman on his arm who'd taken his last name.

'I know you could go yourself, pal,' he advised his son. 'But not today, okay? How about this: If you can go feed Jazz and finish up your homework, that should give me time to get through my last appointment for the day. Then, we can head home, sit down, and eat lasagna. After that, we'll take Jazz for a walk down to the pier and let her drink from that oversized water bowl we call a lake. Sound good?'

Bryce's jaw worked as he mulled over his father's proposition. 'I thought we were going to eat cake?'

The corner of Cohen's mouth twitched upward. 'We'll take two forks with us. That cake isn't going to eat itself.'

Chapter 3

Paige

The second official day of The Cakery being open was just as busy as the first. Maybe even busier, but Paige had lost count of the customers she'd served despite her unsuccessful efforts to keep track. Late into the afternoon, she received a well-deserved moment to herself, her first since she'd unlocked the door at nine o'clock that morning. After tackling the previous day with her witty, nothing-fazes-me cousin by her side, Paige was acutely aware of the void Allison's absence left. She knew she couldn't expect her to abandon her own thriving business every day to help her out, but it had been nice to have the support and camaraderie that came from taking on the world together yesterday, even if it was just in the name of a good old-fashioned sugar fix.

The two of them had been thick as thieves in high school. Inseparable. They were family, but they were best friends, too. Had been for as long as Paige could remember. Even when Paige boldly fled their hometown of Grand Rapids after graduation and set off for New York, while Allison chose to test out her entrepreneurial skills with the Portside Coffeehouse in Port

Landon – a little town Paige had only heard of before moving there – the only distance it created between them ·was in the tangible sense. Thanks to decent long-distance cellphone plans and the aid of Skype, the two women took on their new roles together, despite the eight hundred miles between them.

Both had excelled, but as the years wore on, each one passing by quicker than the last, it had been only Allison that carried the same excitement and contentment in her choice of career. Paige would never in a million years call her life spent in New York City a mistake, and those years would never be something she regretted.

But she was glad she'd listened to Allison's not-so-subtle hints, suggesting she should stop talking about leaving her hectic marketing and design position in New York 'someday' and come back to her home state of Michigan to fulfill her dream of owning her own bakery.

At first, Paige had balked at the idea. She'd thought, *Surely I couldn't do such a thing?*

But, as time wore on and Allison's suggestions became less veiled and more detailed, transforming from hints into full-fledged daydreams, she began to listen to her cousin's ideas of what it would be like to live in the little town of Port Landon. And when Wilhelmina Morrison put her well-known and well-loved bakery up for sale, citing that seventy-nine was as good an age as any to retire and start doing the adventurous things she'd always dreamed of, like taking road-trips and quite possibly skydiving, Allison's incessant prodding became unabashed nagging.

'You always said you wanted to own your own bakery and make pretty cakes and decadent cookies and cupcakes to your heart's content!' she'd reminded her, again and again. 'Here's your chance! Besides, the bake shop building is right beside my coffee shop, Paige. It's perfect!'

That was what scared Paige the most – it *did* sound perfect.

And despite the fact she had been thinking seriously about Allison's proposition, she was petrified to leave the safety net of her executive job in a breakneck-speed city like New York and start over in a small town of only a few thousand people. It was what she knew, her comfort zone. She'd attended college there and built the only adult life she'd ever known.

Until now. Fifteen years after that wide-eyed teenager moved to one of the biggest, busiest cities in the United States, Paige Henley did the unthinkable.

She left.

Paige took her cousin's advice. And in the end, it wasn't because of Allison, or because of her job, or even her own grown-up decision.

It was because of a homemade cake given to a man she could have – no, should have – fallen for.

Her final official board meeting with Livingston Designs was never meant to be her last. It was a meeting like any other, all digital screens and laser pointers and long rectangular tables. Her boss, Alex Livingston, sat to her left, as he always did, and the same team of enthusiastic go-getters surrounded her. The only difference was that the coffee and sweets usually brought in for them was from a new place that had just opened up. Paige couldn't remember the name of the place, but it had been something as light, fluffy, and delectable as the mini cakes that accompanied the coffee.

The coffee was good, but the cakes were downright mouth-watering.

'Oh my gosh!' she'd exclaimed, her eyes fluttering as the sugary explosion burst on her tongue. 'Whoever baked this deserves a medal!'

Alex had merely scoffed, waving a dismissive hand. 'It's a cake,' he replied absently, under his breath. 'Not exactly worthy of awards in my books.'

Mouth still half full, Paige stopped mid-movement. She'd never walked on eggshells before with Alex, but Paige had known better than to bring up something so menial. She knew the pressure he was under to secure the marketing deal they were working on, and it was bringing out his curt side. Still, she couldn't contain her urge to argue. 'You haven't even tried it, Alex.'

He dropped his pen, letting it clatter onto the desk, an indication of how silly he thought this entire conversation was, especially since they were about to discuss a million-dollar advertising campaign proposal. That was the only kind of thing worthy of medals in the eyes of Alex Livingston. 'I don't have to try it to know it doesn't deserve a medal, Paige. It's a cake, nothing more. Besides, anyone who wants to live their lives baking up a storm isn't exactly looking to become award-winning. That's what I'm assuming, anyway. And who would want to live like that?'

The answer hit Paige instantly. *Me.*

Alex meant a great deal to her. They were colleagues in the office and something akin to friends outside it. For fifteen years, Paige had built her relationship with him and with the company, excelling in her career and earning her managerial title. She was acutely aware that Alex felt more for her than just friendship, but Paige had yet to pull the tether and let her heart open up to him. She didn't know why she couldn't seem to do it – they got along well and there was no denying he was an attractive man. She didn't understand why Alex put up with her wishy-washy responses each time he asked her out.

But in that moment, after Alex's thoughtless outburst fueled by stress, Paige suddenly couldn't imagine loving a man who didn't appreciate the little things in life. Who didn't see the value in creating something with your hands even if it didn't result in an exorbitant amount of money or critical acclaim? Wanting to love someone and actually finding love with them were two very different things. And so the sad, vicious cycle continued.

Paige saw things differently, she realized that now. It took his dismissal of someone's gourmet creations for her to realize she didn't care about anything as much as she did her childhood dream. She heard Allison's encouragement, saw the real estate listing in her mind for the rundown bakery her cousin had sent her as clear as if it was sitting in front of her, and felt her blood burn a little hotter in her veins with the physical need she felt to prove Alex wrong.

Me, she thought again. *I want to live like that.* She'd spent the last months teetering on the edge of a precipice, unwilling to make a concrete decision. Now, she felt like the decision was made for her. Paige's heart spoke up, loud and clear, and it told her mind the plan: Paige wasn't going to sit another day idle, wondering what if. She wanted that bakery. Her heart wanted that bakery.

Most of all, Paige wanted to be able to say she'd tried.

It wasn't any one thing that she wanted to run from, more like a series of many things she wanted to run to.

She'd learned so much in New York, about her strengths and about herself. For that reason, she cherished what she'd left behind there, and always would. But because of that moment, that off-the-cuff comment by a businessman she was loyal to and whom she trusted unfailingly, Paige Henley gave a month's notice to him – a move Alex made known he didn't understand but respected. Paige found herself back in Michigan, in the small town of Port Landon, and she was just as eager to see what she could learn about herself there.

This was her new beginning. She didn't see it as starting over so much as switching gears. She'd spent fifteen years doing what she had to do – and she had done her job well, judging by the praise and letter of recommendation from Alex, should she ever need it – but now it was time to do what she wanted.

For better or for worse, Paige had made her decision. Though it wouldn't be easy, she was bound and determined to give it all she had.

And today, she was giving it all she had without the aid of her trusty sidekick, Allison. But being busy had never evoked fear in Paige before. Busy meant there was something to do, something to keep her hands and her mind distracted. It was easier to deal with the loneliness that seemed to creep in now and then, reminding her that those distractions were all she had to keep her company.

Fifteen years of living to work had flown by in a New York minute, but the last five years of hearing about Allison's fun days at the coffee shop and her romantic dates with her boyfriend, Christopher, made Paige open her eyes and realize what her life had become.

Paige wasn't living; she was merely existing.

It was another thing in the long line of things that prompted the move to Port Landon, along with the hefty down payment on Wilhelmina Morrison's old bakery. She wasn't just looking for a new career. She was looking for a new life. A real one. One that included people she cared about, and people who cared about her. One that left her tired in the evenings, but content and happy with the efforts she put forth toward her goals.

And, so far, that was what she had found in the little town of Port Landon. Now, if she could just find someone to share it all with.

The shrill tolling of the bell above the front door broke Paige from her thoughts, and Allison came bounding in as though thinking about her had somehow conjured her cousin up from thin air.

'Paige!' she shrieked. As though it was an afterthought, she glanced around the room, confirming no one else was in the shop. 'Paige, you're not going to believe this!'

The excitement coursing through Allison's veins was infectious, and Paige steeled herself for something huge. 'What's going on?'

Allison stretched her arm out across the front counter,

waving her left hand in front of Paige's face. 'I'm getting married, Paige!'

It took a moment for the words to register, and for Paige to get a look at the shiny diamond on her cousin's ring finger, before both women turned into the squealing high school best friends they'd been so many years ago, holding hands and bouncing up and down like children. Paige's eyes were wide and wet with tears, her joy for her cousin spilling down her cheeks.

'Oh my God, Allison, that's incredible!'

'He finally did it!' Allison laughed, wiping the tears from her eyes with the back of her hand. 'Chris proposed ... and I didn't even see it coming, Paige. At all!'

If that was true, then Paige figured she was the only one blindsided by it. The whole town had probably seen it coming. After five years of dating, even Paige had been waiting with bated breath for Allison to announce her upcoming marriage every time they talked on the phone or had a Skype call. Allison was the most patient person she'd ever known, and from everything they'd ever discussed while Paige was in New York, she and Chris had a good relationship. A solid one.

This wasn't the first time Paige was a teensy bit envious of Allison, but that didn't mean she wasn't going to cry happy tears and jump at the chance to celebrate her big news.

They were best friends. They were family. And family was something that meant the world to Paige.

'I'm so happy for you, Allison.' Paige pulled her cousin into a warm embrace, squeezing her tightly. 'So, so happy.'

'I just can't freaking believe it,' Allison sobbed, letting go of Paige to stretch her arm out in front of her and admire her bejeweled ring finger again. 'I've got a fiancé! A freaking fiancé!'

'Yes, you do.' Paige laughed, reaching out for her cousin's hand to ogle the shiny square diamond in a rose gold setting. 'Just wait until you can call him your husband.'

'Husband!' she screeched, clutching her hand to her chest. 'I'm going to have a husband!'

The theatrics amused Paige immensely. 'Just how long ago did this romantic proposal take place?'

Allison whirled around to glance at the clock. 'About twenty minutes ago! We were having a picnic lunch and—'

'Wait, you left your picnic with your new fiancé, who *just* proposed, to come in here and tell me about it?' Paige stood there, her eyes widened in bewilderment. She couldn't believe what she was hearing, even if it was from Allison.

'I had to tell you! This is time-sensitive stuff, Paige!' She feigned shock, like she couldn't possibly understand why Paige wouldn't understand such a thing. 'Okay, fine, so maybe I'm not a very good fiancée.'

Paige sighed, shaking her head as she reached out and squeezed her cousin's hands in hers. 'It's not that you're not a good fiancée, it's just that you're *too* good of a friend to me,' she explained gently. 'And as over the moon as I am that you're getting married and there's a wedding to plan, I think you'd better go find Christopher and celebrate with him, yeah?'

'I know, Paige, but I just *had* to tell you!' she continued, her gaze becoming a starry-eyed haze. 'I'm thinking a summer wedding. August, maybe.' She held her hands out with a *Just picture this!* gesture.

'That's only a couple of months away!' Paige gasped, surprised. 'That's fast.'

'When you know, you know,' Allison stated, winking at her. 'Besides, there's nothing more romantic than a summer wedding with all the flowers in bloom and the sun high in the sky.' She sighed, obviously picturing the scene in her mind with vivid clarity. 'Wow, that's some serious lovey-dovey voodoo stuff Sonya's been pulling. It's turning me into a complete—'

'What's Sonya got to do with Christopher's marriage proposal?' Paige chuckled.

'That's what I'm trying to tell you!' she shrieked, jumping up and down again. 'Sonya was just saying the other day that it's our time! Something to do with the stars aligning and believing in the power of love, or standing the test of time ...' She shook her head, waving her hand to dismiss her further jumbled thoughts. 'I don't know, Paige, all I'm saying is Sonya predicted it, and then it happened!'

'Or maybe Christopher has been planning this for months and it's just a coincidence?'

Allison, ever the dramatic one, stomped her foot and let out a loud scoff. 'Okay, smarty pants, but what about what she said about you and Dr Cohen?'

Paige arched a brow. 'What are you talking—'

The bell chimed above the doorway again, announcing a visitor. Both women turned to see a young boy enter the bake shop. Paige didn't recognize him. Allison's face, however, lit up and her mouth gaped open. She knew very well who he was.

'And that, I think, is my cue to leave.' She didn't look away from the sandy-haired boy, who was too transfixed by the display of mini cheesecakes in the cooler to notice her stare, but she stepped away from Paige, still wearing a haunted expression.

'What? Why?' Paige was beyond confused.

Allison cupped her hands around her mouth to respond, but whatever she was going to say was quickly interrupted by the bell ringing once more. Cohen Beckett stepped inside the shop, his focus trained on the young boy near the cooler.

'I thought we were walking here, not sprinting like the zombies are hot on our heels.' He wore an amused grin, turning to shut the door behind him. As the door clicked shut, he turned back to face the counter and saw both Allison and Paige staring at him like he had just grown a second head. 'Oh, hello, ladies.'

'Hey there, Dr Cohen.' Allison leaned in toward Paige, lowered her voice, and whispered, 'See? Lovey-dovey voodoo stuff. Sonya knows what she's talking about. We'll chat later ... maid of honor.'

She gave Paige's hand one last encouraging squeeze and disappeared out the front door, letting the bell ring out loudly in her wake.

Paige should have been dancing around like a fool, thrilled to be bestowed such an honor by her best friend, but she was too consumed by the fact that they'd just been talking about Cohen Beckett and then he'd shown up. Just like that.

Almost like lovey-dovey voodoo stuff.

The young boy was still ogling the cheesecake cooler, pointing emphatically at the key lime one with a twisted lime garnish on top, but Cohen was staring after Allison, even after the door had swung closed.

'Should I be worried about the smug little smirk she was wearing?' he asked, turning toward the front counter, where Paige still stood, motionless. His tone was light, but it was enough to break the spell that had rooted her in place, and she rounded the counter, untying her yellow daisy-covered apron and tossing it onto the counter as she went.

'Don't worry about her,' she assured him. 'She's had a long day, and it ended with some really great news, so she's bound to be a little scatterbrained.'

'Great news, huh?'

'Looks like there's going to be a wedding in a few months,' Paige replied, mimicking Allison's gesture and cupping her hand as though it was a secret. 'But you didn't hear it from me.'

Cohen glanced back toward the door where Allison had long since disappeared. 'Wow, Chris finally got up the nerve. About time.' He caught Paige's gaze and chuckled. 'Don't worry, your secret is safe with me.'

She dismissed his comment with a wave of her hand. 'I'm not worried. If the small-town rumor mill is anything like I've been warned, I'm pretty sure everyone and their mother is going to know by tomorrow, anyway.'

'Everyone and their mother's mother,' Cohen corrected her.

'News travels fast in Port Landon, trust me.' He pointed toward the boy, now beside the front counter, hands pressed up against the glass as he *oohed* and *ahhed* over the cookies and selection of cupcakes left over from this morning's baking efforts. 'Speaking of that, this is my son, Bryce. And not only has he heard the rave reviews about your bakery, he fell in love with your chocolate fudge cake last night. Bryce, come and meet Paige, then you can choose your next sugar coma.'

The boy grudgingly peeled himself away from the display case, coming over to stand beside his father. 'Hey, Paige,' he said in a voice that sounded shy around the edges. He nudged into Cohen's side as he spoke. Obviously he preferred to focus on the cakes and cookies rather than her. But his manners were stronger than his timid first impression because the boy stuck a hand out to shake hers.

'Hello, Bryce.' She shook his hand and watched as Cohen wrapped an arm around the boy's shoulders in encouragement. 'I hear you're a pretty big chocolate fan.'

'The biggest.' He gestured wildly to show her just how much. And just like that, the shyness dissipated. 'You make the best cake. Like, ever.'

Paige beamed, stealing a glance up at Cohen, who looked just as amused. 'Thank you. That's the best compliment. Like, ever.' She clapped her hands together, then waved a hand around the room. 'What did you have in mind today?'

In true childlike fashion, Bryce theatrically pressed a finger to his chin, contemplating his choices as he took in his surroundings. 'Something colorful. Something that tastes like … fun.'

She couldn't hold back her soft chuckle. 'Fun, huh? Well, I don't think I've ever had a request for that flavor before, but maybe, since you're the expert and all, you and I can come up with something together?' She held a hand out for him to take, giving Cohen time to intervene if he thought she was overstepping. Cohen only nodded, watching with a crooked smile as Bryce slipped his fingers between hers. 'So, tell me, dear expert, what *does* fun taste like?'

The boy looked up at her, stopping in front of the cheesecake cooler once again, his eyes twinkling. 'It's not any one thing, Paige,' he explained. 'When you know, you know.'

Chapter 4

Cohen

Cohen's day had been jam-packed with back-to-back appointments, not to mention the emergency call that had come in from the Richardsons stating their German shepherd, Lulu, had tried to make friends with a porcupine and it became a prickly situation. Luckily for Lulu, she'd had enough sense to back away at the first cluster of quills in her nose, so there hadn't been many to pull, and the ones that were there were removed easily enough without the use of heavy anesthesia. Lulu even accepted a few treats as a truce with Cohen after the ordeal.

Needless to say, by the time the clinic sign had been turned from *Open* to *Closed*, Cohen was ready to head home and relax. In theory, anyway. His promise to Bryce hadn't been forgotten.

The boy was vibrating with excitement by the time he careened through the clinic door and announced his arrival. The first words out of his mouth were, 'I'm ready to go to the bakery, Dad!' Cohen knew he had no chance of getting out of it today.

Thankfully, there was still a small part of him that was anticipating the trip, which was a fact he couldn't bring himself to contemplate too closely. He fed kibble to Jazz, being careful to put warm water on it and stir it up just the way she liked it before setting it down. He checked her water dish and filled it, too. Jazz slept at the clinic at night instead of trudging through the path in the backyard to Cohen's house. Everyone adored the dog – everyone except Bryce's cat, Norman, who seemed to think Jazz was a little too rambunctious and in-your-face for his liking. Jazz never seemed to mind her makeshift bedroom in the downstairs office. Most days, she was so tired after a full day of greeting clients and being the clinic's entertainment that she was already snoring loudly in her oversized dog bed before they even left for the evening.

With the promise to return and take her for a long walk in a bit, Cohen walked through the back path toward home and changed into jeans and a plaid shirt over a plain white T-shirt. He shoved the on-call cellphone into his pocket, feeling rejuvenated at having somewhere to go. Someone to see. Again, he shook his head, not wanting to ponder that thought.

No amount of rejuvenation was going to help him keep up with Bryce, though. The ten-year-old's energy and ambition were no match for the weariness he currently felt at thirty-six. Most days, he could handle the fast pace of the clinic and the physical demands that came with it, but sometimes it was hard to keep up. Sometimes, the tiredness became too much to bear, something he couldn't see past and couldn't get around. The exhaustion wasn't just what he felt, it was who he was. What he'd become.

When Cohen bought the clinic eleven years ago, he never dreamed he and Stacey wouldn't be side by side to run it together. His wife had been a veterinarian, one of the best as far as he was concerned. Buying the clinic had been a joint venture.

A joint venture he now tackled daily. Alone. Not even his career could give him reprieve from the loss he harbored since Stacey's passing, being just another cruel daily reminder that his life was a jigsaw puzzle with missing pieces that would never be found.

Cohen would never blame Stacey, but the demands of running a veterinary practice, coupled with the struggles of raising an adolescent by himself … it was a lot to handle for one man. He did it, every day, and Cohen thought he did it reasonably well, all things considered. But he lived for the moments when work, responsibilities, and old-fashioned adulting weren't the only things he had to keep him company.

'Slow down!' he hollered after Bryce. 'This isn't a race.' But Bryce had already disappeared around the corner. He believed that's exactly what it was. Cohen chuckled to himself as he rounded the corner, far behind him, and saw the heavy glass door about three shops up swing closed. His son was lightning-fast, he would give him that. And he'd probably have six cakes on the counter ready to purchase by the time Cohen got there to stop him. But it was good to see him excited about something that wasn't electronics related. The kids his age needed more stimulation than just video games and apps to advance their minds, and Cohen was happy to see Bryce so enthralled with something.

Even if it was a place that sold sugar highs.

The bell chimed above his head as he pushed the door open, and while he had expected to see Bryce's wide eyes staring at him as he begged for more baked goods to take home, Cohen hadn't expected the other two sets of bulging eyes that stared at him like he'd just done something outlandish.

While he couldn't be certain, he had a sneaking suspicion they had been talking about him. That's why he'd switched topics so quickly once Allison's big news came up; it was an easy out from the awkwardness.

Things became anything but awkward, though, when Paige took the reins and led Bryce on a hunt for the perfect treat to buy. Watching them together, seeing his son so animated and comfortable, and seeing Paige interact with him so effortlessly – it made his heart ache with a swell of pride and joy. It was good for Bryce to converse with other adults. He was like a little adult himself, so maybe that was why he did it with such finesse. Cohen was still gawking around the shop, taking in the intricate designs and garnishes that topped the tower of cake slices in the countertop display case, trying to pretend he wasn't eavesdropping on Paige and Bryce's conversation about the importance of cream filling in relation to the decadence of a homemade doughnut, when his son's cheering erupted from behind him.

'Eureka!' Bryce cried. Cohen turned to see the young boy holding a silver plate high above his head like a trophy. On it, a massive slice of bright orange cheesecake was displayed, piled high with lush strawberries, blueberries, and an orange slice, all buried underneath a generous dollop of whipped cream. 'Look, Dad, it's fun on a plate!'

Cohen burst out laughing. 'I'd say.' He closed the gap between them, turning the plate in Bryce's hands from side to side, admiring it. 'I think this is where you invite me to share it with you, because, son, I don't think you can eat that whole thing by yourself.'

'Challenge accepted!' Bryce exclaimed, grinning from ear to ear.

'Yikes,' Paige interjected. 'If I'd known this was going to turn into a battle between you two, I would have brought the second piece out quicker.' She held out an identical silver plate for Cohen, shrugging as she whispered, 'I wouldn't want you to have to fight him for it.'

'Good call,' Cohen quipped. 'My bets would be on him.'

'Mine, too.'

'We'll take both pieces!' Bryce took his plate and pushed it up onto the front counter.

Cohen pursed his lips, shaking his head at his son's antics. 'Which, I guess, is code for I'll pay for both pieces.'

'Just one,' Paige insisted. 'My treat. I got you roped into it, after all.'

'Just wait till the sugar high kicks in. I'll be sending him back your way to deal with him until he crashes.'

She chuckled, ringing the sale into the register. 'Good thing it's closing time.'

'It's a small town, Paige,' Cohen joked. 'I know where you live.'

'Yeah, that's not creepy at all,' she replied ruefully.

Cohen pressed a hand to his chest, feigning hurt. 'Damn, creepy, huh? Not my best joke, then.'

'Not the worst I've heard,' Paige countered. 'But definitely not your finest, I'm sure. Besides, everyone knows where I live.'

'See, *that's* creepy.'

She laughed softly, a sound that resonated somewhere deep inside him. 'No, that's just small-town life,' she replied. 'Or so I've been told. Repeatedly.'

'Sounds to me like you're getting the hang of small-town living, Paige.'

'You might be right,' she agreed. 'With a little help, I'll get by just fine.' The twinkle in her eyes made him hear questions she wasn't actually asking, and the flicker of a flirty grin made him wonder if he was seeing things. The expression showed off her natural beauty, a simple femininity that went far beyond the bit of makeup she wore. He let out a long breath.

'Right. I ...' Should say something. Offer her help if she ever needed it. Or maybe—

'Dad ...'

Cohen glanced down to see Bryce bouncing anxiously on the balls of his feet.

'We've still got to walk Jazz before I can dig into this monstrous cake, remember? Can we go now?' The boy's eyes pleaded with his father, but Cohen just patted him on the shoulder.

'Easy, now. Don't be rude. We've got to pay, then we can go

get Jazz.' He pulled a twenty-dollar bill from his wallet and passed it to Paige. 'Keep the change. You and I both know we'll be back before long.'

Paige didn't look prepared to argue that fact. 'You two might just become my best customers.'

'Another challenge accepted,' Bryce assured her. 'Now, let's haul this cake home and get this show on the road, Dad!'

Laughter erupted from Paige's mouth, and Cohen couldn't help but join in. 'He has manners, I swear.'

'It's the cake talking. I get it.' Paige closed the cash register and made short work of putting the cake plates into large takeout boxes. 'Sounds like you'd better get home to Jazz.' She added, 'Whom I just realized is a dog, by the way.'

Cohen's eyes narrowed, humor alight within them. 'Who did you think Jazz was, then?'

'All you said when you were here yesterday was that you had to get back to Jazz, which I just assumed was short for Jasmine or something.'

'Like Princess Jasmine,' Bryce cut in. 'You know, from *Aladdin*.'

Cohen piled one cake box on top of the next. 'Well, Jazz is a princess, I can attest to that. Actually, she's probably more of a diva than a princess. But, yes, she's a dog. And a one of a kind one at that.'

'She sounds wonderful,' Paige said.

'You should come and meet her,' Cohen offered before he had time to talk himself out of it. 'I mean, come for a walk with us. I'm sure Bryce would get a kick out of showing you around town.' He took a breath. 'I would, too.'

What in God's name was he doing?

Paige looked just as stunned as he felt, but she quickly composed herself. 'I'd love to, but I still need to close up the shop and then go upstairs and change into something that doesn't smell like, well, a bakery.'

'I don't know a person in this world who would complain about that smell.' Cohen laughed. 'And those are the perks of living above your shop, yeah? Getting to just run upstairs whenever you need to. I'm thankful every day that our house is directly behind the clinic. It makes things so much easier.'

'I won't argue with you about the convenience,' she replied, turning the lights off in the display case beside the register.

Maybe that was why he'd invited her along on their walk. Because he and Paige had something in common. Even if that commonality was simply a business to run and a home that wasn't far from that business. Maybe she would understand what it was like to struggle to maintain the division between the two. Yes, that was his reasoning for the invite. Nothing more.

'Do me a favor and don't argue with me about the walk, either.' He gave her a faint grin, wondering if his own eyes shone with the amusement he saw staring back at him. 'We still need to take these cakes home and pick up Jazz. Does that give you enough time to close up?'

Paige stared at him, her gaze fixed on his. Whatever she was searching for within his eyes, she must have found it, because she turned back toward the clock, scrutinized it, then whirled around. 'I can be ready in fifteen minutes. How does that sound?'

'I'd say it sounds … pretty perfect to me. Get ready for the grand tour of Port Landon, Paige.'

It had been on the tip of his tongue to use the old adage, 'Sounds like a date.' Even though the woman had proven she could handle a joke, he didn't want to come across as presumptuous if taken the wrong way. Thankfully, he had managed to stop himself in time, before the foreign words slipped off his tongue and caused him to make a damn fool of himself.

Besides, it wasn't a date. He knew that. He hadn't meant it as such when he invited her along. He was just being a friendly neighbor. A good citizen. A friend to someone who had few others to spend time with in a new town. And he didn't *want* it to be a date.

Or did he? No. He couldn't.

No matter what Sonya Ritter thought. The older woman had always been good to him, a friendly face when he needed one, even when he didn't deserve it. That was just how she was with everyone in Port Landon. They didn't call her a mother hen for nothing. But he knew damn well the wheels in her head were turning. They always were, and she didn't need any help with finding reasons to think things were something they weren't.

Paige was just locking the big steel door that led upstairs to her apartment above the bakery as Cohen and Bryce strolled around the corner. From a distance, she looked much younger than her early thirties, and with her long, dark hair, trendy jeans, and sleeveless top, he knew she could easily be mistaken for a woman in her early twenties instead.

The second Jazz caught a glimpse of her up the sidewalk, she pulled relentlessly on the retractable leash, making poor Bryce stumble forwards. Cohen caught him before he fell, fisting the back of his T-shirt in his hand.

Cohen didn't usually allow for it, but once he knew Paige had seen them, he unclipped Jazz's leash from her matching purple collar and let her run full-tilt toward her, running in the bouncy way only Jazz did, with her front paws moving as one, prodding along like a not-so-graceful deer instead of the seventy-five pound dog she was. She plowed straight into Paige's arms, who had crouched down and steeled herself for the dog's weight to hit her. Jazz bounced, and licked Paige's face, and hopped, and licked her face some more.

'Wow, I think she likes you.' Cohen had run to catch up to the dog, making sure Bryce was hot on his heels.

Paige laughed as Jazz attacked her the only way she knew

how – one lick after another with her oversized tongue. 'I think I like her, too.' Paige ruffled the dog's brindle fur, and the dog slowly began to calm, pushing up against her and relishing in the attention. 'Ah, that's what she really looks like. All I could see was the inside of her mouth as she came at me in a furry blur.'

'Dad calls her the Jazzmanian Devil,' Bryce informed her.

'That's a very suiting name, I must say.'

Paige couldn't seem to tear her gaze from the boxer, and the sight of someone else falling instantly in love with the dog warmed Cohen's heart. 'Princess. Diva. Devil. Doesn't matter what you call her, she's still the perfect dog. With some quirks, of course,' Cohen said.

'Well, we've all got some quirks, don't we?' Paige held Jazz's wrinkled face in her hands, talking directly to the dog. 'It's so nice to meet you, Jazz.'

'We'd better be careful, Bryce, or we're going to lose our walking partner to Jazz and her charm.'

Paige looked up, grinning from ear to ear. 'Hey, you can't fault me for falling for her; you're the one who brought her here,' she reminded him. She gave the dog one last pat on the head and rose to her feet. 'She sure is a great dog. You two are very lucky to have her.'

'Maybe Paige can be Jazz's forever home, Dad.' Bryce nudged his dad's arm to get his attention.

'She isn't your dog?' Paige wore a confused expression as she looked between Cohen and his son.

'Well, kind of,' Bryce explained. 'She stays at the clinic because Norman doesn't like her very much.'

'Norman?'

'My cat,' the young boy said. 'Jazz doesn't have a forever home, so she stays at the clinic with Dad and his coworkers because everybody loves her there.'

Paige, to her credit, glanced down at the dog, who was still

45

gazing up at her with loving brown eyes and a waggling tongue, and wilted slightly. 'Aww, Jazz, I'm sorry. That must be so hard, pretty girl.'

'Trust me,' Cohen added, 'She's not upset about it, by any means. That dog gets more attention and love from Bryce and me than the average dog with a real home. And frankly, the staff are crazy about her. We're at the clinic more than we're at home, anyway. As far as Jazz is concerned, we're her family. And as far as I'm concerned, that's exactly what she is, too. Our family.'

'Unless someone special came along to take her home,' Bryce countered quickly, giving his dad a knowing look and trying to discreetly point to Paige without drawing her attention.

Paige chuckled at the boy's antics. 'Jazz is wonderful, believe me. But I don't think the bakery is the place for her, unfortunately.'

'Agreed!' Bryce exclaimed. 'That's why you need to take her home!'

'I can't believe no one has come forward to adopt her.' She looked genuinely perplexed, which only added to Cohen's pride of the dog and her gentle mannerisms. 'She's just so … friendly.'

'Wait till she smiles at you with her lips tucked up, showing off her crooked teeth. She'll steal your heart, then.' He watched Jazz, who watched Paige just as intently. 'The reality is, she's four years old, so her chances of adoption are slimmer than most. People want puppies, not mature dogs.'

'Dad, there's nothing mature about Jazz,' Bryce scoffed. 'She's a puppy trapped in an adult dog's body. Obviously.' The boy did his best Vanna White impersonation, framing his hands around the dog to put her on display, waggling his eyebrows at Paige, silently daring her not to fall in love with the brindle dog.

He couldn't hold in his amusement, and Cohen let his laughter erupt, shaking his head. 'Sorry, Paige. My boy is nothing if not persistent.'

'Gee, I hadn't noticed.'

'We'd better get that ice cream quick.' Cohen pointed down

the street where the water's edge was seen a few blocks away. 'I think it's safe to say it's the only chance you're going to get a moment's reprieve from his relentless badgering about this.'

'I won't forget, you know,' Bryce piped up, handing the leash to his father. 'Even after ice cream.'

'No,' Cohen replied, heading down the sidewalk with Jazz in tow as Paige fell into step beside him. 'I didn't think you would.'

Chapter 5

Paige

Despite officially living in Port Landon for three months, Paige had made little time to really explore the lakeside town she now called home. She had spent every waking minute preparing for the grand opening of her bakery, making sure every detail that she could control was perfect, and that nothing was overlooked. Renovations, remodeling, plans for displays and specials. Paige Henley was a planner, an organizer. And now that the grand opening had come and gone, and been successful, she was glad for it.

Her hope that she would be welcomed in the little town was also fulfilled, it seemed. As she, Cohen, and Bryce ambled their way down the sidewalk, past the stone building that housed the town hall and the old Victorian-style houses that were the pride and joy of most of the population here, they were greeted by a handful of people. Some, she knew; others, she didn't. Most of them, she thought she recognized, but Paige couldn't put a name to the face.

They knew who she was, though. Everyone called her by name, whether it was the middle-aged woman in workout wear they passed on the sidewalk – Amelia Harris, the town's treasurer, according to Cohen – or the older gentleman with sprigs of gray hair tufting out under his straw hat – Old Man Weston, Cohen called him affectionately.

'He was already standing outside your bakery before you even opened the doors yesterday morning,' Cohen advised. 'I saw him on my way into the clinic.'

She had met so many people in the last forty-eight hours that Paige wasn't sure she would ever get everybody's names straight. But everyone she came across seemed to remember her and have a friendly wave or greeting. After only a few months as a resident and a couple of days as an official business owner, that made her feel pretty good.

They turned off Main Street onto Crescent Street, and she marveled at how perfectly aligned the row of tall trees was that lined the road. The leaves, dark green and lush in the high summer sun, created a canopy over the road, only permitting sporadic kaleidoscopic patterns of sunshine to make it through the thick veil. Everything about the town was picturesque, from the vintage-looking red mailboxes that marked the end of each driveway, to the tall houses with their unique moldings and fancy pillars. The downtown core wasn't the only row of buildings to boast red brick and wrought iron pegs that jutted out toward the sidewalk to hold old-fashioned shingles. If the homes in Port Landon weren't tall wooden-sided structures with a Victorian flare, nestled in big yards with feathery shrubs and oversized maple and hemlock trees, they were massive brick estate homes with elegant trimmings and high, pointed roofs. Many had towers, rounded rooms with or without windows. Paige idly wondered what those towers housed. Many places they passed had signs outside on their lawns or hanging beside the driveways – Cindy's Sewing and Dressmaking, Port Landon Dog Grooming, Antiques For Sale.

The residents of Port Landon were industrious, it seemed.

They talked about everything and nothing. With Cohen's prompting, Paige told him about the life she'd left behind in New York. Even as she described it, with its fast pace and its long hours, she realized that it was no kind of life at all. Not for her, anyway. Once she began, the words seemed to tumble easily off her tongue. Cohen was surprisingly easy to talk to, and New York was even easier to talk about. It only fortified her conviction that she had made the right choice. Her life in New York wasn't something she yearned to close the door on and never revisit again, it was just a chapter that had come to a close, allowing her to turn the page and begin a new one.

'I can't imagine what it's like to come from the heart of New York City to a laid-back town like Port Landon,' Cohen said. 'You must think we're all country bumpkins.'

'Hardly,' she laughed. 'I've only been here a few months, but people have been friendlier and more interested in what I'm trying to do than I ever experienced in the city.'

'Most people would call that being nosy.' Cohen didn't miss a step, pointing toward the end of the street where the hill gave the illusion that it somehow ended in the middle of the lake. Paige just caught sight of Bryce and Jazz disappearing over the hill.

'You say nosy, I say it's different, that's all.'

'Do you miss it?'

Paige thought about that. 'I was good at my job, and I lived for it. But there came a point where I had to ask myself … was I really living at all?' For a brief moment, she was embarrassed. It was difficult to confide such a simple truth to someone – that she'd realized the ever-turning hamster wheel of the business world was no longer for her, that she was burned out and exhausted from climbing the proverbial ladder that she would never reach the top of, and that the trajectory of her own path had changed, almost without her realizing it. Especially to someone she barely knew.

That was the thing, though. She might have only met Cohen yesterday, yet the easy back-and-forth between them was effortless. Paige hadn't realized she craved this kind of companionship until she experienced it. Maybe her job in New York had robbed her of more than just her time. Maybe it had prevented her from having the chance of having this kind of social interaction before now, prevented her from putting down real roots and finding someone to share her time with.

'I think if you have to ask, then it's safe to say you made the right decision by leaving.' Cohen stole a glance at her. 'And by moving here.'

A faint blush rose in Paige's cheeks. 'So far, I would most definitely agree with you. It's good having Allison so close by, too.'

'I still can't believe Chris finally popped the question,' Cohen stated following a chuckle. 'It's been years. I was starting to believe he was just holding out in order to drive the town nuts.'

Paige laughed, a whole-hearted sound that echoed off the treed walls of the canopy-covered street. 'I knew it would happen eventually, even though Allison always made such a grand attempt at making it sound like she was okay with waiting to get married. She's been waiting for this moment, she just won't admit it outright.'

'Women,' Cohen quipped. 'Saying one thing, expecting another.'

Paige gave him a playful, narrowed-eyed glare. 'Trust me, I don't think men always want to hear what women are really thinking. We might shock you.'

'Now, that's intriguing.'

The blacktop ended abruptly, making way for the boardwalk that lined the lakeshore, leading out onto the rows of docks. Multiple boats of all different sizes were tied to the metal anchors on either side of the wooden platforms, bobbing in the gentle breeze that Paige hadn't noticed until they broke out from under the canopy of trees.

Bryce's laughter carried through the air like a song, and Paige followed the sound to see the young boy and the dog bouncing happily farther up the boardwalk, which was where she could only assume the pier jutted out.

From here, the town seemed so much bigger, with the expanse of the docks and lakeshore stretching out far in the distance.

'Wow, this place looks like heaven,' Paige breathed out, her eyes locked on the boardwalk. She could feel the warmth of the wooden boards emanating from beneath her feet through her flip-flops.

'It does, doesn't it?' Cohen looked back, realized she had stopped in her tracks, and made his way back to her, staring out toward the mouth of the pier, just as she was. 'Still miss New York City?'

'New York what?' She offered him a coy wink, then shuffled out of her sandals, plucked them from the ground, and took off running in the direction of Bryce and Jazz. There was something magical about having the sun beating down on her, with the boats lined up on her right and the grid of streets and trees swaying in the breeze to her left. Paige had lived for her career in the city – at least, that's what she thought she'd been doing.

Right then, she felt free. Real, true freedom. And it occurred to her that maybe there was a part of her that had been held captive during her time amongst the hustle and bustle. This, right here, wasn't just existing.

This was living.

Paige jogged up to where Bryce stood, waiting impatiently for his father and her to catch up.

'About time, slow pokes,' he taunted. 'Even Jazz beat you here, and she's got a messed-up back.'

Paige was breathless, but it felt good to have her blood pumping through her veins with some fervor. 'What's wrong with Jazz's back?'

It was Cohen that answered her question from behind her. 'Diffuse idiopathic skeletal hyperostosis.'

Paige crinkled her forehead. 'In layman's terms, please, Doctor.'

'DISH, it's called.' Cohen shrugged. 'Basically, her spine has calcification that causes her to move more stiffly than other dogs, and there's no real reason for it. It's common in boxers, and Jazz's case is relatively minor.'

'Is she in pain?' Paige asked, casting a glance at the dog. She certainly didn't look in pain, with her tongue drooping from her mouth and her tail wagging wildly.

'Not at all,' Cohen promised. 'She takes an anti-inflammatory every morning and every evening, but what you see is what you get. She's a happy dog with a solid veterinary team behind her, monitoring her closely. Like I said, she just moves a little differently than other dogs.' The corner of Cohen's mouth turned up. 'But in case you haven't noticed, Jazz isn't exactly like other dogs in any way, shape, or form, so I wouldn't expect anything less.'

Paige chuckled, bending to give the dog an affectionate pat on the head. 'I know, I know. She's the Jazzmanian Devil.'

'That, she is,' Cohen agreed. 'So, we made it to the pier. What's next on the agenda, Bryce?'

The boy made a scene of whirling around as though assessing the situation, but Paige could tell by the gleam in his eyes that he knew exactly what he was going to suggest. 'Ice cream!'

'I knew that was coming,' Cohen assured Paige. 'Lead the way, Bryce. We'll catch up.'

Bryce and Jazz took off ahead of them, and Paige watched as Jazz ambled along with the boy. Now that she knew what she was looking for, she could see the odd way in which the dog moved about. In no way did it seem to be slowing her down any, though. It made Paige's heart swell to see the dog so happy and content despite having so much stacked against her.

'So, with Allison's wedding coming up, I suppose that means you'll have a big, fancy cake to create?'

Paige smiled, eager at the mere thought of it. 'I can't wait. As soon as Allison fills me in on her wedding colors and her ideas for it – and she's going to have a million ideas, I'm sure – I'll be starting on trial runs to get the design and flavor perfect.'

'I volunteer to test out those trial runs,' Cohen offered. 'I know a ten-year-old boy who would be a damn good candidate, too.'

'Duly noted,' Paige replied wryly. 'But I think we should probably let the bride-to-be taste the wedding cake.'

He scoffed at the idea. 'Fine, but I'm not above snatching up the leftovers. Just saying.'

'Again, duly noted.' The playful note in their back-and-forth had her struggling to hide a grin. She wasn't above giving him the leftovers, either. Chances were, she was going to drive herself insane over this cake. By the time she managed to get it just right, she would be tired of seeing wedding cakes for quite a while. At least, ones that resembled Allison's.

Normally, Paige viewed silence between two people as awkward, and the first thing she would do is fear she should be saying something more. But the silence between them was easy, and she didn't feel that anxious tightening in her chest to fill it the way she once did.

'Have you ever been married, Paige?'

Whatever she had expected him to say next, it wasn't that. 'That was blunt.'

'Sorry,' he said, wincing. 'I guess I'm not good at beating around the bush.'

'No need to apologize. I actually think I appreciate that sort of matter-of-factness about you.' Her gaze flitted up toward him for a brief moment. 'And no, I didn't leave an ex-husband or sordid backstory in New York City.'

'Well, damn, because I do love a sordid backstory.' Cohen reached out, pointing at the pavilion they were getting close to. 'Let me guess, no time for dating or relationships due to your breakneck schedule?'

Paige saw the sign for the Old Port Ice Cream Shoppe, and she laughed at Cohen's candid remark. 'You hit the nail on the head. It was hard to find time for other people when I barely had time for myself. Therefore, I'm a cliché – always the bridesmaid, never the bride. Or, in Allison's case, I guess I'm the maid of honor, but you know what I mean.'

'And that bothers you.'

This time, his comment was enough to make her stop abruptly. Paige looked up at him with wide eyes. She didn't know what should have bothered her more, that she wasn't confident that she'd never truly had time for other relationships so much as just never made time, or that Cohen read her like an open book. 'Maybe,' she answered, cautious.

'Sorry.' Cohen held his hands up in mock surrender. 'Innocent observation, I swear. I could hear the tinge of longing in your voice.'

She wondered if she should be angry that he'd called her out on the regret she had a hard time veiling in her tone. The thing was, she wasn't upset at all. There was something calming about having someone else point it out, willing to let her know how evident her want for a romantic relationship was. What Paige wondered was if his ease at picking up on it was because he understood the feeling all too well himself. 'Since I've been here, I've had time to think, and I've been wondering if I've wasted so much time climbing the corporate ladder, I've missed my chances at ever being the woman that has that kind of life.'

'I'm going to assume there was a time in your life when you thought you'd missed your chance at ever owning your own bakery, too, right? But it happened.' Cohen's hazel eyes locked with hers as he stepped ahead and opened the white wooden screen door that led inside the ice cream shop.

Paige sighed. 'Cohen Beckett, you're such a smart man.'

'They don't call me doctor for nothing.' He gestured for her to pass by him. 'Besides, you just have to stay positive. Things happen in their own good time, and everything happens for a reason. That's what I tell myself, anyway.'

Paige stepped inside the shop, and a blast of cool air hit her flushed cheeks. It was frigid in the little storefront compared to the sun-kissed boardwalk outside. She was surprised to see Bryce sitting in the corner booth furthest from the ice cream counter, Jazz plopped down beside him on the floor, panting incessantly with the biggest smile on her jowly face. She didn't think they would allow a dog in here, but she'd learned not to question things like that. Some things were done a little differently in Port Landon.

'That's what you tell yourself, huh?' she countered. 'Like a daily mantra, I assume.'

'Nah, more like a rock.' Before Paige could ask what in the world he was talking about, Cohen pulled a small, smooth object from his pocket and dropped it into her hands. 'I carry that around with me to remind me. Think positive.'

Paige turned the beige stone over in her hands. It was warm from the heat of Cohen's body and smooth to the touch save for the engravings on both sides of it. One side boasted a simple pawprint with a heart in the middle of it. The other had *Think Pawsitive* scrolled across it in dark brown lettering.

'My wife gave that to me a long time ago.'

The words made Paige's head snap up.

'She passed away eight years ago,' he continued, nodding toward the rock. 'But, as I said, it's a reminder to think positive. And, sometimes, all we need is that reminder.'

Paige searched Cohen's face. There was a shadow in his eyes, darkening the brownish green of his irises, but the small hint of a crooked smile proved he wasn't looking for sympathy in his confession. It also proved they shared a common ground – a thinly veiled fear that their time for love had come and gone, and they both clung tightly to the hope that fate would give them a second chance someday.

56

'A little positive thinking can go a long way, Paige.'

Her gaze had migrated back down to the little stone in her hands, along with her thoughts. Cohen's voice pulled her back to the here and now, and she let out a long breath as she held the rock out for him. 'So can ice cream.'

Chapter 6

Cohen

It was almost midnight, but Cohen couldn't fall asleep. Spending a few hours in the fading sun with Bryce, Jazz, and Paige after a full day's work should have left him exhausted, but every time he closed his eyes he could still see the way the sunlight danced as it reflected in Paige's sapphire eyes, and he could still hear the full-blown laughter erupting from Bryce as he joked and enjoyed himself out on the pier.

It wasn't the first time they had gone to the pier after a workday, but it was the first time they'd brought someone else along with them. Usually, Bryce and Cohen were content in each other's company, as they had been for the past eight years. And until today, Cohen believed he was content with the little life he had with his son and the vet clinic.

Until today.

Now, he lay in bed, the covers still pulled back and the bedside lamp still shining dim light across the room, listening to his son's soft, even breathing from across the hall. This was the life they had, the routine they had fallen into. It had served them well, despite being forced into it by tragedy. Work and school, evenings filled with homework and walks, nights spent in bed by ten o'clock at the latest so they could both get up and do it all again tomorrow.

It was simple and easy. And until today, Cohen had thought it was enough. He'd been a slave to his routine for so long he found it hard to remember what it had been like when Stacey had been with them. Not that he couldn't recall the things that mattered – her smile and her warm gaze, her adoration of her son and her unabashed love for him. Those things came to him with a vivid clarity. It was the minutes and days and time spent apart he couldn't remember. Like his tangible distance from Stacey was the deciding factor of what was important enough to remain etched into his brain.

He thought he had coped well following the car accident that took her from him. As well as a man in his twenties with a toddler son could cope. There were days he didn't see how he could continue on, how he could survive one more second with the knowledge of knowing Stacey was gone. But there were more days, as his grief transformed into a simmering bitterness, that Cohen had awoken in the morning, determined to prove to Port Landon's residents that he didn't need their sympathy or charity or help to raise his son. He threw himself into his role as a single father, desperate to prove to them, and to himself, that he could raise Bryce in a way that would have made Stacey proud. He could do right by her through their son, even if he hadn't been able to protect her from the accident that ripped away the life she'd worked so hard to build. The life *they* had built.

It had been eight years – years that seemed on one hand to have been long and drawn out, and on the other hand had gone by in the blink of an eye – and Cohen was proud of the boy Bryce had become as a result of his efforts. He had wanted so damn badly to make Stacey proud. Of Bryce. Of him.

And he had achieved that, Cohen knew it. What he didn't

know was if his own complacency and contentment in being just the two of them had hindered Bryce in some way. His son had talked of nothing but Paige the entire way home after they'd walked her to her apartment door beside the bakery storefront. The boy had relished in having someone else to show off to, someone to tell his jokes to and be a kid around. Bryce and Paige had also bonded over Jazz, and the dog seemed to love Paige just as much.

It had been the perfect evening – ice cream and walking along the boardwalk while the sun disappeared behind the trees, with his son and his new friend.

It had been a long time since Cohen could say he had one of those. Not unlike her, he had spent the bulk of his time intent on running his business and raising Bryce. There had been no time for close friendships. Acquaintances, sure – he had a lot of those in town. But no one he could remember spending time with outside of work hours.

Even now, Cohen wasn't sure if he was being truthful to himself about his reasons for his inactive social life. Maybe it wasn't so much that he hadn't had the time to build one, as that he hadn't made the time to have one. He wasn't even sure he'd realized he needed one. It was just another thing in the long line of revelations that were coming to him tonight.

The wailing of sirens ripped him from his thoughts. With the window open, he knew the emergency service vehicle was heading right past the front of his house. Cohen was one of those people that never could tell the sound of a police siren from a fire truck or ambulance, so he hoisted himself from the bed, clad in blue plaid pajama pants and a white T-shirt, to see if he could catch a glimpse of whatever was coming.

Cohen's little bungalow was situated behind the clinic, and it faced the opposite way, out onto Hemlock Street, which ran parallel to the downtown stretch on Main. When he saw the fire engine career past, with its red and white lights blazing and its sirens screeching in the silence of the night, another revelation hit him deep in the chest.

Maybe Paige's life in New York City had been hectic and chaotic, but he'd bet that when she heard sirens scream in the city, she didn't end up with acid burning in the pit of her stomach because of it. That was both the blessing and the curse of small-town life – when something happened to someone, it happened to everyone. And when something affected someone, it was a given that if Cohen didn't know the afflicted party personally, he would know someone who did. No one was an unknown face in the crowd. People had names, and families, and history within the town limits.

Living in a small town was simple and as good as it got on most days. During nights like tonight, however, it was down-right scary, and Cohen doubted sleep was on the cards anytime soon.

The appointment schedule at the clinic was back to back all day. The day started off with two routine surgeries, then progressed on to a series of appointments that all seemed to carry Cohen further and further away from what he deemed a typical day as each hour passed. He wasn't sure if the disconnect he felt from his brain was due to the challenging cases he was being presented with, or the lack of sleep he'd managed to get the night before. Either way, it felt like there wasn't enough caffeine in the world to get him through the remaining three hours his clinic was open.

'Dr Cohen, there's someone here to see you.' Alice, the receptionist, broke through his train of thought as he stood against the pharmacy counter, reading the lab work results that had just been printed off. 'And she's got coffee in her hand, so I'm thinking you might want to go at least get that from her. You look like you need it.'

'Are you telling me I look awful, Alice?' But even as he joked about it, Cohen set the sheet of paper down and made his way toward the waiting room. If he looked half as bad as he felt, he needed that coffee. Stat.

'Not a chance,' she assured him. 'Just that you look like you're asleep standing up.'

'So, I *do* look how I feel.' He patted Alice on the shoulder on his way past her. 'Thanks for letting me know. Tell my next appointment I'll be right in.'

In the waiting room, Paige stood in the middle of the marble tiled floor with two paper cups in her hands, steam billowing from the hole in the plastic tops.

'I know you're busy,' she blurted immediately. 'I just thought—'

'You have no idea how happy I am to see you.' Cohen reached out for one of the cups in her hand just as Paige held it out to him. *God, did I really just say that out loud?*

'Me, or the coffee?'

'Both,' he replied, glad for the chance to play it down. 'But I won't downplay how thrilled I am to see this cup. Come on back.'

Cohen led her through the pharmacy and into the lunchroom. It was organized chaos. Magazines littered the top of the table, and the chairs hadn't been pushed back into place when the staff used them earlier in the day. There was a desktop computer in the corner on a portable desk, where Cohen attempted to get his notes done throughout the day. It was booted up and displaying a screensaver of a litter of bulldog puppies that had been born in the clinic last year. That litter was the result of a long, drawn-out birth, requiring an emergency caesarean section, but every puppy had lived and the mother was just fine. Rhonda, the veterinary technician, had even adopted one of the puppies when they were old enough to leave their mother. Purses and backpacks were tossed along the far wall where the staff members had left them when they came in that morning.

'It's not the tidiest spot, but I hope it's okay.' Cohen pulled out one of the plastic chairs closest to the table, gesturing for Paige to have a seat.

'It's great,' she assured him as she sat down. 'I won't stay long. I just wanted to say thank you for yesterday. The walk to the pier with you, Bryce, and Jazz was the most fun I've had in a while.'

Cohen pulled the chair away from the computer cart, straddling the back of it as he leaned forward against the backrest. 'Well, thanks, but I feel like I should be thanking you. I think that's the most fun the three of us have had in ages, too. Bryce couldn't stop talking about it last night, or this morning. You'll probably be the first thing he mentions when he comes home from school in about forty-five minutes.'

'I'm glad you all had a wonderful time.' Paige fidgeted with her coffee cup, but she offered him an easy smile.

'We'll have to do it again sometime.' Cohen said it as more of a polite gesture than a concrete invitation, but there was enough uncertainty in his tone that it came out sounding more like a question. The moment the words left his lips, he wondered if he'd made a mistake, if he had been too presumptuous, if he'd made it sound like a—

'I would like that,' Paige replied.

Cohen fought to keep his expression neutral, a battle of relief and hesitancy warring within him. 'Great. Me too.' He let that sink in between them, taking a sip of hot coffee and letting it burn down his throat. 'I know someone else who'd like it as well. Come here, I have to show you something.'

He pushed his coffee cup onto the lunchroom table, knowing the perfect distraction from the awkward conversation that was sure to follow. He led Paige out the open doorway into a hallway at the back of the clinic. To the right, the hall led to the prep room and the surgery. To the left, it led down a flight of four stairs. They went left. Cohen was shocked to discover the temptation he had to reach out for her hand as she descended the stairs. He shoved his hands in the pockets of his jeans.

'Yesterday, you saw the bouncy, crazy Jazz that acts like a typical five-year-old child,' he explained, his lips curling upward. 'But let me show you the real Jazz. The one that no one sees unless they live with her.' Cohen slowly pushed open the door at the bottom of the stairs, which had been left open a crack.

The sound hit them before they could even see her.

'Is she … snoring?' Paige covered her mouth, holding in her laughter.

Sure enough, with the door opened wide, there was Jazz, sprawled out across the biggest, most luxurious dog bed Cohen had been able to find online, snoring like a freight train. Her lips puffed out with each loud exhale of breath, and her eyes and paws twitched as she slept heavily.

'Oh my God,' Paige whispered. 'She's so adorable.'

Jazz's eyes squinted open at the sound of her voice, and she lifted her head, the tip of her pink tongue sticking out as she glanced around, dazed, and tried to reorient herself. Cohen could see the moment of recognition. Instantly, the excitement of Paige's presence took over. Jazz scrambled awkwardly to her feet just as Paige crouched down in front of her. The dog wasted no time in allowing herself to be enveloped by Paige's arms, her tail wagging at sonic speed like a little propeller.

'Hi, Jazzy girl,' Paige cooed, running her fingers through her brown and black fur, nuzzling into the dog just as much as she was nuzzling into her.

'I still maintain she likes you,' Cohen attested with a knowing grin. 'A lot.'

'You told me she likes everyone, so stop it,' Paige said with a laugh. 'Do you still have appointments?'

He had completely forgotten while in Paige's presence. *Damn it*. 'Yes, a few. But no one will bother you in here if you want to stay. It's the payroll administrator's office and she isn't working today, so this room is yours for the taking.'

'Hmm,' Paige said, dodging Jazz's tongue as she tried to lick her face. 'I can stay for a few minutes. There's something I'd like to talk to you about, anyway.'

'That doesn't sound ominous at all.' Cohen narrowed his eyes, a thousand ideas whirling around in his mind of what the topic could be. 'I'll be back as soon as I can.'

Cohen closed the door behind him, leaving Paige and Jazz in their glory with each other. It wasn't lost on him that he felt as though he could have left the room for only a second, and yet he still would have been gone from her for too long.

His remaining appointments got dragged out, stretching well over the course of an hour and a half before Cohen had the chance to step away from the exam rooms and check in on Paige and Jazz downstairs. As he bounded down the steps, he knew he was already too late.

The office door was open, and Paige was gone. So was Jazz. The sight of the empty room and even emptier dog bed deflated Cohen, replacing his anticipation with disappointment. But when he saw the note scrawled on the back of one of the blank sheets of paper pulled from the printer on the desk, Cohen's disappointment quickly vanished.

Cohen,

Sorry, I had to head back to The Cakery, as the note I'd left on the door said I'd only be gone fifteen minutes. Jazz wanted to come with me. Bring Bryce over once the clinic is closed and you've had supper. I'll handle dessert.

- Paige & Jazz

She had drawn a little pawprint beside Jazz's name as her signature. It was a cute touch, he would give her that.

He knew Bryce was going to be elated about their impromptu

dessert plans. If Cohen was honest with himself, he was as well. And while he was on an honesty kick, the truth of how happy it made him was, quite frankly, petrifying.

There were a lot of things that scared Cohen Beckett in Port Landon lately. He just never expected Paige Henley to be one of them.

Chapter 7

Paige

Paige waited at the clinic as long as she dared. Unfortunately, she knew all too well that she had left only a handwritten sign on the door to indicate she would be right back, and her business wasn't going to run itself.

With the dog in tow, she had made her way out the side door marked *Staff Entrance* at the clinic and disappeared back up the sidewalk toward the bakery. The downtown street was bustling with shoppers, and it still mesmerized Paige that such a small town with only a few thousand people could be so busy during the day. She guessed that was what happened when businesses were only open until five o'clock, the diner and convenience store only open until eight. Folks in New York City would have hardly called that convenient. Imagine what they would say if they knew the entire town shut down for the night, silent as a tomb.

There was someone waiting at the front door of her bakery, and she was surprised to see it was Sonya Ritter.

'Are you pulling a Cruella de Vil and stealing that dog, or do you and Dr Cohen have joint custody now?' The woman's spiderweb of laugh lines at the corners of her eyes highlighted the mischievous glint in her dark eyes.

'Hello, Sonya. We're just having a playdate, that's all.'

'You and Jazz, or you and the good doctor?'

Paige couldn't bring herself to look the older woman in the eyes, and she knew her cheeks were flaming red at the assumption. 'Is there something I can help you with?' she asked instead, pushing the door open and gesturing for Sonya to go in ahead of her.

'Allison is on the warpath for some of those apple fritters she saw yesterday. She sent me over to get a few.'

'There are still a couple left, I think. Let me tuck Jazz away in my apartment for a minute and then I will get them for you.'

She made quick work of getting the dog settled upstairs, placing a folded comforter on the floor for her and putting a dish of water down beside it. She wouldn't be gone long, as it was almost closing time. She would have gladly brought the dog into the bakery with her if there weren't some hygienic codes being broken by doing so.

Paige couldn't ease the embarrassment that flooded through her at Sonya's insinuation. So, she – as well as other Port Landon folks, she assumed – were chomping at the bit to find out what was going on between her and Cohen. While she couldn't blame them, since they had done little to hide their budding friendship from prying eyes, the brash assumption that it was more than that was a little presumptuous and, frankly, unfair.

Cohen had been alone for many years. That wasn't news to Port Landon, and they knew exactly why. And Paige – well, no one really knew her, did they?

It was then that Paige realized what was happening. She was getting her first real taste of small-town life. Allison had warned her how it worked: Whatever they don't know for certain, they'll make up. It was harsh, it was stereotypical, and it was the truth.

And, in this case, it was completely inaccurate. Wasn't it?

Paige knew she'd enjoyed walking down to the pier and getting ice cream with Cohen and Bryce. And she had shown up at his clinic with coffee from Allison's coffeehouse because she had a question for him … and because she'd wanted to see him. Paige enjoyed Cohen's company. It was a breath of fresh air to have someone to talk to and someone to spend time with. Her life wasn't all about work for a change.

But that didn't mean she was vying for a date with Cohen Beckett, and it certainly didn't mean she wanted anything more than the simple friendship they had established.

And that was exactly what Paige repeated to herself over and over as she made her way back into the bakery to face Sonya Ritter.

'You're enjoying living in Port Landon, Paige?' Sonya held out the ten-dollar bill, her gaze never wavering as she scooped the box of fritters into her arms. Paige didn't know how the woman managed to say so much with only a look.

She counted out her change and handed it back without faltering. 'It's a lovely town, Sonya,' she assured her with a nod. 'I'm certain I made the right decision by moving here.'

'And that certainty wouldn't have anything to do with Dr Cohen, now, would it?'

Sonya's bluntness took Paige aback. 'Sonya, we've only known each other a couple of days. I'm not sure what you believe is taking place but—'

'What I believe is that everything happens for a reason,' Sonya interrupted, obviously pleased with herself. 'Thank you for the apple fritters. Enjoy your time with Dr Cohen and Bryce tonight.'

Paige just stared after Sonya as she walked out of the shop, sending her one more smug, knowing glance before she let the bell above the door chime, announcing her departure.

She stood there, dumbstruck. It wasn't what she said that rattled Paige, but what she knew.

Paige hadn't told the woman that Cohen and his son would be coming to her apartment tonight, so how did she know?

It was seven-thirty when the doorbell sounded, announcing someone at the bottom of the staircase, waiting to be let into Paige's apartment. The harmonious sound of a lyrical jingle she didn't recognize sounded throughout the apartment, and Paige recoiled at the sound. It was the first time she had heard the doorbell she'd installed, as Allison always texted before coming up and no one else had ever visited. She was going to have to figure out how to change that horrid bell. It sounded ridiculous.

Paige had changed since her visit to the veterinary clinic, opting to wear something other than the dress pants and pastel blue blouse she'd worn under her apron throughout the day. There were worse things to smell like than pastry and sugar, but Paige wanted to put a little effort into her outfit. She had invited her guests over, after all. She'd paired together a long pink maxi skirt that touched her toes and a black cap-sleeved shirt with button-detailing near the hem. Her hair was untied, falling in loose waves over her shoulders. She was comfortable, but dressy. Dressy for her, anyway.

'Jazz, let's go let your family in, shall we?'

The dog lifted her head, looking mighty comfortable on the couch cushions she had migrated to from the makeshift bed on the floor. Earlier, Paige had watched, fascinated, as Jazz circled around numerous times, searching for just the perfect spot, then collapsed into a heap of brindle fur at the far end, facing the window, her chin resting comfortably on the arm. She had promptly begun to snore, despite the fact that her eyes were partially opened. Paige had done nothing to dissuade the dog.

It was evident who was calling the shots.

The doorbell might not have gotten Jazz's attention, but Paige's questioning tone did. The dog dragged herself off the couch and followed her around the corner and down the stairs.

'Jazz, there you are!' Bryce dropped to his knees in the doorway as the dog shuffled over and began to bounce on her front feet like only Jazz could. Paige instantly felt guilty for having taken the dog with her when she left the clinic, wondering if the poor boy had been upset at his dog not being there when he got home from school. But Bryce quickly demolished that fear with his next comment. 'What's the big idea of coming over to Paige's house for dessert without me, dog?'

Paige chuckled as he pretended to give the dog grief about it, and she lifted her gaze to meet Cohen's. 'Hey. Long day?'

'Long enough.' He held out a small bouquet of yellow and white daisies. 'These are for you.'

She thought he sounded like a nervous high school kid approaching his first crush, but Paige didn't know if that was just her own sudden bout of nerves talking, or wishful thinking. The way Cohen's jaw worked, and the way his arm extended slowly, only a few inches at a time, she wondered if he was debating whether to snatch the flowers back and head out onto the sidewalk again. 'Thank you.' She took them, inhaling the sweet scent. 'But you didn't have to.'

'And you didn't have to offer dessert, either.' He shrugged, speaking in a rush. 'It's merely a trade-off. Dessert for flowers. I figure I got the better deal, personally.'

Paige's wishful thinking was deflated. *Merely a trade-off. Ouch.* She played it off, though, nodding toward Bryce. 'Right, tell *him* I didn't need to offer dessert.' She bent and scratched the dog behind one ear. 'Come on, Jazz and I will give you the tour.'

The apartment was a spacious, two-bedroom unit with huge windows and an open concept. Paige had been ecstatic when she found out the building boasted living accommodations as well as the bakery downstairs, so she hadn't had to worry about buying two properties. The apartment suited her well, and she hadn't wasted any time making it her own. The walls were a neutral beige color in the kitchen and dining room, and the living room that looked out over Main Street was a sage green. The counter-tops had been upgraded to a white and sand-colored faux marble, and the cupboards were off-white, to match the color of the oversized plush couch and loveseat in the open living area. There was a television, but Paige couldn't remember the last time she turned it on. That was mostly due to the time it had taken to get the bakery up and running, and due to the overflowing book-shelves that lined the one wall of the living room. She had always enjoyed fictional stories more when she could imagine them in her own mind rather than see someone else's depiction of them on the screen.

'It's a pretty nice place you've got here,' Cohen stated after Paige had led them from room to room, proudly showing off what she had done with the space. To say it had been dated when she purchased it would be an understatement. The apartment had been straight out of the Seventies, along with the downstairs bakery. Seeing as she hadn't even been born yet in that era, it was safe to say she couldn't appreciate the décor.

'Thank you. I'm pretty happy with it.' It wasn't the first time she had seen Cohen in his regular clothes, but once again she was unable to deny how attractive he was in his jeans and simple T-shirt covered by a dark blue and green plaid shirt, left unbuttoned. If the faint hint of cologne she caught a whiff of every now and then was any indication, she'd say Cohen had put a little effort into his outfit as well. 'Who's up for cake?'

Cake. That's what she needed to think about. Not her physical attraction to the handsome veterinarian who'd brought her flowers as a trade-off for dessert.

Bryce was cross-legged on the living room floor, taunting Jazz with pieces of apple and pumpkin biscuits he'd brought with him, making the dog spin in circles around him, much to Jazz's delight. Her docked tail wagged at warp speed, her tongue flop-ping out of her mouth as she played the game. But at the mere mention of cake, Bryce's head popped up, not unlike Jazz's head when she heard the word *treat*.

'Me!' He scrambled to his feet and bolted for the kitchen island that separated the living room from the cooking area, finding a spot on one of the wrought iron stools. Then, all at once, the boy's eyes narrowed. 'Wait, what kind?'

'Does it matter?' Paige arched a brow.

Bryce shrugged. 'Not really. But a man likes to know what he's getting into, Paige.'

Paige stared at the boy, her eyes wide, then snapped her gaze over to Cohen. She wasn't sure whether he looked completely mortified or absolutely bewildered. Either way, she burst out laughing. 'I can't argue with that,' she choked out. 'How does black forest cake sound? I sold half of it to Allison to sell at the coffee house this morning as a special, but I just happen to have a few huge slices to offer up my guests. Like what you're getting into now?'

'No,' Bryce replied, shaking his head. 'I love it.'

'I swear, Paige, I don't know where he gets this stuff from.' Cohen rounded the island and pulled one of the knives from the block on the countertop. 'Plates?'

'In the cupboard to the left of the sink,' she advised, taking the knife from him. 'And it's fine. I happen to think your humor is refreshing, Bryce.' She leaned across the island to close the gap between them, then whispered, 'And I'm just guessing, but I'll bet that sense of humor you've got is pretty similar to your dad's.'

'You're right,' Bryce whispered back without hesitation. 'But don't tell him that. I don't think he can handle it.'

'I'm standing right here, you two.' Cohen's voice was loud and laced with amusement.

Paige didn't know how, but she managed to keep it together while she cut the cake into oversized wedges and passed it out. Bryce was a comedian without even trying. She relished in the game of never really knowing what was going to come out of his mouth next, and he had the gift of being funny without ever being disrespectful or rude. That was difficult to come by nowadays.

She pushed his plate of cake across the counter toward him. The boy's gaze locked with hers as he thanked her, and Paige was overcome with the realization of just how much his son truly resembled Cohen. The boy's cheekbones were a bit higher, maybe, and the angle of his face a little longer, but there was no mistaking the similarities between them. She didn't think those similarities stopped at only their physical appearance, either.

'So, Paige,' Cohen began, pulling out one of the chairs from the dining room table and gesturing toward her to sit, 'You said you had a question for me. Should I be worried?'

Paige set her plate down on the table, went about getting a glass pitcher of water and three glasses passed around, then took her place at the table, adjacent to him. Both adults had their chairs pulled out slightly, turned toward Bryce to include him in the conversation. 'I heard about Helen O'Connor's house,' she said. 'It sounds like the damage is pretty bad.'

It was the topic on everyone's lips, and the news had rocked the tiny town. Helen O'Connor had been one of the first people to come through the door during The Cakery's grand opening, and she'd been nothing but encouraging toward Paige when Allison introduced them. Last night, in the wee hours of the morning, Helen's house had caught fire. No one had been hurt, and Helen's neighbors had been quick to act by calling the volunteer fire department, but there was still extensive damage to the north side of the house despite their efforts.

'I heard,' Cohen replied, solemn. 'The fire trucks passed my house last night, and Rhonda, the technician at the clinic, lives over on Huntington Street, too. Her house isn't near Helen's, but she said the whole one side of the house is blackened. It sounds like Helen is trying to remain upbeat about it – you know, the whole *stuff can be replaced* mentality – but she's been in that house for as long as I can remember. It's sad, to say the least.'

'Very,' Paige agreed. 'Allison came in to grab the cake from me this morning before I opened the shop. She was saying that Helen is staying with her daughter, who lives in town?'

'Not in town, really. Mira's place is in North Springs, about ten miles past the town limits. Close enough that Helen can still be in the town she's known as home for most of her life, at least.' Cohen brought a forkful of cake past his lips, a groan escaping him as the sweet flavors overwhelmed him. 'I'm telling you, Paige, if you keep making cake like this so easily accessible, I'm going to start gaining a lot of weight because I have absolutely no willpower when it comes to your baking skills.'

'I'll take that as a compliment,' she teased. 'And what about you, Bryce?' She turned toward Cohen's son. 'Do you approve?'

Bryce tilted his plate to reveal only a few tiny crumbs left on it. 'Does that answer your question?'

'Loud and clear.' A swell of pride bubbled up within her. 'Which brings me to my question.'

'Do I want more cake?' Bryce quipped. 'You bet!'

'No more cake for you,' Cohen piped up. 'That massive slice you just inhaled is going to have you bouncing off the walls half the night.'

His son feigned disappointment, then cast a glance over at Paige and shrugged, a grin tugging at his lips.

'No, that wasn't where I was going with that,' she replied. 'But it is about cake, in a roundabout way. I was thinking we could band together and organize a fundraiser for Helen. I know she's probably got insurance, but who knows when that's going to kick in, or how much will be replaced.'

Cohen's face lit up. 'Paige, that's a great idea. It really is. Let me guess: You're going to sell cakes, and Bryce and I are going to buy them.'

She almost choked on her mouthful of cake. Struggling to

swallow it down, she exclaimed, 'That's not really what I meant. I want you to help me organize the event. I figure if we had you, Allison, and I spearheading it, that's three downtown businesses that can get involved. With yours and Allison's knowledge of everyone who lives here, and a few hundred decorated cupcakes donated by yours truly, it would be a good start toward getting some well-deserved money together for Helen.'

Cohen stared at Paige for a long moment, long enough that she wondered if she had said something wrong. When he snapped out of whatever trance he'd been in, he held out his hand. 'That's one of the nicest, most thoughtful things I've heard in a long time, Paige. You can count me in.'

There was so much excitement buzzing through Paige, she could barely sit still. She reached out, shaking his hand with a firm grip. 'Yeah? This is going to be fun, Cohen. Looks like we're going to be spending a lot of time together.'

'If that was meant to dissuade me, you're not very good at it.'

Paige hadn't meant to even say it out loud, but Cohen's reply had her rethinking her earlier stance about this truly being only friendship between them. His confession that he wasn't opposed to spending more time with her, mingled with the way his hand felt so warm and comforting wrapped around hers …

A big part of her hoped she wasn't getting in over her head when it came to Cohen Beckett.

Another part of her hoped that was exactly what she was doing.

'You know what's going to be the hardest part of pulling off this fundraiser?' She pulled her hand gently away, steering the conversation away from whatever the heck was happening between them. Her eyes lit up with mischief.

'Decorating a few hundred cupcakes?' Cohen guessed.

'Nah, that'll be a breeze compared to making sure Bryce doesn't eat them just as fast as we can bake them.'

Both Cohen and Bryce chuckled.

'Agreed, Paige,' Cohen said. 'Definitely agreed.'

Chapter 8

Cohen

He had taken a giant leap of faith by admitting he wanted to spend more time with Paige. He didn't know how he felt about it. Somehow, things just came out of his mouth when she was around. Things he knew damn well he should keep to himself. Someone was going to get hurt.

He was going to get hurt.

To anybody else, making a joke about being unable to deter a man from wanting to hang out with a woman would have been just a flimsy comment that held no weight. With Paige, though, his convoluted confession felt more like a leap he'd taken without opening his parachute first. A silly comment that wasn't. He meant it, even if he didn't understand it.

Cohen Beckett didn't take huge gambles with his heart. Hell, he didn't take any gambles with it. He hadn't shown interest in anyone in eight years. No dates, no desire to seek someone else out in hopes of building a relationship. He told himself it was due to lack of time, but he knew better. It was lack of courage. Lack of guts. Until someone lived through the awful pain that came with losing a spouse – and he would never wish that kind of hell on anyone – they wouldn't understand his reasons for keeping love at a distance. He couldn't go through that kind of grief again. He just couldn't.

But there was something about Paige Henley that he couldn't put his finger on. Something that prodded at Cohen's mind and made him believe, even if it were only in brief instances, that there was more to a relationship than inevitable pain.

But it was the *more* he struggled with. And for every brief second he believed in more, there were a thousand other seconds that consumed him, reminding him of what he had gone through. What he'd lost. *Who* he'd lost. Eight years had done little to heal that wound.

It was three days before Cohen's schedule allowed for even a glimpse of Paige again. A few sporadic texts from her confirmed she was just as busy. He had been swamped with appointments and surgeries, and she'd been desperate to keep up with the daily baking for the bakery. There was no rest period for business owners, and nine-to-five was a joke they told themselves in an attempt to remain sane. It was only because Cohen had blocked off a twenty-minute slot on the appointment schedule in the afternoon that he was able to make a run over to the bakery at all.

He knew he looked frazzled. It had been a trying day. Rhonda had called in sick, leaving him to fend for himself when it came to lab work, triage, and drawing up vaccines. And that was just to name a few things. Each day he spent without Rhonda at the clinic – and they were few and far between, thank God – he was reminded just how wholly he relied on her. He would never blame her for needing a day off, but he made a mental note to tell her how much he appreciated her help, just in case he didn't say it often enough.

Between Rhonda's absence, an overbooked surgery schedule in the morning, and a back-to-back appointment schedule in the afternoon, Cohen was drowning. But he made the trek down the sidewalk, anyway, leaving Alice at the reception desk to fend off the clients for a few minutes while he took a moment for himself.

He was disappointed to see two other customers in the bakery when he pushed open the door. The bell clanged above his head, and they turned from the cupcake tower on display to stare at him. So did Paige, her head poking up suddenly from behind the counter. The wide grin that crossed her face at the sight of him was both unexpected and contagious, and he found himself smiling, too, as he crossed the room to close the gap between them.

'I was starting to think you'd moved,' he teased. 'Just jumped in that Maserati of yours and got the hell out of dodge.'

'Maserati?' She quirked an eyebrow, standing up to her full height and pushing the unmade takeout boxes she must have been digging for under the counter onto it, dusting some of the flour off her hands and apron.

'Yeah, isn't that what all the city girls drive in New York City?'

Paige pressed a hand to her chest and gave a hollow chuckle. 'For your information, it's a Volkswagen Golf. But if we're playing the stereotype game, which one are you – the small-town country boy with the souped-up pickup truck, or the uppity doctor with the Lexus for the weekdays and Lamborghini for the weekends?'

He clutched at his own chest, feigning hurt. 'Ouch,' he said, unable to even out his grin. 'I wish I could say I'm guilty as charged to the Lamborghini, but unfortunately there's a two-year-old Honda Civic in my driveway that begs to differ.'

'Somehow, I'm not surprised.'

'What, that I drive a Civic?'

She shook her head. 'No, that you don't fit into a stereotype.'

'Well, that makes two of us, then.'

She glanced past him at the customers near the cupcakes, then went about folding the cardboard boxes, folding the tabs in to make corners. 'How have you been, Cohen? It's been busy here, or else I would have come by to say hello.'

'You don't have to explain,' he assured her. 'It's been insane at the clinic. I think it's safe to say the summer rush has officially begun.'

'Between summer and wedding season, I'm destined to be up to my eyeballs in icing until September.'

'Getting lots of wedding cake orders?' He wasn't sure how that worked, exactly, but figured it must be hectic and time-consuming to have multiple custom orders on top of the everyday baked goods for the shop.

'A few.' She folded the boxes without really looking at them. It was easy to tell she had done it countless times before. 'But Allison's wedding cake is special to me, so I'm driving myself crazy over it. Not to mention, the list of ideas I have for cupcakes for the fundraiser is growing by the hour, so I'm going to have my hands full.'

'Don't feel like you're obligated to pull this fundraiser off.' He ducked down to make sure she was focused on him. 'And you certainly don't have to do it alone.' The conviction in his voice surprised him.

But she waved a dismissive hand. 'I want to help Mrs O'Connor,' she replied. 'I just need to stick to a strict schedule over the next few weeks and we should be able to make it work.'

'Exactly,' he said. '*We*. We'll do it together, Paige.' If the tables were turned, he would want to hear those words. That's why he was adamant about getting that through her pretty little head. And that was the story he was sticking to.

She narrowed her eyes, obviously amused. 'You sure you're up for decorating a mountain of cupcakes between now and the end of the month?'

Yikes, he thought. *That's only two weeks away*. But Cohen nodded his head, feigning confidence in his decision. 'Of course.

You tell me where to be, and when, and we'll decorate cupcakes until we're cross-eyed.'

Paige laughed. 'Don't say I didn't try to warn you.'

'It'll be fun. I'll spread the word. Cupcakes for sale, for a good cause. *Mountains* of cupcakes.'

'Trust me, that won't be an exaggeration. After this, you'll never want to see a cupcake as long as you live.'

'And my waistline will thank you for that, I'm sure.' Cohen pointed toward the scones in the display case beside him. 'Which reminds me, I'd better buy a half dozen of those. The staff at the clinic probably won't let me back in the door without them.'

'You know, you don't have to buy something every time you come in here.' Nevertheless, Paige went about boxing up the apple and cinnamon scones.

'I'm not sure my staff members would agree with you,' he replied with a shrug. 'So, Allison and Christopher have set a wedding date, then? I've heard conflicting rumors about that.'

Paige's forehead crinkled. 'Conflicting rumors?' She slid the box across the counter to him.

'Three different stories, actually,' he advised. People loved to gossip, and the longer the rumors floated around town, the more convoluted the truth got.

'Three, huh?'

With her hand on her hip, eyebrows arched high, Cohen had to press his lips together. He knew she had heard about the steady stream of gossiping that small towns were well-known for, but the mix of surprise and disbelief on her pretty face proved that she'd never really experienced it first-hand until now.

'Yes, three,' he confirmed, leaning against the counter. If he was going to delve into the town's gossip grapevine, which he rarely did, then Cohen was going to damn well enjoy it. 'The first story I heard was that they already eloped and this ceremony will just be for show. But I think you'd tell me if that was true.'

Paige scoffed. 'Of course I would,' she said. Then, in a low, mischievous tone, 'Or would I?'

Cohen rolled his eyes, but he liked that she was having fun with this, too. 'The second story was that the engagement will last forever, with no actual marriage in sight, seeing as it took so many years of dating to get to the proposal in the first place.'

Paige looked appalled. 'Wow, how romantic,' she balked. 'I'll bet the guy who started that rumor doesn't believe in happily-ever-afters.'

'Which is why I tend to believe the third rumor,' Cohen told her. 'I believe they'll end up getting married soon. Fast. No more waiting around.'

'You're *that* guy, huh?' Paige gave nothing away, but her eyes sparkled brightly.

She hoped for the same thing, then.

'I'm definitely that guy. Like a wise ten-year-old boy once said, when you know, you know.'

'Definitely a wise boy,' she said, grinning. 'You believe in happily-ever-afters?'

Cohen didn't look away, and he didn't hesitate. And for the second time that day, the conviction in his voice rattled him. 'Everyone has to believe in something, Paige.'

He could have stayed in that bakery all day. The banter between him and Paige had remained light and easy, as usual. But he managed to learn things about her, little by little, through her comments and answers. Conversations with her seemed to be like that; they said one thing, but the undertones of their words spoke just as loudly as the words themselves.

And when he invited her to come along on his walk with Jazz and Bryce, there was no mistaking the flash of hesitancy that marred her features. Cohen knew immediately what she was thinking, as though she'd said the words aloud. He recognized it, like looking in a mirror.

She felt uncertain and worried that they were getting too attached. That they were getting in too deep after such a short time of knowing each other.

Cohen didn't blame her. He wondered those things, too. Hell, he analyzed them over and over in his head like clockwork, trying to figure out if he was making a mistake by being so friendly.

But that didn't mean he didn't want to keep her friendship. He could tell himself time and time again that it was a dangerous game he was playing, and that it could end badly if he wasn't more careful, but the tether that bound him to Paige didn't loosen despite his concerns. She graciously accepted his offer with shadows in her eyes, and Cohen looked forward to letting Bryce choose what part of Port Landon he wanted to introduce her to that evening. Bryce was always a good one to ease his mind; he hoped his boy could do the same for Paige.

'Boss. Earth to Cohen.'

Cohen's head snapped up. 'Yeah?' Head in the clouds, he had a feeling Rhonda had called his name a few times.

'Sonya Ritter's in the waiting room. She's asking for you.' Her voice carried over to him from behind him, where she was placing a glass slide under the microscope. When he looked up from the textbook he'd been poring over, she was staring at him, curious.

Cohen muttered his thanks and nothing more. He knew why Sonya was here. After he left Paige's shop, he'd ducked into the coffeehouse beside it and ordered four large coffees to go, for himself and his staff members to enjoy along with the scones. Allison, who seemed to be glowing with happiness as she scurried from one end of the ordering counter to the other, always in constant motion, had just been in the process of making a fresh pot, so she promised to bring it over to him at the veterinary clinic when it was done brewing.

Sonya had either been delegated as the deliverer, or she'd jumped at the chance to bring the coffee over herself.

Cohen would bet his salary it had been the latter.

'Sonya, to what do I owe the pleasure?' Cohen offered her a genuine smile. He liked the woman. She had a good heart, was a good friend, and meant well in everything she did. That didn't mean he didn't recognize the mischief in her eyes when he saw it. 'Because I know you can't just be delivering my coffees, and you don't own a pet.'

'Good to see you, too, Dr Cohen.' The woman held out the tray of paper cups to him. 'You know me, I just had to come and see it for myself.'

'See what?' He took the tray from her hands and braced himself, fearful of what her answer might be. It was hard to know with Sonya.

Her knowing look came before the words fell from her mouth. 'Why, the smitten good doctor, that's what!' She made no attempt to lower her voice, and Cohen didn't dare turn around to meet his receptionist's gaze. But he could feel it burning into his back, just as Rhonda's was from the doorway of the lab.

'Oh, Sonya.' He sounded almost apologetic. 'I don't know what you think you know, but—'

'It doesn't take much to see what's blossoming between you and the brunette baker girl down the street,' she announced gleefully. 'A blind man could see that.'

Cohen fought to keep the exasperation from his voice. 'Sonya, my friendship with Paige—'

'Friendship?' The older woman balked at the notion. She mimicked his sympathetic tone. 'Oh, Cohen. Maybe you're the blind man.'

He opened his mouth to retort, or defend himself, or *something*. But Sonya was already partway out the door. She turned just before the door closed, winked at him, and Cohen swore he felt the air change around him. Goosebumps rose on his bare forearms.

Sonya was getting to him. Her meddling made him wonder what exactly she was saying to Paige, and in turn it made him

84

concerned that her incessant desire to play matchmaker was the reason for Paige's hesitation earlier. He made a mental note to remind her that Sonya was harmless. Headstrong and overbearing, but harmless. She was always one to read too much into things, to push a bit too hard and stick her nose in places it really didn't belong.

And no matter how far off course he believed Sonya Ritter was about the relationship he had with Paige, he couldn't deny that there was a small sliver of his heart that wondered, and maybe, possibly even hoped, that she was right.

Chapter 9

Paige

She thought she'd loved Port Landon when she first came here, completely enamored by the vintage quaintness of the harbor-side and the downtown street, awestruck by the natural prettiness of the rows of trees that lined the residential streets and the meticulously landscaped front yards with abundant flowers and shrubs. Flowers had only been in the beginning stages of blooming, and the leaves hadn't been out in full flourish yet.

But now, Paige didn't just love Port Landon, she was *in* love with it. Everything about it. As Bryce led the way, with Jazz trotting along beside him, she took in the mesmerizing array of impatiens, daisies, and lilies that burst in color from the gardens as they passed each house on their way to what Bryce would only refer to as 'the neatest place in Port Landon' – the Hansel and Gretel House. She had tried numerous times during their journey to get the boy to disclose more information, but his lips were sealed. Each time she looked to Cohen for help, he merely shrugged, the same mischievous grin playing on his lips.

Their evening walk became even more intriguing as the paved

road came to an end and they were forced to disappear into the trees, following Bryce along a narrow dirt path. It was only wide enough to allow for single file, but Cohen remained by her side as much as possible, tramping through the overgrown brush.

The forest seemed to envelope them, blocking out the setting sun and casting hazy shadows all around them. Paige focused on the path under her feet, being careful to watch for rocks or uneven ground that might cause her to fall flat on her face.

'I feel like I'm being led into some kind of horror movie scene,' she called ahead to Bryce.

The boy laughed, but his footsteps didn't slow. 'It's just called the Hansel and Gretel House, Paige. It's not like an old witch is really going to try to cook you for dinner! At least, I don't think she will.'

'That's encouraging.'

'Hey, you wanted to see the cool spots in town,' he shouted. 'It doesn't get much cooler than this.'

Cohen barely spoke on the way, and Paige was enjoying the sound of the birds and the gentle breeze that made the leaves and bushes rustle, swaying against each other. He spoke up, then, leaning in to keep his voice from carrying toward his son. 'He's getting a real kick out of this, you know. I promise, it's nothing scary. I wouldn't have let him drag you out here if it was.'

'Oh, trust me, I'm enjoying this, too,' she assured him. 'It's just that I rarely left the city limits for over a decade, so the prospect of traipsing into the middle of the forest is a relatively new one for me at this point in my life.'

'Never underestimate a ten-year-old to make you do things you never thought you'd do,' Cohen quipped.

'I never said I've never done it,' she chuckled. 'It's just been a while.'

'I keep forgetting you're from Michigan.'

Paige tripped on a stone she'd missed while she had been too busy paying attention to Cohen, and his arms jutted out faster than she expected to steady her. Startled, both by the jolt forward and the strength in his hands as they held her firmly upright by her upper arms, Paige went rigid and still, processing the warmth of his fingertips permeating through her thin T-shirt sleeves. 'You'd better believe I'm a Michigan girl.' A failed attempt at sounding steadier than she felt. And that unsteadiness had nothing to do with her clumsy feet. 'I'm not saying I'm the outdoorsy type, exactly, but this?' She glanced around at the picturesque forest that surrounded them. 'This, I could get used to.'

She meant it. She could see herself doing things like this in her spare time – hiking, exploring, maybe even gardening or learning to fish. She'd never done those things before, but it didn't mean she wasn't interested in trying.

There were lots of things she was interested in trying. Lots of things she could get used to. And having the company of Cohen, Bryce and Jazz was high on that list.

Cohen watched her closely as he let his grip on her arms loosen, dragging his fingertips down her arms until his hands reached hers, entwining them together. He moved slowly, methodically, watching for signs he was misinterpreting this, giving Paige every chance to pull away from him.

'I could get used to this, too,' he said.

It was a soft-spoken confession, but it hit her hard and fast, quickening her pulse and robbing her of common sense. She couldn't speak, too stunned to think about anything but those seven words and the handsome man who uttered them. She did manage to squeeze his fingers gently, the only encouragement she could muster in her overwhelmed state. If she tried to do anything more, say anything more, she'd do something crazy. Heck knew her brain was coming up with lots of romantic ways she could respond to him.

'It's a different way of life when compared to city life, I'm sure,' he added. Judging by the sudden throatiness of his voice, Paige wagered she wasn't the only one struck by the warmth of their tangled fingers. 'But it's got its perks.'

'It sure does.' God, even that sounded cheesy, but she couldn't help herself. The synapses in her brain couldn't seem to fire properly when he was touching her, yet she couldn't bring herself to let go. She didn't want to. Because she liked the feel of her hand in his. A lot. 'Have you always lived here?'

A mundane question from her own lips. That was good. She was regaining her wits. It was enough to get them moving again, falling into step side by side, her right hand linked with his left, with matching faint smiles dancing on their lips.

'I'm from Lansing, but once we finished school and—'

'We?'

'Stacey and I,' Cohen explained, his throat moving visibly. 'She was a veterinarian, too. We met in college. Once we finished school and got married, we decided that we didn't want to raise a family in the city. A little research on the internet led us to find out that Dr James Alton was retiring and selling his veterinary practice in Port Landon. The rest is history.'

Paige hadn't expected her line of questioning to head in this direction, but it sobered her. She quickly confirmed that Bryce was far enough ahead and out of earshot before she continued. 'I didn't realize you both had worked together, as well. No wonder it's so busy now.' She immediately regretted her choice of words, because Paige knew it sounded like what she'd really meant was '… now that she's gone.' Because of it, she cut the sentence off abruptly.

Cohen seemed to pick up on it, but he remained unfazed. 'It is busier since Stacey has passed away.' He gave her a sad smile. 'But it's okay. Bryce and I do pretty well, and this little community is the reason we've grieved and moved past it as best we can. It's been eight years, and we're okay, I think.'

'And you attribute that to Port Landon?'

'Absolutely.' He nodded. 'This town came together in the

wake of the car accident. They cooked food for us for months. Hell, some of the elderly ladies still bring casseroles and whatnot to the clinic just in case I don't have time to cook in the evenings. The clinic would have been shut down for those first few months if Dr Alton, the vet I bought the practice from, hadn't taken it upon himself to team up with a locum doctor and fill in for me. Around here, Paige, you don't have to ask for help. It's offered. Without hesitation. Which is exactly why I'm so grateful to you for coming up with the cupcake fundraiser for Helen O'Connor. She helped to look after me and my family when we needed it. Now, it's my turn to return the favor.'

Paige felt her heart swell. This man had been through so much, but what mattered most to him was making sure the residents of his town, the town he called home, were taken care of. The realization that Port Landon mirrored a close-knit extended family wasn't lost on her. 'We'll look after Helen,' she promised, squeezing his hand again. 'We'll turn cupcakes into cash, and we'll make sure she gets every penny.'

'Thank you, Paige.' Cohen's throat moved again, and his footsteps stopped abruptly. It forced Paige to halt, too, and Cohen cupped his other hand over their clasped fingers. 'You have no idea what that means to me.'

She took in a sharp breath as the heat of his palm sank into the top of her hand. Everything stopped. She could no longer hear the chirping of the birds or feel the caress of the breeze. The only thing her brain could register was the cloudy emotion in Cohen's eyes and the warmth in his fingertips as they held hers. 'I think I'm starting to understand.'

'We're here!'

Bryce's voice snapped Paige out of her trance. She stole the opportunity to slip her hand from Cohen's, fearful he would realize the way she was trembling from the sizzle of electricity in his touch. She turned toward his son in hopes of evening out her breaths. Bryce looked about ready to combust, vibrating with excitement. She could relate.

He pulled down on some low-hanging tree branches, revealing the most whimsical old cabin she'd ever seen.

'Bryce!' she cried, shocked. 'This place is phenomenal.'

It was like they had stepped back in time, somehow. The little cabin was no bigger than twenty feet wide, and it was dilapidated and weather-worn, but the building was still standing despite its bowed roof and cracked, crooked foundation. Wooden, grayed shingles still covered the peaked roof, but what parts weren't covered by dark green moss were frayed and chipped, giving them an almost furry look. One rounded window still remained intact to the left of the front door. Others had long since been smashed by vandals or broken over time as the house sagged with age, left with only paint-chipped, broken frames to cover the blackness of the cabin within. The boards that made up the walls were gray and cracked, but they gave the illusion of being smoother than the rough-cut lumber they'd once been, sanded down as the years eroded them away.

'Pretty cool, huh?' Bryce's chest puffed out, his eyes gleaming with pride as he wandered around the perimeter of the house.

Paige couldn't take her eyes off it. 'It's beautiful,' she replied, awestruck. 'In a vintage, forgotten kind of way. And you're right, it looks exactly like I would imagine the old witch's cabin would look in *Hansel and Gretel*.'

'There are multiple stories and local folklore about whose cabin this originally was,' Cohen explained, coming up behind her. 'But the truth is no one really knows for sure, and we may never know.' He was fixated on the cabin, too.

'Whose property is this?' Paige asked, her voice distant.

'It belonged to James Alton.'

Paige's gaze snapped over to meet his. 'The retired veterinarian,' she said. 'Wait. Belonged?'

Cohen's mouth quirked up on one side. 'The house Bryce and

91

I live in behind the clinic was Dr Alton's, too. He sold me everything – the clinic, the house, and his fifty acres of vacant land – with the stipulation that if he visited Port Landon after the sale, he could park his travel trailer on this property while he was here.'

'You own the Hansel and Gretel House.' There was no mistaking the whimsy in her voice.

'I do. I don't think it's safe enough to go inside, so Bryce and I have never tried, but we do like to hike our way out here and visit it from time to time.'

Bryce and Jazz disappeared around the back of the cabin, and Paige stepped close enough to run her fingers along the worn board that made up the top of the railing on the small front stoop. 'And you let other people walk back here, too?'

Cohen shrugged. 'I don't stop people from walking along the path to get out here as long as they don't cause more damage to the cabin. Father Time and Mother Nature are doing a bang-up job of that themselves.'

Paige brought a hand up to cover her heart. 'You're a generous man, Cohen Beckett.'

If she knew him at all, she thought he looked mighty proud of himself for gleaning that compliment from her. 'I try,' he replied. 'But I was hoping you'd be the generous one.'

She stopped near the corner of the cabin and looked back toward him. 'Oh? And what would you like me to be generous with?'

'Your time,' Cohen said. He didn't look away from her as he closed the gap between them. 'I was hoping you'd share some of your time with me. I know you don't have a lot to spare, and I get that. But Bryce has been itching to spend an evening over at his friend's house, and I was hoping you'd let me use that opportunity to … take you out. Just the two of us.'

'Take me out?' She squeaked out the words.

'On a, uh … on a date.' It sounded like a question as it toppled from his tongue. He was just as riddled with nerves as she suddenly was. He didn't touch her, not once, but something about the way the hope and anticipation were blazing in his eyes, mixed with that anxiety, as they burned into hers …

Paige's breath caught. 'Cohen, I—'

'I know you're a busy woman, Paige,' he continued, talking faster now. 'And I know we've got this fundraiser to work on together and that we've already been spending time together on these walks, but I just thought maybe we—'

'I can't.'

Cohen's mouth closed, and he stared at her. 'I … oh.' He hadn't expected her to decline, she suspected. And certainly not so fast.

Paige's chest tightened. She could feel the panic rising in her throat. The words had fallen from her tongue before she could think them through. A knee-jerk reaction. And now she couldn't take them back. 'Cohen, I'm sorry, I just meant that—'

'It's okay.' Despite the fact that they were losing sunlight by the minute, she could see the confusion and disappointment that shadowed his gaze. But he forced a half-hearted smile on his face. 'I totally get it. It's no problem.'

She felt ridiculous. How had this gone so completely wrong, after being so completely right? After he'd taken the chance and held her hand and made her feel so completely alive? 'Wait, Cohen. I just think—'

'Paige.' He reached out and gripped both of her arms as though to steady her again, mustering up an encouraging look. 'You don't have to explain yourself to me, okay?' The sentiment made her feel even worse, but she nodded reluctantly. Cohen released her from his grasp. 'Now,' he added, 'Let's go find Bryce before the old witch does.'

Allison stared at Paige, her head tilted to one side, eyes wide in bewilderment. She had never been one to mince words. 'You've got to be freaking kidding me.'

'I don't know what came over me.'

The coffeehouse was slow for a Saturday morning. Paige was thankful she had the option to open a little later on Saturdays and designate Sundays as her one full day off from the bakery a week, but Allison wasn't so lucky. Coffee shops were meeting spots, hangouts. Most folks wanted to do their hanging out and meeting up on the weekend. So, Allison worked almost every day. She switched on and off with her other staff members, but everyone needed a day off sometime. It was Allison's turn to manage the weekend rush, but as far as rushes were concerned, this Saturday had turned out to be more of a crawl. Paige had been able to use the slowness of the day to her advantage, pulling her cousin into one of the red vinyl-covered booths in the far back corner and telling her everything that had happened the night before with Cohen.

'Let me get this straight.' Allison held her hands out, halting any further conversation on Paige's part. 'He invited you on a walk with him and Bryce, into the woods to show you the cabin that's pretty much Port Landon's pinnacle of folklore, while the sun is setting. Then, he makes the first move to hold your hand and asks super-politely if he can share your spare time and take you out on a real, honest-to-God date ... and you just said – and I quote – *I can't*?' Her hands flailed out on either side of her, her expression exasperated. 'Paige, what is wrong with you? The man suggested a date with you, not that he have his sultry way with you right then and there in the middle of the freaking forest!'

Paige sighed, wishing she knew the answer. She could always count on her cousin to be upfront with her, but hearing it put so bluntly made it sting all the more. 'I know, I know. And the truth is, I wanted to say yes!' she hissed, attempting to keep her voice down so the few other patrons wouldn't overhear. 'I mean, I meant to say yes. I would have said yes if I'd just given my heart a second to catch up with my brain. But, Allison, it was almost like it was the only answer I was capable of giving at the time. I answered so automatically, I don't even think I realized I turned him down until Cohen's face fell.'

'That's because that's what you do.' Allison dragged each syllable out for emphasis. 'I don't even know if you realize it, but it's your claim to fame, my friend.'

Paige crinkled her forehead. She might have realized what she'd done now, which was too late, but that didn't help her to understand what Allison was getting at. 'What are you talking about?' The dark roast coffee at Portside was the best coffee she'd ever had, but somehow she just didn't feel like the caffeine was going to be enough to handle whatever her cousin was about to say.

'Paige,' she groaned, clasping her hands over her eyes and dragging them down her face. 'You've conditioned yourself to believe you don't have time for love. Even in New York, you would mention guys from work that you got along with really well, and then you'd immediately follow it up with some off-the-cuff comment about not being able to pursue it, or having to focus on your work instead, or not knowing where you'd find the time to give the relationship any attention. So, you would push the man away. I mean, does the name Alex ring any bells?'

Paige vaguely remembered some of the conversations her cousin was referring to, though her memories of them didn't seem as full of potential romance as Allison was making them out to be. And she knew very well who Alex was and why Allison was bringing him up. Her ex-boss at Livingston Designs was a clean-cut and successful man she'd both admired and looked up to. He was undeniably handsome in his tailored suits and his unfailing work ethic. She might have pushed the particulars into the recesses of her mind when it came to anyone else she might have been approached by – or convinced herself she really didn't have the time to even think of them again at all – but Paige remembered turning down Alex's numerous suggestions that they see each other outside their long work hours. Her own fears of muddying the waters between their perfect working relationship and a possible romantic one still haunted her from time to time. She couldn't let herself believe she had made a mistake by dismissing him and choosing the path she'd taken to Port Landon. Still, she insisted, 'I'm not that bad.'

'Actually, you are.' Allison reached across the table and cupped Paige's hands in hers. Paige could feel the warmth still permeating from her fingertips from the coffee mug she'd held between her fingers. 'This is classic Paige Henley. You're just doing what you've always done – convincing yourself that you can't do this. That you and love can't get along. And that's the one thing I've never quite figured out about you, Paige. You're always so confident and ambitious and overzealous when it comes to work and succeeding, yet you shy away from anything that might result in you being happy outside of your career.'

'That's not true,' Paige argued. Even as she said it, she could hear the weakness in her words. She wasn't one of those women who had some awful past relationship that marred her confidence when it came to romance. Allison was right, she'd been so driven to succeed since her early years in high school, she'd spent her entire adult life putting her career before everything else. Love included.

'Paige!' Allison gave a hollow laugh. 'It's so true that you turned down Dr Cohen without realizing it! That's how freaking true it is! You're on romantic autopilot.'

Paige opened her mouth to plead her side of the story, found she had no redeeming argument, and slumped forward onto the table, her head in her hands, narrowly missing her half-full coffee cup. 'What have I done, Allison?'

'Nothing you can't fix,' she replied softly. 'Just go talk to him.'

'And say what?' Paige exclaimed, sitting up straighter. 'That I panicked? That I actually do like him, but I am too emotionally inept to know how to handle it?'

Allison shrugged, looking amused. 'There you go. Now we're getting somewhere. You've got the truth figured out, and you're finally past the denial stage, so there's nowhere to go but up from here.'

Paige ran her hands through her hair, letting out a long breath. She knew her cousin was trying to be funny, but there was a sincerity in those words as well. 'Thanks, Allison. How am I ever going to repay you for these impromptu therapy sessions?'

'Oh, please,' she replied, pulling her long auburn hair up into a ponytail just as the door chime announced the arrival of another customer. 'I'm going to want every juicy, romantic detail, my friend. That'll be payment enough.'

Saturday had always been Paige's favorite day of the week. Not only because the bakery opened a bit later in the morning, but because there was a calm that the weekend evoked, making her waking hours seem somehow less full. She did all the same things, but the day itself held more promise of downtime with Sunday just around the corner. That's what Saturdays were to Paige, a day of promise.

This particular Saturday was no different. Sunlight streamed in the windows, and if she looked out the storefront windows at just the right angle she could see slivers of the water glistening as the breeze pushed it in easy ripples and the sun reflected off it. Customers meandered in slowly, taking their time to peruse Paige's displays. During the week, there was less of that simple perusal; people had places to go and things to do. Transactions were quicker. It was just another reason Saturdays appealed to her so much – she had a bit more time to chat and mingle, and her customers had more time to appreciate her efforts. Heck, she had more time to appreciate her efforts.

She also had more time to think, which wasn't necessarily a

good thing. The more she contemplated her kneejerk reaction to Cohen's suggestion, quickly followed by her cousin's swift explanation, the more Paige realized how right Allison was. She didn't want to outright admit that, but she was beginning to understand what she was talking about.

Does the name Alex ring any bells? Allison was never going to let her forget that her boss had attempted numerous times to take her out on dates. She could practically hear her cousin's voice screeching at her through the computer screen on one of their many Skype calls, demanding to know why she wouldn't at least give the guy a chance, why she wouldn't walk out that office door with him and have dinner, just to see where the conversation led. Why she wouldn't give herself a chance to find love with a handsome, successful man like Alex Livingston.

It should have been easy. She and Alex were similar in many ways – holding marketing degrees, thriving in the hustle and bustle of New York, married to their work and unafraid to burn the midnight oil to accomplish their goals. They were so much alike, yet just different enough to complement each other. Whereas Alex wasn't afraid to let his opinions be known or to verbalize his determination, Paige had always preferred her actions to do the talking for her. She spoke up when she needed to, but one look at her completed projects or work schedule, and it was pretty clear what was important to her and where she stood when it came to her own goals. She and Alex were great together, and there was no denying he was attractive. Somehow, though, it had never seemed like the right time to try to take things further.

Allison's vehemence was enough to make Paige contemplate it, but Paige always held back. In her mind, she didn't think she should have to make the choice to love someone. Perhaps she had watched one too many chick flicks during her college days, but Paige wanted to believe real love happened without thought. Thought suggested it was governed by the mind – Paige didn't buy that. True love was felt from the heart, not thought up or decided upon.

Her own mother, happily married to Paige's father for more than thirty-five years, had once told her, 'I knew your dad was the one the day I met him. Ask me to think about it, and I'll tell you he's far from perfect. But ask me to tell you how I feel about him, and that man is as perfect for me as they come. When it comes to love, it's the heart that counts, Paige, not the mind.'

Because of that, Paige politely turned down Alex, again and again. She just couldn't let her mind – or Allison's, for that matter – persuade her to ignore her mother's powerful words.

Now, if she could just remind her heart of that fact and get it back on track, maybe she could refrain from automatically turning men down before she'd realized she did it.

Not men. Cohen. Just Cohen. Paige didn't think she'd ever reflexively turned down someone before, but if Allison's theories were any indication, she might have. One thing Paige did know for sure was that it had never plagued her the way her dismissal of Cohen's suggestion did.

She figured that had to count for something.

As she smiled at an elderly couple who milled about at the cupcake display case, Paige vowed she was going to rectify this. She was going to apologize to Cohen Beckett, and she was going to be honest with him. Dating had never been her thing, and she frankly didn't have a godforsaken clue how to go about it.

But his easy mannerisms and kind face made her want to try.

Paige raised her head and nodded to herself. There, she had a solid plan: Brutal honesty at the expense of her own humility. She wasn't ashamed of her lack of knowledge when it came to romance and dates. If she'd learned anything from her glimpse of time with Cohen, she thought he would understand. He would forgive her hasty dismissal and give her a second chance to—

For a moment, she thought he was merely a mirage, an image her brain had conjured up because of his constant presence in her jumbled thoughts. Blinking rapidly and still finding him there in her line of vision, she realized that wasn't the case.

Outside the bakery, Cohen had stopped in front of one of the huge bay windows that jutted out onto the sidewalk. He glanced back toward the veterinary clinic, his hand raised to shield his eyes from the unyielding sun. A moment later, Bryce appeared, bouncing on his heels as he caught up with his father. Paige watched as the man's hand came to land on his son's shoulder affectionately, and they both laughed at something. Presumably something Bryce had said, if Paige had to wager a bet.

Paige didn't think he was going to look her way, seeing them both take the first steps past her bake shop. In response, she was the one to take a step forward, wanting nothing more than to close the gap between them, both physically and situationally. This was her second chance. She would explain and they could move on from her lapse in judgment.

Cohen's head turned, facing into the bakery window. Through the glass, his eyes scanned the interior, causing Paige to halt mid-step, her heart leaping into her throat. Cohen stopped, too, on the other side of the window, his eyes squinting in the afternoon brightness.

Could he see her, standing there? Could Cohen and her customers hear the incessant beating of her heart as she stood, still, silently pleading for him to come through the door and give her a chance to say what she needed to say?

If he saw her silhouette through the glass pane, Paige wasn't about to find out. She held her breath, watching as Cohen slowly shook his head and mumbled something to Bryce, a resigned sadness etching his features as he forced a smile and tugged his son onward, proceeding down the sidewalk.

As she swallowed, Paige couldn't look away as Cohen disappeared past the window. So many questions whirled in her head, so many scenarios. Things she should have said, things she should have done. There had to be something she could do to heal whatever wound her accidental rejection had caused him. The fact that she wanted so irrevocably to mend whatever this was between them spoke volumes to Paige. She couldn't ignore it. She wouldn't. Because for once it wasn't her mind calling the shots; it was her heart.

That counted for something, too.

Chapter 10

Cohen

Sunday, the only day of the week the veterinary clinic was closed to the public. Cohen was still on call – that wouldn't change unless he managed to hire a second veterinarian – but the folks of Port Landon were generally good about only calling him in cases that were real, true emergencies. Therefore, it was rare he got called into the office on a Sunday.

Sunday mornings were the only mornings where he left Bryce to his own devices. Every other morning during the week, his son was forced to get up for school and come with Cohen through the backyard to the clinic where Bryce's friend Hunter and his mom would pick him up and drive him to the school in North Springs, about ten miles away. Saturday mornings were spent alongside Cohen at the clinic, either doing his homework in the back office or hanging out with Jazz until the clinic closed at noon. Cohen felt like the boy was always being tugged to one place or another, never given the time to do what he wanted without some sort of schedule to adhere to. So, Sunday mornings were Bryce's time to fill however he sought fit. Sometimes, he slept in until almost eleven. Others, Cohen would find him huddled under the covers playing one of his handheld video games until hunger forced him out into the kitchen in search of food. At other times, Bryce would disappear into the backyard for hours, backpack slung loosely on his back, and he would hide out in the treehouse Cohen had built for him four years ago. It'd taken Cohen months to construct that thing around his clinic schedule, but it was worth it – his son utilized that treehouse more than he ever dreamed he would.

Today was one of Bryce's video game days. Even from the kitchen table where Cohen had the *Port Landon Ledger* opened, the town's own newspaper, and his third cup of coffee sitting on a coaster, he could hear the digital zapping sounds and bomb blasts of the game. Now and then, Bryce would let out a muffled 'Yes!' or 'Take that!', making his father raise his eyebrows and chuckle to himself. It was well past one o'clock in the afternoon, but Cohen wasn't going to rouse Bryce from his bedroom if he didn't have to. Besides, he had two weeks' worth of newspapers to skim through and a half pot of coffee to be drank before he had to think about doing any real adulting today. It would help to keep his mind from replaying his conversation with Paige at the Hansel and Gretel House over and over in his head like he'd been doing since Friday night. He had wondered constantly since then how he'd managed to get up the nerve to ask her on a date. Where the hell had that desire come from, and how had the thought bypassed his brain completely, tumbling off his tongue like an instinctive reaction? Better yet, why did those instincts tell him it was a good idea to hold her hand? He'd seen the fire in her eyes, so he didn't understand how it had all gone so damn wrong, so quickly.

Those same instincts were what made him second-guess whether or not to step foot in her bakery yesterday when he and Bryce took a twenty-minute break and walked to the convenience store for milk and eggs. Okay, and a small tub of chocolate ice cream. Anything to get a few minutes' reprieve from the appointments that seemed to be piling up on his short weekend schedule. The clinic was only opened till noon on Saturdays, but noon had come and gone hours ago and the phone just kept ringing.

His moment of reprieve had quickly turned into the inner turmoil of deciding whether or not to say hello to Paige or not. Something so simple, so innocent. In the end, Cohen couldn't let his instincts steer him wrong again. He let his logical mind win the war, and he trudged on without so much as a word to her, despite Bryce's protests. And his own.

He needed to give her space and time. It was only fair. Cohen had held out a branch for her to wrap her fingers around, and he needed to let her grab a hold of it when she was ready. At least, that's what he'd told himself as he walked away from the bakery, the *Open* sign glaring at him in the window just as stoically as if Paige herself were staring in his direction, watching, waiting.

It took every ounce of patience he had to walk away, letting her words echo in his ears.

I can't. Why not? Was it him? Or was it a matter of timing?

These were the questions that were going to take up his entire day, as they had done for the past two. Whether he liked it or not. He vowed not to let them ruin his only day off. Bryce wasn't the only one who was a big fan of Sunday mornings. Especially Sunday mornings that dragged lazily into the afternoon.

Which was why, when a soft knock sounded at the front door of his house, and Cohen was still clad in only his worn jeans and a plain black T-shirt, still barefoot and sporting messy bedhead, he groaned. His relaxation was about to be interrupted by an urgent veterinary emergency.

'Paige.' Cohen couldn't have been more shocked if the Queen of England herself were standing on his doorstep. 'I wasn't expect—'

'I didn't mean it.'

'Excuse me?' Cohen held the edge of the door, his brows

furrowed. He was still reeling over the fact she was there, on his doorstep. He couldn't keep up with the conversation. He stood there, still, unsure what to do, or what was happening. 'Didn't mean what?'

'I didn't mean what I said to you at the Hansel and Gretel House,' she repeated quickly. 'I wasn't thinking. Or, rather, I was thinking too much.'

The weight that lifted from Cohen's shoulders at the sound of her confession was massive. For the past two days, he had replayed their conversation, dissecting everything he'd said to her, trying to decipher where he went wrong. How he could have been so mistaken. He just couldn't figure out how he had managed to misread the signals so badly.

'Will you come in?' he offered, opening the door wider. 'We can talk about this over coffee.'

She let out a relieved sigh, her shoulders sagging with the effort. It made him wonder if she thought he might have slammed the door in her face instead of hearing her out. 'That sounds wonderful. I'll just be one sec.' She turned and promptly hopped back down the front stairs.

'Where are you going?'

She whirled around to face him. 'I brought cake. It's in the car.'

Of course she did, he thought, amused. *The woman sure knows how to apologize.*

Cohen's kitchen was modern in style, with stainless-steel appliances and a logical, industrial feel to it. A stark contrast to the comfortable style of jeans, T-shirts, and plaid tops he usually wore when he wasn't working. The cupboards were wooden and white, but the rest of the room boasted metal-legged furniture and sleek gray countertops that resembled concrete. He wasn't blind to the fact that the room – as well as the rest of the house, for that matter – begged for a woman's trendy touch.

But the house was tidy and well-kept, and there was a swell of pride that washed through him as he watched Paige glance around, taking in her surroundings.

'Quite the place you've got here,' she remarked, taking a seat in the chair he gestured her toward. 'It's really nice.'

'Thank you. It's weathered a few storms with us.' Okay, some of those storms were more like category-five hurricanes, but it was their home and it had been their sanctuary through those tumultuous times. Cohen pulled a pile of three plates from the cupboard above the dishwasher, followed by a few forks and a knife from a drawer nearby, then went to work cutting into the two-layer Dutch chocolate cake Paige had brought with her. In a bid to keep the conversation light, he tilted his head toward the hallway. 'Have you ever seen that commercial for cat treats when the cat runs through the wall at the mere sound of the treat bag being shaken?'

'Of course. Why?'

'Watch this.' Cohen served a slice of the cake onto a plate. 'Bryce! Cake!'

A strangled sound that sounded an awful lot like 'Oh, yikes!' came from down the hallway, and his son emerged from the depths of his room like his pajama cuffs were on fire.

'Paige, I didn't know you were here.' He turned to his dad. 'Oh, wow, that cake looks insane!'

Her hand came up to cover her tightly pressed lips, but Paige managed to keep her eruption of laughter at bay. 'Thank you, Bryce. You're more than welcome to it, as long as your dad says it's okay.'

'You yelled,' the boy reasoned. 'Therefore, you must be willing to fork over a slice or six, right, Dad?'

Cohen shook his head. Where on Earth had his son inherited such negotiation tactics? He was pretty sure this was where his own mother would remind Cohen of just the kind of ten-year-old he had once been. 'One slice, but it comes with two conditions.'

'That doesn't sound fair, but I'm listening,' Bryce replied, hands on his hips.

Cohen didn't dare steal a glance over at Paige, whom he knew would be fighting not to laugh out loud. 'I didn't say it was fair, I said the cake came with conditions. This isn't a negotiation.' He pointed a finger at Bryce, which the boy promptly pushed away, chuckling.

'State your conditions, Dad.'

'The first one,' Cohen rhymed off, holding one finger up again to count them down, 'is that you thank Paige for bringing it in the first place.'

'Thank you, Paige,' Bryce recited immediately. 'It's a great surprise, having you here *and* bringing a cake with you.' His son's tone had changed, and he heard the sincerity in his voice, which made Cohen proud.

'You're very welcome, Bryce.' Paige nodded at the boy. 'It's my pleasure.'

'And the second condition?' Bryce questioned, impatient.

Cohen handed him the plate and a fork. 'You've got to eat it in your bedroom and let us adults talk for a bit,' he advised. 'I will come and get you when we're done. Cool?' Cohen held out his hand, waiting for Bryce to shake on it.

Cohen could almost see the wheels turning in his son's head. He was smart, and the way his gaze flitted from Paige to Cohen and then back again, Cohen knew the assumption Bryce was going to make. It made his chest constrict, but he planned to talk to Bryce about it.

Right after he talked to Paige.

'Cool.' Bryce balanced the cake plate with one hand and shook his dad's hand with the other. 'See you later, Paige.'

She gave him a little wave and Bryce retreated down the hallway, cake in hand, stealing furtive glances over his shoulder as he went.

When Cohen heard the bedroom door shut, he turned to Paige. 'I don't know where he gets it all from, I swear.'

'He's a good kid, Cohen.' She accepted the plate he held out to her. 'And a smart one. I think it's safe to say he's going to be asking some questions in the near future.'

'I'll bet,' he replied wryly. 'But before that happens, I've got a few of my own for you.' Cohen served himself up a slice of cake, then filled a mug with coffee for Paige, sliding it across the table to her before he sat down to face her straight on. 'Will you tell me what's going on?'

She moved the cake around on her plate, focusing on it like it might get up and do tricks. 'I made a mistake,' she said finally. 'I said I couldn't go on a date with you … made it sound like I didn't want to.' She looked up at him. 'And that's just not true, Cohen.'

The look of distress on her face prevented him from offering her a smile. 'I can't deny I'm glad to hear that, Paige. But if that's not the truth, then what is?'

'The truth is …' She pushed the cake around again, then huffed a sigh as she put the fork down. 'The truth is that I'm not sure how to date, because I've never really done it, and I'm scared.'

'Scared of what, exactly?' Cohen was surprised, to say the least. Surprised that she hadn't dated much, and that she was fearful enough of it to steer clear of all things surrounding it. Including him.

'Scared of the fact that … I like you. And that I might mess this friendship up because of it.'

This time, he couldn't fight the grin tugging at his lips. 'I like you, too. And, personally, I think it means more to me that you are afraid to mess up our friendship, than if you weren't.'

'You don't think I'm being silly?' This obviously wasn't how she expected the conversation to go.

'Not at all,' Cohen assured her. 'But maybe that's the difference between you and me. I took a chance by asking you out. I'd be lying if I said I was ready for more than just friendship. With anyone.' God, he hoped that didn't come out wrong. 'But maybe

I never will be, Paige. My wife died. It was tragic, and unexpected, and it ripped me apart. Hell, some days it still does.' Cohen paused, unsure if he had ever voiced that truth to anyone before now. 'So, if you're not ready to take that leap, I'm the last one who will begrudge you that. And I certainly won't pester you about it. But, just know, I'm here, and the offer still stands. Whenever you're ready. Or not ready. Maybe we can be not ready together.' He laughed hollowly at his own ridiculous explanation. But it was the best he had, and it was the truth. That had to count for something.

She looked stunned. 'You've been so nice to me. And you're still being so nice to me, even after I declined your offer. Allison said you don't really …' She trailed off, her cheeks flushing into a deep crimson.

'Allison said I don't date much?' He finished the sentence for her, the corner of his mouth lifting slightly. 'She's not wrong. I don't date. There's no denying that losing Stacey plays a factor in that, but I've also just never really had the time since, I guess. Or never really made the time – that's probably more accurate.'

'Me too!' Paige looked about ready to jump out of her chair. 'I think it's just so easy to get caught up in work and obligations that spending time with someone else can get shoved onto the back burner without realizing it.'

'You're preaching to the choir, Paige.' He shrugged. 'That doesn't mean we can't try to change that, though. We can take baby steps. If we find the time to spend an evening out with each other, then that's great. If not, I promise you, it's not the end of our friendship. All right?' Cohen never thought he would be the one sitting there, advising a fellow workaholic that they had to take time to smell the proverbial roses. He certainly never thought he would be vying for a date with someone. Because Cohen Beckett didn't date. There was a time he believed that he, Cohen Beckett, was no longer himself as a whole. He was merely what was left over after losing the love of his life. A piece of something that could never be put back together again. There was a time that he had been resigned to the fact that the dating ship had come and gone from the harbor of his life.

But that time was before Paige Henley.

'So, I'm just overthinking this.'

'You're definitely just overthinking this,' Cohen chuckled. 'But I mean it. I do appreciate the fact that our friendship means enough that you're fearful of ruining it. That, in itself, tells me a lot about you. And you know what else it tells me?'

'What?'

'That I would love to take you on a date even more.' He had to say it, because he meant it. In that moment, Cohen felt no apprehension about the prospect. He needed to use that fleeting moment of conviction to his full benefit.

Paige snickered, plucking her fork back up to spear a mouthful of cake. 'Despite the fact that I overanalyze everything?'

He paused for a moment, then leaned back and dug in his jeans pocket, pulling out the familiar stone he'd shown her a few days ago. 'Like I said before, you've got to just think about the positive stuff. *Think Pawsitive*. Besides, the fact you're over-thinking this isn't the most important part of what you've said since you sat down.'

Her eyebrows furrowed. 'It's not? Then, what is?'

Cohen leaned in. 'The part where you said you liked me.'

She tried to cover her wide grin. 'I meant that part.'

'And the part about wanting to go out with me?' It was a bold step for him. One he would probably overanalyze himself later on. But he asked, nonetheless.

'I meant that part, too.' Her eyes were bright. 'But where would we go?'

Cohen lowered his fork onto his plate, giving Paige a steady stare. 'You just leave that up to me.'

Chapter 11

Paige

She couldn't believe she was doing it. Paige Henley was really, truly going on a date.

With Cohen Beckett.

She didn't even fully know what that meant since Cohen insisted on letting him surprise her with the details, but she had to admit …

She was excited. And proud, if she was honest with herself. For a woman who shied away from every romantic relationship opportunity that had come her way up until now, pretending to need work and only work to keep her company, Paige was bursting with pride that she'd not only confessed to Allison that she really wanted to spend time with Cohen, and then listened to her when she gave her good advice, but she'd taken the bull by the horns and pursued Cohen herself. Six days ago, she'd confronted him. Sat in his kitchen with cake and coffee to fortify her, and she admitted her fears about the entire thing.

And Cohen had calmed those fears. With ease. She found solace in knowing he had that kind of ability, and genuine comfort in knowing she hadn't messed things up between them permanently.

The only thing Cohen advised her was to bring a jacket. Everything else was left in his hands. The idea of leaving the fate of the evening to someone else made Paige's stomach twist. It was a mix of uncertainty and anticipation, though, so she knew that, while the notion scared her, it was fear of the unknown that she feared, not the time with Cohen itself.

It wasn't like she had never dated at all. Paige had a few dates in high school and college, but there was a difference between being taken out to the local burger joint or the campus pub with a man led by the hormones of a teenager, and being asked out by a man who had his priorities in check and didn't expect anything from her other than to give him a chance.

Nothing about Cohen Beckett could be compared to a teenage boy. Hell, he was only a few years away from being the father of one, though she would never remind him of that fact. Kids grew up too fast as it was. Cohen didn't need it thrown in his face.

Paige didn't need the continual reminder that Bryce wouldn't be there with them tonight, either. A formal date with Cohen was so much different than the evening walks and the dessert they'd shared at her place with Bryce before. She had been comfortable then, never viewing it as more than it was, never expecting more than that moment.

But was that because she just didn't know *more* when she saw it, or because she and Cohen were so connected that the *more* came without thought or a conscious choice?

She was doing it again. Overthinking it. Overanalyzing it. She could practically hear Cohen's deep voice telling her to take it easy. Could see his hazel eyes with flecks of amber glinting the way they did when he found her neuroticism amusing.

He's right, she thought, letting out a long, steadying breath. *Just relax and enjoy it.* The thought was quickly followed by, *And think pawsitive.* She smiled.

Paige slipped on her favorite leather sandals just as the doorbell chimed out the first few bars of a pretty classical-sounding jingle. Much better than the previous chime. It was eight o'clock on the dot. Cohen was punctual. Just another thing to add to the list of things she liked about him.

'You look beautiful.' Cohen's eyes gleamed as the outside light above her entryway door at the bottom of the stairs reflected in them.

Paige had stressed over what to wear. Knowing she needed to bring a jacket hadn't helped her very much in deciding what to wear underneath it, so after tossing half her closet out onto the bed, she'd decided simple was best, pairing black capris with a cap-sleeved emerald green top. She knew it made the hue of her eyes pop without the aid of makeup, and she'd added only some faint lip gloss and foundation. Less was more when it came to makeup, as far as she was concerned.

'Thank you.' She gestured toward his ensemble of his signature jeans and T-shirt covered by a dark forest green plaid shirt he'd left open. 'You don't look too bad yourself.'

'Thanks.' He held an arm out for her to take. 'I contemplated dressing more formal, but I didn't want to freak you out. And, honestly, I didn't want to be uncomfortable all damn night.'

Paige appreciated his candor, having thought along the same lines. 'I happen to like your casual look. It suits you just fine.'

'Seeing as you opened the door, I'm assuming you haven't completely talked yourself out of this yet. So, what do you say we go before you change your mind?'

He might have said it in jest, but Paige wondered if he'd truly thought she would cancel their plans before now. She didn't blame him for thinking that. She let out a long breath, pulled her denim jacket from the hook by the door and folded it over one arm, then hooked her other arm around his. 'Lead the way.'

Outside, Main Street was buzzing with action. Well, as much action as a small-town downtown could on a weekend evening when almost all the businesses were closed and people were forced to make their own entertainment. Wrought iron lampposts lined

113

both sides of the street, casting soft shadows in the glowing lamplight. The sky was clear, and the stars twinkled and shone like diamonds across the blackened backdrop. The moon, though brighter and whiter than the yellow halogen light glowing from the streetlamps, was large and round amidst the stars, and it cast a romantic, storybook ambience onto the scene.

Paige rarely went out after dark, either working late into the night to prepare the next morning's baked goods or heading to bed early with a good book and falling asleep after a chapter or two. She was mesmerized by the activity around her. Couples were out walking hand in hand, peering into the shops and murmuring amongst each other. Through the shrubs and tree trunks, she could just make out the blinking lights and the ripple of the water where boats glided smoothly through the harbor, leaving gentle, rolling waves in their wake. A handful of vehicles passed by, going in both directions, their occupants either out for a scenic drive or heading toward their weekend plans.

In Paige's mind, it reminded her of the constant hustle and bustle of New York City, but on a smaller scale. Okay, a ridiculously smaller scale. But the idea that Port Landon resembled a mini New York in a small-town, easy kind of way held a certain charm that she couldn't deny she loved.

It made her ache for her old life in the big city for a split second. But just as quickly, Paige fell in love with her new life just a little bit more, tipping the scales in the small town's favor.

'So, this is what's going on while I'm slaving away in the kitchen or hiding out in my apartment.' She still held Cohen's arm loosely, allowing him to guide her from the sidewalk, down the cement stairs beside the bank, and onto the wooden boardwalk that would lead out to the pier they'd visited last week.

'There's always something to do, Paige. Something to see. Even in a small town.' He gave her hand that rested on his forearm a little squeeze. 'We just have to be willing to take the time to do and see it.'

114

'Spoken like a true workaholic.'

'It takes one to know one.'

She didn't take it as an insult. Rather, it was something they shared, something they understood about each other. Paige relished in the fact that Cohen was just as ambitious and hardworking as she was, albeit for different reasons. She liked that she didn't have to explain that side of herself to him. 'Do you ever wish you could change that about yourself?' she wondered out loud. 'Your workaholic ways, I mean?'

Cohen stayed quiet long enough that she wondered if she'd overstepped. Then, 'Even if things were different ... even if there was a second permanent veterinarian at the clinic alongside me, I think I'd still struggle to step away from my business. I don't delegate well. I think that's just the kind of person I am,' he said. His gaze met hers. 'But that doesn't mean I wouldn't like to try.'

The longing in his voice didn't go unnoticed. 'Ditto,' Paige replied. His words washed through her, lifting a weight from her shoulders. She wasn't sure she could have phrased her own thoughts better than he did.

'Ditto?' Cohen raised an eyebrow. 'What are we, in a scene from *Ghost*?'

'The fact that you even know the correlation between ditto and that movie just awarded you more brownie points than you know, Cohen Beckett.'

He fist-pumped the air theatrically. '*Please* tell me those brownie points get me actual brownies.'

'Oh, the perks of owning the local bakery.'

'Bryce is going to be ecstatic,' he quipped. 'Looks like I'd better brush up on my '90s movie trivia. It seems to have its perks, too.'

'You are too much.'

'Hey, you're the one who mentioned brownies.' He pointed down the length of the boardwalk toward the Old Port Ice Cream

Shoppe. 'This way.' He led her off the boardwalk and closer to the shop, which Paige could see was very much closed for the evening. It was dark, all the lights were off, and the sign on the screen door had been flipped to read *Closed*.

There were less people out this way, and Paige wondered idly why they were there at all. 'It's closed, Cohen.'

'It is,' he agreed, guiding her around to the back of the building that faced the waterfront. 'But not for us.'

He pulled a small keyring from his pocket and let go of Paige's arm only long enough to unlock the back door. Situated beside it was a small wooden patio boasting two Adirondack lawn chairs. He pushed the door open, revealing a dimly lit room. He waved a hand. 'Ladies first.'

Confused, Paige stepped past him. It took her eyes a few seconds to adjust to the dim light. As she looked around, the light in the room grew brighter. She spun around to see Cohen turning a dimmer switch on the wall, a crooked grin on his face.

'I knew we wouldn't make it to North Springs in time to have dinner at one of the fancier restaurants there. You deserve better than the diner here in town, which closes at eight o'clock, anyway. So, I did the only thing I could do.' He pushed away from the wall and held a hand out toward Paige. 'I brought one of those North Springs restaurants to you.'

She still didn't quite understand until she took Cohen's hand and let him lead her through the back entrance and into the ice cream storefront.

Except, it wasn't the storefront she'd experienced the day they'd come here. The round tables and steel-framed chairs had been removed, leaving only one long table against the far wall and one round table with two chairs in the middle of the room. Even in the soft light, Paige could see that the table nearest the wall had a couple of warming trays and pitchers set out on a crisp white tablecloth. The table in the middle of the room was set with two place settings, and a single rose was perched in the middle of it in a thin crystal vase. There were small tealight candles on both tables, their bright flames the only movement in the room as Paige stared at the entire scene, awestruck.

'You had dinner brought here?' She couldn't seem to get the words out clearly.

Cohen sprang into action, guiding her toward the table of warming trays. 'You've heard of Marcello's, I hope? It's the Italian restaurant in North Springs. I wanted to take you there, but there wasn't enough time in the day to make it happen. So, I had them deliver a variety of different appetizers and entrees, then I called in a favor to Ben, the owner of this shop. He helped to keep everything warm until we got here, so hopefully there's something here that you'll like. Do you even like Italian?'

She heard the panic as it grew in his tone the more he spoke. 'Cohen, this all looks ... fabulous. I love Italian food, but ... but ...'

'But what?' Uncertainty etched his features. 'Is this all too much?'

'What? Oh my God, no!' she gasped. 'It's just ... there's enough food here for the two of us to eat for a week!'

Cohen clasped a hand to his chest, evidently relieved. 'Paige, if that's the best complaint you can come up with, I think I must've done something right.'

'Right?' She looked at him as though he had sprouted a second head. 'More like you've done something perfect.'

'So, I'm definitely getting brownie points now?'

'To heck with the points. You're definitely getting brownies.' Her eyes met his. 'Cohen, this is amazing. Really. Thank you.'

It may have been a trick of the candlelight that flickered in his shining eyes, but Paige thought she saw more emotion in that hazel gaze than just relief. 'Come and sit down, Paige. You don't even know what you're thanking me for yet. Just wait till you try the gnocchi caprese and the fusilli primavera. Then you can thank me.'

'I think I've eaten more bread and pasta tonight than I've consumed in ten years.' Paige set her napkin down over her plate. She couldn't manage to eat another morsel if she tried. 'But it was worth it. Cohen, I think I've found a new favorite restaurant.'

'I told you Marcello's was fantastic.' He pushed his chair out slightly. Looked like she wasn't the only one who'd had their fill. 'But as good as that tiramisu was, I'll bet yours would rival anything they serve.'

'You're too kind.' Paige watched as Cohen rose from his chair and headed to the table near the wall, filling the small stainless-steel carafe that sat there with steaming hot coffee from the industrial coffeemaker. He brought the carafe back to their table in the middle of the room, and she smiled. She was thoroughly enjoying being wined and dined, a concept she'd only heard of in movies and through people she'd overheard at work in the city. 'Cohen, I'm not complaining, but you've already done too much. You don't need to serve me after-dessert coffee, too.'

'I don't need to ...' He filled one white ceramic mug with coffee and handed it to her. 'But I want to.'

'This has been so wonderful.' She meant every word. As always, the conversation between them had come easily, their anxiety about the first-date formalities dissipating as the decadence of the food took over. Paige enjoyed hearing about the mundane things like Bryce's spelling bee win and the science fair entry he was working on.

The thing was, those things weren't mundane at all. They were real life – Cohen's real life. She was overcome with gratitude that he felt he could share those bits and pieces of his life with her. In turn, she filled him in on the line of gluten-free goodies she was working on for the bakery, and they bounced ideas back and forth about the ways they could decorate the cupcakes for Helen O'Connor's fundraiser coming up next weekend.

'It's not over yet.' He leaned forward on his elbows. 'Unless, of course, you want it to be.'

'I was fearful of this whole date idea, Cohen. You know that.' She took a sip of her coffee, getting her bearings. She could be honest with him. She needed to be, because she wanted nothing less from him in return. 'But I'm serious. This has been one of the most wonderful evenings I've had in a long time. And I have you to thank you for it. So, no, I can't say I'm ready to call it a night just yet. As long as you're okay with that, I mean.'

'Not a chance. I've got one more trick up my sleeve, Miss Henley.' He stood, coffee cup in one hand. He held out the other. 'Bring your coffee and follow me.' Someone was enjoying playing the host.

She did so without hesitation, taking one last longing look at the spread of delicious food on the table and the candles that still flickered, though the wax had dripped enough now that they were less than half their height. The dim lights, the candlelit dinner, the amazing food and soft background music from the soft rock radio station Cohen had turned on in the kitchen area before they sat down …

It was the most romantic gesture anyone had ever done for her.

Cohen led her toward the door they'd come in, stepping to the side just beyond it to indicate the small patio they'd passed on the way in. He set his coffee mug down on the flat arm of one of the lawn chairs.

'Take a seat, Paige. I'll be right back.'

He ducked back inside. When he emerged, he was carrying her jacket over one arm and gripping the crystal candleholder in the other, the flame flickering and bobbing with his movement. He placed the candle on the railing, then carefully draped Paige's jacket over her knees. 'Wouldn't want you to get cold.'

'Thank you.'

He settled into the chair beside her, coffee mug in hand. 'This is the most serene spot in town, Paige. I know it's not much in comparison to the lights and glitz of New York, but for tonight, this spot is ours.'

She looked out over the water, watching as a series of boats floated silently in all directions, using the harbor as their own personal highway. The lights shining from each of them reflected off the rippling water, stretching like long, colorful shadows that danced in the breeze. It was far from cold, but Paige welcomed the warmth of her jacket to protect her from the gentle wind that came off the water's edge.

'This spot is perfect, Cohen.' She tore her gaze from the waterfront to turn toward him. 'I don't think there's anywhere else in the world I would rather be.'

Something changed in Cohen's eyes, his features softening. He said nothing, setting his mug down before he nodded, as though he'd made some kind of decision. 'Me neither, Paige.' He spoke in a low voice, and she knew the words were meant for only her, and her alone. 'Me neither.'

Chapter 12

Cohen

Another Sunday came and went in the Beckett household. It didn't carry the awkwardness that Cohen had expected after his date night with Paige the night before. Somehow, he'd expected Bryce to question him about it. Cohen hadn't quite known how he would approach the subject if he did. But his son said nothing. Instead, he chose to discuss his friend's video game selection and the endless junk food they'd consumed during his sleepover at Hunter's house the night before. The thought of the sugar rotting his teeth and the games rotting his mind made Cohen cringe inwardly, but he was glad his son had a good time.

He noticed Bryce's furtive glances, though. And those glances said more than any words from his mouth could. The boy wondered about his relationship with Paige. Cohen knew he would. Bryce was a smart kid, and he knew his father had never taken anyone out on a date in the past eight years.

Cohen wondered about his relationship with Paige, too.

If there was contention about it, however, Bryce didn't show it. The look in his eyes was laden with curiosity, not malice or hurt. Call it cowardice, but Cohen decided to let his son come to him when he was ready. Maybe by then he would be ready to talk about it himself.

He had no idea what he would tell the boy, mostly because he was still trying to sort through his thoughts and emotions on his own. One thing was for sure, though ...

Cohen liked Paige. More than he knew how to deal with. He not only liked her, he admired her. Admired the way she took charge of her life and danced to her own beat. Admired the way she seemed so fearless in the name of her search for happiness, yet had her reservations about jumping into anything with someone she had only known for a few weeks. He respected that. More than she knew. Paige wasn't someone looking for a quick fix on the road to contentment, and she sure wasn't someone who was looking for someone to provide it for her.

She understood what had taken Cohen years to figure out – happiness wasn't something someone else could give; it was something people had to allow themselves to find, experience, and accept. Only then could they let someone else in to share it with.

Was Cohen ready to take that leap and let Paige in?

Even more, was Paige ready to let him in? Sure, she'd had a good time last night, but she had been honest about her hesitation from the beginning. He'd been planning to call her later today, but maybe he should take a step back and leave the ball in her court. Maybe he should let the next step be hers. He didn't want to come across as overbearing. Maybe he was overthinking this.

That sure was a lot of maybes. And all those maybes made him wonder if *he* was the one truly not ready.

Bryce ambled into the living room, where Cohen had sprawled out on the sofa with a list of town residents he planned to approach about helping out with the silent auction he'd had the idea to include on the fundraiser day for Helen O'Connor. The clinic emergency phone sat on the coffee table, and he sent it warning glances, silently pleading for it to stay silent just a bit longer. He was enjoying the peace and quiet around him, even if his mind was anything but.

'Hey, that's my spot.' Bryce dropped himself into the oversized armchair beside the couch, eyeing up the cushions his father sat on.

'You snooze, you lose.' Cohen tossed a gray corduroy throw pillow at him. 'Finally decided to make an appearance, huh? I could hear you hissing out threats from here.'

'I was playing Fortnite with Hunter. Things were getting intense.'

'Obviously,' Cohen said. 'I guess I wouldn't understand.'

'Yeah, you're too old.'

'That was harsh.' But a grin danced on Cohen's mouth. 'You're lucky I don't have another pillow to throw.'

'You'd miss anyway, old man.'

Laughter bubbled up from his throat. The kid was on fire today. 'Did you just come out here to make fun of me? You're doing a bang-up job of it.'

'I aim to please,' Bryce quipped, giving a half-hearted bow without getting up from the chair. 'Nah, I actually wanted to talk to you about something.'

Oh, here it comes. 'Sure, what's up?'

'It's about Paige.'

Cohen may have been expecting it, but that didn't make his son's words any less ominous. 'I figured you would have questions about her.'

'Yeah?' His son tilted his head. 'Then why didn't you say anything before now?'

Good question. Mostly because I'm a coward. 'I figured you would come to me when you were ready.'

'And are you?' Bryce countered, sounding a lot more like an adult than Cohen wanted to admit. 'Ready?'

He let out a long breath, surprised by his kid's blatant inquisition. 'Ready for Paige? Bryce, I don't know, buddy. But that doesn't mean I don't want to see where things are going, you know? She seems really nice, and she's taken a shine to you, I think—'

'Wait, what are we talking about?'

Cohen stared at the young boy, confused. 'About Paige. You asked me if I was ready to talk about her.'

'Technically, I didn't,' Bryce explained. 'I meant to ask you if you were ready for my questions, but at least now I know what you're really thinking, Dad. You like Paige, and you finally admit it.'

Cohen just stared at his son. Had the boy really just tricked him into admitting his feelings for Paige Henley? One glance at the crooked grin on Bryce's face and Cohen knew he had been duped. And the boy had done it purposely. And perfectly.

How sneaky.

'You purposely confused me, didn't you?' Cohen was shocked. Not just because his ten-year-old had the capability to talk circles around him, but because he'd fallen for it.

'Hey, it's not my fault you can't keep up in your old age.' Bryce raised his hands in mock surrender, his smirk now a full-fledged smile. 'Dad likes Paige,' he taunted in a sing-song voice. 'Dad likes Paige.'

'You are far too devious for your own good, boy.' He shook his head, wondering how in the world Bryce had grown up so fast. 'And far too smart.'

'I get it from you, Dad.' He shrugged. 'Besides, it's okay. I like Paige, too.'

'You do?' Cohen was too surprised by his son's admission to show his pride at having his son believe his brains came from him.

'Yeah, of course. She's pretty cool.'

Cohen let that register in silence. He liked Paige, and he'd unwittingly admitted it to Bryce. And Bryce liked Paige, too.

The boy had even given him his blessing to pursue something more than the friendship they'd formed, in his own roundabout way.

'Besides,' Bryce continued, 'She bakes the best chocolate cake ever. What's not to like?' He stood and cast a glance in the direction of the clock in the kitchen. From his vantage point, he would be able to read it clearly. 'I'm going to go play with Jazz in the backyard for a bit.'

And just like that, Bryce disappeared out of the room, leaving Cohen with only his jumbled thoughts to keep him company. Bryce's confession hit him like a bombshell. It wasn't that it was a huge surprise. He knew his son was a fan of Paige. And it wasn't that he had expected him to react in a negative light.

What Cohen hadn't expected, though, was that his son would be the one to instigate the conversation and expertly coerce Cohen's own convoluted confession from him about his feelings for her.

'Wait!' Cohen hollered, springing from the couch and following Bryce out to the back door. 'If that wasn't what you were trying to talk to me about, then what did you want to talk about regarding Paige?'

Bryce was crouched down on one knee, tying up his running shoes. When he stood to his full height, the mischievous grin was back in place. 'Oh, just school. My class is doing a project on local businesses and we're supposed to pick one to interview the owner and ask questions about it. I wanted to ask you if it was all right if I chose Paige and the bakery instead of the vet clinic. Hunter says he wants to interview you, anyway.'

Now, Cohen knew for sure that his son had purposely been vague in order to extract information from him. There was no reason he couldn't have just come out with it. Instead, he had danced around the subject, focusing his carefully chosen words on Paige and not the school project.

Well played, son.

'I'm okay with it if Paige is,' he said. 'You'll have to ask her, though.'

'Is she coming over later?' The boy held his gaze with the expertise of a master negotiator. It scared Cohen immensely that at only ten years old his son knew how to get him to divulge answers to questions without actually having to ask them.

'Not tonight,' he replied carefully. 'But I have to talk to her about some fundraiser stuff for next weekend, so we can stop in during Jazz's walk tomorrow night after the clinic closes and we've had supper. When's the project due?'

'End of next week.' Bryce clapped his hands together. 'So, that works perfect.'

'You sure?' Cohen swallowed, then added, 'If you want, you can stop in at the bakery on your way home from school.'

'Alone?' Bryce went still, waiting and watching with bated breath.

Cohen knew he was stepping over a precipice he couldn't crawl back from. But he had to loosen the reins a little at some point. His son was a responsible kid, always had been. He couldn't think of a better time to give him a little freedom than when he had a school project he was interested in that would send him in Paige's direction. 'Sure. But you're there for school, not to coerce chocolate cake from Paige.'

'Deal. Thanks, Dad!' He high-fived him with overzealous enthusiasm, making his father chuckle.

Cohen watched Bryce amble out the door. He didn't look away until he saw him disappear into the back entrance of the clinic. All he could think about was that his son had chosen Paige over him. The thought didn't hurt his feelings. How could it? He could relate. Mostly because he was pretty sure his own heart had chosen Paige, too.

The next day, the bell clanged overhead as Cohen slipped into the bakery. As usual, a handful of customers mingled amongst the display cases and coolers. Immediately, he noticed a new glass case set up to the right of the counter, with a fancy calligraphy sign announcing the new gluten-free cakes, cookies, and breads Paige had been agonizing over for the past few weeks. He was proud of her. She had finally taken the plunge.

'Well, hey,' he said by way of greeting. 'We've really got to stop meeting like this.'

Paige whirled around. Today's apron boasted oversized roses and a damask background. A white smudge of flour or baking powder was smeared on her cheek, and her long locks were pulled up into a messy yet stylish bun on the top of her head. She looked downright adorable.

'You're right.' Her eyes lit up. 'Perhaps we should just meet at ice cream shops after hours and eat to-die-for Italian food instead.'

Cohen quirked an eyebrow. It was the first time she had openly flirted with him. At least, he thought she was flirting. It had been a while since he'd played that game. 'I must admit, I like the way you think, Paige.' He nodded toward the cake on the back counter behind her, partially covered with pale blue, pink, and white flowers and leaves made of frosting. No wait, fondant – that's what she'd told him it was called. 'That's pretty.'

'Thank you.' She turned back to the cake, spinning it on the turning cake pedestal to show the designs from all sides. 'It's my umpteenth attempt at Allison's wedding cake. Now that she's officially picked a date and everything—'

'She has? I hadn't heard that yet.'

'Well, I am closer to the source than most of Port Landon,' she laughed. 'So, I would hope I would know before the coffee drinkers at the diner.'

'I won't tell them you said that.'

She levelled her gaze on him, narrowing her eyes until they were only slits. 'You wouldn't,' she said with a sly grin. Then, with a nonchalant shrug, she added, 'Besides, they probably wouldn't believe you, anyway.'

'You're probably right,' he chuckled. 'Hell knows they seem to have the inside scoop about stuff before it even happens.' He matched her shrug. 'But, either way, whatever you say, it's safe with me. Locked away in the vault. I promise.'

Paige paused and regarded him with a curious stare. Then, as though she'd made some kind of decision about him, she snapped her fingers. 'Good. Let me help these customers, then I've got a quick favor to ask of you.'

It was on the tip of his tongue to respond with, 'Anything,' but she was gone, wiping her hands on her ruffle-edged apron. She boxed up an entire black forest cake topped with rich red maraschino cherries – a mirror image of the one they'd dined on in her apartment – while he stood there admiring how far her business had come.

He remembered fondly the old-school décor of Wilhelmina's bake shop before Paige took it over, with its red and white checkered curtains over the windows, the old melamine tables and cases that displayed her baked goodies. The linoleum on the floors had been a battered beige color, and they had long ago lost their shine from the decades of traffic they'd been subjected to. The bread, muffins, and baked goods had always been top notch, and treats from Wilhelmina's were at the top of the list for anyone visiting Port Landon. The shop itself, however, had begun to look rundown and in need of some desperate tender loving care.

And that's exactly what Paige Henley had done. New barn-board-inspired laminate flooring had been laid down, and the chipped melamine tables and cases had been replaced with glass-doored display cases and coolers with shiny enamel, and silvery hinges. The walls had been painted a soft sage green, a color he thought resembled that of her living room upstairs. Off-white curtains hung from wrought iron rods above the windows. The two huge floor-to-ceiling bay windows that faced out onto the sidewalk were open, and a white bistro set sat in front of each of them for customers to enjoy their purchases if they wanted to indulge immediately.

It was a simple yet classy little spot, and he thought it matched Paige's personality to a tee.

'Okay,' Paige said, heading to the sink around the corner to wash her hands after handling the money. 'I need your help.'

She waved him behind the counter to where the cake sat, and Cohen followed her silent instruction as she placed her hands on his forearms, guiding him to the spot in front of her. 'So, here's the thing. Allison has given me her ideas for the cake and I've come up with numerous variations of those ideas, but haven't quite knocked it out of the ballpark yet.'

'What's been wrong with the past attempts?' He eyed the cake, looking for something that might be considered untoward. It still looked like a pretty wedding cake to him.

'Let's see …' She spun the cake around slowly to the side where the floral décor hadn't been added. 'The wedding colors are gray and purple, so I've tried numerous times to create a floral motif on the cake, but Allison's changed her mind a few times.' He could hear the exasperation she tried to hide, and he suppressed a smile. 'Then, the flavor hasn't been up to par. She wanted vanilla, but not a regular vanilla. Her words, not mine. She wants something closer to the vanilla bean flavoring they use in the lattes at the coffeehouse. Again, her words, not mine.'

Cohen couldn't help it. He laughed. 'You're a good friend, Paige. I can hear the frustration in your voice, and still you don't complain. You just forge ahead toward perfection.'

'I'm just trying to do what she wants. It's her day, not mine.'

'And that's what makes you such a good friend.' He nodded at the cake beside him. 'So, this is vanilla bean cake with the perfect flowers?'

'In theory,' she replied. 'The flowers are small and intricate, but they're forget-me-nots. A symbol of true, faithful love and good memories, and the cake is what I call a Paige Henley original, made specifically according to Allison's well-meaning ramblings.' She set about lopping off a small wedge of the cake onto a dessert plate and stabbing a forkful. 'So, here's what I need you to do. I want you to close your eyes and pretend this is your cake. Your day.'

'You want me to pretend it's my wedding day.'

Immediately, Paige winced. 'Oh God, I'm sorry. I didn't even think—'

Cohen reached out and touched Paige's arm, steadying her. 'It's okay.' He hadn't meant to mortify her, reminding her that he had, in fact, had a wedding day once upon a time. He frankly found her request a bit amusing. 'Let's do this.'

'Are you sure?' Paige's arm was rigid and motionless beneath his fingertips.

'Of course,' he insisted. 'I get cake from it, don't I?'

She held up a finger, rolling her eyes. 'Fine. Just shush. Now, it's your day, and all you wanted was a vanilla bean cake with a light, airy frosting that complements the flavors. I said close your eyes, Cohen.'

He did, but not without an exaggerated sigh. 'Okay, okay. It's my day, my cake ... I get it.'

'As I was saying, you've just eaten your meal and this cake is supposed to go perfectly with the after-dinner coffee and tea being served. Not too sweet, not too heavy. And you're sharing it with ... the person you love. Your best friend.'

Cohen suddenly felt like all the air in the room had evaporated. He hung on her every word. Not just on the words themselves, but on the soothing voice he'd come to appreciate. He opened his eyes; he couldn't help himself. He needed to correlate the comforting voice with the intriguing sapphire eyes he'd craved to see since he got up that morning. 'Keep going,' he encouraged her softly.

Something shifted in Paige's eyes as they locked with his, and he saw her throat move visibly. 'The cake has been cut,' she continued in a gentler tone, 'And you're staring into the adoring eyes of that one person. Your true love. Your forget-me-not.' She lifted the fork up. 'Your gaze doesn't waver as you lean in and open your mouth slightly ...'

Cohen was mesmerized by her. He leaned in just as the words tumbled from her lips.

'And, together, you share that first bite of the cake that signifies the celebration of the life that awaits you.' She guided the fork to his mouth and Cohen tasted the sweet, decadent flavors as they burst on his tongue. He moaned, overcome by the cake as well as the moment itself.

It was perfect. The cake, the moment ... and Paige.

'Paige, you've done it,' he said once he managed to find his voice. 'That cake is pure perfection.' When he opened his eyes, he came face to face with her. Only inches separated their faces. And their mouths. He couldn't breathe, his gaze flitting down to her pink lips and up again to her eyes, round and wide and locked on his. He could feel the damp warmth of her breath against his skin, coming out in shallow pants as she watched him, waited for him ...

'Well, would you look at you two!'

With deer-in-the-headlights looks, both Cohen and Paige snapped their gazes away from each other and toward the door. Without thinking, Cohen took a step away from Paige. He realized just as quickly that she did the same.

'Aww, come on, you guys,' Allison snickered, clapping her hands together happily. 'Don't break up the romantic ambience on my part.'

How had she even made it into the shop without him or Paige hearing the damn bell chime? Had he really been that lost in Paige Henley that his senses had shut down?

She was really doing a number on him.

He could see the blush creeping up into Paige's cheeks, and he knew very well that it looked like exactly what it was. He and

Paige had been taste-testing someone else's wedding cake. He was pretty sure he hadn't been the only one pretending it was their own. Then, there was the fact that he had been a fraction of a second away from kissing her. So close, so warm and inviting …

'Dr Cohen, you'd better be treating that girl nicely.' Sonya's voice sounded from behind Allison just as she shut the shop door behind her. 'Heaven knows we want her to stick around Port Landon. Looks to me like you do, too.'

He could have groaned at the sight of Sonya Ritter and her overbearing matchmaking attempts, but he was too engrossed in the truth of her statement. Paige wasn't only doing a number on him, she was doing a number on the others in Port Landon as well. She belonged here, and it was Sonya's interpretation that he held the power to keep her here.

That was fine, because Cohen Beckett had every intention of keeping Paige Henley within the town limits. All he could hope was that her intentions were the same.

Chapter 13

Paige

She meant it innocently enough. In the beginning, anyway. Allison's wedding cake was driving her nuts, and she'd only wanted someone else's opinion as to where she stood in baking and designing the perfect one. Other than the bride-to-be herself, Cohen was the only real friend Paige had in Port Landon. She had been resourceful in recruiting him for his say on the matter.

Until, suddenly, it wasn't about the cake at all. At first, she was only trying to explain the level of perfection she was going for. How perfect she wanted the moment and the cake to be for her cousin on her wedding day.

Then, her guided visualization had quickly turned into Paige's own personal fantasy of her own romantic wedding day. Having Cohen standing before her, his eyes glassy and fixated on her the moment they opened, like she was the only woman in the world ...

She'd gotten lost in the illusion. Lost in his gaze, cognizant of the way it kept lowering to her lips. He was a breath away, only a mere breath.

And, of course, it just had to be Allison and Sonya who appeared out of nowhere and ruined it all.

'Aren't you guys just the cutest?' Allison was gushing, batting her eyelashes. She was putting on a theatrical show Paige didn't care to see.

She rolled her eyes. 'We were just discussing your wedding cake. You should be thanking Cohen for even attempting to help me perfect it before I shove another feeble try under your nose.'

'There's no one in the world who's going to turn down cake, Paige.' Allison was still looking between her cousin and Cohen. 'I take it you told the good doctor the news? That Christopher and I have set a date?'

'She mentioned it.' Cohen cast a furtive glance toward Paige. One that screamed he was trying to diffuse the situation and save her from it, just as much as himself. He put down the fork he'd taken from Paige's fingers when they'd been interrupted, setting it down on the edge of the plate with a soft clatter. 'I should probably be going—'

'The first of August,' Allison interjected, leaning her elbows onto the counter and peering at him and Paige with wide, dreamy eyes. 'That's the big day.'

Cohen looked a bit shocked. 'That's only three weeks away.'

Paige knew all too well the short timeframe. Hence her reason for losing her sanity when it came to the wedding cake and her maid of honor responsibilities.

'That's right.' Sonya spoke up, pointing a finger at Cohen. There was an assertiveness in her tone Paige hadn't expected. Judging by Cohen's expression, he hadn't, either. 'So, you'd best be getting around to asking this lovely girl to be your date for the wedding reception.'

Paige's jaw dropped at the same time Cohen's did. Allison, however, clapped her hands together like an enthusiastic school-girl and jumped up and down.

'How did I not think of that?' she exclaimed. 'Paige, Cohen can be your date for my wedding!'

If she thought she was mortified before, Paige knew she must be seventeen shades of cr

only thing she could do was

bulging eyes, her mouth openin

couldn't seem to voice.

She was going to kill her cousin. I

She snapped her gaze to Cohen, her eyes

Cohen. It seems these ladies forgot to brin

them.'

'It's fine,' Cohen assured her. He waved a dis

gesture which eased her mind a bit. Then, he tug

piece of paper from his pocket and handed it to her.

over. It's a list of the people I've talked to about the silent

for the fundraiser, and a few I haven't. I really do need t

back to the clinic, but maybe we can meet up with you tonigh

'Tonight?' She couldn't keep up. The change of topics was

giving her whiplash, and Paige was even more humiliated by the

realization that Cohen was changing the subject and pretending

like being her wedding date had never even been suggested.

'For an evening walk with Bryce and Jazz,' he explained. 'And

me, of course. We can iron out the final details for the fundraiser.'

'Oh.' She shook her head, hoping to clear it, and plastered a

half-hearted smile on her face. 'Of course, sure.'

'Perfect.' Cohen clapped his hands together and rounded the

counter, leaving Paige standing beside the wedding cake alone.

His absence left a palpable void in the empty space he occupied

only moments before. 'Well, ladies, it's been a pleasure.' He nodded

his head toward Allison and Sonya.

Paige couldn't take her eyes off him. And when he made it to

the door and turned around to face her once more, she was still

fixated on him, like she knew he couldn't possibly leave the

conversation on that note.

'Oh, and Paige?'

'Yeah?'

Cohen flashed her a crooked grin. 'For the record, if I'm invited ore than to be

e opened the

ll chiming in

d had since

played on

rom being

candor, to

ing every-

played it

n hadn't

d made

exactly where

imson by now. Words failed her. The
stare at her cousin and Sonya with
g and closing on the excuses she

was official. 'Allison, I ...'
pleading, 'I'm s-so sorry,
their manners with

missive hand, a
ged a folded
Look that
auction
get

...u love nothing more than to be her date. He'd said it in front of everyone. It was one thing to go for walks together at night, or to have a quiet dinner together without the prying eyes of the other people they interacted with every day. But Allison's wedding was going to be a community affair. Everyone and their uncle would be there.

And Paige would be there, too. On Cohen's arm.

The giddy teenager within her was squealing with delight. The more time she spent with Cohen Beckett, the more Paige knew she cared about him. In only a few short weeks, he and his exuberant son had managed to sneak their way into Paige's heart. And they had done it with a quiet and gentle kindness.

That's what she liked about him so much – his gentle nature. Cohen was a man; there was no denying his rugged handsomeness, or the chiseled muscles of his forearms that peeked out from the sleeves of his scrub tops. But he was also a gentleman. Polite to a fault. He'd raised his son the same way.

That was another thing – Cohen had raised his son. On his own. After befalling a tragedy that some people might never dig themselves out of. After losing the woman he'd both promised and expected to spend the rest of his life with. But their time together had been abruptly shortened, stealing Cohen's role as a husband and compounding his role as a father drastically. He became not only a father, which was difficult enough, but a single father. His efforts had resulted in an adolescent boy he should be extremely proud to call his son.

She was still thinking about Bryce when he suddenly materialized as though from thin air. The bell chimed and there he was, his lanky limbs dressed in a plain green T-shirt, jeans, and Converse shoes. A Michigan Wolverines hat was atop his head, his sandy hair sticking out from under it in little wisps.

'Hey, Paige.'

'I was just thinking about you,' she admitted by way of greeting.

Bryce pushed his backpack farther behind him. 'I really hope that means you were thinking of feeding me chocolate fudge cake.'

She laughed. How could she not? 'I think we both know what your dad would say about that.' She cast a glance at the clock behind her. 'Especially since you haven't eaten supper yet.'

'Can't blame a guy for trying, right?' Bryce shrugged cheerfully.

She shook her head, chuckling as she cleaned out the display case on top of the counter. The banana bread and lemon poppy-seed loaves she'd made the night before had sold out before noon, much to her delight. 'Has anyone told you yet that your sense of humor is adorable, Bryce?'

A hint of pink shone in his cheeks, but the boy scoffed, pretending it was no big deal. 'I was going for rugged and manly, actually.'

She pressed her lips together until she could safely get words out without bursting into laughter. She continued, 'I won't tell anyone I called you adorable, then.' She tossed the paper liner from the bottom of the display case into the trash can. 'What brings you by? It's slim pickings around here today for sugary leftovers, I'm afraid.'

Bryce glanced longingly at the lone éclair on the top shelf of the display case as he spoke. 'I actually came here to see you.'

She wasn't quite sure if he was talking to her or the éclair, but she plucked the treat from the case and put it on a pale purple napkin, sliding it across the counter toward him. 'That's our little secret,' she advised, her heart swelling a little at the sight of his eyes growing wide. 'Now, what's on your mind?'

Bryce wasted no time digging into the éclair, and the cream filling was smeared across his top lip as he struggled to talk around the dessert in his mouth. 'I have this school thing. A project about a local business. I want to do it on your bakery.' He swallowed, then quickly added, 'Would that be okay?'

'You don't want to do the project on your dad's vet clinic?' She arched a brow.

'I talked to Dad about it already. He's cool with it. Said I should talk to you.'

She was touched. The boy had come in here on his own to ask her if he could do a school project on her business. He'd chosen her own business over his dad's. He probably did it because of the goodies he could nab while working on it, mind you, but he'd chosen Paige's bakery, nonetheless. 'I don't know what to say, Bryce. I'm flattered you'd want to.'

'Just say yes. That's all you need to say.' He took another bite of the éclair and held out his hand.

'You drive a hard bargain, Bryce Beckett.' She shook his hand, grasping it firmly as though he was an adult. 'You've got yourself a deal.'

'I might need some more treats like this to keep me going while I work on the project, though. Just saying.' He pointed to the éclair like it was the key to sustaining life. Or getting good grades on a school report.

'I'll see what I can do,' she replied. 'But, again, your dad might have something to say about that. Just saying.'

He shrugged again. She couldn't blame the kid for trying. She let him bask in the sugary goodness of his éclair as she worked on cleaning up the storefront in preparation of closing for the evening. He seemed content, which is maybe why she didn't expect what happened next.

'Dad likes you.'

Paige looked over at him from across the storefront, where she'd just turned the lights off inside the glass display cases near the window. 'Yeah?' She was caught off guard but did her best to test the waters of what the boy was really saying. 'Well, I like your dad, too. He's a nice man.'

'Like, more than friends, though, right?' He seemed genuinely interested in her answer. 'Because I think that's the way Dad likes you.'

This was uncharted territory for Paige. She didn't know the protocol when it came to dating in general, much less the ins and outs of dating a man with an inquisitive son. Her instincts told her to cut him off at the pass, advise him as politely as possible that this wasn't something they should be talking about. But Paige felt as though Bryce had something he wanted to say. She gave him the safest opening she could. 'And how do you feel about that?'

The boy looked bewildered that she would consult him, but his hands came up as he spoke, fingertips covered in chocolate and cream filling. 'I feel like … like, *finally*.'

She would have found it funny if it wasn't such a serious matter. And if the matter didn't concern her. 'Finally?'

He was as enthusiastic as ever. Once she'd allowed him the inch he needed to explain, he took the mile. 'Like, finally Dad's not alone all the time, you know? I know it's because Mom died and everything, but I even heard Hunter's parents say Dad's lonely.' Paige waited for him to continue. 'I mean, we do everything together, but I go to friends' houses and on school trips and stuff, so I can't be there all the time. And he works all the time, I know that. But if he's not at the clinic, then he's just … by himself. So, maybe he won't be now?'

Paige felt her heart break for the poor boy. Not because he could ever want for anything more than he already had, but because he'd unwittingly taken on the role of supervisor for his father, thinking he had to try to protect him from his own loneliness.

She wondered if Cohen had any idea that his son was trying to protect him just as much as he was trying to protect his son.

'You're such a good kid.' She was at a loss for words but decided to stick with the truth. 'Your dad is lucky to have you, Bryce.'

'I know.' He made a show of brushing his knuckles on the front of his T-shirt, wearing a smug grin. 'He's pretty cool, though. You know, for an old guy.'

If she'd been taking a drink of the coffee she kept tucked behind the counter, she would have spat it all over. 'Easy now. If he's old, then I'm old.'

'If the shoe fits.'

His sense of humor never ceased to amaze her. 'Careful, I'm going to tell your dad you called him old. No, wait, I'm going to tell him you called *me* old.'

His smirk vanished and he froze, suddenly wary. 'You won't tell him I told you he liked you, though, right?' Bryce winced. He was just as aware they probably shouldn't have been having this conversation.

She waved a hand, making light of it. 'Don't worry. Your secret is safe with me.'

'Thanks, Paige.' He crumpled the purple napkin and tossed it over the counter into the trash can with perfect form. 'I'd better head to the clinic before Dad wonders where I am.'

'Sounds good. I'll see you and Jazz tonight, okay?'

He stopped after slinging his backpack up onto his shoulder. 'You're coming for a walk with us?'

'Only if that's all right with you.' She waited, letting him realize he had just as much say in this budding relationship as his father did. They were a package deal, and after the conversation they'd just shared, Paige didn't want Bryce to ever feel like she was taking over in any way.

Something shifted between her and the young boy as his eyes locked with hers. Then, he nodded, confirming whatever decision he'd come to. 'Yeah, that's all right.' And just like a few hours earlier, Bryce took the same path toward the door to leave as his father had, turning at the last minute. 'Paige?'

'Yeah?'

The corner of Bryce's mouth curled up. 'You're pretty cool, too. You know, for an old person.'

Chapter 14

Cohen

Once the sun dipped into the horizon, it became chilly enough that Cohen was actually starting to feel bad for inviting Paige out with them. Bryce didn't seem to notice the briskness of the evening air, bundled up in a hoodie over a long-sleeved shirt and jogging pants as he pretended to have mini fifteen-step races with Jazz, much to the dog's delight. But Cohen noticed. One glance at Paige, arms wrapped around her middle as she struggled to hold in the warmth from her thin jacket, confirmed she noticed, too.

'Oh, to be a kid again, huh?' They had been talking comfortably off and on since they rounded the corner and left Main Street, but there was a lull so he focused on the one thing he always reverted to – Bryce. He meant it as a joke, but Paige's answer was laced with sincerity.

'I wouldn't go back,' she said. 'I think it took me too long to get where I am.'

Interesting. 'In Port Landon, you mean?'

'In general.' She faced him as she walked. 'I don't feel like I wasted all those years in New York City, but there is a relief that comes with knowing I made it through them and ended up where I should be. Here.'

'Everything happens for a reason, right?'

'Exactly,' she replied. 'There was a winding, concrete jungle path to get here, but I finally made it.'

'You're that content with Port Landon?' Cohen didn't mean to sound skeptical, but most people their age had either sprinted for the town limit sign long ago or were still hoping for the day they could. He'd lived away from here, so he believed that's what made him appreciate the vast differences.

'Of course.' Paige's forehead crinkled. 'For the most part, anyway. I will admit there are days when I still think I'm crazy for uprooting myself the way I did. And when I still think there's no way some city girl is going to make it in a little town like this without a whole heap of luck. But it's turned out pretty well, don't you think?' Thinly veiled amusement quirked at the corners of her mouth. Cohen decided that that kind of smile was his favorite of hers.

'I couldn't agree more.' He had the strong urge to reach out and wrap his arm around her shoulders, to hold her close and keep her warm. Keep her safe. Or he could entwine his fingers with hers and hold her hand again, bask in the warmth of her fingertips. Anything, as long as she was close to him. But that might be too much, too soon after the incident at the bakery. Or misconstrued that way. He was acutely aware she had yet to mention their almost-kiss, or to reach for his hand, either.

'Did Bryce tell you he came to visit me today?' She stared far ahead, watching the antics of his son and the brindle boxer as Jazz sniffed at a spot near a large maple tree, and Bryce tried without success to steer her away from it.

Cohen nodded. 'I told him he had to ask you himself about the project. He was pretty shocked when I suggested he could go to the bakery alone to ask you, though.'

'I was a little surprised, too.'

He nodded, trying to act nonchalant. 'I hold on tight, I know that. But every now and then I remember that he's growing up and he's not a baby anymore.'

'He'll always be your baby,' she said simply. 'There's no shame or blame in that, Cohen.'

'You're a woman after my own heart, aren't you?' The phrase slipped off his tongue before he realized he'd said it out loud. He couldn't be sure in the fading light, but he was almost certain Paige was blushing in response.

'You're a good dad, Cohen,' she replied. 'And he's a good kid. I'm sure everyone around here would tell you the same thing.'

'Yeah.' He nodded, watching as Jazz stopped trotting along like a miniature horse long enough to make sure they were following. 'But their opinions don't seem to matter to me the way yours do,' he confessed. 'So, thank you.'

Yeah, Paige was definitely blushing now. 'You're welcome,' was all she managed to say. Her loss for words left a satisfied grin on Cohen's face. It was nice to know he could affect her the same way she affected him.

'So, I take it you agreed to be Bryce's project subject?' He thought maybe it was better to get back onto more solid, platonic ground.

'I did,' she said. 'After I confirmed you were okay with it, of course.'

'Don't worry, I can handle knowing my son thinks you're cooler than I am.'

'Oh, I am,' she teased. 'For an old person, anyway.'

Cohen stared at her, eyes wide. 'What?'

'Your son's words, not mine.' She laughed.

'He said that to you?' He pointed ahead, where Bryce was tugging on the leash to try to keep Jazz from being too curious about Mrs Appleton's tabby cat, confirming they were talking about the same kid.

'Oh, don't worry, you're old, too,' she added. 'We're in the same boat in your son's eyes.'

'I'm liable to put him in that boat and take away the paddles.' Cohen shook his head. 'What a kid.'

'Come on, it's kind of funny,' Paige insisted. 'Remember when we used to believe thirty was old?'

'Isn't there a song about that?' Cohen turned his body in an attempt to block her from a particularly brisk gust of wind.

'First you make a reference to *Ghost*, then you know the lyrics to *Strawberry Wine*?' Paige's eyebrows rose. 'Color me impressed, Cohen Beckett.'

'I'm a man of many talents.'

'I'd say.' She pulled her jacket tighter around her, tugging the collar higher up against her chin. 'Speaking of that, are you ready to show me what you're made of in the cupcake decorating department? Because I've got nearly a hundred and fifty made, just begging to be frosted.'

The fundraiser was scheduled for Sunday morning. It was the only day the vet clinic wasn't open, and the last thing Cohen wanted to do was help to set up this fundraiser and then leave Paige to handle the event day by herself. Being on call was another thing altogether, but all he could do was hope things stayed quiet for a few hours.

'I almost forgot we still needed to do that. Between you, me, and Bryce, we should be able to decorate that many cupcakes in an evening, right?'

Her face wore an expression somewhere in between a frustrated parent and the humor of a school teacher about to prove him wrong. 'Cohen, that's *half* the cupcakes,' she explained. 'I've made a few batches a day and frozen them. But there are another hundred and fifty or so to be baked, giving us three hundred in total.'

'Three hundred?' Cohen wasn't sure he even knew what that many cupcakes looked like in one room. 'Do we really need that many cupcakes?'

Bryce had stopped once he heard the exasperation in their voices. Or maybe it was the mention of cupcakes. 'Dad, honestly, there can never be too many cupcakes. What's wrong with you?'

'I'm going to have to side with Bryce on this one.' There was no hiding the faint grin on her lips. 'But seriously, if even a quarter of Port Landon's population shows up – and you know they will – and they each buy a half dozen cupcakes – and you know they will – then we're going to need a huge number of cupcakes, Cohen.'

'Three hundred,' he replied doubtfully.

'Three hundred.' She held his gaze. 'I've done the calculations.'

He would have completely balked at the idea if he didn't find her so attractive as she stood her ground, shoving logic and facts at him. 'You did the cupcake calculations. I didn't know that was a thing, Paige.'

'It is now.' She placed her hands on her hips, amused. 'So, tell me, Beckett, are you in or are you out?'

Bryce, ever the cupcake confidante, stepped up beside Paige, arm to arm, facing his father with a dutiful stare. Jazz followed suit, sitting on her haunches beside Bryce, panting happily.

He was outnumbered, clearly. 'I've been betrayed by my own flesh and blood,' he snickered. 'It looks like we've got three hundred cupcakes to decorate.'

Bryce turned to Paige, triumphant. 'Yes!' He high-fived her just as Jazz gave a gleeful woof of victory. 'When?' The boy's excitement was vibrating through him like a sugar high.

'We've only got a few days.' Paige cast a glance at Cohen. 'Are you free Thursday, Friday, and Saturday night? I'll bet we can have everything done in three nights if we stick to it.'

'Sure. Whatever it takes.' Instinctively, his hand lowered to the on-call cellphone in his pocket. 'As long as I don't get called for an emergency, I'm all yours.'

That hint of pink rushed into Paige's cheeks once more, and

she nodded. Bryce, however, rolled his eyes, scoffing at both of them.

'You guys are flirting again,' he whined.

'Sorry, buddy,' Cohen said, his eyes gleaming as they connected with Paige's. 'She brings out the worst in me, I guess.' He paused, then tipped his head toward her. 'And the best.'

The golden lamppost light reflected in Paige's gaze. She didn't look away from him. 'Ditto.'

The next day came and went in a blur. Cohen wasn't sure he was even thinking straight on any one topic, let alone the thousand that seemed to be whirling around in his head. Paige, the fund-raiser, Paige, the clinic, Bryce's school project, Paige, the invitation to Allison and Christopher's wedding that conveniently showed up in his mailbox that morning – it hadn't been mailed, just set inside for him to find.

But the only thing he could focus on was Paige.

She'd come quietly into town and turned his whole world on its axis. He felt like a schoolboy with a teenage crush.

That wasn't what it was, though, was it?

No, there had been other women who moved to Port Landon only to be caught up in Sonya Ritter's web of matchmaking chaos. Some had been keen enough to want to date him, but Cohen had shown little interest. He wasn't kidding when he told Paige he hadn't completely moved on from Stacey's death, which had left him grief-stricken and broken. He wasn't kidding when he said he didn't know if he ever would. That's how he had felt during each of Sonya's matchmaking fumbles, and that's how he felt now. He was a believer that a connection between two people couldn't be forced. The difference between then and now was Paige Henley. She was the only one who made him want to try.

Besides, those newcomers hadn't lasted in the harborside town, citing big box stores and closer amenities as their reasons for leaving almost as quickly as they'd come.

Small-town living wasn't for everyone, Cohen knew that. But it suited Paige Henley, and he truly believed that was because she'd chosen to embrace it rather than point out the differences in her city life versus its slower, simpler counterpart. She seemed made for this kind of life.

Made for *his* kind of life.

Cohen shook his head. *Get yourself together, man.* He had never been one to envision a picture-perfect life for himself. He had that once and it had been torn away from him. But eight years later, for the first time in history, Cohen felt like he might actually agree with Sonya's perspective on this one.

She wasn't the only one seeing Paige as the glue that just might have the chance of putting his and Bryce's family back together. They would never have the life they'd lived with Stacey, and Cohen tried hard not to compare the two women. But maybe, just maybe, they could build a new kind of life. One different from the life he'd lost along with his wife, but one that put the broken pieces of him back together and gave him the strength to start over again. *Really* start over. Every time that thought niggled its way into the forefront of his brain, it hit him like a punch to the chest.

Cohen was falling for Paige. He didn't know how he had let it happen, but that was the kicker about these things, wasn't it? He hadn't *let* a damn thing happen. It happened regardless of how he felt about it.

She had to know it, too. Hell, it was probably written all over his face.

That didn't mean she felt the same, though.

There he went again, round and round in the vicious circle of wondering where he really stood with her. He had only tonight to get the things he needed done out of the way. He was about to spend three solid evenings, plus the entire day on Sunday, with her. Yet, there he was, worried about what she thought of him. If she was falling for him just as much as he was falling for her.

Beckett …

Good God, he needed to stop being so hard on himself. Thinking about this wasn't getting him anywhere except further into a state of torturous mind games. He'd never been one to let something – or someone – permeate his well-being to the point of becoming unproductive. Cohen wasn't an overthinker. He was a doer. Always had been.

So, why was this any different? Why was Paige different?

Cohen didn't know the answer, but he did know one thing – she *was* different. That didn't mean he had time to drop the ball by being idle, conjuring up catastrophic thoughts before he even had a reason to be thinking them.

He'd never wasted time with negative thoughts before, so he wasn't going to start now. He didn't even realize he'd dug in his pocket for the smooth, dappled stone until he was squeezing it between his fingers.

Think Pawsitive.

That's what he needed to do. Think positive and *do* something. Don't just think about it, but actually do it.

Cohen glanced over at the computer to his left, confirmed his next clinic appointment wasn't scheduled for another fifteen minutes, then picked up the phone beside it and dialed.

He didn't know exactly where Paige's heart was when it came to him. But that didn't mean she needed to question his feelings for her.

Chapter 15

Paige

Paige was stressed.

Rarely did she get so caught up in the whirlwind of being busy that it became overwhelming, but as the layers of undecorated cupcakes piled up in the fridge, and she continued to put more pans of them in the oven, she knew she might have gotten in over her head with this fundraiser idea. Paired with the steady stream of customers coming and going from her bakery, which meant she had to stop what she was doing in the back to go help them – and even then, it was only half-decent service – Paige was a bundle of frustration.

She couldn't keep up. She'd taken on too much. The worst of it was that she had no one to blame but herself. She'd spearheaded the entire event a few weeks ago, not only because she truly did want to help the poor woman whose house had burned, but also for selfish reasons. She could admit that to herself now.

Paige wanted the residents of Port Landon to like her. She wanted Dr Cohen Beckett to like her, too.

Now, weeks later, Paige was more confident that she'd earned her place in the community. Her business had only flourished because of it. She was also more confident that Cohen liked her just as much as she liked him.

That didn't make her fluctuating fears about furthering their relationship any easier to contend with. As she fought through the hours of the morning and made it into the early hours of the afternoon with the aid of copious amounts of coffee, Paige couldn't shake the reasons that bounced back and forth through her mind as to why something as great as her friendship with Cohen could quickly come crashing down around her.

There was the obvious city versus small town dilemma. Sure, she was comfortable and content in Port Landon now, but it had only been a few months since she officially left the city. Would she stay happy here like she hoped? The sporadic texts from Alex, her former boss from Livingston Designs, sure made it seem like he hoped she would get tired of the 'small town fad' and come back to New York, and to the company, where she belonged. It was nice to feel wanted, and even nicer to have that safety net, but Paige wanted to believe she belonged in Port Landon just as much as Alex believed she belonged under his employ.

Then, there was the fact that the whole town, led by the effervescent Sonya Ritter, was all googly-eyed and convinced that she and Cohen were destined for a big, sappy, happily-ever-after. That was a load of pressure to live up to.

The worst part was that she was convinced that pretty soon Cohen was going to realize Paige had no experience whatsoever in raising a child. She knew nothing about kids. Zilch. Nada. She had no siblings, and her family was small. Children were a foreign entity in her childhood. And that little voice in the back of her mind kept telling her that once Cohen figured that out – a man who lived for his son, who probably deserved the Best Dad Award if there was one – he would turn on his heel and leave her lonely and broken-hearted in the middle of her bakery.

That sad thought was still careening around in her head when she heard the bell above the door chime for the gazillionth time that day. She whirled around, prepared to plaster a big, fake smile on her face and be the business woman she'd trained herself to be.

Only it wasn't a customer. She honestly couldn't even tell if the person was a man or a woman due to the humongous bouquet of red and white roses in front of their face.

'Paige Henley?' The voice was deep and distinctively male, and he sounded disgruntled at having to navigate into the shop with such a large arrangement in his hands.

'That's me.'

'Then these are for you.' He set the bouquet down on the front counter, revealing his face. But Paige didn't see his face at all. She was too enamored by the gorgeous rose collection sitting before her, their scent wafting through the air, immediately reminding her of an easy summer day.

'You must be someone pretty special to somebody, Ms. Henley,' the delivery man said. He tipped his hat. 'You have yourself a good day, ma'am.'

'Thank you,' she replied absently. 'You too.'

He left her alone in the empty storefront, staring at the flowers like they were about to do cartwheels. The card was tucked between the stems and leaves, and she pulled the cream-colored envelope from its spot to unveil it.

It turns out there are no real flowers that match the pretty blue of your eyes, Paige. So, I went with something beautiful and classy – something that reminds me of you just as much.
Thank you for being such a good friend to Bryce and me.
Cohen

Paige had never been more thankful that there was no one around. She didn't know what to say, or do, and she just stared at the card as though more words could be found between the lines if she just concentrated hard enough.

Her first reaction was to melt into a warm puddle from having such a romantic gesture bestowed upon her. She could feel her entire body wilting with the weight of how thoughtful – and completely over-the-top – Cohen's gift was.

Paige's second reaction, however, was to analyze the bits and pieces of what he'd done, pointing out that he'd not only referred to her as a friend but also mentioned that the flowers were from Bryce as well.

Was this one step forward in their path from friendship to something more, or was Cohen just one for overwhelming gestures, even for platonic friends?

Somehow, she didn't think he was the type of guy to go to such lengths without his entire being guiding the way.

And his heart.

The thought made her giddy. If she was right, and this embarrassing bouquet was any indication, then Cohen was letting her know exactly how he felt about her. The hope that bloomed deep in her chest proved that, regardless of what her brain said, she felt the same way about him.

It was frightening and mortifying to have overzealous butterflies fluttering inside her over a man. It was also exhilarating to feel that kind of delicious anticipation.

If she had been excited before about their cupcake decorating rendezvous tomorrow night, Paige was counting down the hours now.

She may have locked the bakery door and turned the sign to read *Closed* at five o'clock sharp, but it was almost nine before Paige managed to turn the ovens off. It was only then that she felt prepared to reopen the shop's door tomorrow morning. Another eighty cupcakes had been baked and cooled in between her other duties throughout the day, stowed away in the fridge overnight, leaving only a few more batches of batter to be made, scooped into tins, and baked before tomorrow evening. She could do that.

Paige turned the lights off and disappeared out onto the sidewalk. It was almost completely dark, but the streetlamps that lined Main Street were glowing brightly along with the moon, reflecting in the shop windows and off slivers of the harbor she could see between the downtown buildings and shrubbery. She turned the key in the lock, about to sidestep to unlock the door to her apartment, when she heard someone holler.

'Paige!'

She turned to see Allison and Christopher trudging up the sidewalk, hand in hand. The chilliness from the night before had warmed a bit, but once the sun sank there was no escaping the need for at least a sweatshirt. Both her cousin and her fiancé were wearing dark ones that zipped up at the neck. She would never say it out loud to Allison, but Paige thought they looked an awful lot like they were dressed alike. How cheesy, and just a bit adorable. 'Hey, you two.'

'So, is it true?' Allison blurted out the question. Christopher gave her a narrowed glance.

'Ally, we could say hello before we grill her for information.' Christopher, more than a foot taller than the two women and boasting a dark, well-trimmed beard, turned to Paige, eyes alight with mischief. 'Hello, Paige. Now, tell us, is it true?' He said it in his best girly voice, obviously mocking his soon-to-be wife.

'Is what true?' She laughed. Allison and her fiancé were just too damn cute sometimes.

'Did Dr Cohen send you a gi-freaking-normous bouquet of roses today or not?' Allison couldn't get the words out fast enough.

Paige's jaw dropped. 'How ...' She shook her head. 'How did you know that?'

'Eek! So, it *is* true!' Her cousin let go of Christopher's hand so she could clap hers together excitedly, jumping up and down. It was quickly turning into her signature move when it came to Paige and Cohen's budding relationship milestones.

'Don't ignore the question,' Paige stated, holding up her hands in an attempt to calm Allison. 'How do you know Cohen sent me flowers?' She had told no one about them since they showed up, and Paige had taken five minutes earlier that afternoon to take them upstairs into her apartment, so she knew there was no way anyone could have seen them by coming into the bakery.

'Oh, Paige.' Allison rolled her eyes. 'I've told you a million times – it's a small town, and everyone knows everything.'

Paige swallowed hard, but she didn't respond, waiting for a real answer.

'Calm down, dear cousin. It's not like I have your place bugged or anything.' She scoffed at the idea. 'Christopher's cousin's wife works at the flower shop in North Springs. When Cohen ordered them this morning, he talked to her. She texted Christopher's cousin, who then texted Christopher, and Christopher called me.' She shrugged like it was no big deal.

'Wow, you weren't kidding when you said everybody knows everybody, huh?' She couldn't hide the slight annoyance in her voice.

'I wasn't exaggerating,' Allison said. 'People here love to have something to talk about. And whatever they don't know for sure, they make up. It's harmless.'

'Yeah, until it's not.'

Allison's eyebrow quirked up, and she cast a quick glance at her fiancé. 'Paige, it's just flowers.'

That was the problem, though. To Paige, it wasn't *just* flowers. It wasn't *just* anything. Those flowers meant something to her, and she had a strong feeling that they meant something to Cohen, too, or he never would have sent them. The look on her face must have conveyed the inner battle going on in her head, because Allison cocked her head and offered her a sliver of a grin.

'You really like him, don't you?' The woman may have been in her mid-thirties, but she was practically vibrating as she waited for Paige to respond. Paige was starting to think she was just as bad as Sonya.

'I'm still trying to come to terms with it,' she admitted.

'Oh, Paige!' Allison leaped forward, wrapping her arms around her cousin in a tight hug. 'You're falling in love! Finally! I feel like I've waited my whole life for this!'

Paige couldn't contain her laughter. 'Aren't I supposed to be the one saying that?'

She didn't let go. 'Maybe by next summer we'll be planning *your* wedding!'

'Now you're just getting ahead of yourself.' Paige pushed her away. 'Just don't contribute to the gossip chain, all right? That's all I ask.'

Allison made a show of zipping her lips shut. 'My lips are zipped. But Paige?'

'I know, I know,' she huffed. 'People are going to talk either way.'

'That's true, but it's not what I was going to say.' Allison shifted from one foot to the other, facing her cousin squarely. 'Remember what I said about people gossiping? That whatever they don't know, they make up?' She paused, forcing Paige to give her her undivided attention. 'It's not the stuff they know that you've got to worry about, girl. It's the stuff they make up to fill in the gaps. Remember that.'

Chapter 16

Cohen

Cohen wasn't sure what he was waiting for, but it felt like that's exactly what he was doing. Waiting for something. And he was sure that something would ruin the high he felt at having taken the chance, wearing his heart on his sleeve and sending the roses to Paige at the bakery. He didn't know if roses had been too much, but his only other idea had been to ask about sending her forget-me-nots seeing as she'd explained their symbolism of good memories to him, but it was their representation of true love that stopped him, thinking it was too presumptuous. Too much. Roses seemed more appropriate, somehow.

Maybe he was waiting for her response to his gesture. Maybe he was second-guessing the grandness of his ploy, just a bit. Maybe he was waiting for something, anything, to ruin his chances at getting to see her tonight for the cupcake decorating. He was looking forward to their evening, and it was all Bryce had yammered on about at breakfast that morning.

The Beckett household was definitely under Paige's spell.

Two surgeries and a handful of appointments later, Cohen was starting to think he'd never get through the day and reach seven o'clock. Everything went smoothly, thank God. He was greeted with wagging tails and smiling faces as he went about his clinic appointments. He met with no real emergencies, but the minutes seemed to drag on slower and slower as the day went on. At one point, he'd been convinced Bryce would be crashing through the back door soon, home from school. He'd looked up at the clock, only to realize it was barely noon.

The day hadn't gotten any better. On top of the clocks that seemed to be turning backward instead of forward, he caught his veterinary technician giving him the side eye a few times when she didn't think he was looking.

The fourth time he noticed, he called her on it. 'Something up, Rhonda?'

She cleared her throat as she stuck a label on a prescription bottle. She seemed to mull over whether or not to answer, then turned to face him, leaning her hip against the pharmacy counter. 'Have you noticed how every client who's come in here today has been giving you little smirks, or whispering to Alice at the front desk?'

'Can't say I have,' he replied. 'But I've noticed you doing it, if that means anything.'

'That means I'm the only one who seems to be getting through that lovey-dovey fog that's taken over your brain.' She counted out a few more pills. 'I've never seen you like this, Dr Cohen.'

'Like what?' He did his best to keep his expression neutral.

'Like a man who's doing more than just going through the motions.' She held his gaze. 'You've got a gleam in your eye, boss, if you don't mind me saying so. And I haven't seen that there in the time I've known you.'

Rhonda had been employed at Cohen's clinic for seven years. She was the one who'd helped him carry on the weight of the work following Stacey's death. The previous veterinarian who owned the place, James Alton, had stayed to help as long as he could, but it wasn't a permanent arrangement. In stepped Rhonda Weaver, a registered veterinary technician with mocha skin, deep brown eyes, and a height of five feet one inch. She was tiny in stature, but the woman was a force to be reckoned with. Her work ethic knew no bounds, and she'd stuck by Cohen through the long hours and the painful adjustment of being a one-veterinarian clinic. She was a godsend, a hero, and she didn't mince words.

Which was why Cohen was paying attention now. Rhonda wasn't one for menial small talk. She didn't say things unless they needed to be said.

'Surely that's not what the clients are whispering about.' He meant it as a joke, but Rhonda placed her hands on her hips.

'No. But it's because I know you better than they do.' She pointed through the doorway into the waiting room. 'They're saying you're wooing this baker girl like a true Casanova. I'm calling it a gleam in your eyes, but they're seeing hearts bugging out of 'em and waiting on the engagement ring.'

Cohen leaned around the corner to see his last client still hunched over the front desk, speaking in hushed voices with Alice, the receptionist. 'Tell me you're joking. That's Gerald Simkins. The man is seventy, Rhonda. He's got to have more to focus on than my personal life.'

The woman snickered. 'If you think that, boss, you really don't understand small-town life at all.' She grabbed the prescriptions she'd made up and headed for the doorway. 'That seventy-year-old man is the first one to make it to the coffee club at the diner each morning, just so he can get the gossip from the night before. He's also the one who filled Alice in on the roses you sent Paige. Was the bouquet really two feet wide and all long stems?'

'What? No ... Rhonda, what the ...' Cohen looked flabbergasted.

'My point exactly, Dr Cohen.' She pointed at him with the bottle still in her hand. 'You've got the whole town talking. You might be used to that kind of thing, but your girl isn't. So, while they're talking, boss, you'd better be listening.'

Rhonda's words reverberated through his head the rest of the afternoon, and well into suppertime with Bryce. It never occurred to him that he might have to protect Paige from the unruly side of the gossiping crowd. Before now, he had never said or done anything to be on that side of them. But now that it had been brought to his attention, there was nothing he wanted to do more than just that – protect her.

People were talking. They always would. But were their words, regardless of the truth in them, affecting Paige? Did she listen to them, and did they bother her? He was well aware that Paige Henley was a strong, independent woman who didn't need a bodyguard.

He planned to mention it, anyway, just as a precaution. Just so she would know he was there for her if she needed him. He kind of liked the idea of her needing him.

'Are you ready, Dad?' Bryce's voice carried from the top of the stairs just before he bounded down them two at a time. 'I'm going to go get Jazz.'

'Jazz?'

'Yeah, Jazz. Cute brindle boxer with an attitude, remember?' He made motions with his hands, showing Cohen approximately how big the dog was.

'I know who she is, smart guy. I'm asking why you're going to get her.' Cohen tucked his wallet in his jeans pocket.

'Because she's coming with us to Paige's house.' The boy seemed genuinely confused by the whole conversation.

'Did Paige say that was okay?'

'Paige knows we're a package deal, Dad.' Bryce bolted out the back door toward the clinic without another word.

Cohen couldn't argue with that kind of logic, and he doubted Paige would, either. He was starting to think Bryce could get away with just about anything in Paige's eyes. Within reason. He'd wrangled her into helping him with his school project, called her old, and was now showing up with a seventy-five-pound dog without notice. It was a dog that Paige had already hijacked once from his possession of her own accord, mind you, but Jazz was coming with them without notice, nonetheless. Bryce's bond with Paige made Cohen's chest tighten with the sentiment.

The boy was back in a flash, Jazz trotting along happily beside him, ready and raring to go.

'Has she been fed?' Cohen asked.

'Yes.'

'Been given her medication?'

'Yes, Dad.' Bryce let out an exaggerated sigh. 'Let's just go, okay?'

'All right, all right.' He waved a hand. 'Lead the way with your trusty mutt.'

Bryce shook his head, leading the dog back outside with him while Cohen closed the door. 'Did you hear that?' Bryce pretended to whisper to the dog. 'He called you a mutt. Don't worry, we'll pour kibble in his shoes later on to retaliate.'

Jazz looked far too keen about the idea.

From the street, Cohen could see the soft glow of light coming from Paige's upper apartment windows. The curtains were pulled wide and it occurred to him what an amazing view she must have from there first thing in the morning with the sun just coming up as she took her first sips of coffee. He rang the doorbell and waited. Jazz sat and waited, too, but her tail was wagging at super speed. She knew exactly where she was.

When the door opened and Paige swung it wide, Jazz ambled to her, her entire backend wagging from side to side with excitement. Paige crouched down, pulling the dog in for a hug.

'Jazzy girl! What a pleasant surprise!' Paige's gaze raised to meet Cohen and Bryce after Jazz got in a lick of her chin. 'Oh, hey. Jazz brought you guys along with her, did she?'

Bryce gave his father a levelled look. 'Told you.'

Paige arched a brow as she held the dog in place. 'Do I want to know?'

'Nah,' Cohen replied. 'He was right and I was wrong. That's all you need to know.'

Bryce leaned in toward Paige. 'It happens more than he'll admit to.'

Cohen let his head lull forward, feigning defeat as Paige grinned. She unclipped Jazz's leash and let her clamber up the stairs, letting her lead the way.

'Come on.' She followed closely behind Jazz.

Upstairs, the scent of warm cake filled the air. Combined with the soft lighting in the living room and the candle that was lit in the middle of the coffee table, Cohen wasn't sure he'd ever experienced a more welcoming scene.

'Since I know there's a certain dog here that's going to want to taste test every cupcake that comes out of the oven, and a certain doctor who's going to frown upon it to the hundredth degree, I made sure I was prepared.' Paige ducked under the cabinet beneath the sink and pulled out a wrapped Dentabone treat. 'Come here, Jazzy girl.'

Once again, Bryce leaned over to Cohen and whispered, 'Told you.' Cohen gave his son a crooked smile. The kid was good, he would give him that.

Paige was busy unwrapping the bone, and once she handed it over to Jazz, the dog held it gingerly between her teeth and scampered off, finding a quiet spot on the throw rug in the living room where she would be uninterrupted to gnaw on her new treat.

'I didn't figure you wanted dog hair in the cupcake batter,' Paige explained, shrugging. 'But I didn't want her to feel left out.'

'That was very sweet of you.'

Bryce let out an audible groan. He didn't say it outright, but Cohen heard him loud and clear. *Dad, you're doing it again.*

Sorry, son, but if that was flirting, you're going to have to deal with it.

Instead of acknowledging his son's displeasure, Cohen clapped his hands together. 'Okay, Paige, you're the boss. Tell us what you need us to do.'

Paige's eyes shone brightly. 'We'll get to that, but first, I have something for you. Well, both of you.'

'Is that so?' Cohen was a little worried she was going to try to feed them a sugar-laden dessert before getting down to work, in which case he'd probably be so stuffed by the end of it he wouldn't want to decorate cupcakes and Bryce would be the definition of an impending sugar crash, but he couldn't voice his concerns. He didn't want to be the reason for that brightness in her sapphire eyes to dull.

She whirled around to the kitchen island, where he noticed for the first time that tea towels were spread over something. Cupcakes, he assumed. But why would they be for him and Bryce?

Paige gripped the edge of the towels. 'I got the flowers you guys sent me, and I didn't know how to say thank you for being so thoughtful,' she stated, a shaky quality edging its way into her voice. 'So, I thought I'd make you a little bouquet of my own.' She pulled the tea towels away in one smooth move.

If that was a little bouquet, Cohen didn't understand the meaning of the word. On the countertop, she had arranged forty or fifty cupcakes of various colors to depict flowers and stems. Four daisy-like flowers, with pink centers and vanilla petals, were created on the countertop canvas, with long, green stems.

'Thank you for the roses,' Paige added shyly. 'Both of you. They're beautiful.' She pointed toward the end table near the sofa where the bouquet had been tucked into a crystal vase, displayed where she could see it at almost any angle in the apartment.

'We sent you roses?' Bryce piped up, his forehead crinkled.

'*I* sent roses,' Cohen corrected. 'And may have mentioned your name on the card.' Something he was starting to regret quickly.

Another groan escaped Bryce's mouth. 'Dad, roses? Really? You could have done something more manly.' Bryce turned to Paige, a very forced-looking, sincere expression on his face. 'Don't worry, Paige, I'll have a talk with him.'

Paige's eyes grew wide right before she began to laugh, tears brimming at the corners of her eyes. Cohen, on the other hand, put his head in his hands, shaking with the amusement he tried to contain.

'You never cease to amaze me, Bryce,' he mumbled.

'You know what amazes me?' his son countered. 'Paige's flowers. These daisies are the bomb.'

'Thank you, Bryce,' Paige managed to utter. 'And don't worry, Cohen, I thought your roses were very sweet.' She winked at him. 'The bomb, even.'

Bryce high-fived her on her superb use of teenage slang, making Cohen's chest constrict even tighter. Just when he thought he was falling for Paige, he saw the effortless way she interacted with his son and he knew he was wrong.

He'd already fallen.

Chapter 17

Paige

Baking and decorating a couple hundred cupcakes was no easy task. Add in a ten-year-old boy with a zest for the sugary things in life, and it was even more daunting. More than once, Cohen had to chastise his son for sneaking a cupcake or two when he thought no one was watching.

'You can't eat those! They're for the fundraiser!'

Bryce held up the half-eaten cake. 'But, Dad, this one had a piece broken off of it. I'm not eating the profits … it's quality control!'

Cohen scoffed, leaning in toward Paige and whispering, 'The kid's going to be a lawyer, I just know it.'

'Or a taste tester for Hershey's,' she joked.

Bryce perked up. 'That's a thing?'

'Look what you've started now.' Cohen pretended to scold Paige, then turned to Bryce. 'If your argumentative talents don't work out, maybe Paige can use your chocolate connoisseur ways in her bakery.'

Paige saw Bryce's eyes light up and she figured he must like the idea. 'If law school doesn't pan out, we'll work something out.' She smiled wide as she handed him another bowl of green icing she'd just mixed up.

'I'm not going to go to law school,' Bryce announced. 'I'm going to be a firefighter.'

Paige picked up immediately on the way Cohen's eyebrows shot up, so she knew this must be a new revelation. 'That's a very honorable, respected profession, Bryce.'

'It's also very dangerous.' Cohen's mouth was a tight line. 'What brought this on?'

Bryce didn't look at either of them. Instead, he focused intently on the cupcake he was decorating, placing candy googly eyes on the green frosting to make it resemble a frog. 'Maybe if Port Landon had more firefighters, we could've saved Mrs O'Connor's house,' he explained simply. 'So, I want to be able to help the next time something like that happens.'

While Paige hoped nothing as tragic happened here again, she couldn't deny the flood of sympathy she felt at the boy's conviction. Only ten years old and he loved this town just as much as his father did. The dedication they had to their home hit her like a tidal wave. 'You'll be an amazing firefighter, Bryce.' She cast a quick glance at his father, whose eyes had softened at the boy's explanation, too.

'For now, how about we help Mrs O'Connor the only way we can?' he said, clearing his throat. 'With cupcakes.'

'With cupcakes,' Paige repeated, holding one without icing up and tapping it against the one in Cohen's hand in a *Cheers!* motion. 'Lots and lots of cupcakes. As daunting as this is, it's going pretty well, I'd say.'

'Agreed.' Cohen glanced over at the pile of containers waiting to be trudged downstairs to the coolers in the bakery, filled with iced cupcakes of every color, design, and flavor that existed. 'When you said this could be done in three evenings, I was skeptical. But we've made a pretty big dent in only a few hours, and you've got them all baked, too.' Pans of cupcakes sat on every available surface in the kitchen, some long since cooled and others still emitting billows of steam. 'It's going to be a breeze getting these done by Sunday.'

'Your confidence tells me you haven't frosted enough cupcakes,' she chuckled, watching as Bryce slid off his bar stool and made his way into the living room to check on Jazz. 'Keep going, then tell me how you feel in another two hours.'

In three hours, they'd managed to not only bake the remaining cupcakes needed but also decorate almost one hundred cupcakes, and package them up. That was an average of a half a cupcake every minute since they'd started, so Paige was thrilled with their progress. Cohen was right. They could definitely finish this by Sunday if they kept up the momentum. But she understood it was ten o'clock at night, and all three parties had work or school in the morning. She also understood the stress that would occur on Saturday night if they were behind in their bid to complete the decorating phase with only hours to go before the event.

'Are you getting a bit overwhelmed, Paige?' Gone was the humor in his tone. Cohen looked sincerely concerned. 'We've got time.'

'I know.' She felt silly even admitting her fear of not finishing in time. After all, it was just a cupcake fundraiser for a small community. But it was a fundraiser she had organized with Cohen, and it was her community now, too. She wanted it to go off without a hitch. 'I'm a bit of a perfectionist, though, in case you didn't notice.'

'I couldn't tell,' he replied wryly. 'Don't worry, we can pull this off.'

'I keep telling myself that, but there's that little piece of my brain that keeps telling me something is going to go wrong.' She hated to admit it, but it was the truth. And she wanted to be honest with him.

Cohen set down the spatula in his hand and took a step away from the counter. He shoved his hand in his jeans pocket and pulled out the familiar stone he'd shown her once before. 'Sounds like you need this more than I do right now.'

Paige let him drop the smooth sand-colored stone in her hand, letting the warmth of it seep into her palm. *Think Pawsitive*. She read the words silently on repeat until a faint grin tugged at her mouth. 'How is it that you know exactly how to make things better with only a few words and a stone?'

'Impressed? I've got other tricks up my sleeve, but I'll save them for a rainy day.'

'You never cease to amaze me.'

Cohen leaned forward. 'Ditto.'

She blushed. She couldn't help it. Paige gave the stone one last squeeze and held it out to him, but Cohen promptly waved it away.

'Hold on to it.' He reached out and closed her fingers around it again. 'It's helped me out of a few stressful situations. Let it do the same for you.'

She was floored that he would want her to keep it. She knew it meant so much to him. She knew who had given it to him. 'Cohen, no, I can't—'

'Just till Sunday,' he interjected. 'Once the event is done, and you see that everything went fine and all is well, I'll take it back. Deal?'

She met his eyes. After a moment, she sighed. 'Deal.' She tucked the stone into her apron pocket for safekeeping. 'Maybe we should stop for tonight?' She had a funny feeling neither Cohen nor Bryce would end the evening themselves. She could see the heaviness in Bryce's eyelids, and Cohen looked worn out from his long day at the clinic. She felt bad enough taking up their evening as it was, let alone running them ragged on the first night. 'We can pick up where we left off tomorrow.'

'You sure?' Cohen asked.

Before she could answer, Paige heard the bleep of her cellphone, announcing a text. She stepped closer to it, using one finger to touch the screen and display the text. She swallowed down a groan, choosing to ignore it. She didn't have the time and effort to deal with Alex Livingston at the moment.

'Everything okay?' Cohen watched her, eyes narrowed.

'Oh, fine.' She waved a hand, dismissing it. 'Just a text from a friend in New York. I'll reply later.'

Cohen seemed skeptical, but he dropped it. 'I can help take these cupcakes out of the tins and put them in containers.' He already had one of the cupcakes extracted from the tin and was working on the second.

'You don't have to do that.' Paige pulled the plastic container closer and began to use a butter knife to free the cupcakes from the tin.

'Maybe I don't have to,' Cohen said. He reached for the same cupcake she meant to grab, and his hand rested on hers, warm, inviting, and full of an electricity that made her glance up at him, surprised. 'But I want to,' he added quietly.

Everything seemed to halt. Paige could no longer hear the clock ticking on the wall, could no longer see the flickering of the candle out of the corner of her eye. The only thing she registered was Cohen – the heat that emanated from his skin against hers, the gleam in his hazel eyes that confirmed he felt the same sizzling connection.

'Let me be there for you, Paige.' His words weren't more than a whisper, but they hit her with the impact of a semi-truck. 'That's all I ask.'

Paige stood there, taking in the sight and scent and heat of him. All the things that made up Cohen Beckett. The flecks of gold in his eyes that twinkled with the promise in his words. The light shadow of a beard that covered the contours of his cheeks and jaw. The way his lips pressed together and then released, allowing the seductive warmth of his breath to caress her skin and render her weak while giving her strength at the same time. She found herself nodding before she realized it, too enthralled with letting his words wash over her to consciously comprehend her movements. 'Okay.' Her simple answer came out shaky and breathless, but it was an answer, nonetheless. His hand didn't move. Neither did hers. 'On one condition.'

She wasn't sure but it looked like Cohen was holding his breath. 'Name it.'

Paige swallowed, fighting to even out her pounding heartbeat. This was too much. *He* was too much. Paige wasn't sure how they had gotten here, to this moment, but she cherished it more than she could put into words. 'Don't change,' she whispered to him. 'The man you are – the man I see – doesn't exist anywhere else but inside you, Cohen. You're almost too good to be true, and it scares me that that could change.'

The upturn of his mouth wasn't exactly a grin, but more of an understanding one. 'Who I am is who you've seen since the beginning, Paige. I wouldn't change a thing. I couldn't. Not me, not you, and definitely not us.'

Something settled inside Paige's chest as she basked in his words and the voice that delivered them straight to her heart. Her eyes met his, and the smile within them was just as genuine as the one donning her lips. 'Ditto.'

Paige couldn't believe the difference a few short weeks could make. In fact, she found it hard to believe she'd still been on the hamster wheel in New York City only a handful of months ago. Still contemplating what it would be like to fulfill her childhood dream of owning a bakery instead of actually doing it. Still subjecting herself to Allison's relentless nagging during their Skype calls about how perfect it would be to own side-by-side businesses on Port Landon's Main Street.

And it was. Perfect. At thirty-three, the prospect of new beginnings was something almost unheard of in her world. Until now.

Now, she was following her dream, being the gourmet baker she'd always wanted to be, living in a small community that supported her and helped her to feel like she didn't just exist. She belonged.

And she had fallen in love. It was the most unbelievable part of the entire scenario. Cohen Beckett had come quietly into her life, fitting perfectly into the puzzle she hadn't known had been missing a piece. She wasn't sure she knew what love felt like, but the butterflies in her belly and the tingles on her skin she felt with just his presence or the faintest touch, coupled with the way he seemed to be beside her – not in front of her, and not behind her – every step of the way …

Paige hoped that was what love was. She loved the way Cohen made her feel, about him and about herself. She loved the way he understood their differences and worked with them instead of trying to transform them into similarities. She loved his devotion to his son, and his easy way of just being.

She cared deeply for Cohen, and she knew in her heart that it was love she felt for him. She didn't understand it, and she had nothing to compare it to, but Paige knew it had to be love. Nothing else came close to describing her feelings where he was concerned.

Everything since she had come to Port Landon had been hard work – remodeling the bakery and the upstairs apartment, fine-tuning recipes and acquiring bulk inventory for her business, branding and professional marketing to get the word out.

But falling for Cohen had been effortless. Easy. She hadn't been expecting him, had been downright anxious about his interest in her from the beginning. Yet, he had managed to become the man she knew she could build a life with, which was something Paige couldn't believe she was even thinking about. The fact that she was said more about the way she felt than words ever could. The Paige Henley from New York never would have thought along those lines. About anyone. The Paige Henley from Port Landon, however … she wanted to try something new. She wanted to be open to giving love a chance.

Paige was shuffling plastic containers full of cupcakes around in her glass-doored cooler to get to the bread dough she'd refrigerated yesterday. With two evenings of cupcake decorating done, and only a few dozen cupcakes left to finish, there was no reason why they shouldn't be able to complete everything in time for the fundraiser tomorrow. She had also designated her shop as a drop-off spot for items in the silent auction Cohen was spearheading, and she was relieved the business owners had dropped off everything on the list Cohen had provided her with.

The afternoon had been steady with customers, but not the overwhelming crowds she had become accustomed to each day during the workweek. A lot of shop owners and their employees popped in to buy an afternoon snack if they had the chance, but today seemed less hectic. She wasn't complaining. When the doorbell rang loudly, she was still half obscured by the refrigerator door.

'Hey, Paige.'

She turned, recognizing the voice instantly. 'Bryce, hey. What brings you by?' It was then she realized Bryce wasn't alone. A boy who looked about the same age stood near the display table nearest the door. His hair was inky black. Though she could only see the back of him, Paige had a feeling she knew who he was. 'And who's your friend?'

'Oh, that's Hunter. I wanted to show him all the cool stuff you have in here.' Bryce tossed his backpack down on the floor before joining his friend at the table.

Paige felt a swell of pride, pleased with the idea that Bryce would want to show her bakery off to a friend. 'Hello, Hunter.' If there was any table to show off the largest amount of sweet treats in the smallest amount of space, they had picked the right one. She'd spent a lot of time in the morning arranging a variety of squares, butter tarts, and cookies so there would be plenty of selection for a Grab N' Go bag if customers wanted to try something new. All day, she had kept an eye out to see which kinds were being chosen over others, but so far only a few of each goodie had been purchased, and only three of the twenty takeout boxes beside the tray had been used.

'Hey, Ms H.' Hunter only offered her a quick glance, obviously too busy taking in the mountains of sugar that surrounded him. Paige didn't mind. It was nice to see someone appreciating her efforts, even if he didn't plan on purchasing anything.

'Have you got those interview questions ready for me yet?' She fought the urge to hover, instead choosing to shout from the opened refrigerator in hopes of getting the bread dough unearthed from its deepest depths.

It took Bryce a moment to answer. 'Uh, no, not yet. Dad told me I could wait till this weekend once we had all the cupcakes decorated.' He whispered something to his friend that she couldn't make out. 'I'll bring them to you soon, though, okay?'

'Of course.' She felt bad. She wasn't trying to push Bryce about it, and she certainly didn't want him to think she was harping on him about schoolwork. That wouldn't keep her in the cool books with him at all. 'Is your dad swamped today?' she shouted, crouched in front of the fridge as she pulled two bags of dough from the bottom shelf while holding up the containers on top of it.

'Haven't ... haven't been there yet,' Bryce shouted back. 'I should probably get over there, though, and see what's up, okay? We'll see you tonight after supper.'

She heard shuffling and tossed the bags up onto the countertop before rising to her full height. Bryce slung his backpack over his shoulder. 'Sure. I didn't mean to make you think you had to leave.' Hunter was already at the door, clutching his backpack in one hand and the doorknob in the other.

'It's no problem, Paige.' Bryce turned to give her a crooked smile, but his feet were still moving him backward, toward the door behind him. 'Dad and I will see you tonight. Later!'

Paige barely got the chance to wave goodbye before the two lanky boys were out the door and gone, so fast that the doorbell still tolled faintly long after she couldn't see them on the sidewalk anymore.

She walked across the storefront, a tea towel in her hands as she dried her fingers from the cold condensation on the refrigerated plastic bags of dough. There was no sign of the boys as she peered out the window, and she shook her head as she turned back around.

Adolescent boys are such an awkward species, she thought to herself. She wondered what Hunter must have said to him to make Bryce want to run from the shop without looking back. Maybe they were late for one of their video game things on the computer, or maybe Hunter had to be home for supper. Or maybe—

Her gaze landed on the table near the door as she passed it, and Paige stopped dead in her tracks. That couldn't be right. She had been so meticulous with keeping track today. There was just no way.

But as Paige went about counting the takeout boxes piled near the tray, dread sunk in her stomach like lead. Only fifteen boxes remained in the pile. Two less than when she counted earlier, and there had been no one else in the bakery since then. Not only that, but almost all the butter tarts were gone, and part of the circular arrangement she'd made with the chocolate squares was missing.

Bryce wouldn't take items from her store without asking. Would he? She couldn't even bring herself to use the word *steal* in the same sentence as his name. It just didn't sound right.

There was no other explanation, though. She had kept tabs on that table's inventory all day, and it answered the question as to why the two boys had been so eager to race out of there.

Paige would talk to him. Tonight. Maybe. She groaned to herself. There was no way she could delicately ask him if he knew what happened to the missing baked goods. Maybe she would be better off talking to Cohen. She could ask him what she should say. Maybe Bryce wasn't really a part of the heist, or he panicked when he realized what his friend was doing.

She would find out tonight. Get it all sorted out and they could move on. It wasn't a big deal.

But suddenly, she wasn't looking forward to the evening nearly as much as she had been. That realization hurt almost as much as the fact she'd been the victim of theft.

Chapter 18

Cohen

Cohen didn't care if he ever saw another cupcake as long as he lived. He didn't know how Paige did it, baking and decorating them to perfection day in and day out. And he didn't know how Bryce still had an unfailing need to consume every one of them as they packaged them in containers for the fundraiser tomorrow. He might be the only one, but his appreciation for baked goods was dwindling after being surrounded by them for two back to back evenings from the moment he finished supper until the minute he laid his head down on his pillow. He could do without cupcakes for the foreseeable future.

He did care if he saw Paige, though. His appreciation for her had only grown over the course of their fundraiser preparations. Cohen considered himself a workaholic, but he was certain that Paige's work ethic and perfectionism rivaled his. She worked efficiently and effortlessly, never missing a beat in their conversation and never slowing down on the tasks she took on.

Cohen was impressed. He was brimming with respect.

And he was pretty sure he was in love with her.

Every time she blushed that faint crimson, every time she

offered him a sliver of a smile that said more than words ever could, every time she joked with his son and included him, Cohen fell a little harder and a little faster. He liked that she made him feel like those glances and grins were solely for him, like she'd never looked or smiled at anyone else like that before. Cohen liked that he could affect her in subtle ways, the same way she managed to make his heart beat quicker just by saying his name.

He could do without the cupcakes, but there was no denying that he wanted to see Paige tonight. And every other night from then on, if he was honest.

There had been enough said between them, both verbally and in their mannerisms, for him to know she had feelings for him. He also knew Paige was just as cautious as he was. Maybe more. He wondered if putting a label on their relationship would be too much for her. Hell, maybe it was still too much for him.

But Cohen had spent the past eight years with only his son for companionship. He owed it to himself, and to Bryce, to take a gamble with his heart and set it free. Paige Henley had come in like a silent hurricane and battered down the walls he'd built up around his broken heart. It was Cohen's turn to try to do the same for her. He was going to tell her the truth. To hell with the fact that it was scary and foreign and overwhelming. He was in love with her. And he needed to leave no room for doubt in her mind. Saying it aloud would be therapeutic for him, too. The proverbial jump off the precipice into the land of the living.

If this was real – and he knew it was – then he needed to set aside his fears and tell Paige the truth. He would confess how far he had fallen for her.

Tonight.

'Please tell me that's the last of them.'

Both Cohen and Paige turned to Bryce with wide eyes, surprised by the boy's statement. 'Well, I never thought I would see the day,' Cohen quipped, using his oven mitt covered hands to take the last remaining muffin tin from the oven and set it on top. 'Are you finally sick of seeing cupcakes?'

Bryce feigned hurt, clutching his hands to his chest and screwing his eyes shut. 'It pains me to admit it, Dad, but yeah, I guess I am. Not the cupcakes themselves, I'm just running out of ideas for decorations.' He gestured toward the table full of cakes in front of him, all frosted with a rainbow of colors and candy toppings. 'I'd still eat them, though.'

'Didn't see that coming at all.' Paige stole a knowing glance at Cohen. 'But, yes, Bryce, that's the last tray of cupcakes. I promise.'

'Hallelujah!' Bryce exclaimed.

'I'm not going to lie, I would like to second that hallelujah.' Paige held her hands up in mock surrender. 'I've never been so happy to see only a few dozen cupcakes left to be frosted.'

'I'm right there with you,' Cohen added. They were nearing the end, and he knew now that they had bitten off more than they could chew with their fundraising efforts. If there was a next time, he would mention recruiting some help. He knew a few people in town who would be glad to do this kind of thing. 'Although we've done pretty well, if I do say so myself. Three days, three hundred cupcakes, and a silent auction that even I can't wait to get my bids in on? Yeah, we nailed this, Paige.' He held up a hand, still covered in an oven mitt, and high-fived her.

Paige reciprocated, grinning widely. 'We make a pretty good team.'

'Agreed,' Cohen replied. He turned to Bryce, hand raised. 'Right, son?'

'Yeah, Dad.' Bryce high-fived his dad. When Paige raised her palm to initiate a high-five of her own, Cohen didn't miss the moment of hesitation in Bryce's eyes. He gave her a half-hearted clap, but there was a resigned quality to it. It wasn't the first time tonight that he'd noticed Bryce watching Paige out of the corner of his eye. He looked wary, like he was waiting for her to say something. Do something.

Cohen wondered if it was his son's way of trying to make sense of the budding relationship between him and Paige. He couldn't blame the kid for that. Hell, he was still trying to figure it out himself. He might have come to terms with the fact that he loved the woman and admitted it to himself, but Cohen still didn't have a damn clue what to do with that information, or how to react to it. Or how Paige would react to it.

Once he talked to her about it, he made a mental note to talk to Bryce, too. He wanted to keep the lines of communication open, just as they had always been.

Paige didn't seem bothered by Bryce's uncharacteristic antics, if she noticed them at all. She, herself, seemed quieter tonight, though, but Cohen attributed that to the impending fatigue that was blanketing their trio after three late nights and early mornings. Tomorrow was the finish line. All they had to do was get the fundraiser over with, then a well-deserved nap was on the cards for everyone involved.

A soft whimper sounded in the living room. Cohen followed it to find Jazz prancing near the doorway. It was time to go outside. He knew Jazz enough to know that there was no waiting – when Jazz said go, he moved. Cohen knew who owned who.

'I'd better take her outside.' He pulled the oven mitts off and set them on the counter.

'Nah, I'll go,' Bryce announced, dropping his butter knife, coated in sunshine yellow frosting, with a clatter. 'We'll be right back.'

It was dark outside, and later than Cohen felt completely comfortable letting Bryce wander the streets alone. But he was trying to give the boy some independence, trying to loosen the reins a bit and let him grow. Besides, it was Port Landon. 'Sure,' he agreed, against his better judgment. 'Thanks, buddy.' Cohen passed him the purple leash and watched as Bryce slipped into his shoes. 'Don't take her past the park though, okay? There's not enough street lighting past the corner. It's not safe.'

'I know the drill, Dad.' Bryce attached Jazz's leash and gave the two adults a parting glance before opening the door and clambering down the stairs with the dog in the lead.

Cohen listened to his son's footsteps grow further and further away, then the door at the bottom of the stairs slammed behind him. He turned back to Paige. 'Okay, what's next, boss?'

She held up an undecorated cupcake. 'The same thing we've been doing for three days,' she advised with a chuckle. 'I can see the light at the end of the tunnel, so just keep going.'

'Whatever you say,' he replied, washing his hands under the tap after handling the leash. 'I was hoping we could talk while we decorate these godforsaken things.'

Her eyes met his. Cohen saw a renewed cautiousness in them once again. 'Me too, actually.'

Her serious tone caused a ball of dread to form in the pit of Cohen's stomach. 'Ladies first, then.'

'No, you go ahead.'

She sighed when Cohen only quirked a brow and waited patiently. He wasn't going first, especially not now that he could see the turmoil distorting her pretty face. Something was up, and watching her fidget with the cupcake in her hand was only adding to his unease.

'Okay, I don't …' She trailed off, and Cohen was relieved when she sat the cupcake back down. Her constant tinkering with it was going to demolish it. 'I'm not really sure where to start.'

'How about the beginning?' Cohen suddenly didn't know what was going on, but he could feel the tension in the room, so thick it was almost tangible. 'Take your time, Paige. Just tell me what's on your mind.'

'You!' She blurted it out like it was the hardest thing in the world to admit, then laughed uneasily. 'And Bryce. You two seem to be all I think about nowadays, in some form or another.'

Her distress would have been comical if Cohen didn't hear the unspoken *but* that seemed to follow after it. 'I can relate to that, more than you know.' He hoped it would ease her mind. 'So, now, tell me the part of it that's worrying you.' He took a step closer, but Paige took one step back, keeping him at arm's length.

'I need to talk to you about Bryce.' It came out in a whoosh.

'All right.' Cohen nodded, encouraging her.

'He came to see me earlier today. At the bakery. With Hunter.'

That was news to Cohen. However, it didn't strike him as the catastrophic breaking news Paige was making it out to be. 'He didn't mention it,' he said carefully. 'Did something happen?' Cohen quickly worried that Bryce had said something untoward to Paige about their relationship and hurt her feelings. Maybe his son wasn't as okay with things as he thought.

'I don't know.' She shook her head vehemently. 'Well, yes. I mean, I didn't see it—'

'Paige.' Cohen stepped forward and touched her forearms gently. He was close enough that she was forced to tilt her head up in order to see his face. He tried to convey a comforting expression despite the anxiety that gnawed away at his insides. 'Just tell me.'

'Bryce and Hunter came into the bakery,' she began again. Paige took in a deep breath, held it, and released it slowly. 'I was busy, so I wasn't paying much attention at the time. But after they left, that's when I noticed.'

'Noticed what?' She wasn't making sense to Cohen.

Her gaze fixed on his. 'That there were a couple boxes of tarts and squares missing.'

'What would Bryce know about that?' He couldn't fully register what she was getting at. The idea was that preposterous to him.

Paige's throat moved visibly but her body was still, posture stiff. 'I think he was there … when it happened,' she admitted. 'When the items were taken.'

Hearing the accusation fall from her lips hit Cohen straight in the gut with the force of a hammer. 'Wait. You think Bryce stole from you?'

'I don't …' She was struggling to string a coherent sentence together. 'I set that table up in the morning, Cohen. And watched all day to see what sold.'

'But you didn't actually see him take anything.'

'Well, no.' She shook her head. 'I would have said something to the boys then—'

'And have you?' Cohen couldn't believe what she was suggesting. Surely she realized his son would never do such a thing? 'Mentioned this to Bryce?'

'What? No. I wanted to talk to you first.' This close, Cohen could see the glimmer of tears brimming her eyelids.

'You mean you wanted to accuse my son of stealing.' He spat out the words as though they left a bad taste in his mouth. He couldn't believe her audacity. 'Bryce wouldn't steal from you, Paige. Or anyone. I raised him better than that.'

'Cohen, I'm not questioning that at all,' she pleaded with him. 'I said it wasn't just Bryce there. Hunter was involved, too. Maybe he talked him into it or something.'

'So, let me get this straight.' Cohen stepped away from her, holding a finger up to count out the points she'd made. Acid rose in his stomach, burning in his throat. 'Not only are you telling me my son stole from you, but now he's impressionable, too? A follower of the masses?'

'Please, Cohen,' she pleaded. 'I didn't come to you to start trouble.'

'My son is not a thief, Paige.' Cohen scoffed at the ludicrous idea. 'This isn't New York City, you know.'

Her eyes widened, appalled. 'What does New York have to do with this?'

'Not everyone is out to get you here,' he explained, venom tainting in his voice. 'You might get away with accusing people of ridiculous things there, but that kind of thing doesn't fly around here.'

Paige's mouth gaped open. 'Cohen, that's not fair.'

'Neither is spreading lies about my son. You said you never saw it happen.'

'I didn't, but—'

'So, you have no proof,' he stated. 'My son wouldn't steal from you. I know that. And, frankly, I'm hurt that you don't.'

'You're making it sound like I'm insinuating he's a convict waiting to happen.' Her eyes narrowed. 'Kids will be kids, Cohen. I thought you would be more reasonable about this.'

A hollow laugh escaped his throat. Was she serious? 'You'll have to excuse me if I'm not *reasonable* about you accusing my kid of something he didn't do.' He made air quotes with his fingers. This was getting out of hand. He didn't need to stand here and listen to these absurdities.

She huffed a loud sigh, turning away from him. 'This is not how I thought this would go at all.'

'Trust me, I'm feeling the same way about tonight.' All the things he yearned to say to her, all the feelings he harbored for her that he wanted to confess – it was all tossed out the proverbial goddamn window by her allegations.

He had been waiting to tell her he'd fallen in love with her. She had been waiting to tell him she believed his son was a thief.

'Cohen, I don't want to fight with you.' She spoke with a more even tone. 'I know I don't have children of my own but—'

'No, you don't.' He cut her off, fueled by the outrage simmering inside him. 'You don't have kids, so I can't expect you to understand, Paige. But I can tell you one thing – you don't have a damn clue what you're talking about.'

'No?' Paige's jaw was clenched. Any other time Cohen might have thought the fire in her eyes was attractive, but not now. 'What I *do* know is that two boys came into my bake shop, acted strangely, then bolted for the door with guilty looks on their faces as they left. After that, two takeout boxes were missing from the pile I'd set out that morning, and a bunch of tarts and squares had miraculously vanished. Bryce and Hunter were the only two people in the shop then, Cohen. That's what I do know, all right? Whether or not you believe it, that's your prerogative.'

'Well, I don't believe it, Paige.' He swallowed hard, afraid to look away from her in case his fears shone through the foundation of his anger. Fears that what she was saying could be plausible. Fears that he didn't know his son at all.

Fears that he didn't know Paige at all.

'I'm a liar, then, is that it?' Her voice cracked. Cohen's heart cracked along with it.

The words toppled from his mouth before he had the sense to stop them. 'My son is not a thief, Paige. So, you can take it how you want it.' Cohen immediately regretted that vindictive jab the moment it left his mouth. But it was too late. He shook his head, wondering how this evening had taken such a horrendous turn for the worst. 'Maybe it's best if I go.'

'It is,' she agreed, the first of her tears toppling down onto her cheeks. 'I don't need your help to finish up.'

Cohen heard what she was really saying. She didn't need *him*. And as angry as he was, as hurt as he was, it cut through him with the force of a thousand daggers, slicing through the battered but mended heart he'd given away to her. He left without another word.

Chapter 19

Paige

She had spent the past few weeks looking forward to today. Now that it was here, Paige wished she could fast forward through it completely. Even more, she wished she could rewind to last night and change the way the evening had concluded.

Paige should have never brought up the incident with Bryce and Hunter. If she had just kept her mouth shut, kept her suspicions to herself, things would still be good between her and Cohen. At the very least, she could have said something different, been gentler about the topic when she approached him.

Who was she kidding? She knew very well it didn't matter how she said it. Cohen was too protective of his son to hear what she was really saying. She didn't blame him for wanting to protect Bryce from slander. She would never say he was overprotective either, because Paige wholeheartedly believed parents should protect their children at all costs. But she was hurt that Cohen would think she would go to him with her concerns without being certain Bryce was actually involved in some way. It had been hard enough to talk about it to Cohen in the first place. Hard enough to admit she believed sweet, exuberant Bryce was even capable of such a thing. So, to have Cohen completely shut down on her and retaliate with hurtful words, portraying her as just some city slicker with no common sense and even littler knowledge about children …

Cohen Beckett had hurt her. She had hurt him, too. And that left them in a place Paige wished they didn't have to be.

Apart.

Cohen and Bryce might only be down the street, but they might as well have been a million miles away. She could still hear the echo of the door at the bottom of the stairs slamming when Cohen had slipped his shoes on and left to go in search of Bryce and Jazz. She wasn't sure her apartment had ever felt so empty and lonely. The colorful array of cupcakes that littered every surface did little to help, creating a stark contrast between their vibrant colors and her bleak mood. She hadn't been able to tell one color from the next by the time her tears took over, anyway.

By morning, nothing had changed. Cohen was still gone, her apartment still carried the emptiness left by the space once occupied by him, and her heart remained in the shattered pieces it had crumbled into as he had walked away from her the night before.

So much for the day she'd been looking forward to.

In the early morning light, Paige tackled the remaining tin of cupcakes she'd set aside before going to bed last night, accompanied only by her coffee cup. She'd brewed the coffee strong and bold. She was going to need it. She ignored the texts on her cell, unable to handle Alex Livingston in her current state of mind, and instead turned on the radio app on her phone, thinking the melody and morning talk show hosts would help to ease her cluttered mind. But it was no use. No amount of guitar riffs or heated debates was going to fill the void left by Cohen and his anger.

She was so conflicted about the entire interaction. Maybe she should have regretted mentioning Bryce and Hunter's odd behaviors at her shop yesterday, but she didn't. Not completely, anyway. Sure, she never wanted to upset Cohen or drive a wedge between him and his son, or her and him. But Cohen needed to know what his son was up to; she believed that. She was a firm believer in taking responsibility for one's own actions, and though she might not have the first clue about parenting or raising a child, Paige believed that, if the roles were reversed, she would want to know the incident had happened. All she had were hypothetical beliefs to go on, but she was confident she would want to know, all the same.

That didn't mean she wouldn't go back in time and fix this, given the chance. If she could, Paige never would have let Cohen disappear down the stairs and out into the night. She would have said something to make him stay, done something more to repair the damage she had done.

But Cohen did leave. And he didn't call or text her to take back his hurtful words. She didn't, either. Which left them at a standstill, wishing things were different, with broken hearts and bruised pride.

And four hours together at a fundraiser. Perfect.

Cohen was nowhere to be found when she opened up the bakery, intent on arranging the cupcakes and boxes for the event. The shop wasn't open on Sundays, but the *Port Landon Ledger* had donated an advertising spot each week for the past three weeks announcing that the fundraiser and silent auction would be located at The Cakery. She had two hours to transform the storefront into an inviting, organized landing for half the town to mill about in.

'Up and at 'em, are you?'

Allison poked her head in the door, setting off the doorbell. Like the reliable hero of a cousin she was, she held a tray of paper coffee cups in her hand, sugar packets and creamer containers stuffed into the two hollows that were empty.

'I have never been so happy to see you.' Paige sighed, reaching for one of the cups. 'And you, too, Allison.'

'I'll let that one slide.' Allison held the tray out, let Paige retrieve her coffee, then set the tray on the counter. 'You okay? Don't take this the wrong way, but you don't look so hot.'

She groaned. Hot wasn't what she was going for, but Paige had hoped her sleepless night wasn't written all over her face. Unfortunately, she should have known there wasn't much she could keep from Allison. There never had been. 'I didn't sleep much.'

'Trouble in paradise?'

Paige rolled her eyes. 'Wow, the town is already talking, are they?'

'No.' She drew out the word slowly. 'Lucky guess. But you just confirmed it, so spill the beans, Paige. What happened?'

'Cohen Beckett happened.' Paige took a long sip from her coffee cup just so she wouldn't have to elaborate. She didn't know what to say, didn't know the words to choose to convey how conflicted she was over the outcome of last night's talk with him.

She arched a brow. 'If he hurt you, I swear, I'll steal drugs from his own damn clinic and make it look like an accident.'

'Allison!' Paige covered her face. She was grateful that her cousin would commit a felony in her honor, but the mention of stealing had a thick lump forming in her throat. 'Careful, your crazy's starting to show.'

'You say crazy, I say family's gotta stick together.' Allison shrugged. 'But fine. How about you talk, and I'll pull the gazillion containers of cupcakes out of the coolers. Sound good?'

The bell above the door chimed again, sounding loud in the otherwise silence of the room. Paige turned and saw Cohen standing there in his faded jeans and plain blue T-shirt, a box tucked under one arm and a backpack slung over his other shoulder. Her mouth became dry at the sight of him.

'Am I late?' His gaze was fixed on hers as he spoke. Paige couldn't bring herself to look away. Maybe it was just wishful thinking, but she thought she heard apologetic uncertainty in his voice.

'Good morning.' She did her best to sound chipper, but it sounded hollow even to her own ears. 'You're right on time. The folding table where the silent auction items will be on display is over there.'

'Got it.' He let the door close behind him. His eyes lingered on hers as though trying to convey something to her without verbalizing it, then he let the eye contact break, heading over to the table and allowing the backpack to slip down his arm to the floor.

Paige stole a glance at Allison. She was watching the two of them with marked interest, eyes narrowed each time they landed on Cohen. She swore she could see her cousin mapping out a mental target across his chest. Paige shook her head, hoping Allison would get the drift that their conversation was over for the time being, and that she wasn't to do or say anything regarding what little Paige had confided in her. Allison just shrugged again, but Paige knew that shrug all too well. It meant she understood what Paige was saying, yet she could promise nothing. It was Paige's turn to narrow her eyes, warning her beloved cousin to stand down and keep the murder plotting to a minimum.

It wasn't Allison that Paige had to worry about, though. Seconds later, the bell tolled once more above the door. This time, Sonya Ritter waltzed in. She might not have known what happened with Cohen and Paige the night before, but she definitely assumed she had the scoop on their relationship status.

'Let's raise some money, shall we, lovebirds?' Sonya's arms were full of Portside Coffeehouse shirts and coffee mugs for the silent auction.

It was obvious she was referring to Cohen and Paige, but Cohen barely looked up from the table he was unfolding. Allison

– thank God for her! – ran with the joke to take the limelight off Paige.

'Sonya, my hunky lovebird isn't here right now, so do me a favor and don't rub it in, okay?' Her sarcasm only made things worse. Not only was it enough to pique Sonya's interest when it came to Cohen and Paige, but Allison's attempt at defending Paige's dignity would undoubtedly confirm to Cohen that she'd confided to Allison about last night's argument. Which she hadn't. Kind of. At least, not yet.

The moment of awkwardness that followed only heightened Paige's anxiety about the entire situation. She was overthinking it, overanalyzing Cohen's every movement out of the corner of her eye, and downright petrified that Sonya's appearance was only going to make things worse.

If they could get worse.

Allison must have noticed her discomfort because she clapped her hands and made her way into the middle of the room. 'Okay, troops! We're a team of four, we've got three hundred cupcakes to display, and we've only got a couple hours to do it. Game face on, folks. No time for idle chit-chat.'

Which was Allison's way of saying, *Don't talk about Paige and Cohen, just do your freaking job*.

Paige could have hugged the woman. Boldly, she stole a quick glance in Cohen's direction and saw him let out a long, relieved breath. She would bet her week's profits that he could have hugged Allison, too. When his eyes met hers and a faint grin tugged at the corners of his lips, she wanted to sigh from relief as well. This was a rocky patch between them, but maybe there was still hope, yet. Cohen's smile always seemed to evoke that in Paige – hope. She wanted nothing more than for this time to be no different.

Under Allison's careful – and sometimes overbearing – watch, not one person said a word to Cohen or Paige about, well, anything. If it wasn't fundraiser related, she wasn't allowing for it. Paige figured that was the ultimate measure of their friendship; her cousin didn't have a clue what was bothering Paige when it came to Cohen, and yet she still guarded her like she was harboring Paige's deepest, darkest secrets. And threatening murder, evidently.

The moment the clock hit the top of the hour, the entire population of Port Landon seemed to awaken from their slumber and pour out of their homes and into the downtown shop. The Cakery was packed within fifteen minutes of opening its doors, and cupcakes began to be boxed up a half dozen at a time.

People oohed and ahhed over the colors and designs, struggling to box their goodies up because they were too busy showing them off. It might have taken days of baking and three solid nights of dishing up frosting, but Paige was over the moon about the town's reaction to her bite-sized masterpieces.

Cohen kept to himself over the course of the fundraiser, sticking instead close by Bryce as they both manned the silent auction table, handing out pens to those who wanted to place bids. Now and again, Cohen's melodious laugh met Paige's ears, and the sound did something to her heart, making her chest constrict tightly. The sight of the smile that accompanied it all but undid her completely.

She craved to hear that sound and know it was her who caused it. At that moment, however, the cheery sound only reminded her of the frustration in his voice the night before. She had been the cause of *that* sound.

She shook her head, hoping to shake the sad thoughts into the back of her mind. Cohen and Bryce looked as though they were having a good time. So was the guest of honor, silver-haired Helen O'Connor, who was perched atop a black folding chair near the front counter, dressed in her Sunday best, watching the entire spectacle with a gleam in her eyes and a paper cup of coffee in her hand. That was what mattered most right now. This wasn't about Paige, and it wasn't about Cohen. And it certainly wasn't about Paige *and* Cohen.

One of the five tables that had been set up earlier in the morning was completely empty forty-five minutes into the fundraiser. By the time there was only one hour left of the event, all the remaining cupcakes had been shuffled over to one table. Cohen helped to fold down the empty tables to make room for the people still trickling in off the sidewalk. He bumped into Paige while trying to put the table up against the wall out of the way.

'Sorry.' He glanced up, surprise on his face. 'Oh, hey.' He obviously hadn't expected her to be the one behind him. 'This is going well, huh?'

'Better than I ever expected,' she admitted, pushing a stray strand of hair behind her ear. 'Port Landon has really outdone themselves in the name of Helen O'Connor.'

'So did you.' He offered her a crooked grin. 'You did a good thing here, Paige. You should be proud of yourself.'

Something more than pride swelled inside her. 'You, too. I couldn't have done it without you, you know. And Bryce, too.'

Cohen's eyes burned into hers. She didn't know what she expected him to say or do, but when he pulled his gaze away and stepped away from her, taking the heat that emanated from his body with him, she felt foolish for thinking they would simply apologize and pretend like nothing had happened. 'I should go,' he said. 'I've got to announce the silent auction winners.'

'Of course.' She waved a hand, but he had already retreated toward the table, picking up a conversation with someone he knew like he'd never left it in the first place.

After that, Paige buried herself completely in the task at hand. She was bound and determined to make every last one of the cupcakes disappear. She listened with only partial attention as Cohen's loud, booming voice echoed above the constant hum of chatter, silencing everyone.

'As you all know, this event is to help out one of our own.' He turned to share a dazzling smile with Helen, who looked as though she was about to be charmed right off her chair. 'Mrs O'Connor, it was a tragic thing that happened to your house, ma'am, but be sure that Port Landon has every intention of helping you rebuild what you lost.'

Cheers erupted throughout the crowd, accompanied by clapping and a few shrill whistles.

'We can't replace some things,' Cohen continued, 'But we'll sure try to help you start anew.'

More cheering and clapping ensued, making Paige smile widely.

'Of course, this event wouldn't be possible today without the generous efforts of a few key players. A huge thank you goes out to all the local businesses who donated items to the silent auction.'

Everyone clapped, and one bold man shouted out, 'Tell us who won the prizes, Dr Cohen!', resulting in a fit of laughter amongst the crowd.

Cohen chuckled. 'We'll get to that, Todd. Hold your horses, will you?' He waved a hand toward Paige, who stood across the crowded room from him. 'But first, we must give credit where credit is due. A special thanks needs to go out to the baker extraordinaire, Paige Henley, who not only spearheaded this colorful, sugary event, but also slaved over the ovens tirelessly for the past few weeks to make every one of the tasty treats you've purchased today. So, Paige, on behalf of all of Port Landon, I'd like to thank you for your endless generosity.'

Allison let out a whoop beside her, and Paige blushed bright red as the applause rang out for her. Through the throngs of people, she could just make out Helen O'Connor peering at her. The old woman nodded her head and mouthed, 'Thank you,' which brought tears to Paige's eyes. The moment was in her honor, but all she could think of was Cohen, whose eyes were fixed on hers twenty feet away. He didn't have to do that, didn't have to put her on a pedestal and thank her publicly.

But he did. There was that hope again, swirling up inside her stomach and making it hard for her to breathe. They may have argued about something, but it was passing. Things were going to be okay. Surely, he wouldn't have made such a heartfelt announcement in front of half the town if it wasn't? She was certain he knew just as well as she did that the gossipmongers would end up making more of it than it truly was.

And he had done it anyway.

It was Paige's turn to say, 'Thank you,' to Cohen, but it came out as only a whisper in the chaos of the crowd. Still, Cohen gave her a soft nod. He might not have heard the words, but he knew she'd said them. Maybe he felt them, as she did. The softness in his hazel eyes confirmed he knew she meant them, too.

The rollicking laughter and banter that followed as Cohen and Bryce announced the winners' names of the silent auction items was so comical it brought tears to Paige's eyes. One by one, the winners were called, and each announcement ended in some kind of anecdote or story that would be later embellished and discussed by the town. It wasn't just the colorful cupcakes and chance at winning prizes that people were enjoying – it was the camaraderie. The intricate way every person was knitted to the next. Everyone knew everyone to some degree, and the event brought them together to chit-chat and enjoy each other's company. The baked goodies were just a plus, Paige decided.

To see so many people come together for an event in the name of one elderly woman was beautiful to Paige. The folks who filed through the doorway weren't there to buy cupcakes, though they would gladly take a box home. They were there to help out Helen. Because Helen O'Connor wasn't merely a woman. She was one of them. A neighbor, a friend, and a part of their home. Judging by the way Helen's eyes scanned the crowd, rimmed with tears, taking in her surroundings with a keenness that belied her advanced age, she was taking mental inventory of each and every person who attended. She would attempt to return the favor, no doubt. It was the Port Landon way.

By the time the last of the attendees left the shopfront, Paige was dead on her feet. Any other day she could work eight or more hours without batting an eyelash. Today, she'd run a marathon in the course of four hours. She flipped the lock on the door, locking herself, Allison, Bryce, and Cohen in the room to clean up and count the money raised by their efforts.

'That was a phenomenal success, I'd say.' Allison pulled the cashbox off the last remaining table and set herself up on a stool by the front counter to start counting. 'I haven't counted yet, but it's safe to say we made a big chunk of money for Helen.'

'I hope so,' Paige replied, setting the folded chairs up against the wall. 'The woman is a sweetheart. She deserves every penny. Cohen, you have the silent auction proceeds?'

'Counting them now.' He opened the cashbox at the other end of the counter and started counting it out.

Paige had done rough calculations. She knew with three hundred cupcakes at two dollars a piece, there should be a smooth six hundred dollars in the cashbox. She and Allison had managed to keep track of the community members who offered cash donations over and above the cupcake sales, so they'd kept that money separate from the cupcake proceeds. Paige was still wiping down the tabletops and changing out the trash bin bags when Allison spoke.

'We sold all the cupcakes, right?'

'Every one of them,' Paige answered. 'Which is pretty freaking cool, by the way.' She was damn proud of that fact. Not only had the event itself been a success, but her baking had been well received as well.

'It is,' her cousin said absently. 'How are you making out over there, Dr Cohen?'

Paige turned away from the trash bag she was tying up. She heard the distance in Allison's voice.

'All good here.' Cohen pressed a few more numbers into the calculator app on his phone, smiled to himself, then wrote down the final tally on the bottom of the sheet of paper in front of him and circled it. 'Everything adds up perfectly for the silent auction. We raised five hundred and sixty-four dollars. Every penny accounted for.'

'Whoa, that's awesome!' Bryce exclaimed, peeking over his father's shoulder to see the written number. He high-fived Cohen, a wide grin on his face.

'It's more than awesome,' Cohen insisted. 'It's phenomenal. Did everything add up on your end, Allison?'

Allison's forehead was wrinkled in concentration. She tapped numbers into the calculator again. 'We sold every cupcake at full price, right? Two dollars?'

'Yes,' Paige replied.

'And your pre-calculations are correct?'

'Of course.' She had checked them numerous times to make sure. She knew exactly how much they had started with before the event began.

'Then, we're out by ... fifty dollars.' Allison raised her head to give Paige a confused look.

'That's impossible.' The words were out of Paige's mouth before she could stop them. 'We were so careful.' She slipped in beside her cousin and Allison pushed the calculator toward her, letting her recheck the tally. Sure enough, her final numbers mirrored Allison's. Her head swam as she tried to think back throughout the day. She glanced past her cousin to Cohen. 'Any ideas where it might have gone?'

She realized her mistake the moment the words tumbled from her lips. She had meant the question so innocently, but a second later when Cohen's gaze narrowed and darkened, she knew how he was interpreting her inquiry.

'None, actually,' he replied, tight-lipped. 'But if you're suggesting what I think you're suggesting, you should be ashamed of yourself.'

Paige felt the blood drain from her face. Bryce was the furthest thing from her mind when she had asked him about the missing money. He had been at the forefront of Cohen's, though. 'What? No, Cohen, I—'

'Go on, Bryce.' Cohen stood, nodding toward the door. He placed a firm hand on his son's back and led him toward it. 'We've done our part. Looks like it's time to be heading home.'

'Cohen, just wait.' Paige sounded as exasperated as she felt. 'That's not what I asked, and you know it.'

He pointed toward the door, giving Bryce no room to argue with his stance. The boy obeyed silently, giving Paige and Allison a little wave before unlocking the door and disappearing out onto the street. Cohen pulled his backpack up over his shoulder, then leaned in closer to Paige. 'You didn't have to ask, Paige. I know what you meant.' His chiseled features may as well have been stone, his gaze made of steel. He pushed the cashbox from the silent auction closer to her. 'You'd better keep that wad of cash, too. I wouldn't want Bryce accused of anything else.'

'Cohen, I didn't mean—'

'Congrats on today, ladies.' He nodded toward Allison before making his way out of the store, leaving the bell chiming shrilly in his wake.

Both Paige and her cousin stared at the spot Cohen had been only moments before, eyes wide and mouths agape.

'What in the blazing hell of glory just happened?' Allison asked, bewildered.

Paige couldn't bring herself to respond, but she knew the answer all too well. She might have thought he'd left her heart-broken before, but Paige was wrong. Cohen Beckett had just shattered her heart completely, with no regard for the shards he left it in.

Chapter 20

Cohen

Summer had definitely hit Port Landon. In Cohen's line of business, he always judged the beginning of the season by the flare-ups of allergies, fleas, ticks, and other untoward conditions. The heat of summer mixed with the pollen and weed growth had a way of creating a playground for those kinds of things. In their small town, it was up to Cohen to control it for the furry population and their owners.

But that was his job – to aid animals with their ailments. What he couldn't heal or fix, he would do his best to ease and control.

It seemed to be the only thing he could control these days. He had never been one to want to control his surroundings, and he'd always done well at taking things as they came. In the same vein, he wasn't one to ruminate on what others thought of him or how he was perceived through the eyes of others.

That wasn't the case when it came to how Bryce was perceived, obviously. Or maybe what mattered to him most was that it was Paige Henley's perception of his son that was in question. Okay, so there was no maybe about it. If another person in their town came to him and accused Bryce of doing something like—

No, it wasn't possible. Because Bryce wouldn't do something like that. The fact that Paige could accuse Bryce of stealing not once but twice made his stomach twist in anguish every time he allowed himself to think about it. She had come to him, blaming his ten-year-old for some missing baked goods, and then she had the audacity to insinuate he was the culprit of the missing fifty dollars at the fundraiser as well?

Well, technically she hadn't said it out loud. But he knew what she was getting at. And that didn't sit well with Cohen. Not only because it was his own flesh and blood in question, but because he never would have expected it from Paige.

And maybe that was what hurt him the most.

He couldn't let it get to him. It was easier said than done, especially seeing as everything reminded him of how good things had been for him over the past few weeks, and everyone he talked to mentioned Paige by name. The fundraiser had made her a local celebrity … and the town's own sweetheart. Port Landon loved her.

The problem was, so did he. Still. She accused his son of the unthinkable, yet she was still at the forefront of his mind no matter how hard he tried to push the thoughts of her away. He felt like he was betraying Bryce in some way, and that made Cohen's heart hurt even more.

Bryce, however, was more interested than ever about Paige. Two days had passed since the fundraising event. His son had grown quieter over that time, but when he did open his mouth, it was questions or comments about Paige that emerged.

'Are you and Paige okay?' Bryce had asked the evening before while they lounged in the living room watching *Home Alone*. It was their favorite movie, one they had watched together more times than Cohen could count. They could both recite lines from it word for word.

His question caught Cohen off guard but he played it down as much as possible. 'Everything is fine, buddy.'

'That's not what I asked.'

The kid was smarter than he gave him credit for. 'You don't need to be worried about me or Paige, Bryce. We'll be okay.'

'Are you guys still going to go on dates?' Bryce didn't miss a beat, and his eyes pleaded with Cohen to be honest with him. Not for the first time, Cohen was rudely reminded that his son wasn't the baby he still saw him as.

'Paige and I are just friends,' Cohen explained carefully. 'That's all we've ever been.' The words tasted like lies on his lips.

Bryce scoffed. 'Yeah, right.'

'What?' Cohen quirked an eyebrow. 'It's the truth.'

'Dad,' Bryce said, obviously fed up with his father's insistent denial, 'I'm not stupid.'

'Maybe not, but you're ten years old,' Cohen reminded him. 'We're not discussing this.'

'Because you and Paige broke up?' he countered. 'Or because you don't want to admit it to me?'

Cohen stared at his son, as though for the first time. There was something in his son's eyes that scared him. Vulnerability, maybe? Incomprehension? He couldn't bring himself to ask the boy about it, but one thing was certain. He sure didn't want to believe that look in his eyes was guilt.

He didn't answer the question. Instead, he pointed at the television screen. 'Just watch the movie, Bryce.'

The boy huffed a loud sigh. 'We need to talk about Paige, Dad.'

If he hadn't been so upset when it came to her, Cohen would have laughed out loud. Bryce was making it sound like he needed an intervention or something. 'No, we don't. There's nothing to talk about, my boy.'

'There is, though.' Bryce's hands came up in exasperation, but Cohen sat up straighter, holding up one hand to silence him.

'Enough, Bryce!' He shook his head. 'This is between Paige and me, all right?'

'But, Dad—'

'No,' he stated more sternly. 'I mean it, Bryce.'

His son tossed himself back against the couch cushions again, defeated. 'Fine.'

Finally. Cohen remained silent, easing back into his spot on the couch. Kevin McAllister was ordering pizza in the movie, but he didn't think his son was paying much attention to the television, either. Rarely did he argue with his son, and Cohen knew how lucky he was to have such an easy relationship with him at that age. He wasn't naive to the fact that strain was coming as the boy got into his teenage years – Cohen had been a teen once and he had given his own father a run for his money. Cohen and Bryce's journey would be no different.

He never fathomed that they would argue about Cohen's dating life, however. Mostly because Cohen had never had a dating life up until now, and because he hadn't thought of the repercussions for Bryce if things didn't work out with Paige.

Now, he had a boy who wanted to know about adult things. Things that Cohen wasn't interested in telling him. Not to mention, there was no way he was confessing to Bryce that Paige believed he'd stolen goods from her shop. The notion would crush the boy. He couldn't allow for that. He was the adult in this duo, and he would handle it himself.

As far as Cohen was concerned, it *was* handled. Paige knew where he stood on the matter, and Bryce now knew that he had no need to concern himself with anything regarding Cohen's personal affairs. Bryce was a kid, one that would never get caught up in the things he had been accused of. And Paige, well, she was a friend that he didn't have as much in common with as he thought.

If Cohen kept telling himself that, maybe he would eventually believe it.

After the movie ended, Cohen did his best to smooth things over. He hadn't yelled at his son, but a loud, stern voice was pretty much the equivalent in the Beckett household. Bryce rarely heard it, and Cohen rarely had to use it. And now he felt guilty about talking to his son in that tone.

Which was why he let Bryce coerce him into taking Jazz for an extra-long walk. It was later than usual thanks to the length of the movie, but Cohen relented. It would be good for them, as well as the dog, to get out and get some fresh air.

The pier was eerily quiet, especially considering how many people milled about, either strolling along the boardwalk or standing at the water's edge to watch the moon rise steadily in the sky, casting a distorted reflection across the rippling lake.

Bryce was quiet, too. He focused on Jazz as they walked, which was exactly how Jazz preferred it. Cohen didn't try to force the conversation, intent to let him do short sprints with the dog and laugh when she lopped along like a deer instead of the canine she was.

Let him be a kid, Cohen told himself. That's all he ever wanted for the boy. To have a decent, normal childhood. He had been so young when tragedy struck. When he lost his mother. Cohen was determined to counteract that with as much love and devotion as he could while he had the chance. He didn't think it was possible to love his kid too much, but he wasn't afraid to try.

Which was exactly why he had such a damn hard time understanding Paige's stance on the supposed theft at her bakery. Paige had said herself that she knew Bryce was a good kid. So, how in the hell could she justify accusing him of something that suggested the polar opposite of that? He didn't get it. He sure didn't appreciate it, either.

Still, he knew he had been rash in his reaction. Okay, he had outright overreacted. Guilt tainted the anger he still harbored toward her because he knew he had been quick to shut down on her, and even quicker to leave. Now that he'd cooled off a bit, he knew he could have – hell, he probably should have – stayed and tried to talk it through. He could have made her see how wrong she was about Bryce.

Except, Paige had been adamant in her convictions. That had only hurt Cohen more, which in turn, he expressed as anger. It was no excuse, but he had been plagued by fatigue and unprepared for a conversation that pointed fingers at his one and only son as a common thief. What he *had* been prepared for was to confess his feelings for Paige. Instead, he'd had to protect his son from her accusations. Her false accusations.

So, in the end, he had taken it out on her. Blamed the ruining of a perfectly good and romantic evening on her because she'd wrongly signaled out Bryce.

And she *was* wrong. She had to be. That's why Cohen hadn't even bothered to question Bryce about it. There was no need to put him through that when the whole idea was completely ridiculous.

And it *was* ridiculous.

Why, then, was he so damn petrified to question Bryce about it? Why did guilt ball up in his stomach like lead every time he thought about the things he said to Paige?

He knew why. It wasn't that he hadn't bothered to question Bryce about Paige's allegations, it was that he couldn't bring himself to. He wasn't sure he could handle knowing he had unfailingly defended his son against the one person who had been his friend, his partner in fundraising crime ... and potentially his something more, and ruined everything, purely because he wasn't brave enough to face the whole situation head on.

Cohen let out a defeated sigh. There were some things he just wasn't ready to face tonight. Things he couldn't bring himself to face. Instinctively, he dug into his pocket to clutch the small, smooth stone he had carried there faithfully for almost a decade. It wasn't there. The second his brain registered its absence and where the stone was, he groaned loudly.

Without it, Cohen felt a sense of lostness he couldn't put into words. Paired with the absence of Paige, however, the combination created a vast wave of sadness he hadn't expected. Which was suiting, seeing as he hadn't expected Paige Henley at all in the first place.

It seemed Paige had left his life in the same unexpected way she had come. And, if he was honest, he had no one to blame for it but himself.

Chapter 21

Paige

At the grand opening of The Cakery so many weeks ago, Paige wouldn't have been able to come up with one good reason why her bakery wouldn't be open and ready for business on a weekday. It was in her blood, the need to run her business smoothly and be reliable and available to her customers on a daily basis. She never liked to let anyone down.

But she didn't want to let Allison down, either. That was why, for the first time since she had opened her shop, Paige had turned the sign to *Closed* early, locking the door at noon so she could meet up with her cousin and go dress shopping in North Springs. By the end of the afternoon, a gorgeous white wedding dress and pretty bridesmaid dresses would be chosen.

Paige anticipated the outing more than she would admit. The idea of sifting through all the satin and chiffon and silk to unearth the perfect gown for her cousin's big day was both whimsical and romantic to her. She loved the idea of hearing Allison say 'This is the one!' and seeing the excited gleam in her eyes. Paige wanted that for Allison.

Someday, Paige wanted that for herself.

But today wasn't that day, and every time she reminded herself that this wasn't about her, and that she was going to try extra hard to make this outing perfect for her cousin, Paige's mind managed to conjure up Cohen again. It was a sad, sad reminder of the state of their friendship.

Was it even that anymore? She didn't know. Dwelling on it wouldn't change anything, and letting it ruin her day with Allison wouldn't solve anything, either. Paige planned to keep the conversation as far away from the attractive veterinarian as possible. She wouldn't mention his name. Instead, she would focus on the fabric swatches and multiple dresses she'd need to try on while making memories with her cousin – that was going to be Paige's day in a nutshell.

Too bad she hadn't made Allison aware of her plans. The first thing out of the woman's mouth the moment Paige opened up the car door and got into the passenger seat beside her was, 'Ready for our girls' day?' When Paige responded with an enthusiastic nod, Allison didn't hesitate to follow it up with, 'Good, now tell me everything that's going on with you and Dr Cohen.'

Paige groaned, loudly and on purpose. 'Allison …'

'She's been going on about it since I got in the car.'

Paige whirled around to find Allison's friend, Kait, in the backseat. She had forgotten there would be another person on this outing, which was silly on Paige's part. She had known she wasn't the only member of the wedding party on the bride's side, but somehow her muddled brain hadn't put two and two together.

That meant there were more ears to hear the sordid details of her argument with Cohen.

'Oh, hey, Kait,' she said politely, having only met her briefly once or twice before, and only in Allison's presence. The woman's straw-colored hair was up in a twist on top of her head, and her emerald eyes shone, highlighted with dark mascara. She looked light and carefree in her paisley peasant top and denim skirt, ready to hit the town. 'I love your outfit.'

'We both love her outfit,' Allison interjected hurriedly. 'Now, we've got a fifteen-minute drive ahead of us, Paige. Twenty if we're lucky and there's midday traffic. Start talking.'

'Like I said,' Kait cut in, leaning forward between the front seats. 'She's been relentless about this since I got in the car.'

Paige sighed. Only Allison would think getting stuck in traffic would be lucky, giving them more time to talk. 'Can't we just talk about something fun instead? I don't really think—'

'Kait's lips are locked tight, if that's what you're worried about. She won't say a thing. I only surround myself with the best people in the world, you know that.' Allison peered into the rearview mirror, giving her friend a cheeky grin.

'Well, thanks for that,' Kait said. 'But, yeah. Anything said today stays between us. I promise.'

Paige appreciated the oath of confidentiality, but that didn't make it any easier. 'I appreciate it, you guys. I do. I just don't want to dampen the fun of today by talking about an argument that happened days ago.'

'So, you do admit there was an argument.' Allison didn't miss a beat. 'And that it happened days ago. That's the problem, isn't it? You're my cousin – the maid of honor, for God's sake – and we've both been busy enough that we haven't even had a chance to talk about this yet. Until now. Besides, if you don't talk to us about it, who are you going to talk to?' She cast a quick glance toward Paige, knowing she had hit the mark with her statement. 'Now, do us all a favor and get it off your chest. I know you well enough to know it's been eating away at you.'

'Allison, I don't want—'

The woman scoffed. 'Is it because I said I would murder him if he hurt you and make it look like an accident? Because I didn't mean it.' She stole another glance at her passenger. 'Unless he did hurt you. Then, I did mean it.'

'Allison, no one's murdering anyone.'

'You're right. Gotta keep my lips zipped on that. You guys could be arrested for being an accessory if I'm convicted.'

'Allison!' Paige's eyes were about to bug out of her head. 'Geez, you're officially banned from watching true crime shows on TV.'

Kait giggled in the backseat, but Allison just waved a dismissive hand. 'Fine. All I'm saying is, talk about it now, in this car. Once I park at the bridal boutique, the topic can be tabled and we won't discuss it again if you don't want to.'

She was right. Her thoughts of Cohen had been eating away at her, and the days that had passed without so much as a word or even sight of him did little to ease her mind. Maybe talking about it would help. 'Once we're out of the car, you'll let it go?' Allison was like a dog with a bone. She knew saying she would table the subject of Cohen was different than actually doing it.

'I promise.'

Paige glanced over at her cousin, then into the backseat where Kait sat quietly with her hands in her lap. 'Fine.'

At first, Paige's words came out jumbled and all over the map. She didn't know where to start. Didn't know how to put into words the course of events that led her to the pain her heart was feeling. After a few pauses, sighs, and attempts at starting over at the beginning as Allison patiently suggested, she began to find her rhythm and the truth began to fall from her lips. She went from struggling to explain to not knowing how to turn off the tap. Everything – how good things had been going between them, the romantic candlelit date at the ice cream shop, the teamwork as they prepped for the fundraiser, the events that led her to suspect Bryce and his friend, as well as the ensuing argument about it between her and Cohen – poured from her like she had been awaiting the chance to let the dam break open.

'And you're sure Bryce and Hunter were the only ones who could've done it?' Allison asked. Paige could hear her trying to tread lightly, but she didn't take the question as a rebuke.

'I didn't see them take the tarts and squares, but the fact that I watched that table so closely that day, mixed with their actions as they left the shop … yeah, I'm sure. I wouldn't have said anything, otherwise.'

'Then you were right to go try to talk to Dr Cohen about it,' Kait piped up from the backseat.

'Definitely,' Allison added with a nod.

It felt good to hear others agree with her choice. It meant she hadn't been completely off base. 'I mean, it's not like I was telling him I was going to charge the kids or something. All I wanted to do was talk.'

'Dr Cohen has been a pretty protective dad—'

'Overprotective,' Kait insisted, cutting Allison off.

'I'm not saying his reaction was appropriate,' Allison added quickly. 'I'm just saying I could see how he would struggle with hearing that Bryce did something like that. He's such a good kid.'

'I never said he wasn't a good kid!' Paige threw up her hands. That wasn't what she had been insinuating at all. 'I was trying to be open and honest. Isn't that what people do when they're—' She stopped abruptly, her cheeks flaming up in an instant.

Allison snapped her gaze sideways. 'Dating? No wait … in love?' A devious grin spread across her face. 'Please tell me that's what you were about to say.'

Paige remained silent.

'In a relationship. Maybe that's what she was going to say?' Kait sounded like she was trying to help Paige get her foot out of her mouth, but again, she remained quiet. All she could think was that Allison owned the coffeehouse and Kait worked full-time at the diner on the other side of Main Street. Yes, they had both guaranteed secrecy of the topics brought up in the car, but Paige couldn't fathom how humiliated she would be if the gossipmongers got a whiff of the word love being tossed around.

'I'm just saying I thought openness and honesty was a good idea,' she replied, defeated. 'Obviously, I was wrong.'

'You weren't wrong.' Allison pulled up to a red light, the first double-laned intersection Paige had seen in a while. They were getting close to town. 'Cohen got his hackles up about the situation. It's been just him and Bryce for so long that Bryce is just as much his best friend as his son. So, he didn't take it well to hear he'd done something Cohen didn't know about. *That*'s not your fault.'

'When's the last time you talked to him?' Kait asked.

Paige turned. 'At the fundraiser.'

'Well, that *is* your fault,' Allison stated bluntly, punching the accelerator when the light turned green. 'You need to go talk to him, Paige.'

'And you need to keep your eyes on the road,' Paige insisted. 'Your driving is starting to freak me out.'

Allison rolled her eyes, changing lanes with the skill of a race car driver. 'No need to worry. Dale Earnhardt has got nothing on my mad skills. But seriously, you need to try to talk to him again.'

'The dress boutique is right there!' Kait called out, tapping viciously at the window beside her. Allison veered into the turning lane, taking the turn fast enough that Paige gripped the handle on the side of the passenger door.

'Where did you get your driver's license, in a Happy Meal?' The car came to an abrupt halt in a parking space just outside Bianca's Bridal Shoppe. It was a quaint little shop with only one tiny front display window. The long, lacy wedding dress in it was absolutely to die for. Surrounded by sparkly diamond tiaras and jewellery, with two pale peach strapless dresses on mannequins at each side, the display was lovely, evoking every little girl's dream.

Despite the high anxiety amongst the women in the car because of almost missing their turn, and coupled with Allison's questionable driving skills, Paige wasn't the only one who let out a sigh of appreciation toward the storefront display.

Allison turned the key, killing the engine. Her eyes never wavered from the front window of the store. 'We're really doing this.' The words were barely audible.

Paige smiled, reaching over to give her cousin's hand a squeeze. 'You're really doing this,' she corrected. 'You're going to marry the man of your dreams, and Kait and I will be right there by your side when you do it.'

Kait unbuckled her seatbelt and leaned forward, squeezing Allison's shoulder. 'Wouldn't want to be anywhere else, Allison.'

'And I wouldn't want anyone else there with me.' Tears brimmed Allison's eyes, which only summoned up tears in Paige's eyes, too. She blamed her raging emotions.

The collective pause that ensued needed no words. It was a defining moment in Allison's life, but it was a memory that both Paige and Kait would hold on to tightly as well. They relished it, giving Allison the time she needed to compose herself.

'Okay, girls, we said we were going to make this a girls' day, so let's do this.' She sounded like she'd put herself back together, so Paige patted her hand and began to unbuckle her seatbelt, too.

Excitement was reverberating off Kait in waves from the backseat. 'Judging by the front window of that shop, Allison, we're going to be doing this in style.'

Paige was starting to feel a little bad for the bridal consultant. Three hours and what felt like a gazillion dresses later, they were still no closer to finding the perfect dresses than when they had arrived.

The consultant's name was Mira, and she had been exuberant in their initial greetings as they got started with the overwhelming task of making Allison's dreams come true. It had been three hours since the introductions, however, and Mira was looking more frazzled and frustrated than buoyant. Her perfectly styled red hair now exhibited flyaway strands, and Paige heard the sighs she tried to hide under her breath.

Paige was beginning to feel a little bit like that herself, but she understood both sides. The bridal consultant was trying her hardest to find dresses that matched the requirements Allison outlined for her – her wedding dress would be simple but long and classy, not revealing too much skin and not harboring a lot of bling, and the bridesmaids' dresses would be long and simple as well but in a deep gray color. Basically, she would know the perfect dresses when she saw them.

'Allison, you looked stunning in that last one,' Kait assured her, pointing at the discarded pile of creamy satin slung over a chair. There were dresses everywhere, draped over every bench and chair and surface around them. The change room area looked like Cinderella's ballgown closet had exploded. A wedding warzone.

It was a battle that the three women were bound and determined to win.

'I liked it,' Allison replied. 'But I didn't love it.'

As far as Paige was concerned, her cousin looked like a Disney princess in every one of the dreamy dresses she had tried on. She could just imagine her with her hair done in fancy curls and her eyes made up in soft hues as they glimmered with anticipation of her soon-to-be husband seeing her at the other end of the aisle. Allison was such a beautiful person inside and out already, but Paige understood the importance of loving one's wedding dress. This was a one-shot deal – it had to be perfect.

'Let's recap.' Paige clapped her hands once to get everyone's attention. 'You really liked the simplicity of that one, but not the neckline.' She pointed toward one of the dresses slung on the bench beside Kait. 'And you thought the sweetheart neckline of this one here was great, but you didn't like the feel of the rough overlay.' She ran her fingers across the beaded belt of the dress tossed onto the chair beside her. 'The length wasn't okay on that one, and the fit of that one over there wasn't comfortable ...' She pointed at each dress, amazed at herself for being able to keep track of each and every flaw after seeing so many white dresses in such a short span of time. 'So, where does that leave us?'

Allison huffed out a sigh as she looked over each of the dismissed wedding dresses. 'Where it leaves me is wishing they were as perfect as ...' She snapped her head up, eyes wide as she stared beyond Paige to Mira. '... the one in the window.'

Mira looked genuinely affronted. 'The window?' She turned, following Kait and Paige's gazes where they were staring hopefully in the same direction as the bride-to-be. 'Oh, that dress is only the display model, ma'am. It's a discontinued line. We can't order it anymore.'

'I want to try it on.' Allison's hope was rejuvenated by the dress on display.

'But, as I said—'

'Let her try the dress on!' Both Paige and Kait exclaimed the words in exasperated unison, then looked at each other in horror. 'Please,' Paige added weakly, shocked by her own bluntness. They were desperate. If Allison thought there was a chance the display model would fit, she wouldn't deter her.

'Of course.' Mira scampered away, undoubtedly wanting to get the trio out of the shop sooner rather than later.

'And bring the peach bridesmaid dresses on display beside it,' Allison called after her.

Kait and Paige said nothing as they watched Mira fumble to undress the mannequin and bring the satin and lace dress back to the change rooms. There was too much riding on whether or not the dress would suffice.

But as Allison took the dress in her hands, holding in gingerly as though the mere touch of her fingertips might damage the intricate lacy overlay, Paige felt different about this one. She knew Allison did, too.

'This is it,' Allison whispered to no one in particular. She was transfixed by the fabric slung over her hands. 'This is the one, girls.'

Paige stepped closer. 'You haven't even tried it on.'

Her cousin raised her head to meet her gaze. 'When you know, you know.'

Paige watched as Allison disappeared back into the cramped change room, still hanging on the five words she had uttered. Five words that kept coming up from different sources, yet still made such an impact every time she heard them.

'Is the long peach bridesmaid dress only a display model, or can it be ordered in any color?' Allison's voice rang out over the change room door, making both women turn toward Mira for an answer.

The bridal consultant had just tugged the second peach dress from the mannequin, and she was looking beyond flustered. 'These dresses are available in almost any color you could want, ma'am.'

'Dark gray?' Allison hollered.

'A few variations of gray are available.'

'Good,' Allison shouted. 'Paige … Kate … try 'em on.'

Neither woman was going to argue. Mira deposited one dress into each of their hands after checking the tags and determining which might be closest to the size they would wear. 'Like I said, I can order in any color and any size, so these dresses are just to try on and see what you think.'

Paige made it in and out of the change room beside Allison's in record time. The strapless dress was a little on the bigger side, but that only aided her in being able to shimmy it around and do up the back zipper herself. She smoothed out the fabric and held the top of the dress up as she retreated from the change room.

'Wow.' Allison was out, too, and the sight of her in the long-sleeved satin dress with a delicate lace overlay stopped Paige in her tracks. 'Allison, that dress … it fits you perfectly. Absolutely perfectly.'

'It really does, doesn't it?' She whirled around again to face the mirror, admiring her reflection with dreamy stars in her eyes. 'I told you.'

'You were right.' Paige shook her head, amused. Leave it to her cousin to try on every dress in the store and end up finding perfection in the very first dress they'd laid eyes on before they'd even gotten out of the car. 'It was made for you. You look like a princess.'

'I feel like a princess.' Her smile was contagious. Allison nodded her head toward her cousin just as Kait emerged from the room behind her. 'You should, too.'

Paige and Kait turned simultaneously, shifting one way then the other as they took in their reflections. In seconds, everyone in the room was smiling from ear to ear.

'Well, Mira, if you can get those dresses ordered in gray, then I think we've managed to find the dresses we want to buy.'

The bridal consultant looked elated, and Paige was confident it wasn't just from the commission she was about to make.

The women turned to head back into their designated rooms to change. 'This whole time, the perfect one was right under our noses,' Paige chuckled.

'Yeah.' Allison beamed. 'Sometimes, we just have to get a little closer to realize how perfect something really is. You could learn from that, too, Paige.'

Paige halted in front of the opened change room door. 'We're not talking about dresses anymore, huh?'

Allison shook her head. 'Just go talk to him.' She pulled the train of the dress up into her hands. 'You felt better earlier when you talked to me and Kait about it all. Just imagine how relieved you'd feel if you did the same thing with Cohen.'

Paige knew her cousin was right, but that didn't stop the ripple of anxiety from coursing through her. 'Fine, but the deal was we wouldn't talk about this here, remember? How did we even get on this topic again?'

'Simple,' Allison said, smirking. 'I saw you in that dress and knew Cohen was going to love it. He's your date for my wedding, Paige, so you'd better get your butt over there and at least try to make this right. It's just a lovers' quarrel, nothing more. You and Cohen aren't over. Not nearly.'

Paige didn't want to think so, either. This couldn't be the end of her budding relationship with Cohen Beckett. It sure wasn't the beginning, though, either. And knowing they were somewhere in between … that was what worried her the most.

Chapter 22

Cohen

Some days were busy at the clinic, with appointments keeping things running steadily until five o'clock rolled around.

Other days were insane. Today was one of those days. There was no other way to describe the craziness that ensued with walk-in appointments that couldn't wait until the next available appointment slot, or the already packed schedule that had awaited them first thing that morning. Cohen felt bad for his staff. They had been run off their feet since they arrived. He was pretty sure they hadn't even been able to stop and take their full lunch breaks yet. He wasn't sure, because he hadn't had a moment to stop and find out.

No moment was sweeter than when Rhonda shouted, 'I'm locking the front door.' That meant the last client had left for the day. Cohen glanced at the clock. The clinic had technically closed more than an hour ago. What a day.

He remembered seeing Bryce shoot in through the clinic's back door like a blur, but he couldn't recall how long ago that had been. It seemed like hours in some respects and only minutes in others. He faintly recalled giving him permission to take Jazz out into the backyard to play. Which was humorous, seeing as everyone knew that constituted Bryce tossing toys into the air while Jazz stared at them as they hit the ground, wondering who was going to fetch them for her. Jazz was more human than dog – she didn't play dog games well. She adored the attention, nonetheless.

'Anybody seen Bryce?' He was trying to run one last lab work panel, otherwise he would have checked on his son himself.

'In the backyard with Jazz and Hunter. They're fine,' Rhonda assured him. 'You got another visitor, anyway, boss.'

Cohen was about to advise her to make them an appointment for tomorrow if it wasn't an emergency, but from the corner of his eye he saw movement. He looked up from the slip of lab results printing from the machine to see Paige standing behind the veterinary technician. 'Paige, hey.'

'Hello.' He could hear her anxiety. 'I know you're busy. I'm sorry to show up like this.'

'It's okay.' He waved a hand to display the vials and paperwork, and now-cold coffee cup beside the computer. 'It's been one of those days.'

'Obviously. I've been here twice and could barely wade through the waiting room. I guess the third time's the charm.'

'You have?' That perked Cohen's interest. He waited for Rhonda to fade into the background, knowing full well she was hanging on every word. 'Is something wrong?'

'No,' she said quickly. Then, 'Well, yes. This.' She motioned between them after looking around to confirm no one was eavesdropping. 'Us. It's all wrong.'

He knew exactly what she meant. Wrong was a good way to put it. The way things had been so good between them, then in the blink of an eye it had all turned sour. 'I know,' he admitted.

'You agree.' She sighed with relief, her shoulders sagging. 'Can't we talk this through? Cohen, all I want is for things to go back to the way they were before.'

Before. Paige's confession was heartfelt, but there was something that irked him about her choice of words. She made it sound like it was his fault things had gone so off track. He leaned back in his chair. 'That makes two of us,' he replied truthfully. 'I hadn't heard from you since the fundraiser, so I just assumed we were past the point of talking.'

'We're only past the point if you want to be.' Her eyes said she hoped that wasn't the case, but Paige's tone held an assertive air. She was just as desperate to hold on to some semblance of control as he was. Even if it was a fake bravado that gave the illusion of control.

'Of course I don't want that.' He snapped out the words, his fatigue getting the better of him. He sighed. 'What I want is to have never heard you accuse Bryce of stealing in the first place, Paige. But unfortunately we can't turn back time.'

Her jaw tightened. 'No, we can't,' she agreed. 'But maybe we can talk about this like adults, then talk to Bryce and get everything cleared up—'

'You still think Bryce did it.' Cohen couldn't believe what he was hearing.

'Of course I still believe Bryce *and Hunter* did it,' she exclaimed. 'Cohen, I wouldn't have come to you in the first place if I wasn't sure.'

'You've got to be kidding me right now.' Cohen pushed his chair back, tossing the lab results on the counter as he stood up. 'You haven't even tried to apologize for this yet, and now—'

'Apologize?' Paige's eyes grew wider. 'The only thing I'm going to apologize for is thinking you would handle this rationally. Because that's obviously not the case.'

'You can't just come in here and suggest that my kid—'

'Cohen!' She held her hands up. 'We've been through this. I told you already, Bryce is a good kid. He really is. And you know I care about him. That's why I came to you about the missing stuff at my shop. Not because I want to crucify the boy, but because I care about him. Why can't you see that?'

'Because you can't see that he wouldn't do that in the first place!' Cohen argued back. He paced the floor, which only fueled his frustration. 'Bryce thinks the world of you, too, and what thanks does he get for that? You came to me spewing lies about him.'

'Did you ask him about it?'

He stopped pacing. 'What?'

'I said, did you ask Bryce about the day he and Hunter came into the bakery?'

'No!' He shook his head vehemently. 'I'm not bringing my ten-year-old son into this witch hunt, Paige. He doesn't deserve it.'

'He doesn't deserve it?' She arched a brow. 'Or you can't admit to yourself that his answer might not be the one you want to hear?'

'That's enough,' Cohen warned.

'He can be a good kid and still make mistakes, Cohen. It seems he's not the only one who needs to learn that.'

A hollow laugh fell from Cohen's lips. 'You know, if this is your way of trying to make things better, you're not very good at it.'

Paige scoffed, her spine straight as a fencepost. 'Yeah, but there is no way to make things better when I'm dealing with someone who doesn't *want* to make them better.' All the frustration had gone out of her voice, leaving her sounding defeated. 'And I don't think you want to, Cohen.'

He swallowed. It had come to this pivotal moment, and once he replied, there would be no going back. But there was one fact that remained. One thing he couldn't sweep under the rug. 'I can't be with someone who doesn't trust my son, Paige.'

He saw her throat move, struggling to keep herself composed. A very similar struggle was making it difficult for Cohen to keep his expression blank.

'I never said I didn't trust him.' The waver in her voice made his chest tighten.

'You're right, you didn't say it. But you didn't have to.' Cohen's own anger crashed down around him, leaving him with only his exhaustion and jumbled feelings to guide his way. 'I'm sorry, Paige.'

He wasn't sure how to read what was simmering in Paige's eyes. It wasn't just hurt or sadness – he could distinguish that from the tears brimming her bottom eyelids. And it wasn't full-fledged anger. There was some of that, sure, but that wasn't all. What was that? Cohen's conflicted, tired brain wasn't capable of deciphering it at the moment.

She sniffed, shaking her head as though this was some kind of tragedy he would never understand. 'Yeah, me too.'

It was a tragedy. But Paige didn't understand tragedy the way he did. She couldn't. And that was something he could never explain to her. She would never understand his need to protect Bryce ... because he was all he had left. Call his reaction irrational, over the top, even explosive. Cohen knew his son had the ability to evoke those severe emotions in him. But he had to put Bryce first. No matter how much it cost him. No matter the consequences.

Paige looked away, and Cohen felt the connection between them snap apart like a lifeline strung too taut. She fished around in her jacket pocket, held something tightly in her hands, and then set the stone down on the counter beside him.

The words *Stay Pawsitive* cut through Cohen's cognition like a hot knife.

'I'd better give that back to you,' Paige said. There was no mistaking the hurt in her eyes now. 'But I should warn you, I don't think it works anymore.'

She turned to leave, raising alarm bells within Cohen's mind. If he let her walk out now, this was it. He would lose her for good. He was certain of it.

'Paige, wait.' The words about choked him as he stepped forward, but she turned on him, holding up a hand.

'That's all I've done,' she replied, her tears toppling down her cheeks freely. 'For days. So, I came to you, Cohen. And look what it got me. A broken heart.' She shook her head vehemently, obviously frustrated with herself for confessing her heartbreak. 'Goodbye, Cohen.'

This time, Cohen was so shocked by her outburst, and by the pain in her eyes, he didn't try to stop her. It hadn't registered immediately, but finally Cohen recognized the emotion he'd seen shrouding her gaze earlier. It was the same one that took the forefront as she stared at him for the last time before turning away and disappearing out the front door.

Regret.

It petrified him to think how deep that regret went. Was it regret about the time she'd waited for him? The time she had spent with him? Did she regret meeting him at all? He didn't know, and he didn't want to know.

Cohen ran his hands through his disheveled hair. He was making so many mistakes, and those mistakes were hurting other people. People he cared about beyond words.

And himself.

He turned around, intent on grabbing the sheets of lab results and taking them home with him to interpret. He couldn't stand being there one more minute now that the clinic was as empty and desolate as his emotions. His gaze landed on three pairs of eyes in the other doorway, however. Bryce stood there, eyes wide and face ashen, with Rhonda's hands clutching his shoulders for support. Jazz sat solemnly beside him, her own face more serious than Cohen had ever seen it before.

It looked like he had managed to break more than just Paige's heart.

Chapter 23

Paige

Paige loved her apartment. It was her home, the space she had single-handedly transformed into the perfect refuge from a busy day. It was her sanctuary from the tireless hours she put into her work, the peaceful place she ran to when it all seemed to be too much.

But now? Now, all Paige wanted to do was put a sledgehammer through the walls to make it bigger, more open, less confining. She wasn't sure how it was possible, but the apartment seemed to be closing in on her, growing smaller and narrower as the hours ticked by.

Then again, maybe it had something to do with the trays and pans and dishes that were piling up on every available surface, resting on racks and potholders as they cooled. It was the one thing Paige had always done when she needed time to herself or needed to think – she cooked. She had the next couple days' worth of doughs and baked goods prepared and stowed away in the coolers and freezers for the bakery. Two lasagnas, a meatloaf, and a shepherd's pie were cooked and cooling on top of the stove. She would cut the nine-by-thirteen pans into meal-sized portions and freeze them. She could eat for weeks.

And all because she needed to stay busy. Needed to keep her mind occupied. If she didn't, she would dwell on how quickly everything had begun to fall apart.

Paige should have known better than to approach Cohen with her concerns about Bryce. Especially without solid proof. The truth was, she thought she had been doing the right thing. Helping the boy in the long run. She wasn't a mother, and hadn't been raised with a handful of children around, but Paige felt in her heart that dealing with the matter head-on would have been a much better strategy than pretending it didn't happen at all.

She wasn't dumb. She knew the real issue wasn't that Bryce had been involved in something untoward, or that she had been the one to suggest his involvement. The problem wasn't even that she hadn't seen it happen.

The problem lay with Cohen himself. If anyone had gone to him and stated similar concerns about Bryce, he would have come unhinged with them, too. She was sure of it. Maybe not to the extent he had with her, stating negative things about her life in New York City and making her feel like she didn't have a clue how to interact with kids, but he would have clammed up and shut down in the same manner.

Cohen wasn't prepared for Bryce to grow up, and Paige would never begrudge him that. She couldn't fathom how hard it must be to love and nurture a child for ten years, most of those spent caring for him on his own, only to find that he had become a young man in the blink of an eye. That heavy conglomerate of pride, fear, excitement, and unpreparedness must be hard to bear.

Paige was hurt and saddened that Cohen had ended their friendship over it. Heartbroken was probably more accurate. Still, she couldn't help but feel sorry for him. She was hurting for her own loss of what could have been, but Paige also hurt for him, fearing his heart might remain too closed off for anyone to ever get through to him. She had tried, and she had failed. His walls were still constructed high, and Paige didn't see how anyone would ever succeed in breaking through them.

In that regard, her heart pained for him just as much as herself.

She shoved another pan of oversized oatmeal raisin cookies into the preheated oven and set the timer, knowing her clientele would go crazy for the special treat tomorrow when the bakery opened. Another thing she knew was that she had fallen too quickly for Cohen Beckett. Fallen too hard. Paige wished she could say she had known better, and pretend like she had something to compare her feelings to, but the truth was that she hadn't known better. She had never met someone so easy to be with – so easy to love. Paige felt like she didn't have a choice in the matter. Maybe she never did.

Back in New York City, she had found it easy to ward off the men who pursued her. She'd never had a problem keeping a balance between her work and her personal life. Because her work came first. Always.

She sighed. That was her biggest mistake. Paige moved to Port Landon with one item on her wish list – she wanted to be a part of a community and lead a life that didn't resemble a constantly spinning hamster wheel. She had accomplished that, but it had come at the cost of mixing her work and personal life together. Something she didn't understand, something she had never done before. In her small town life, there was no balance she fought to keep because Paige had nestled into a routine where she could maintain it all at once, working around her social life and blending her passion for baking with her desire for simplicity.

Now, she didn't know where her work life ended and her personal life began. Hell, she didn't even know if she still had a personal life now that she didn't have Cohen, Bryce, and Jazz to spend her time with. She had Allison, sure, and maybe even Kait after the dress-buying outing they'd survived together, but the

Beckett duo and their dog had become such an integral part of her days. Paige didn't know how she was going to pretend like the past few months had never happened.

And in a town as small as Port Landon, the residents weren't likely to forget the past few months, either.

Paige sighed. Without consciously doing it, she found herself daydreaming about the anonymity that New York City had allowed her. There was never any worry about who would say what about something that happened. The city never slept, and it could always be relied on to produce something more newsworthy and eye-catching fast enough that yesterday became old news long before tomorrow began.

That sounded pretty good to her at the moment.

There was also something safe in knowing her old life in the city revolved around her career. Paige never had to worry about whether her merchandise would sell, whether she was appealing to the masses. She had been well-respected in her old position. And her ex-boss, Alex, at Livingston Designs had done little to hide the fact that he would welcome her back with open arms if she chose to close up shop and retreat back to the concrete jungle.

But Paige had come so far. Was New York City and the rat race of a lifestyle she'd once lived something she wanted again? She didn't know anymore. She didn't trust herself to make any decision about anything right now. Her heart was too battered, her brain too fatigued from rehashing her argument with Cohen over and over like a Lifetime movie on repeat.

It didn't hurt to keep her options open, though. Alex Livingston had remained in contact since she took her leave from his company. A handful of texts had passed between them in the subsequent months, and all of them were innocent inquiries as to how things were going, laced with hopeful intent that he could lure her back into his employ. The lines of communication stayed open. There was a mutual respect between the two of them. Even a sense of friendship. And Paige was thankful he had been so gracious about her departure. She was even more grateful that he'd thought highly enough of her to check in and see how she was doing. Their bond, though purely professional, remained intact. And that meant more to Paige than she could explain.

On a whim, she pulled her cell from her purse and tapped the screen a few times to bring up Alex's text window. She typed out a quick message to say hello, making small talk and asking how things were going. Her sudden need to reconnect with the city life she left behind was indescribable, and she let out a loud sigh when a reply came almost instantly.

Your ears must have been burning. Gerald and I just mentioned you after yesterday afternoon's board meeting. You're missed, Paige.

Gerald was Alex's uncle, and the founder of Livingston Designs. He had always been an intimidating man in Paige's eyes. Knowing he had brought her up in conversation piqued her interest.

She replied to him.

You were mentioning good things, I hope? And thank you – I miss many things about NYC, too.

She could just imagine Alex's eyebrows raising when he read her response. Paige had ignored his last few texts to her, and this was the first time she had replied to him with anything remotely resembling nostalgia for the life she had walked away from. His reply only confirmed his interest in the real meaning behind her words.

Such as Livingston Designs?

Possibly.

There was no use denying it. The prospect of being hundreds of miles away from Port Landon right now was tempting. Hundreds of miles away from the town meant hundreds of miles away from her heartbreak.

And from Cohen Beckett.

Do you miss it enough to discuss it with me further, Paige?

His text came in fast. Alex had seen an in, and he was taking it.

Paige stared at the screen, willing the words to part and give her insight into what was between the lines so she would know what to do, know how to handle it. But there was nothing between the lines to read. She knew what Alex Livingston wanted to discuss. She knew she had options if she wanted them.

She wrote back a simple, to-the-point reply.

Call me.

Chapter 24

Cohen

The evening following Cohen's final argument with Paige at the clinic was a quiet one. Bryce said little to his father, and Cohen gave him the reprieve of his silence, if only because he didn't know what to say. The following morning and evening were the same, broken up by Bryce's school day and Cohen's day at the clinic. Once at work, even Rhonda and Alice seemed to have lost their enthusiasm for words. It wasn't until the next morning, almost two days since Bryce had witnessed their argument, that his son finally brought up the topic. Cohen wasn't sure whether to be relieved or scared out of his damn mind.

'So, you and Paige have really broken up this time?'

Cohen sighed into his coffee mug before taking a sip. With only a half hour before his son had to be on his way to school and Cohen had to be heading to the vet clinic, he wondered if that was the safest subject to be discussing. Especially without a full cup of coffee running through his system. 'I really wish you wouldn't call it that.'

'Breaking up?' Bryce said it again, his head hovering over his bowl of Frosted Flakes as he spooned another spoonful into his mouth. 'Well, what would you call it?'

'I'm not calling it anything. Mostly because we don't need to be discussing this.' Cohen was sure there had to be some kind of rule about discussing his love life with his ten-year-old son, but even as he outwardly attempted to steer the conversation in another direction, he did want to know what Bryce was thinking about it. The boy hadn't said more than a handful of sentences to him since he'd turned around and seen him standing there at the clinic. Because of that, Cohen had automatically assumed his son was angry with him for not telling him that it was a subject regarding him that he and Paige had fought over. Cohen had always been honest with Bryce. Always kept him apprised of things that affected him. He figured Bryce was upset because, while this affected him on a few different levels, his father had kept it to himself. The jury was still out as to how wise that decision was.

'I want to talk about Paige, Dad.' He said it with such an air of maturity that Cohen's gut clenched. Not because of what his son had said, but because of the grown-up way he'd said it.

'There really isn't much to say, Bryce.' He didn't know how to assure him that this wasn't something he needed to be worried about. They'd been fine before Paige Henley, just the two of them. They would be fine now.

'You guys were arguing over something to do with me, right?' Bryce's spoon stopped midway to his mouth. He waited, unblinking.

'Paige thought it was something to do with you, but it wasn't.' Suddenly, Cohen's curiosity about his son's stance on Paige Henley didn't matter anymore. All he wanted to do was end the conversation and walk away without having to admit the truth.

Bryce's eyes stayed fixed on his father long enough that Cohen shifted in his seat from his discomfort. The boy put his spoon down, leaning back in his chair. It didn't go unnoticed that his son's posture mimicked his own. 'And that's why you and Paige don't talk anymore.' It wasn't a question.

'We have our reasons,' Cohen replied.

'Yeah,' Bryce said quickly, meeting his father's gaze. 'Me.'

The notion that his son believed he was to blame shot right through Cohen's heart. He leaned forward, reaching for Bryce's arm. 'This is not your fault.'

'Yes, it is.' Bryce flinched away from him, pushing his chair back. He stood so fast Cohen thought he was going to bolt from the room, but he didn't. Instead, he stood tall, running his fingers through his hair. 'Dad, it's all my fault.'

'Bryce …' He stood as well, if only to try to calm his son down.

'Dad, I did it.' The exclamation came out in one rapid breath. 'Hunter and I took that stuff from Paige's bakery.'

Cohen could feel the blood drain from his face. 'What?'

For a boy who hadn't spoken much in the past few days, the words suddenly began to topple from his mouth like he couldn't get them out fast enough. 'We didn't plan to do it, I swear. But we stopped in, and Paige was busy with her head in one of those big coolers behind the counter. She was talking to me, but not really paying attention, you know? Hunter, like, nudged me and pointed to the table where the boxes and stuff were. I kept talking to Paige, and Hunter put a bunch of stuff in the boxes and shoved them in his backpack.'

It was true. Damn it, it was *true*. His son had helped his friend steal items from Paige's shop. Paige wouldn't have witnessed it, but according to Bryce, everything happened exactly as Paige had suspected.

She was right, all this time.

'Bryce …' Cohen wasn't equipped to handle the onslaught of emotions storming through him. He was too rattled, too shocked. 'But, why?'

'I don't know.' Bryce shook his head. He looked close to tears.

231

It was obvious the weight of his guilt had been heavily carried on his shoulders. 'I know I shouldn't have let him do it, Dad. And I know I should have said something. I should've gone to Paige and told her. But I didn't want Hunter to be mad at me. And I was just scared.'

'It's reasonable to be scared of the repercussions, Bryce.' Cohen hoped he sounded steadier and sterner than he felt. 'Speaking of that, you're going to be grounded for a long while, you know that, right?'

Bryce hung his head. 'I know.' The tears had begun to fall onto his cheeks, his chest heaving as he struggled to hold in the sobs that lodged in his throat. 'But that's not what I was scared of.'

Confusion pushed to the forefront of Cohen's ever-churning mixture of emotions. What else could a ten-year-old boy possibly be afraid of, if not the loss of a childhood friend or being grounded until he's in college? 'I don't understand.'

Bryce threw his hands up, obviously flustered by his father's incomprehension. 'Dad, I didn't want to let you down!' His hands clenched into fists. 'Or Paige. Instead ...' A sob wracked his body, erupting from him as he clenched his fists against his eyes to unsuccessfully hold back the tears. 'Instead, I tore you and Paige apart.'

No, Bryce, I tore us apart. The realization sunk like lead in his stomach. All the cruel words he'd said to her, all the animosity he'd harbored toward her. Cohen blinked fast, trying to keep his own tears at bay. His own mistakes crushed his chest relentlessly, but his son's turmoil was breaking his heart into shards, not just pieces. 'Bryce, you didn't—'

'I did!' Bryce cried, letting Cohen pull him against his chest. 'It was stupid and ended up ruining you and Paige.'

'Bryce, it's okay.' Cohen clutched the boy to him, holding him so tight he wasn't sure he could breathe properly. Cohen didn't believe his own words – it was far from okay – but, in that moment, he wanted to do something, anything, to take away the pain his son felt. If he couldn't take it away, he at least vowed to ease it.

'But it's not, Dad,' Bryce sobbed. 'It's not okay. I like Paige. *You* like Paige.'

No, he loved Paige – there was a difference. He loved her and he'd betrayed her. He feared her because of that love, because of what that love could do to him. Cohen had been so hell-bent on pointing fingers in her direction, so quick to label her as the one guilty of deception, that he hadn't realized he was the one deceiving everyone, himself included. He let that fear grab a hold and squeeze him, in the end using his fear to do away with love before it once again had the chance to do away with him.

But Cohen knew he couldn't explain that to his son. Something told him he didn't need to, anyway. The boy was wise beyond his years, but he was still just that – a boy. 'Let's just deal with this whole stealing thing first, then—'

'But, Dad, you don't get it.' Bryce reared back, his reddened, wet eyes glistening up at Cohen. 'You and Paige would still be okay if me and Hunter had never taken that stuff from her shop. And you wouldn't have had that big argument the other day.' Bryce paused, then stepped out of his father's arms to wipe his eyes. 'Wait, you knew this whole time, because Paige told you. Why didn't you ground me a long time ago?'

Because you weren't the only one who was scared, he thought. *Because I felt that, if it was true, then I was the one who had let you down, not the other way around.* He'd sure as hell let Paige down, too.

'I don't know, Bryce.' He glanced up at the clock on the wall. They were both going to be late. 'I guess we both should have said something before now.'

'I'm sorry, Dad.'

Cohen stared at his son as though for the first time. He knew he wasn't just sorry because he got caught. That's not the kind of kid Bryce was, and it wouldn't be the kind of man he would become. Bryce was hurting because he had hurt others, and it pained Cohen to watch as he learned for the first time that his actions had consequences. Sometimes, those consequences affected others just as much as himself. 'I know you are, buddy.' Cohen gave him a faint encouraging smile. 'But you were caught stealing, which means you're still grounded until you're eighteen.'

'Figured as much,' the boy replied, shoulders slumped. 'But you can still fix this, right?'

'You'll need to apologize to Paige face to face, and you'll have no weekly allowance until you've paid her back in full for what you took.' Cohen held his fingers up, counting each point one by one. Bryce, however, had others points to make and he waved his hands dismissively to shush his dad.

'Yeah, yeah, I know all that, Dad,' he stated, a renewed sense of determination in his gaze. 'But what are *you* going to do?'

'Me?' Cohen's forehead wrinkled.

'Dad ...' Bryce was obviously frustrated with his inability to keep up. 'You've got to say you're sorry to Paige, too.'

He hadn't expected the boy to start rhyming off a to-do list for him as well. After all, he wasn't the one who'd just been grounded for the rest of his adolescent and teenage years. 'I will, but—'

'No buts.' Bryce seemed older to Cohen, somehow. More grown up. 'I think I know why you didn't tell me that Paige told you I stole that stuff.' He paused, but Cohen didn't know what to say to that. He just stood waiting with bated breath as his son continued. 'You were trying to protect me, right, Dad? That's what you've always done. And you're good at it.'

'I'll always protect you,' he whispered, not trusting his voice to get any louder. 'But I was protecting myself, too, I think.'

'I know,' Bryce replied without a hint of hesitation.

His son's simple answer hit Cohen with the weight of a

transport truck. When had the roles reversed? When had his son begun to realize his own father's fear of the unknown? Or his fear of living life itself?

'I don't remember much about Mom, but I know you do,' Bryce said softly. 'And I know you've been happy with just the two of us for, like, ever.' He steadied his gaze on his father, shrugging. 'But you were happy with Paige, Dad. Like, really happy. A different kind of happy. Probably the same kind of happy you were with Mom, huh?' He paused, his shoulders shrugging slightly again, as though he couldn't explain his reasons for his beliefs, but he knew they were as close to the truth as he was going to get. 'I think Mom would want you to be that kind of happy with Paige.'

Every wall Cohen had built around his heart came crumbling down as his son spoke of the things he believed, the things he knew, even if he didn't fully understand them. But that was love, wasn't it? Believing in something so strongly and so completely that it didn't matter if it made sense or not. Sometimes love didn't make sense, and that was okay. Because it didn't make sense to be getting advice on love from a ten-year-old, either, but Cohen was doing it, and he was proud of his son for standing up for something he believed in so strongly.

'Thank you.' Cohen reached out and pulled his son in for another embrace, this time holding him against him while having to wipe away tears of his own. 'I'm so lucky to have you, Bryce.'

'Agreed,' the boy quipped, making Cohen choke out a laugh through his tears. 'You ain't the only lucky one, though.'

Cohen pulled back, savoring every second of this moment, memorizing every inch of his son's face. He knew something was changing in their dynamic. Though Bryce would always be Cohen's baby, it was the first time Cohen knew in his heart that his son was becoming a man. A good man. One he would be proud of. *Was* proud of.

'I'm still calling Hunter's parents,' he added, trying to gain some ground as the parent in the situation again.

'Fine, Dad,' Bryce groaned. 'Just do it *after* you go see Paige.'

It was too late to let Bryce walk to school on his own, so Cohen drove him there to make sure he arrived before the first bell rang. Cohen was late getting to the veterinary clinic because of it, which had never happened in all the years he had owned the business, and his staff members noticed. So did the clients, as the first two appointments of the day had already shown up and were waiting in the exam rooms.

'Late?' Rhonda was the first to comment. Cohen wouldn't have expected anything less. 'I didn't think that was possible, boss.'

'First time for everything, I suppose.' Cohen changed into the running shoes he wore inside the clinic and checked the patient files, pulling each one up on the computer screen. 'I had to drive Bryce to school. Wait, Rufus is back?' He squinted at the computer screen. 'We just removed those sutures yesterday.'

'Yeah, and the wound has dehisced a little,' Rhonda explained. 'It's not bothering Rufus at all, and it looks clean, but Shelly thought we should take a look, just in case. I think Steri-Strips will do the trick, but he'll be back wearing the good ol' cone of shame.'

The Irish wolfhound in question had had a benign lump removed from his hind leg two weeks ago because it kept getting bumped against things and causing him discomfort. He wasn't a rambunctious dog, and he'd been a perfectly well-mannered patient thus far, so Cohen felt bad that the dog was back in the clinic once again. Especially if he had to resort to making the dog wear a plastic cone once more to keep him away from the incision.

'I'll check on him first,' Cohen advised. 'It shouldn't take long. Then, Viola is in the other room for vaccinations?'

Rhonda nodded. 'The Richardsons are heading to Canada next

week and will need signed proof of vaccines as well in order to cross the border.'

'You got it.' Cohen made a note on the Post-it notepad he always carried in his scrub shirt pocket. 'Anything else?'

'Then, you can tell me what's happening between you and the baker girl so I don't have to keep hearing everything from two miles down the gossip chain.' Rhonda stood, hands on her hips, glaring at Cohen like he'd done something wrong by keeping his private life ... well, private.

He resisted the urge to roll his eyes. Rhonda knew him well. Well enough to know he wasn't one to partake in the gossip, or one to converse about his own life save for the goings-on of Bryce and his amusing antics. Besides, on the subject of Paige, Rhonda knew all there was to know. She had been standing there two days ago when he had ended things with Paige so unfairly. Because of that, he found it a little unfair that she was asking for more. It was like pouring salt in a wound. 'There's nothing to tell, Rhonda.'

'You're telling me that—'

'Dr Cohen!'

Both Rhonda and Cohen whirled around at the sound of his name being shouted from the waiting room. Sonya Ritter came ambling toward the opened door of the pharmacy. He really had to do something about the view into the pharmacy from the front door.

'Sonya, is everything all right?' She didn't look perturbed to him, but with Sonya it was never safe to assume.

'How's the good doctor today?' Sonya brightened as soon as he gave her his undivided attention. She held a sealed envelope in her hands, but made no movement to hand it over just yet.

'Busy, but doing well,' he replied. His smile probably looked as false as it felt, but he couldn't guess what might come out of the woman's mouth next and he had clients seated in the waiting room. An audience, just what Sonya loved. 'What brings you by?'

She finally held the envelope out in front of her. 'I swung by The Cakery on the way into the coffeehouse, but Paige hasn't opened up yet. Which is odd.' She paused, as though waiting for him to give her an explanation. When he only raised his eyebrows, she continued. 'Anyway, I wanted to drop this off to her, but perhaps you can give it to her?' She held out the envelope.

Cohen could see the word *Fundraiser* scrawled across it in Sonya's elegant handwriting. His eyes narrowed, curiosity piqued, but he just shook his head. 'You might be better to wait until Paige opens the shop up. It's for the fundraiser?' He couldn't help himself. Cohen thought that had all been dealt with already.

'It's the fifty dollars I borrowed from the fundraiser money to cover the float for the coffee we were selling at the coffeehouse. All the proceeds went to Helen's rebuilding fund. I plum forgot to return it before the fundraiser was over.'

Sonya looked just as curious now, having sensed a morsel of contention in the words he obviously hadn't chosen carefully enough. Cohen, however, was staring at the plain envelope like it might burst into flames at any moment.

The missing fifty dollars from the fundraiser. The missing money he had immediately and unfairly accused Paige of blaming Bryce of taking.

Sonya had been the unwitting culprit all along.

First, he found out Paige had been correct in her assumptions about Bryce and Hunter, and now he found out he'd lashed out at her over the missing fundraiser cash unfairly. Well, he already knew he had been unfair about that, but still. Today was turning out to be a hard pill to swallow.

'Thanks, Sonya.' He took the envelope, shoulders sagging under the weight of his grim mood. 'I have to head over there later on, so I'll give it to Paige then.'

That made the older woman's eyes twinkle. 'Glad to hear it, Dr Cohen.'

How did she manage to make such a mundane reply sound

so scandalous? He didn't dare to ask her. 'I should get back to work,' he said, hoping to put an end to the social interactions that were becoming harder and harder to keep on solid ground. Talking to Sonya was like talking to a rattlesnake. You never knew when she was going to strike with the venomous statement that rendered one speechless and left you rethinking everything you'd said and done.

'You got a second for a harmless old biddy?' She paired the innocent request with a soft smile, but Cohen knew better. Under it was the sharpness in her gaze and the firmness in her tone. She wasn't asking. The rattlesnake was about to strike.

'Sonya, I really don't—'

She pinned him with a glare that had him leading her toward the closest examination room, shutting the door behind them. Whatever she had to say, it didn't need to fall on straining ears.

'I have work to do,' Cohen reminded her as the door clicked closed.

'Sounds like it.' She didn't blink. Didn't even bother to try to hide the gravity she felt the situation warranted.

Sonya wasn't talking about his clinic appointments.

Raking his hands through his hair, Cohen all but growled under his breath. 'I can't handle your cryptic affirmations today, Sonya. You're going to have to either spit it out or save the conversation for another day.' He hoped like hell she chose the latter, but again, it was Sonya, and he knew better. Either way, he was out of patience and his day had barely begun.

The older woman's eyebrows raised. 'Must be your charm that Paige loves about you so much.'

Cohen knew sarcasm when he heard it. It didn't make hearing *Paige* and *love* in the same sentence any easier, though. 'Sonya ...'

'She does love you, you know.' Gone was the sarcasm, replaced by a soft and unwavering sincerity he rarely heard in the woman's voice. Sonya was damn good at being the loud and feisty spitfire who stuck to her guns like what she was preaching was the gospel truth. But that boisterous quality was absent now. 'And you love her, too.'

This side of her was frightening in a whole different way. He swore she was peeking into his soul. Reading his thoughts. 'I made a mistake,' he confessed. Damn it, she really was doing some of her lovey-dovey voodoo crap on him, coercing confessions from him without lifting a finger. 'Multiple ones. Too damn many.'

'Cohen,' she began, and the way she addressed him made a lump lodge at the base of his throat. Sonya never referred to him as anything but Dr Cohen. It was the community's nickname for him, as unoriginal as it was. 'You forget, I stood beside you eight years ago and watched you lose the woman you loved. The woman who loved you back just as deeply.'

The mention of Stacey only tightened his throat further. 'I haven't forgotten.'

A sad smile flickered at the corners of Sonya's lips. 'Stacey Beckett was a good woman. A beautiful person, inside and out. And she loved you.'

'I know.' He could barely choke out the words through his emotions.

'She loved you,' she repeated. 'Flaws and all.' Her smile widened, though her tone remained gentle, as though dealing with a skittish animal. 'If Paige Henley is half the woman I think she is – half the woman you *know* she is – she does, too.'

Cohen's chest ached with his need to believe the woman was right. He reached out to press his hand against the wall for support, his legs weak with the emotional upheaval. 'Sonya, you don't understand,' he all but whispered.

'Make me understand, then.' Her gaze pleaded with him, holding him in place without so much as a single touch. 'Is this because you're comparing her to Stacey?'

'I'm not comparing her to Stacey.' He spoke in a rush. There wasn't much Cohen could be certain of at the moment, but he knew damn well he'd never once compared the two women to each other. Not once. No one could compare to Stacey, not in his mind. And he certainly could never, and would never, try to replace her with someone else.

'Didn't think so.'

'What?' Good God, was she just playing games? He didn't have time for this. 'What are you getting at, Sonya? Please, get to the point.'

The woman crossed her arms, steeling herself against his foul mood. 'I agree with you,' she continued. 'I don't think you're comparing her to Stacey, Cohen. But I do think you're comparing her to your memory of her.' She stopped, holding up her hands. 'Maybe comparing is the wrong word. More like, you're putting Stacey on a pedestal no one else is ever going to be able to reach.'

Cohen gave up, shaking his head. 'You're wrong, Sonya.'

'Stacey was flawed,' Sonya continued, her gaze never wavering. 'Just like you, and just like me. We've all got flaws, Dr Cohen. Paige is no different.' Her eyes narrowed. 'Or Bryce, for that matter.'

He went still. Did Sonya know about the allegations toward Bryce? He didn't think she did. Until that moment, at least. But it would make sense, since Paige could have confided in Allison, and then Allison could have possibly mentioned it to Sonya at the coffeehouse. Or Sonya was just doing that creepy know-it-all stuff she always seemed to do at the most inopportune times. He figured there was probably a better chance of that than a line of gossip that began with Paige and Allison. 'I know, Sonya.'

'Then do me a favor and sort out whatever is making your heart ache so bad with regard to our resident baker, will you? Because the last thing I want to do is stand by and watch you lose the woman you love all over again.'

Her choice of words, coming from a woman who had been a friend and unwavering support to him through the hardest and worst days of his life – they hit Cohen in the chest with the weight of a sledgehammer. He couldn't speak. Couldn't think about anything except Sonya's statement. It crushed his soul and broke his battered heart all over again, but there was a sliver of light that those words had managed to let in, too.

'There's nothing you could have done to save Stacey,' Sonya continued softly. 'And nothing you could have done to save yourself from the grief you endured by her loss. But Cohen …' She reached out for his hand, grasping it tightly between her own, the thin skin and gnarled knuckles a stark contrast to the large size and strength of his own. 'You can save yourself from losing Paige. And save her from losing you.'

She gave his hand one last tight squeeze and left without another word about it.

Rhonda's eyes were firmly fixed on him once he made his way back into the pharmacy. However, he knew by the expression she wore that the storm of turmoil he'd just undergone with Sonya hadn't yet passed.

'Is something wrong?' he asked.

'Paige Henley,' she said after he closed the door between the pharmacy and the waiting room.

Cohen stifled a groan. Rhonda didn't have to remind him twice.

'You're lucky Sonya hasn't heard about your little spat with her yet. If she already had, she would have flown in here on her broom and turned you into a frog.'

The comparison of Sonya to the Wicked Witch of the West was amusing to him, but Cohen didn't laugh. Rhonda's mention of the argument she'd witnessed put him on edge. While he wasn't entirely convinced Sonya didn't already know about what he'd said to Paige, Rhonda was right. The conversation he'd just had with the older woman could have gone worse. A lot worse. 'I've got enough to worry about without adding Sonya Ritter's nosiness into the mix, Rhonda.' It was the best he could come up with in order to keep Rhonda from knowing all the gut-wrenching things Sonya had laid out on the line for him.

'You're telling me.'

'What's that supposed to mean?' He snapped out the words harsher than he meant to, but he had a full day ahead of him, and a lot of things on his mind. His emotions were running high, simmering just below the surface. If Rhonda felt the need to press him about this, she was bound to be the one he would take it all out on next if he wasn't careful.

'You told Sonya you were going to see Paige tonight.' Rhonda's hands landed on her hips, waiting.

'I will,' he replied. 'I mean, I'm going to.'

'Does she know that?' Rhonda asked. 'Paige, I mean? Have you even talked to her since you acted like a jerk?'

Leave it to Rhonda to put him in his place. He might have been her boss, but Cohen also knew her summation of the events was pretty accurate. 'I haven't,' he said evenly. 'But I will tonight. What are you getting at, Rhonda? You don't think I should?' He was getting fed up with the common practice of talking in riddles that seemed to be going on around him today. 'Just tell me. Please.' He added the last word as an afterthought.

Rhonda bit down on her bottom lip. Cohen didn't know if she was trying to hold something back or simply debating what to say next. 'What I think is irrelevant, boss. But I'd say you should've tried to talk to her before now.' She paused. 'Mostly because I heard she's leaving.'

'Leaving?' Cohen felt like the room was void of oxygen. 'What are you talking about?'

He had never seen Rhonda at a loss for words, but her mouth opened and closed a few times before she spoke. 'Randall Conlin came in this morning. Blatantly asked about Paige and her bakery. Made some comment about her not lasting very long 'round these parts. It seems the coffee drinkers at the diner were talking about only one thing this morning. That Paige is closing up her shop and moving back to New York. I don't know how they know that, or if it's just good old speculation on their part. But Sonya just said the bakery isn't open yet this morning, and that's not like Paige. You know that. So, it sounds to me like there's some truth to it, Dr Cohen.'

He wanted to tell her she was wrong. That there was no way Paige would do that. She wouldn't give up everything she'd built for herself here in Port Landon. Not because of an argument. Not because he had been so damn unfair to her and ended things so abruptly.

Then, it hit him. Maybe she would, because of a broken heart. And he'd been the jerk to break it.

If the rumor was true, not only had Cohen broken Paige's heart, but he had ruined all that was good in Paige's eyes about her new home. A place she had fallen in love with. That notion pierced Cohen's own heart just as deeply.

'She wouldn't do that. She wouldn't.' There was no conviction in his voice. Cohen knew what a broken heart could do. He remembered all the times in the first few years after losing Stacey that his unending pain and sadness had driven him to contemplate packing up and leaving Port Landon as well. To start over. To have something and somewhere that didn't remind him of his wife. Of his loss. Of the torture of being without her.

But he'd stayed, and, now, he was glad of it. Which was exactly why he had to make sure Paige stayed, too. Not just because she would be losing everything she had thought she found in their little town, but because he didn't want to lose *her*. He couldn't. Not like this. Sonya was right. He couldn't lose the woman he loved, not when she was in arms' reach of him and he still had a chance to remind her that a lot of good things still remained here. That the town needed her, and loved her.

So did he.

Chapter 25

Paige

Paige flipped the sign on the bakery door to read *Open*, hoping she hadn't missed too many customers in her tardiness. Maybe no one had noticed. Maybe no one had realized the bakery hadn't been open for the past hour. It was after ten o'clock, and ...

Who was she kidding? Paige knew someone would have noticed. Probably multiple someones. This was Port Landon, after all. Small town extraordinaire. If she didn't know what she was doing, or was supposedly doing, someone would fill her in. She was sure of that.

And that's what she was afraid of. Not because the shop hadn't been opened on time, but because of *why* the shop hadn't been.

It had all seemed so innocent the night before. One simple phone call with Alex Livingston. After the text messages he had sent her since she left his company, she owed him that much. And Paige had expected him to offer up her old job on a silver platter. She'd done her job well in New York City, and she was a go-getter. She was an asset to any design company. Livingston Designs knew that. Alex knew that.

Which was why, over the course of their hour-long phone

245

conversation, Alex went a step further. He sweetened the deal. Not only did he offer her old position back if she wanted it, but he offered higher compensation than she had previously received, increased commissions, and the opportunity to spearhead a bunch of new projects they had on the horizon.

Livingston Designs wanted her back. Alex wanted her back. And they were willing to pay what was needed to achieve that.

At least, that was what Alex Livingston said to her, face to face, this morning when he showed up on her doorstep, ready to prove how serious he was. At eight o'clock, Paige's cellphone rang. She didn't know who in the world would be calling her at that time of day. When she saw Alex's number on the display screen, she'd become even more confused.

He could have knocked her over with a feather when he said that Main Street was nice. Quaint, even. And yes, he was standing outside her storefront, waiting for her to let him in. Baffled, she scurried down the stairs and ushered him in off the sidewalk, unable to comprehend how her New York life had just collided with her new hometown.

Eight hundred miles was nothing when you were the young and powerful Alex Livingston, apparently.

He spent the next hour explaining his stance over the pot of coffee they shared at her kitchen table. After their phone call the night before, he had made the split-second decision to hop on a red-eye flight and offer up his business proposal in person. Dressed in an Armani suit that cost more than half of Paige's entire wardrobe and a red silk tie that knotted tightly and effectively at the base of his throat, Alex was the epitome of professionalism. He pulled files, spreadsheets, and typed documents from his briefcase to outline his plan for Livingston Designs going forward, producing hard, cold facts and numbers to back up his plans, and highlighting exactly how he hoped Paige would play a crucial part in bringing those plans to fruition.

Many times, she had seen Alex's negotiation tactics at work, and every time she was awestruck by his abilities. He was a businessman by trade, but a businessman by heart as well. He lived and breathed the corporate life. Though only a year or two older than Paige herself, she knew there would never come a day when Alex Livingston would walk away from the company his family had built in search of something smaller, quieter, and less New York-like. The family business had built him just as much as the family had built the business.

Alex talked for more than twenty minutes straight, pausing only to sip from his coffee cup. Paige admired his zest for the proposal, but halfway through she was only catching every third or fourth word. This was the first time she'd seen him from this side of the negotiations; as a man with every intention of having his studious preparation awarded with the acceptance of what he was expertly proposing. A man who had every intention of getting what he wanted.

They were similar in age, and similar in vocational background. But that's where it ended. Paige had never viewed her ex-boss as a potential love interest, though she knew Alex's side of things was another story – and Allison's, apparently. It had gone nowhere, mostly due to Paige's explicit rules about mixing her career and personal life together. Despite his chiseled good looks and their comfortable working relationship, there'd never been a spark between them. Not like that.

And the inner romantic in Paige, though submerged and buried deep inside her so as to let her career shine, hoped there was some kind of spark that jumpstarted her heart when it came to real love. Her mother's words echoed in her head, never far from the forefront of her thoughts. *When it comes to love, it's the heart that counts, Paige, not the mind.*

As she listened to him and watched his mannerisms, admiring his clean shaven, handsome face and pale crystal eyes, Paige realized with a bit of a start that she couldn't see herself with someone so devoted to the corporate hustle. Not anymore. She had nothing against Alex and his enthusiasm to become a business mogul, but that wasn't who Paige saw herself with. No, not anymore.

Because that wasn't who she was. Not anymore.

Paige let Alex put forth his entire spiel, not interrupting him until he asked her thoughts about it.

Her head spun, filled to the brim with all the facts and figures and hopes and dreams he'd planted in her brain. 'It's all a bit much to take in, Alex. I'm going to need some time to think about it.' After all, she had a life here now. One that would need to be packed up and moved eight hundred miles if she chose to accept his extravagant offer.

And Paige couldn't think about that. It was too much to process. Besides, she had a bakery to run.

She'd told Alex as much, which quickly ended the impromptu job interview. Thankfully, he had 'a couple of phone calls to make', which was probably the understatement of the year. His phone had beeped a steady string of text alerts along with countless missed phone calls that he had ignored while sitting at her kitchen table. His gaze landed on the phone every time, and she'd seen his fingers twitch, aching to reach for it. A kneejerk reflex. Paige had been a slave to her cellphone once, too. Now, though she carried it with her, she could go more than half the day without even glancing at it.

So much had changed in such little time. Sure, it had only been months since she left New York, but now that life seemed like it was someone else's. She didn't feel like she was the one who'd lived it. Breathed it.

Paige had Port Landon to thank for that. She had the entire community to thank.

She had Cohen Beckett to thank. And right now, she didn't want to thank him for anything. She wanted to walk down to the shoreline, write his name in the sand, and let the water wash away every letter, along with all the hurt and sadness she associated with him.

Paige might have known she could never be with someone like Alex, but look at what she got by finding someone she thought she could. Finding someone who ignited that elusive spark within her.

Heartbreak.

It was the sadness she was feeling that made New York City look so enticing. She could see that now. Alex made it sound like the sun rose and set more beautifully in the cityscape. There were things she missed about the city, sure. She would never say otherwise. But if Paige left Port Landon, she would miss it, too. Terribly. She would miss so many things.

She would miss Cohen.

Paige silently chastised herself. Why did everything have to come back to him? Why was her mind still consumed by him when he had made it perfectly clear she wasn't fit to be a part of his and his son's life? She knew exactly where she stood when it came to him. It was time to make a decision that would help her get past him, the same way his decision had been made to move on without her.

But first, she had a couple loaves of multigrain bread to get in the oven and a batch of death-by-chocolate brownies to whip up. She would feel better once she did that.

Paige had to get her head back in the game. If not for herself, then for her cousin, who was about to get married in only four short days. Paige had a thousand things to do to help with the wedding – the decorating, the organization of the favors, confirming timely delivery of the flowers …

The cake. Being the one to bake and decorate the wedding cake was both a blessing and a curse at this point. Agony had plagued her over the thing. So much so that if Paige ever saw another wedding cake with purple and gray fondant decor again, it would be too soon.

The wedding itself was weighing on her. She blamed that on Cohen Beckett, too. Paige loved weddings, always had. And this was her cousin's wedding. Her cousin, who was also her best friend and most trusted confidante. She should have been over the moon with excitement and practically bursting at the seams to wear the gorgeous gray dress and watch with joyous tears in her eyes as Allison pledged her love and devotion to Christopher.

Instead, she was constantly reminded that her date for the wedding wouldn't be coming. She never should have let Sonya and Allison wrangle poor Cohen into it in the first place.

Poor Cohen. She was doing it again. Feeling bad for all that had happened to him when she was supposed to be letting it go. Letting him go. Moving on. She would have even settled for just being able to pretend the whole thing hadn't happened.

Donning her favorite purple damask apron, Paige threw herself into her work. If she couldn't forget about Cohen, she would work her fingers to the bone and make sure she was so exhausted by the end of the day that she would be too tired to speak his name, let alone contemplate the meaning of life with or without him in it.

Each time a customer came in, she was relieved when they didn't mention she'd been late to open the shop this morning. She was even more relieved that no one asked her who the tall man in the swanky business suit standing outside her apartment had been. She had already made the mistake of mentioning last night's phone call to Allison during her impromptu trip to the coffeehouse before she opened the bakery. Although her cousin would eventually find out all the juicy details, Paige hadn't had it in her to dish on the fact that Alex had flown there to win her over. She would misconstrue it as more than it really was. She could practically hear Allison's over-the-top, mushy comments now. The woman would swoon until she collapsed, thinking the gesture was the most romantic of all romantic gestures. Which it wasn't. That wasn't what this was about. At all.

Paige ran the risk of people hearing only bits and pieces of the story if she spoke about it, so she was better to just keep it to herself. For now, anyway. She didn't need, nor want, others' input on the matter just yet, anyway. All she'd wanted at the time was good coffee, not a chance to feed the gossipers.

The entire bakery smelled wonderfully of fresh baked bread and warm sugar by the time the hours rolled into the afternoon. Paige was starving, but she had been productive and felt better for it. The lunch rush resulted in selling out of all the oversized oatmeal cookies. She was right; they were a hit. Most of the bread and biscuits had flown off the shelves, too. Many residents of Port Landon were going to be indulging in comfort food tonight. She was just pulling the last loaves of whole wheat bread out of the oven in hopes of having something to cover the bare bread shelves with when the bell above the door chimed. She glanced out around the wall, intent on promising she would be with the customer in a minute. She was met with the hazel gaze she hadn't been able to stop thinking about.

'Cohen.' She recovered from her shock, quickly adding, 'Hi.'

'Hey.'

He looked disheveled, to say the least. Paige wagered a guess that his day at the vet clinic had been a trying one. But there was something else hidden amongst the fatigue and stress in his eyes. Sadness. It pulled at her heart strings and messed with her resolve. Setting the bread pans on the stovetop and removing her oven mitts, she headed out to the front counter. 'What brings you by?'

'I, uh ...' He held a stapled stack of papers out for her. 'I brought the interview questions for Bryce's school project. If you still want to do it, I mean.'

She had completely forgotten about Bryce's project. Her answer was out of her mouth before she even realized she was saying it aloud. 'Of course, yes.' Inwardly, she cringed at her own neediness. How unattractive was it to hold on to such a small sliver of a connection between her and the Beckett family like it was a lifeline? 'I mean, unless you want to answer the questions about the clinic instead.'

'I can't,' he replied. 'I filled out Hunter's questionnaire a few days ago.'

'I'm glad to help.' She reached for the sheets of paper.

Cohen stepped forward and held it out, but not before taking her hand between his fingers, sending every nerve ending in her fingertips into a fiery frenzy. 'Paige, I need—'

Paige wasn't sure if she would have heard what he was about to say over the incessant pounding of her own heart. Unfortunately, she didn't get the chance to find out. The front door swung open wide, sending a loud toll of the bell ringing through the air. Alex Livingston sauntered in, his gaze assessing the quaint storefront with a look of thinly veiled amusement.

'So, this is the childhood dream you left me for?' Alex mused.

Paige pulled her hand out of Cohen's grip, thoroughly unprepared to deal with both New York and Port Landon personified in the storefront of her suddenly very cramped bakery. 'Alex, hey. I didn't … expect you back so soon.' It sounded ridiculous as soon as she said it, but the truth was that she didn't know what to expect from him at all. She certainly hadn't expected him to jump on a plane and come all the way there to offer her a dream job in the heart of New York City.

There was no mistaking the way Cohen was looking Alex up and down. He wasn't even trying to hide it. Taking in his pressed suit and shiny shoes, the expensive cellphone in one hand and the leather briefcase he held in the other, Cohen's posture stiffened. Paige watched as his eyes widened, registering Alex's poor choice of words, which Paige realized too late could have easily been misconstrued. Eyes narrowed, Cohen obviously had come to some kind of presumption.

She stifled a groan, fearful of how wrongful that presumption might be.

'I didn't leave you, I left Livingston Designs.' Paige chuckled, trying to pretend it was no big deal. Just a simple joke. Anything to diffuse the awkwardness in the room. Which wasn't working.

At all. 'Alex, this is Cohen. Sorry, Dr Cohen Beckett,' she corrected, meeting Cohen's gaze. 'He's ... a friend of mine. Cohen, I'd like you to meet Alex Livingston, my boss from New York.'

Ex-boss. But she realized her mistake too late, and it was too late to take it back. Alex was running with it, and he was in full sprint, in it for the win.

'We're friends, too,' he said, enunciating the words to give them the full effect of blatant insinuation. He grinned like the Cheshire cat as he held his hand out to Cohen, shaking his hand firmly. 'It's good to meet you, Dr Beckett.'

'Likewise.' The edge in Cohen's voice was sharp as a knife, his knuckles turning white with the pressure he exerted in the hand-shake. There was very obviously nothing good about meeting Alex Livingston as far as he was concerned. His stunned expression only fueled the tangible tension between them.

'Alex, I was ... I mean, I ...' She couldn't get the words out, sputtering as she tried to explain. Explain what, exactly? She didn't need to explain a thing to Cohen concerning Alex's presence. And she surely didn't need to explain to Alex that while, yes, they were friends, the obnoxious way he'd said it was very much on purpose. Goading Cohen.

Ugh, men.

Both men were going to do what they wanted, and think what they wanted. Paige was through with putting everyone else first all the time.

'I should go, Paige.' Alex pulled his hand away from Cohen, leveling his gaze on her. 'Meet me for dinner, though? Before I head back to New York later tonight? We've still got so much to discuss.'

Paige's head was swimming with so many flustered thoughts. All she could do was nod. Anything to get him and his fancy suit out of there. 'Yes, of course. Call me in a bit and we'll arrange something.'

'I'll text you. See you tonight.' He flashed her a smug smile, then nodded toward Cohen, who still stood there with a flabbergasted expression plastering his face. 'Again, nice to meet you, Dr Beckett.' Alex left the bakery as quickly as he'd come, his wry grin never once faltering as he closed the door behind him. The bell chimed loudly, shrill as a siren in the deafening silence that ensued.

If she hadn't been so completely bowled over by the absurdity of it all, Paige would have laughed out loud. But there was nothing funny about the hazel eyes that stared back at her, and there was nothing funny about the desire that coursed through her veins to run into his arms and beg him to ask her to stay.

It was on the tip of her tongue to explain. To tell him everything Alex had offered. But she didn't trust herself to start talking, knowing too well that more words would come out. Things she couldn't let herself say aloud. Knees weak, Paige felt powerless against her own swirling emotions. There was no way she could contend with his right now.

'I should get back to work,' she said, taking a step back.

Cohen's eyes never wavered, fixed on her. Watching. Waiting. 'Yeah, me too.'

Heat crept up into Paige's cheeks. She felt too much, too strongly. She couldn't do this. Cohen had made his decision, and she had to abide by it. 'I'll get this questionnaire filled out for Bryce and email it to the clinic for you to give to him. Thanks for dropping it off.'

Whatever Cohen expected from her, it wasn't that. He seemed confused. Blindsided, even. 'Sounds perfect.'

She nodded as she backed away from him, rounding the front counter to put distance between them. She let the uncomfortable silence hang between them after that, not trusting herself to say anything more until she saw him retreat toward the doorway.

'Cohen?'

He turned, hand resting on the door handle. Hope swarmed his eyes, and it caused a painful twisting in Paige's stomach knowing she'd given him that thread to hold on to with only a single word.

'It was good to see you,' she said. Then, she disappeared back behind the dividing wall and hid there, back up against the cool drywall, until she heard the bell chime as Cohen left, walking out of her life. This time, for good.

Chapter 26

Cohen

It was good to see you. Paige's words reverberated through his mind, overtaking his brain and wiggling into his subconscious. The way she said it had seemed so … final.

He knew then that he'd lost her, although the obnoxious bigwig in the expensive suit should have been his first clue. That guy's haircut probably cost more than Cohen had paid for his lifetime of haircuts combined.

We're friends, too. Those few words had kept making their way into his mind as well, etching themselves into his thoughts and making him crazy. Alex Livingston had been enjoying himself, there was no denying that. He'd known he had the ability to entice Paige into leaving. To steal her away from him.

Except, Paige had never been Cohen's to steal in the first place, and he had given her every reason to want to be persuaded to walk away from Port Landon and never look back. Hell, he may as well have packed up her vehicle for her and filled the tank with gas.

In his haste, Cohen had forgotten all about the envelope of fundraiser money he'd said he would deliver. Thankfully, he did remember Bryce's school project questionnaire. It was a flimsy excuse, but good enough to get him in the door. Cohen could have filled it out himself if he'd been intent on keeping his distance from Paige. But distance was the last thing he wanted. He knew he needed to fix this. He needed to stop Paige from running back to New York.

And from taking his heart with her.

That's why he'd gone into the bakery in the first place. Not to hand over Bryce's assignment, but to apologize to Paige, once and for all, and to confess to her that he wanted a chance to make things right. He wanted to tell her he loved her, like he'd planned to that night before the fundraiser.

Somehow, that night seemed like a lifetime ago.

Even with the knowledge of what Rhonda had told him this morning, though, Cohen never expected to come face to face with his worst nightmare. Not only was it true that Paige was negotiating her move back across the country, but she and her old boss were friends – whatever *that* meant – and he was here in Port Landon, riding in like a white knight on his trusty Armani steed, ready to convince her to go back with him.

And they were having dinner. Tonight. He was some corporate tycoon that had everything to offer a beautiful woman like Paige. Not just a career, but a life with all the glitz and glamor she could ever want.

Cohen couldn't compete with that. Hell, he'd had an Italian eatery from ten miles away cater their meal in to a closed ice cream shop. That was his wholehearted attempt at a first date. Weak when compared to Alex Livingston's likely extravagant ideas.

Cohen was far from a man capable of glitz and glamor. Besides, he'd hurt her enough already that it didn't matter what he had to offer. She was through with him, and she was moving on without him.

And it looked like Alex Livingston was all too eager to help her do that, smirking the whole way.

The four days preceding Allison Kent's wedding went by in a busy blur. Cohen made sure of it. Whether it was an extra appointment tacked on to his workday, or an impromptu outing with Bryce to the Hansel and Gretel House, or to North Springs to see the newest Marvel movie, he was bound and determined to fill his days with something, anything, to keep his mind just as occupied as his body. He needed to keep his thoughts free of Paige Henley. He needed to give her what she wanted. And that didn't include him.

The cardstock invitation with calligraphy and sunflowers on it was still tacked to his refrigerator. Cohen felt a pang of guilt knowing he had RSVP'd to attend the reception, and knowing there would be one less person in attendance. He had always been a man of his word. The idea of not following through on something made his thoughts restless and his pride ache.

But the idea of actually going to the wedding reception, especially with the possibility of seeing Paige there on the arm of someone else … well, that was almost too much to bear. Still, he couldn't bring himself to toss the invitation away, and every time he passed by the fridge, he caught it in his peripheral vision like a beacon in the night. He couldn't not see it, and he couldn't look away once he'd turned to stare at it.

He noticed that Bryce arched an eyebrow at the invitation each time he passed it, too. The boy never said a word about it, just looked at it with a questioning glance, turned to see if his father would say anything in response, then looked away. The invitation was the big ole' pink elephant in the room, and they didn't speak of it.

But Bryce broke his silence on the morning of the wedding. Still donning his Ninja Turtles pajama pants with a hooded sweatshirt tossed over his shoulders, he stopped at the refrigerator, scrutinizing the invitation with renewed interest. Cohen sat at the kitchen table, coffee cup in hand, watching his son out of the corner of his eye.

Bryce stood there, quiet, long enough to read each word on the card at least twice.

'Allison's wedding is today, Dad.' The expression he wore when he turned to face his father gave nothing away.

Cohen set his mug down. 'It is. I'm on call, but we could head into North Springs and check out that new arcade downtown.' It was better to lead with the arcade offer – that would get Bryce off the topic of the wedding faster.

The boy seemed to be having an internal struggle about something, his lips pursed and his jaw tight. 'Raincheck?'

Cohen hadn't seen that coming. Either the boy had grown out of the video game phase overnight, or …

He had something else planned. Immediately, Cohen's eyes narrowed. 'You bet,' he said. 'But, I must admit, I'm a bit surprised by that. So, you're going to have to tell me why we can't go today.'

It might have been Cohen's imagination, but he thought his son's face paled slightly. 'Because … you have to go to Allison's wedding.'

The poor kid was growing up way too fast. 'Bryce, I'm not going. It's fine—'

'And you're not on call,' he blurted out in one rushed breath. Bryce's eyes widened, waiting for … what?

Cohen was on high alert now. He was always on call. There was no one else to be on call for him, and Bryce knew that. 'Of course I am. Bryce, why wouldn't I be?'

'Because Dr Alton is going to be instead.' It was full-blown fear in his son's eyes now, but he continued. 'I called him.'

That didn't even make sense to Cohen. Bryce didn't know James Alton well enough to call him, and he certainly didn't have the elderly veterinarian on speed dial. 'What are you talking about?'

Bryce sighed, his shoulders sagging. 'You had his phone number in that address book you keep by the computer at the clinic. Rhonda helped me get—'

259

'Rhonda.' Cohen groaned. He should have known. If there was something going on behind his back – and there obviously was – then he should have known Rhonda would be involved in it.

'Yeah,' Bryce continued. 'I told her I needed to find Dr Alton—'

'Why?' Cohen blurted, panic rising in his throat.

'I'm trying to tell you.' The roles had reversed once again, and Bryce looked exasperated by his father's continuous interruptions. 'I got his number from the address book and I called him. I said you needed to go to a wedding, and you needed somebody to cover for you.'

'You didn't.' This was getting worse by the minute.

'Yeah, I did.' Bryce puffed his chest out. 'Now, you can go to the wedding with Paige.'

His ten-year-old son had gone behind his back and planned a date night for him and Paige. To rekindle the relationship he thought he'd torn apart, no doubt. It would have been heart-warming if it wasn't so unbelievably sad.

'Bryce, I don't think Paige and I are going to see much of each other anymore.' He spoke carefully. 'She's not expecting me to show up at the wedding today.'

'That's an even better reason to go!' Bryce exclaimed, his hands waving wildly. 'You can surprise her. If you say you're sorry, then she'll forgive you. I know she will.'

Oh, to be an adolescent boy again. Cohen wished it was as easy as apologizing. And he wished a mere apology held the weight it did on the playground at ten years old. 'That's not really how it works, son,' he said. 'I know you're trying to help, and I appreciate that. I do. But I don't think this is going to work out the way we want it to.'

Bryce pointed to his father like he'd just caught him in a blatant lie. 'You just said *we*.'

'Bryce …'

'Just go talk to her, Dad!' The boy pointed emphatically at the invitation on the fridge. 'You've got an invitation to do it and everything. Nothing's going to change if you don't say you're sorry.'

He had to give his son props – his pep talk execution was on point. And he was right, which was difficult to admit. 'When did you become the teacher, little grasshopper?'

'I'm just saying stuff you'd say,' Bryce said with a wink. 'And you always say to think positive and try my hardest. Take your own advice, old man.'

Cohen laughed. Sometimes, his kid was just too much. 'Did you really call James Alton?'

His son nodded. 'Sure did. He'll be here by lunchtime.'

The wedding ceremony was scheduled for three o'clock, with the dinner following at four-thirty and the reception starting at seven. If what Bryce said was true, then he would have time to brief Dr Alton on the ongoing cases he might hear from, explain that he knew absolutely nothing about his son's meddling plans, and still be ready for the wedding reception with time to spare.

Was he really going to do this? His son had intervened, for crying out loud. Given him one last chance to tell Paige how he truly felt. Could he get through to her before she was gone from his life forever?

Something swelled in his chest, making him feel like he couldn't quite get in enough air.

Bryce was right. He had to think positive and try.

'Is this just your way of trying to get your grounding sentence shortened?' Cohen quipped, arching an eyebrow.

Bryce waved a hand. 'Nah. I'm just saying sorry, and trying to help.' He paused. '*Did* I just get my grounding sentence shortened?'

'We'll talk when I get back from this wedding.'

'You're going?' Bryce fist pumped the air. 'Yes!'

'Like you really gave me a choice.' Cohen stood, pushing his coffee cup away. He stepped forward, pulling his son in for a tight hug. 'Thank you, Bryce.'

261

Bryce hugged him back, squeezing him dramatically. 'I did it for both of us, Dad.'

'You really do like her, too, huh?'

His son nodded against his chest. 'Yeah. So, a guy's gotta do what a guy's gotta do.'

Cohen pulled away to give his son a weathered look. 'Tell me that's not what you told Dr Alton.'

Bryce shrugged, stepping back. 'Nope. I told him you were going to the wedding to make up with the woman you love. And I told him she makes the best chocolate cake in the whole world.'

Yeah, it was official. His son really was too much.

Dr James Alton was all too eager to be a part of the romantic scheme to aid Cohen in confessing his love to the woman Bryce had told him about. A romantic scheme, that's what he'd called it when he arrived. Looking similar to a silver-haired Albert Einstein, with a fancy for buoyant colors and busy patterns on his button-up shirts, the elderly doctor shone with the energy of a man half his age. His bright blue eyes twinkled, watching Bryce usher Cohen toward the back door of the clinic.

'You're going to be late.' Bryce had exclaimed it numerous times while his father unnecessarily walked Dr Alton through a handful of patient files he probably wouldn't need and a recap of how to use the computer system he probably wouldn't boot up. Cohen was stalling. He knew it. But he struggled with handing over the business he'd singlehandedly maintained for over eight years, even if those reins were given to the man who had taught him everything he knew.

But if Bryce could see through his time-wasting tactics, that meant James could as well, and Cohen didn't want his own insecurities to be mistaken for the belief that his mentor couldn't handle the clinic for an evening.

'Thank you for this,' he said to the older man. He meant every word. Cohen might never have had it in him to make that call and ask him for help, but he was more grateful to Bryce than he could ever explain. Bryce knew him too well, and he'd known Cohen would make flimsy excuses to avoid having to face Paige again. The boy had done the only thing he could – he removed the excuses from the equation. That, to Cohen, showed more courage and selflessness than he thought a ten-year-old should possess. It only made Cohen prouder.

'Don't mention it, Cohen.' Dr Alton beamed, making hand motions to shoo him toward the back door. 'Jazz, Bryce, and I have got this. You just get yourself to that wedding on time.' God, he made it sound like it was his wedding he was going to be late for. 'Go on, now.' Jazz bounced excitedly at the older veterinarian's feet, thrilled with a new audience to show off to.

'I'll do what I can,' Cohen promised.

'Oh, and Cohen?'

He turned around to face James Alton again. 'Yeah?'

'When you make up with your lady friend, I'll gladly be paid for my time in chocolate cake.'

Bryce laughed the whole way home, bouncing through the path between the clinic and the house like an adolescent on a sugar rush. 'Dad, do you even own a suit?'

He playfully pushed the boy in through the door of the house and up the stairs into the master bedroom. 'You really have no faith in my abilities to handle this, whatsoever, do you?' Wryly, he tossed the closet doors open and pushed the hangers aside to reveal a few garment bags hidden in the back of the closet.

'You can use all the help you can get.' Bryce shrugged but there was a glint in his eyes when he said it. 'You've got a tie?'

'Yes, I own a tie,' he replied, feigning disbelief that his son would even need to ask. 'A few, actually.' He pointed to the top drawer of his dresser, where Bryce set to work laying each one out on the bed.

'Which one are you going to wear?'

Cohen stared at the selection after unzipping the garment bag in his hand to reveal a simple black suit. It wasn't fancy, or expensive like the one Alex Livingston wore, but it was all he had to work with. 'The purple one, with the silver pinstripes.' He thought back to the day Paige had shown him the wedding cake, and he was sure she'd said Allison's chosen colors were purple and gray.

His quick response obviously piqued Bryce's interest. 'Does that match what Paige is wearing or something?'

'It might.'

'Good job, Dad.' His son held his hand up for a high-five. 'Attention to detail – I like it.'

'Impressive, huh?' He grinned. A moment later, his smile faltered. 'But maybe I'd better go without a tie.'

'Why?' Bryce's forehead crinkled in confusion.

He couldn't bring himself to admit that he hadn't had a need to wear a suit since the boy's mother was alive. Stacey had also been the one to tie his ties for him, and there had been no reason to learn how to do it himself before now. 'I'm not very good at tying them up,' he said instead. 'I'll just go without.'

Bryce seemed to mull his explanation over, then pointed to the en-suite bathroom. 'Go get dressed. I'll be right back.' The boy bounded down the staircase without another word.

Cohen obeyed him, changing into the suit. He was relieved it still fit him well after all the years that had passed. He vowed to update his formal wardrobe once this night was over. He stepped out of the bathroom and took in his reflection in the floor-length mirror behind the bedroom door. The man who stared back at him looked confident and prepared to handle whatever the night threw at him.

Cohen hoped he could pretend to be that man long enough to confess his feelings to Paige.

Bryce clambered up the stairs sounding like a herd of elephants, bursting into the room with his tablet in his hand. He stopped, staring at his father. 'You look weird in a suit.'

'Weird?' That wasn't a good sign. It was a white dress shirt and a black suit. How bad could it be? 'Good weird or bad weird?'

'Just … weird.' He assessed him quizzically. 'You don't look like a veterinarian. You look like one of those guys on the shoot 'em up movies that pretend to be waiters at a fancy restaurant, but really they've got guns in their ankle holster, ready to take down the mafia guys at any second.'

He was saying he looked like an undercover agent? 'First of all, I don't know if that's a good thing or a bad thing,' he said. 'And second, how do you know about shoot 'em up movies with mafia guys?' He certainly hadn't been watching those kinds of movies in Cohen's presence.

'Dad, this isn't about me, it's about you.' Bryce waved his hands, dismissing his question. 'Just get over here so I can fix your tie.'

Intrigued, Cohen sat on the bed in front of his son and let him wrap the tie around his neck. It took two tries, but when Bryce stepped back to assess his handiwork, he looked satisfied.

'There.' He motioned toward the mirror. 'I think that's how it's supposed to look, right?'

Cohen stood and crossed the room to the mirror again. The knot at the base of his throat was perfectly aligned and expertly tied. 'How in the world do you know how to do that?'

Bryce held up his tablet, shrugging again. 'YouTube.'

Well, I'll be damned. 'You never cease to amaze me, son.'

Bryce made a show of pretending to polish his knuckles on his chest. 'Glad to help, Dad.'

He reminded himself that he wouldn't even be doing this if it wasn't for Bryce. He wouldn't have been brave enough on his own. 'Thank you,' Cohen told him. 'No matter what happens, thank you for helping your ol' dad summon up the strength to try.'

Bryce stretched his arm out and plucked the smooth, sand-colored stone from on top of the dresser, holding it out to Cohen. 'Just gotta stay positive, right?' The boy knew who had given him the stone, and he knew his father had carried it with him daily for many years. When Cohen didn't immediately take it from between his fingers, Bryce leaned forward and dropped it into the front pocket of his suit jacket. 'You love Paige, right?'

The sincerity in his son's voice made Cohen's chest constrict. It also compelled him to be completely honest with him. 'I do, Bryce.'

'Good. Now, since you finally admitted it out loud to me, how about you go admit it to her?' Bryce reached out and made sure the knot in Cohen's tie was straight, then stepped back. He motioned toward the bedroom door. 'Go get 'er, Dad!'

Chapter 27

Paige

Paige remembered why she loved weddings so much. From the moment she woke up to the sound of her alarm – that's right, even the screech of the alarm couldn't curb her heady anticipation – and took those first sips of hot coffee as she bustled around to get ready for her breakfast with Allison and Kait before their hair appointments at ten o'clock, she had visions of silk and satin and fairytale flowers mixed with vows of love and adoration, and happy memories they would all cherish when they looked back on this day.

Today was Allison's day, a day she'd dreamed of since she was a little girl. And Paige promised herself that she would do everything in her power to make sure it was exactly the perfect day her cousin had wished for.

Not that she'd had to ward off any negative energy or diffuse any chaotic situations. The hair appointment was just as carefree and buoyant as Allison's mood. The bride was enjoying every moment of her big day as it came, and even though Paige, always the worrier in their lifelong duo, kept an eye out for things that could quickly go sideways, the schedule of events went off without a hitch.

The photographer, a woman named Sasha from Detroit that Allison had met at one of the entrepreneurial conventions she'd attended before officially taking over ownership of the coffee-house, floated along as though on the breeze, always a stone's throw away and ready to capture a candid moment, yet she wasn't overbearing. There were times when Paige didn't even know she was there.

Everything fit perfectly. Paige and Kait both oohed and ahhed at each other as they emerged from their respective makeshift dressing rooms in Allison's house, completely enamored by the classy charcoal gray color Allison had ordered the dresses in.

Paige had expected nothing of this day, and yet she expected everything at the same time. It was important to her that her cousin's wedding would be perfect. Probably just as important to her as it was to Allison herself. But there wasn't a thing she would have done differently, and Allison repeatedly said the same thing throughout the course of the festivities.

With her hair done up in loose curls piled on top of her head, and her makeup done by Kait – although it looked like it had been done professionally by a makeup artist – Paige felt like a movie star. Add in the gorgeous dress that complemented the subtle makeup highlighting her eyes, and the reflection that stared back at her in the mirror looked like someone else. Paige didn't just look like a movie star, she felt like a princess.

That was nothing, however, to the way she felt the moment Allison walked out from behind the door of her en-suite bathroom in her wedding dress. Allison looked nothing short of Cinderella. Scratch that. Cinderella had nothing on her. She was something out of every little girl's fairytale wedding. Even after the ten thousand dresses they had sifted through in order to find it, Paige knew without a doubt that the delicate lace dress Allison wore now was the perfect one. Christopher was going to be shocked when he saw his beautiful bride-to-be at the other end of the aisle. Allison was a hard worker, always had been. Rarely did she take the time out of her busy schedule to do more than toss her auburn hair up into a ponytail and slip on one of the coffeehouse T-shirts with a pair of jeans. Her style was simple, and it reflected Allison's content personality and way of life. No nonsense, no fuss.

But today was a different day, a special day, and Allison Kent looked like she just stepped out of a bridal magazine. Paige had to blot away the tears that brimmed her eyelids, fearing they would ruin her mascara, so joyous to see her cousin finally looking like the princess she had always dreamed about being on her wedding day.

Paige made a mental note to remind Christopher just how lucky he was to have Allison. Something told her, however, that he already knew.

Even though she had helped with decorating the church and community hall, Paige was still completely blown away by how much some tulle, ribbon, and garden lights could transform such a previously bland space. The church was minimally decorated, with only a few white candles with purple and gray ribbons sitting on the guestbook table, and little bursts of tied gray ribbon with purple lilies as well as pale blue, pink, and white forget-me-nots decorating the end of each pew. A dark purple runner lay up the middle of the pews, accenting the aisle. But the community hall where the reception would take place – there was nothing drab about it now. Little strings of white lights twinkled amidst carefully twisted ribbons and lace, with a mix of similar lilies and delicate forget-me-nots overflowing from crystal vases in the center of each round table, each covered by crisp white tablecloths. Eight chairs surrounded each table, each one boasting white and gray ribbon and lace decorations that Allison, Paige, and Kait had spent two nights prior putting together by hand.

She had never been so relieved to know the community hall

was just up the street from the white steepled church on Lansing Crescent. In true Paige fashion, she had checked and rechecked the decorations, the flowers, and the food as it arrived. The night before she had made the same trek across town to confirm things were in order, not wanting Allison to have to do it herself when she was busy spending time with her parents who'd just arrived in town the night before. The morning of the wedding, though, she walked back and forth between the hall and the church numerous times in her long satin dress, practically wearing a path into the sidewalk with each anxious step.

But everyone involved was just as determined to pull today's fairytale event off without a hitch. The flowers that arrived from the florist in North Springs were on time and absolutely perfect. The woman delivering them even offered to help set the centerpieces up where they needed to be. The catered meal from the Mirage, the restaurant Christopher had taken Allison to on their first date, showed up with time to spare. The cooks said they only needed to know when the ceremony would be over and when the dinner would commence – they would do the rest.

Paige knew she was flustering herself over the little things more than she had to. She was the maid of honor, sure, but the people who'd been paid and delegated to aid in the different parts of the dinner and reception were more than capable of handling it. She only had to concentrate on two things – making sure Allison was happy, and the wedding cake.

That wasn't enough to keep Cohen's absence far from her conscious mind, though. Knowing he wouldn't be a part of this special day, after all the weeks of anticipating it, made her sad. Sad for him, because she knew he would have enjoyed himself. Sad for Allison and Christopher, because they'd invited him, and Allison had been so excited to have him join in on the fun and festivities. And sad for herself, because, even after everything, she still wanted him there.

270

A few nights ago, Allison had cautiously suggested that maybe she could ask Alex to stay in town one more night and attend the wedding with her. Paige had quickly quashed that idea. For one, she didn't want to give Alex – or the other wedding attendees, for that matter – the wrong idea about her intentions when it came to him and his lavish business proposals. Mostly because Paige knew now, without a doubt, that Alex's proposal wasn't all about business. His cocky innuendos in front of Cohen at the bakery had been the final straw for her. And when she had called him on it, Alex had simply laughed.

'Couldn't help myself, I guess. The man was clearly sizing me up, ready to stake his claim or something.' Alex had sounded almost disgusted by the idea.

'So, you thought you would pretend you'd already done it?' It was a bold statement, coming from Paige. Especially with the proposed career plans on the line.

'Paige, really, it was no big deal.'

'It was to me,' she'd insisted, put off by his simple shrug. 'You made Cohen think something that wasn't true. Something that hurt him even more than he was already hurting.'

Alex jerked his head back, letting out a hoarse scoff. 'You're making more out of this than there is, Paige. Besides, did you explain to him that there was nothing going on between us?'

Her cheeks had burned so hot then, Paige thought she was going to ignite from the shame she felt. She hadn't set the record straight. That was her mistake, one she had to live with. 'I didn't,' she'd stated matter-of-factly, 'But that doesn't mean I'm not going to. It's on my list of things to do, Alex. After you leave. Without me.' She had lots of mistakes she had to live with, but this didn't have to be one of them.

She may as well have slapped him, judging by the shock on his face. 'You can't be serious,' he'd said. 'Paige, there's nothing here for you in this town.'

'You're wrong.' The words had slipped off her tongue, surprising

Paige with her own vehemence. 'I don't expect you to understand, Alex, but Port Landon is … it's my home now.' That was the thing, though, and it had taken until that moment for her to realize it – no one else needed to understand. It made perfect sense to her, and that was all that mattered.

'This is ludicrous.' Alex wore a shell-shocked expression. The man clearly thought she'd lost her mind. 'After everything you and I have accomplished in New York … everything I just sat here and offered you …' He shook his head. 'Paige, I can't let you make this kind of monumental mistake.'

'That's the beauty of it, Alex; you don't have to *let* me do anything. I didn't have to explain anything to Cohen about you and me, and I don't have to explain my reasons for wanting to stay here. The difference is, I want to explain the truth to Cohen, Alex. And I guess, in a way, that explains one of the big reasons why I'm staying here, too.' Pretty good for a woman who'd originally shown up hoping to make people like her. Now, Paige knew better. She just needed to be herself, and do what made her happy. The rest would come in time.

Alex's eyes had narrowed. 'You're staying for him.'

'No, Alex, I'm staying for love,' she'd announced proudly. 'Love of this town. Love of my own business. And love of all the people in it, including a man, his son, and their rescued dog.' She'd smiled so brightly despite the defiance in her eyes, Paige knew she must have looked positively unhinged. 'No job offer or amount of money can replace that. So, thank you for the offer, Alex, but I'm going to have to politely turn you down.'

Paige had let him stand there, still and bewildered, giving him the time he needed. She knew enough about Alex Livingston to know rejection wasn't something he had to deal with much, always the one to offer the sorts of business deals that were hard to decline. Finally, he'd reached up and run his hand through his perfectly styled hair, mussing it up as he blew out a long breath. 'Never had a woman choose an entire town over me, Paige.' Defeated, one corner of his mouth turned up. 'Especially not with a job offer on the table like the one I offered you.'

She knew a corporate-minded man like Alex would never understand her motives. And that was okay. Because no amount of money could ever compete with the sense of belonging she had found within Port Landon's town limits, or the spark she had found within the heart of Cohen Beckett.

'First time for everything,' she'd replied, hoping to soften the blow a bit. She was taken aback when Alex reached out and enveloped her in a hug. Another first. But, somehow, it only added to the finality of their conversation.

'I only hope you know what you're getting yourself into, Paige.'

'I don't,' she'd admitted with a half grin. 'But I think that's part of learning to really live. For me, anyway.' Live. Not just exist, but *live*.

Paige realized now that she probably should have confided in Allison about her conversation with Alex, but she hadn't felt right dumping that kind of heavy truth on her cousin when she already had so much on her plate. Either way, Paige had refused Allison's notion to bring someone to the wedding with her just to have someone. Besides, Alex Livingston wasn't the someone she wanted there with her. There was little use in pretending. As much as she wanted to believe it was because she was too proud to invite somebody else as a second choice, Paige knew better. If she were truly honest with herself, she still held out the tiniest sliver of hope that Cohen would show up. That was reason enough for her to attend the celebration solo.

Think pawsitive, she found herself thinking without realizing it. Then, she immediately sighed. Even in his absence, Cohen managed to sneak his way into her innermost thoughts. There was something sad about that. Something she refused to ponder. Which meant it was time to put those thoughts on the back

burner again and get back to work. She had a wedding extrava-
ganza to pull off.

With or without Cohen Beckett.

The ceremony was beautiful. As Allison had rhymed off her vows,
staring lovingly into Christopher's eyes, Paige had stood just
behind her, holding her bouquet and wiping away tears that
managed to stray past her fingers as she struggled to discreetly
wipe them away. Thank God for waterproof mascara.

Christopher wasn't quite so subtle about his flooding emotions,
breaking into sobs the moment Allison said, 'I do.' Seconds later
when they were announced husband and wife for the first time,
Allison wrapped him in a hug, chuckling softly as he struggled
to pull himself together and kiss his beautiful bride properly.
Paige didn't hear what he whispered in her ear just before he
kissed her, but when Allison finally pulled away, she was crying
happy tears, too.

The ceremony, although to the point and sweet as honey, was
reserved and mellow. The dinner and the reception that followed,
however, were anything but. Much to Allison and Christopher's
initial amusement, then eventual thinly veiled frustration, the
attendees all around the room kept clinking their forks and knives
against their wine and water glasses, eager for the newly married
couple to kiss. Again, and again, and again.

'Don't get me wrong, I love the man,' Allison snickered under
her breath to Paige. 'But I've barely eaten a thing all day, and this
roasted chicken is looking even better than the prospect of a
gazillionth kiss from him. One more clink of a fork on a glass
and I'm going to personally take away everyone's utensils and
make them eat with their fingers.' But she was still smiling when
she said it. Not even hunger could dim the brightness in her
cousin's eyes today.

The laughter and happiness that swept through the hour-long

dinner turned into full-blown excitement as the wedding cake was revealed. Paige had gone overboard. She knew it. But the widened gazes of Allison and Christopher, paired with the gasps and admiration from the other attendees made every painstaking minute she'd put into it worth the effort. Three tiers, each one above smaller than the next. Paige had decorated every fondant leaf and flower on it by hand. A filigree pattern encircled the bottom tier, allowing for the intricate flowers to peek out from gray and purple strips of fondant ribbon, like the cake was wrapped in it. The top boasted larger versions of the ribbon-tied flowers, their petals and leaves folding over to mimic the real lilies and little forget-me-nots that were incorporated in Allison's bouquet.

'Paige, it's beautiful.' Allison choked out the words. 'It's absolutely perfect.'

Relief washed through her, followed by more emotion than a cake should have elicited. 'I'm so glad you like it.' She hugged her cousin tight, hoping to convey the happiness she couldn't put into words.

'What do you say we kick this party into full gear?' Allison pulled back, giving her cousin a rueful grin. It was the moment the bride had been waiting for. Sure, she wanted to marry her best friend and eat a fancy meal in the company of all her friends and family, but Paige knew the one thing Allison loved to do more than anything.

Dance.

The coffee and tea had already been served during the ceremonial cake cutting, which resulted in both Christopher and Allison having to go wash their faces free of the icing they'd managed to smear on each other, and the deejay had already given Paige the thumbs-up to confirm he was ready to go. Paige wasn't going to make her cousin wait any longer. It was still ten minutes shy of the designated time for the reception to begin, according to the strict itinerary she'd followed to a tee thus far.

But it was Allison's day. If she wanted the music to be played, the music would be played.

She and Kait got some help from Christopher's best man, Adrian, and his other groomsman, Lucas, to move the round tables off to the sides of the room, opening up the impromptu dance floor. Allison didn't hesitate to be the first one on it. She had never been able to resist the riffs of *Old Time Rock & Roll*.

Paige wasn't much of a dancer, but she joined her cousin for a few songs, along with Kait and a few of her staff members from the coffeehouse. Sonya even broke out her best moves, which looked a lot like someone trying to start a lawnmower.

The entire crowd stared with stars in their eyes as Allison and Christopher shared their first slow dance as husband and wife. That was the part of weddings that always choked Paige up the most – the first dance. To her, it was like watching a couple taking their first steps together, in perfect synchronicity and harmony. The first glimpse of the honeymoon. There was just something about the first dance, with so much love in their eyes and hope in their hearts, that moved Paige to tears. She was wiping the tears away when she heard someone say her name over the slow, melodic rhythm of the music.

'Paige.'

She turned toward the voice. Her eyes were still blurry, but there was no mistaking that voice. Or the man, despite how different he looked in a crisp, black suit.

How undeniably handsome he looked.

'Cohen?' She couldn't believe her eyes.

He looked … transfixed. 'Wow, you … you look amazing.'

Cue the blushing. 'You do, too,' she managed to say. 'You look so … different.'

'Not weird, though, right?'

'What?'

Cohen's mouth turned up, waving his hand to dismiss the

notion. 'Nothing. Long story.' He paused, running his hands through his hair. Halfway through, he must have remembered there was gel in the strands and stopped, blowing out a long breath. 'Would it be all right if I asked you to dance?'

She was overwhelmed by his presence. Surely she would combust from the fire in his touch if he held her against him. Shock flooded her mind, stunned by the fact he was really there. He had come. Just like she hoped he would. She hadn't even noticed the song had changed and that people were pairing off to dance alongside the newlyweds. All she could do was nod, dumbfounded, and let Cohen lead her away from the sidelines and out onto the dance floor.

Like a true gentleman, he held one of her hands, entwining their fingers, while his other hand fell to her waist, guiding her effortlessly around their little piece of the dance floor.

'Paige—'

'I'm glad you came.' She hadn't meant to blurt it out, but there it was. The real and honest truth.

'I needed to,' he explained softly. 'I needed to see you.'

'I don't care what your reasons are, I'm just glad you're here, Cohen.'

The corner of his mouth quirked up. 'As happy as I am for Allison and Christopher, I didn't come here for them. I came here for you. And I need you to know that, Paige.'

Okay, maybe she did care. She was just so acutely aware of his close proximity that she couldn't focus. Couldn't think straight. 'You did?' Immediately, she felt ridiculous for saying it out loud, but Cohen chuckled.

'I did.' He twirled her around like he'd practiced the move a hundred times before, bringing her back in just a tiny bit closer to him than she'd been previously before he spoke again. 'Paige, I'm so sorry. So damn sorry. For the way I acted, and for not believing you. Bryce told me everything.'

'He did?' She knew she sounded like a broken record but

hearing that Bryce had confessed to him about taking the baked goods was another shock to her system. The surprises just kept on coming.

'Bryce also sent me here to tell you he's a good kid and that he's sorry for what he did.'

'Of course he is. I would never contest that. You can tell him I forgive him, Cohen. I forgave him the moment it happened. Water under the bridge.'

'He's still going to pay you back every penny he owes you. And he's grounded until he's in college.'

Paige couldn't help but let out a soft laugh. 'Go easy on the kid, Cohen. Maybe only ground him until he can drive.'

Cohen smiled. 'We'll talk about that later. I'm more concerned about how things are going to be left between us before you leave.' He paused, his expression growing more pleading. 'Paige, please stay.'

'Before I leave?' Her brows furrowed, confused. 'Where am I going?'

'To New York.' He suddenly didn't sound so sure of himself. 'With that—' He cleared his throat. 'With your boss.'

'Cohen, I never said I was going back to New York.' She stopped dancing, unable to pay attention to her footsteps and the muddled conversation at the same time. 'I'm not leaving Port Landon.'

'But Rhonda heard from …' Cohen looked genuinely confused now. 'And you and Alex Livingston …'

'Cohen, look at me.' Paige's hand was still entwined with his, and she gave his fingers a little squeeze. 'There's nothing going on between Alex and me. I called him, yes. But I had no idea he was going to take it upon himself to show up here.' She shook her head, still astounded by her former boss's determination. 'But that's not important. What is important is that I turned down the job offer he came here with, Cohen. He's gone back to New York, and I'm staying here.' Her gaze never wavered as she searched his eyes for a sign of understanding. 'This is my home.'

The way he stared at her, so deep and intense, Paige felt as though he was trying to decide if she was real.

'So, you're staying in Port Landon?'

'Yes,' she said again, fixated on him. She should have known someone would have seen Alex on her doorstep and asked questions. And God knew what Alex himself had idly said to people he met in town during his stay. He had been so certain he would have Paige packed up and heading back to the city with him. 'I can't leave, Cohen. I love it here.'

'And I love you, Paige.' Cohen's words came out in a hurried breath. 'That's another thing I need you to know. Another thing I should have said long before now.' He clasped her hands in his, and Paige tilted her chin, taking in the striking contrast of her mauve nail polish against the creamy white of his palm. 'I've made so many damn mistakes. But, I swear, I don't want you and me, *us*, to be one of them.'

His confession robbed her of her breath and stole her ability to speak. Paige had spent so much time steeling herself against the prospect that Cohen would never forgive her. That they were over before they started. But she was wrong. Cohen was standing before her, telling her they were far from over. Paige didn't think she'd ever been so relieved to be so wrong. 'Cohen, I—'

'I don't want to lose you, Paige,' he continued, squeezing her hands tightly in his, scrambling for a lifeline. 'All you ever wanted me to do was let you in. But I see now that you were already in my heart, long before I ever admitted it to myself.'

'Oh, Cohen.' Paige leaned forward as he leaned down, pressing his forehead against hers. Her eyes clamped shut, desperate to hold on to his beautiful words and his steadying hands.

'God, I thought I lost you,' he whispered again, his breath caressing her lips with the softness of a downy feather.

'You didn't,' Paige choked out quietly. Her emotions were rising within her like the tide, bubbling to the surface and threatening

279

to capsize her composure. 'It was just small-town gossip you heard. You know how people love to talk.'

'Yeah,' he breathed. Cohen slipped one hand away from hers and brought it up to wipe a stray tear away from her cheek with his thumb. 'Paige, what do you think those people would say if I kissed you right now?'

As far as she was concerned, there was no one else in the room with them at that moment. Through the sound of her own racing heartbeat, Paige whispered, 'Only one way to find out.'

He leaned forward and touched his lips against hers, cupping her cheek with his hand. Every overwhelming emotion – joy, happiness, sorrow, regret, guilt, relief – melded together and radiated through his kiss, conveying the feelings for her he had held in for too long and flooding Paige's resolve in one vast wave. Saying all the things their words couldn't.

When Cohen finally pulled away to gaze into her eyes, Paige's eyelids fluttered, completely consumed by the man before her and the intensity of his mouth on hers.

'Want to know another piece of gossip?' he asked gently, running his thumb across her bottom lip. He lowered his voice to barely above a whisper. 'Cohen Beckett isn't the only one who loves Paige Henley.'

Paige's eyes shone. 'Hmm, I wonder if that rumor is true.'

'Bryce and Jazz adore you. But not as much as I do. Not nearly.'

'Is that right?' The corner of Paige's mouth curved upward, basking in the warmth and promise of the moment.

'If that kiss didn't confirm it,' Cohen said, 'I will kiss you again. And again and again, until you do believe it.'

She knew her cheeks must be seven shades of crimson, but she didn't care. She didn't have to hide her feelings for him. Not anymore. 'Want to know a secret?' Without waiting for his response, Paige turned slightly in his arms and pointed through the throngs of people still dancing around them. People she had forgotten all about until now. 'I think we're being watched.' Across the room, Allison and her pretty white dress were huddled together with Sonya and Kait, watching her and Cohen with lovestruck, wistful stares.

'I don't think that's much of a secret,' Cohen reasoned.

Cohen and Paige's gazes met theirs, and all three women waved unabashedly. Sonya, ever the lovey-dovey voodoo queen, nodded toward them, a sincere smile lighting up her features. Then, the woman placed one hand over her heart, left it there for a split second as her eyes fluttered shut, and then released her hand, opening her eyes again slowly before blowing them a kiss and disappearing into the crowd.

'Fine, then I think Sonya just put a spell on us.'

Cohen lowered his chin, a wry grin on his lips. 'Again, tell me something I don't know.'

She stood on her tiptoes and kissed him again, wrapping her arms around his neck. 'I love you. In every sense of the word.' She pulled away, the heat from her gaze emanating into his and igniting something comforting within his hazel eyes. 'Do you believe that secret?'

Cohen's throat moved, but he never looked away. 'Trust me, Paige, I'm starting to.'

Epilogue

Cohen

One Year Later ...

There was a sense of calm that settled over Port Landon in the evenings of summer, transforming the hot and bright dog days of August into warm, starry-skied nights. Midday, folks milled about on the streets and sidewalks, but the fading sky ushered people away from Main Street and toward their patios and backyards to enjoy the heat they had waited all year for. Autumn would be upon them again soon enough, and there wasn't a Michigan resident who failed to remember that.

Cohen unlocked Paige's apartment door for her and stepped back to let her go first. For Christopher and Allison's first wedding anniversary, the happily married couple had invited them over to celebrate with a backyard barbeque and ice cream. Bryce had been ecstatic to go, being a big fan of Christopher's original Nintendo system. He called it 'vintage', which made every adult in the vicinity groan.

The evening had gone later than they had planned, ending only when Allison announced that she and Christopher were going to miss their movie in North Springs if they didn't leave soon.

Cohen and Paige's own plans included a long walk out to the Hansel and Gretel House. Cohen had suggested it, since it was usually too long to do that route during their busy weekdays with the vet clinic and the bakery. Bryce had quickly backed up his father's decision. Paige was outnumbered.

Not that she minded. Paige loved the longer walks on the weekends just as much as he and Bryce did, and the Hansel and Gretel House had since become their spot, a place where they didn't have to be the veterinarian, the baker, or even members of their community.

They could just be Cohen and Paige, together.

'We'll round up Jazz, then we can head out.' Paige embarked up the stairs to retrieve her trusty canine friend, who was no doubt snoozing on the end of the couch like she always did when Paige left her for a few hours.

Paige had surprised everyone by asking to officially adopt the brindle boxer last year, only a few days after Allison's wedding. The fact that she wanted Jazz to live with her permanently wasn't the surprise. To Cohen and Bryce, it was that it had taken her so damn long to admit to herself how in love with the dog she really was.

Cohen liked to think she'd had to admit to herself that she loved him first, then she could deal with her adoration of Jazz.

Either way, Paige was gracious enough to make room for Jazz in her home. She was even more gracious to make room in her heart for Cohen and Bryce. They came from different backgrounds, had been through things that shaped them into who they were, flaws and all. But they had overcome obstacles that

Cohen was proud to see long behind them. He planned to leave the past exactly where it was, and he hoped that meant he could focus on the future.

Their future.

'Paging Paige Henley and her diva dog! We're running out of daylight!' Cohen cast an amused glance at Bryce, who obviously found humor in his dad trying to rush Paige. The boy was eleven, and he knew better – women couldn't be rushed.

'I couldn't find Jazz's collar,' Paige announced, breathless as she bounded down the stairs with the dog following close behind her. 'She likes the purple one.'

'*You* like the purple one,' Cohen chuckled. 'Jazz doesn't care whether her collar and leash match.'

Paige quirked a brow down at the dog. 'Do you hear this? Are you going to tell him, or should I?' Jazz glanced over at Cohen, and he swore if the dog could talk she would have told him he didn't have a clue what he was talking about. 'Come on, Jazzy girl. Let's go before the Hansel and Gretel House gets dark and creepy.'

The shadows stretched out long in front of Cohen and his entourage as they made their way to the edge of town and along the tree-lined path into the forest. By the time the old cottage came into view, the sun was peeking through the trees, creating patterns of shadow and light all across the grassy opening, reflecting brightly off the dirty windowpanes. There was a sense of beauty in the old, dilapidated cottage, a long since forgotten charm that wasn't in the residential structures of modern times. One glance over at Paige, who still held his hand even though they'd stopped to take in the sight of the house, and Cohen knew she felt the same way about it.

'It really is the perfect spot, isn't it?' He said it in a low voice, as though speaking too loudly might awaken whatever ancient entities inhabited it when they left.

'It really is.' She gave his hand a gentle squeeze.

Bryce tramped through the leaves around to the other side of the cottage with Jazz in tow. The boy had practically run the entire way, forcing Paige to take Jazz's leash from him because the poor dog couldn't keep up with the stamina of an eleven-year-old.

Cohen's stomach knotted, but he was thankful his son had made it out of sight without alerting Paige to his overflowing excitement.

'What do you think it would be perfect for?' He tried to sound nonchalant, but even to his own ears he knew he'd failed.

Paige's forehead wrinkled, confused. 'What do you mean?' She eased her hand from his grasp and turned away, about to trudge around and explore, dismissing his odd question.

Cohen reached forward and clasped her hand in his again, tugging her playfully to him. Her free hand came up to land on his chest. 'I said, what do you think it would be perfect for?' He couldn't keep the smile out of his voice.

'I don't know,' she chuckled. 'It's just … perfect.'

'It is,' he replied. 'But is it perfect for us?'

'For us?'

God, she was adorable when she was bewildered. 'I think this should be our place, Paige.'

'I thought it already was.' She laughed, but Cohen could see that she was starting to realize something was going on.

He leaned down and placed a gentle kiss on her forehead. Then, he entwined his fingers with hers and pulled her along to where he hoped Bryce was set up and ready.

His son didn't disappoint.

Rounding the corner of the rundown cottage, Bryce stood there with a rustic makeshift table set up. It was an old wooden crate he and Cohen had found the day before when they'd come there during the day while Paige was still working, but Bryce had set the table up with three place settings. The dishes were gold-rimmed, bone china that Cohen's grandmother had given him, the glasses cut crystal with starburst motifs from the same era. It was rustic meets classic, and he and Bryce had been planning it for days.

It wouldn't be the bone china or the crystal that Paige would be talking about later, anyway. The topic of conversation wouldn't even be the raspberry iced tea Bryce had poured into the glasses or the silverware he'd brought from home.

The cake stopped Paige in her tracks. It had taken a few white lies to get her recipe for the Oreo fudge cake with chocolate fudge icing – the same cake Paige had sliced up for Bryce on the first day Cohen met her – but he and Bryce had managed to borrow the recipe card and bake a cake of their own. One layer, still in the nine-by-thirteen glass dish, but they'd baked and decorated it themselves. And Cohen wasn't sure whose eyes were wider, Paige's or Bryce's.

There was a stunned silence as she took in the scene and read the words Bryce had painstakingly written out in bright white frosting on the chocolate iced cake.

Paige, will you marry my dad?

By the time she whirled around to face Cohen, eyes brimming with tears and hands cupping her mouth to hold in the gasp, he'd dropped to one knee. Her gaze lowered to meet his, and Cohen presented a small red velvet box, opening it to reveal a glistening solitaire diamond ring with a white gold band.

'Paige Henley …' He tried to continue, got choked up, and had to clear his throat to start again. 'Paige, you've had my heart since before I even realized I'd given it to you. Will you do Bryce and I the honor of being my wife?'

When Cohen had sat down to talk to Bryce, man to man, about his desire to marry Paige, the boy's only stipulation was that he got to help pull it off in a fun way. To Bryce, that purely meant double fudge chocolate cake. But to Cohen, that meant the world, because the boy realized they were a package deal. The Beckett men stuck together, no matter what, and Cohen couldn't put into words what it meant to know that Bryce wanted Paige to be a Beckett, too.

'Oh my … yes!' Paige threw her arms around Cohen's neck just as he was trying to stand, and they both almost toppled over, causing laughter to erupt from Bryce behind them.

Paige held him, sobbing into his chest until Cohen pulled her back to make sure she was all right. There was a smile amongst the flood of tears, which calmed his fears a bit. 'You okay?'

'Of course,' she sobbed. 'I just … I don't even know what to say.'

'You said all you need to,' Cohen assured her. '*Yes* was all I needed to hear.' He leaned down and kissed her softly, wiping away a stray tear from her cheek before sliding the diamond ring on her finger. A perfect fit. Bryce made a gagging noise from behind them, but not even adolescent antics could ruin their moment.

'So, that's what you meant when you said you wanted this to be our place.'

'Partly.'

Her eyebrows shot up. 'I'd hate to sound like a broken record, but once again … what do you mean?'

'Bryce, you're up, buddy.'

His son sprang into action, digging a roll of legal-sized foolscap out of the backpack they'd stashed out there yesterday. He unrolled the sheets and held them out for Paige to see. 'Dad wants us to live here.'

'In the cottage?' The mortified expression on her face was almost worth the less-than-stellar lead-up to Bryce's explanation.

'No,' Cohen laughed. 'I want to recreate the Hansel and Gretel House. We could build a new house out here. Put the driveway in along the path we came in on.' He pointed back toward the rocky path, then showed her on the building plans where it would be. 'You could choose all the finishing touches, of course. And anything in the plans can be altered. This is just a rough idea.

Basement, library, pool – hell, I don't care if you want it to have a clock-tower. We can make it work.' Cohen nudged her lightly. 'We could even put in a professional-grade kitchen,' he added, pointing to the building plans again to show her he'd already thought of that himself and included it in the preliminary drawings.

Paige's gaze scanned the plans with the excitement and anticipation of a child on Christmas morning. 'Cohen, this all sounds amazing,' she said. She raised her head, her gaze flitting between him and Bryce. 'But what about your house?'

He exchanged a knowing glance with his son. They had already discussed that, too. 'We've talked about it, and we're ready to have a new beginning. A real one. We want to build a new home with you, Paige. We want to build a life with you. Just you, me, Bryce, and the Jazzmanian Devil.'

'And Norman,' Bryce interjected. 'Jeez, Dad, you always forget about Norman.'

Cohen rolled his eyes, but he couldn't help seeing the humor that, even in the midst of a marriage proposal, his son was hellbent on assuring his ornery cat's place in their family. 'Yes, of course. And Norman.'

Paige burst out laughing. Especially when the brindle dog came ambling around the corner as if on cue. 'Are you sure about that?'

Cohen gave her a crooked grin. 'Pretty sure.'

'And are you sure you want to get married and build a new house at the same time?'

He shrugged. 'Pretty sure.'

'There are a lot of unknowns in an equation like that, Dr Cohen.' She stepped closer to him, wrapping her arms around his waist to hold him tight.

'Paige, the only thing I know for sure is that I love you. Everything else will fall into place as it comes,' he assured her, kissing the top of her head. 'We've just got to *think pawsitive.*'

Cohen and Paige pulled Bryce into their hug, letting Jazz nuzzle her way into the middle of the circle at their knees.

Whatever the future brought to Port Landon, they would handle it the only way that mattered from now on …

Together.

Acknowledgements

Thank you to Erica Christensen. There are many reasons to thank you, but to keep this short, I will simply thank you for being you. To the rest of the team at Metamorphosis Literary Agency, thank you for your guidance on this journey. Thank you to Belinda Toor at HQ Digital for taking a chance on me and my stories, and for polishing this book until it shines. Thank you to the rest of the team at HQ and HarperCollins UK for loving this story as much as I do. It's a dream come true to work with you. Thank you to my family and friends for all the support and encouragement. A special thanks goes out to my husband for believing in me, even when I didn't believe in myself. Also, thank you to Jazz for being my brindle partner-in-crime. We're a package deal, diva dog, and I'm blessed to be your mama.

Most importantly, thank you to everyone who has read, reviewed, and recommended this book. You're the reason authors get to do what they love, so thank you for giving me that opportunity.

Dear Reader,

We hope you enjoyed reading this book. If you did, we'd be so appreciative if you left a review. It really helps us and the author to bring more books like this to you.

Here at HQ Digital we are dedicated to publishing fiction that will keep you turning the pages into the early hours. Don't want to miss a thing? To find out more about our books, promotions, discover exclusive content and enter competitions you can keep in touch in the following ways:

JOIN OUR COMMUNITY:
Sign up to our new email newsletter: hyperurl.co/hqnewsletter
Read our new blog www.hqstories.co.uk
🐦 : https://twitter.com/HQStories
📘 : www.facebook.com/HQStories

BUDDING WRITER?
We're also looking for authors to join the HQ Digital family!
Find out more here:
https://www.hqstories.co.uk/want-to-write-for-us/
Thanks for reading, from the HQ Digital team

HQ

If you enjoyed *The Forget-Me-Not Bakery*, then why not try another delightfully uplifting romance from HQ Digital?

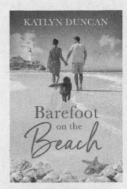

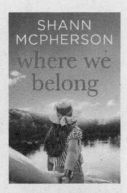

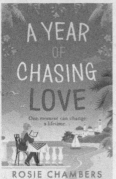

WEARING THE
RANCHER'S RING

BY
STELLA BAGWELL

Published in Great Britain 2014
by Mills & Boon, an imprint of Harlequin (UK) Limited,
Eton House, 18-24 Paradise Road, Richmond, Surrey, TW9 1SR

© 2014 Stella Bagwell

ISBN: 978-0-263-91320-0

23-0914